FROM CHINA TO ENGLAND
A TUMULTUOUS AGE BEGINS ...
SWEEPING A CHOSEN FEW
TO FAR-OFF PLACES
OF MYSTERY AND DESIRE

PRINCE HENRY—Third son of Portugal's "Bastard King" John, he waited for a sign from God as he punished himself with the scourge. And that sign would tell this most pious of princes to send his ships on a sacred mission to find the legendary islands at the edge of the world.

ZARCO—The unscrupulous "Blue Eyes," pirate captain of Prince Henry's fleet, he would discover what Henry prayed for: a lush, bountiful island that one careless act would destroy.

PEDRO—A servant boy who dreamed of being a sailor, he would have his chance to see not only the wide reaches of the world but the limitless cruelty of his fellowmen.

INÊS ALVES—Daughter of the noble Dom Martim Alves who hoped to replenish his family's fortune by discovering a land of gold, her only dowry would be a letter with a devastating truth....

ALESSANDRO CAVALLI—Heir to a merchant fleet and a family fortune, he would end up feeling the slaver's lash on his back. Now he was chained in a Genoese galley, bound for wherever the ship took him, living on hate and dreams of escape.

THE TURK—A huge, mysterious muscleman who shared Alessandro's oar, both his flesh and his mind were scarred by the whip, but he held the key to Allesandro's freedom and a plan for revenge.

THE SLAVE GIRL—A frightened Greek beauty on the auction block, she was sold to become a harem girl in some pasha's seraglio ... and would haunt Alessandro's dreams until he could find her again.

TOM GILES—A weaver's apprentice who preferred women to work, he was nearly thrown in gaol for sampling the sweet favors of his master's wife. Instead he's headed for Bristol's docks, a distant city, and another pretty lady's delightful—but risky—embrace.

MATHILDE—Youngest of three sisters in the city of Bruges, she spun wool for a living, but it was Tom of Bristol's irrepressible charm that was winding round her heart ... and catching her in a dangerous web of intrigue.

CHENG HO—Head eunuch and admiral of the Imperial Treasure Fleet, he served the Yung Lo Emperor in the Forbidden City. Now he needed that emperor's favor to carry out his grand scheme ... to dominate the world by sailing the seas.

YUNG LO—Despotic emperor of the Middle Kingdom, his power was absolute and displeasing him meant a slow, terrifying death. So he'd give Cheng Ho one chance to succeed at conquering the entire earth ... before having him killed.

BANTAM BOOKS BY PAUL KING

The Dreamers

THE DREAMERS

A Novel of Adventure and Discovery

Paul King

BANTAM BOOKS

NEW YORK · TORONTO · LONDON · SYDNEY · AUCKLAND

THE DREAMERS

A Bantam Domain Book / December 1992

DOMAIN and the portrayal of a boxed "d"
are trademarks of Bantam Books,
a division of Bantam Doubleday Dell Publishing Group, Inc.

ISBN 0-553-29242-0

Published simultaneously in the United States and Canada

Bantam Books are published by Bantam Books, a division of Bantam
Doubleday Dell Publishing Group, Inc. Its trademark, consisting of the
words "Bantam Books" and the portrayal of a rooster, is Registered in
U.S. Patent and Trademark Office and in other countries. Marca Reg-
istrada. Bantam Books, 666 Fifth Avenue, New York, New York 10103.

PRINTED IN THE UNITED STATES OF AMERICA

RAD   0 9 8 7 6 5 4 3 2 1

PROLOGUE

December 1418, Sagres

The sounds coming from behind the Prince's locked door were so terrible that the kitchen boy, Pedro, almost dropped the tray he was carrying as he instinctively tried to cross himself.

He could not bring himself to knock and call out to the Prince, as he had been sternly instructed to do, and now he was afraid even to set the tray outside the door, in case the Prince should hear the rattle of dishes and confront him.

A moan came from within and then the sharp crack of leather followed by a cry of pain, and Pedro distinctly heard the Prince call out the name of Jesus.

He backed away from the door, his eyes growing wide. Still balancing the heavy tray, he retreated a short distance down the corridor and around a bend, until he could think what to do.

It had been three days since Prince Henry had shut himself up in his chapel, refusing all food and not answering those who tried to talk to him through the door. The trays that were left outside remained untouched, and the Prince himself, as a further act of self-abasement, emptied his own slops late at night. The strain was beginning to tell on the servants, who walked on tiptoe and spoke in whispers when they passed the chapel wing.

Pedro was only fifteen and the son of a simple fisherman; a dark-eyed, well-muscled boy who was more comfortable pulling an oar or hauling his father's nets than pussyfooting around the high and mighty. To Pedro, even the country *fidalgos* who lorded it over this coastal district in Portugal's southernmost province were grand and distant figures. It was no part of his job to serve a royal personage—and certainly not to wait on the *infante* Henrique, the renowned third son of the well-loved Bastard King, John the First.

But the Prince's servitor that day, a page named Dinis who was the pampered son of a knight of Avis, had balked at the intimidating task, and the seneschal's eye had fallen on Pedro, who was cleaning fish in the scullery.

"It doesn't matter," the seneschal, Dom Álvaro, had grumbled. "He won't see who leaves the tray anyway, and even if he did he doesn't care who serves him or what is set before him. The art of fine cooking is wasted on him—he fasts like an anchorite half the time as it is, and won't drink wine. Go on, boy, and don't linger—you stink of fish."

Dom Álvaro, a haughty, Lisbon-bred *cavaliero* from the household of Henry's older brother, Duarte, did not bother to hide his disdain for Prince Henry's modest establishment or for the backwardness of the rustics with whom he was forced to deal. He was on loan from Duarte for only as long as it took to get things running smoothly at Sagres, and he could not wait to get back to the glittering court of the heir apparent.

It had been less than a month since Prince Henry had returned, covered with fresh glory, from North Africa. The gathering Moorish forces had fled at the sight of his fleet and had refused to fight, though Henry had loitered at his prize town, Ceuta, for three months, hoping to draw them out.

But Henry, the hero of all Christendom since his famous victory over the Moors at Ceuta three years earlier, had declined to bask in his new celebrity. He had refused the honors of the pope and the crowned heads of Europe. Instead, he had unaccountably decided to retire in obscurity to the bleak and windswept promontory of Sagres, where the world ended and the chin of Portugal jutted out into the Ocean of Darkness.

He had swooped down on poor, startled Sagres with only a skeleton household and settled into this rather modest cliffside manor house until a new village, the *Vila do Infante*, could be built around the naval observatory he had already started to construct on the headland. There weren't enough servants to do the work, and Dom Álvaro had been forced to recruit local labor for the rougher tasks. Pedro had been thought lucky to be hired as a *mancebo de cozinha* at a rate of two copper *dinheiros* a day.

All had gone well at first. The Prince, despite his eminence, was a frank and kindly man who treated his servants with punctilious courtesy. But he seemed very remote. He liked to take solitary walks on the high cliff and brood out over the enigmatic western ocean, as if God had given him the power to see past the horizon to the boiling waters that marked the rim of the world.

Even Pedro could see that the Prince was possessed by some great melancholy. As the days passed, the melancholy ripened into a despair that infected those around him. Work on the observatory slowed to a standstill. The ships of his fleet rode idly at anchor, while the mariners, deprived of his orders, loafed in the taverns of Sagres and Lagos.

And now, for three days, he had been acting as if he were a penitent, punishing himself for some sin.

Pedro heard a muffled groan from the chapel, and the voice of a man in anguish crying hoarsely, *"Christo, salvador, forgive me, I have failed you!"*

And again there was the crack of leather.

This time Pedro did set the tray down on the stone corridor floor and cross himself. He had known the Prince was a pious man, but this was beyond piety. This was a soul in torment.

It was utterly beyond Pedro's understanding why the Prince should have plunged into this frenzy of grief and

remorse. How could the conqueror of Ceuta believe that
he had failed the Lord in any way? Centuries past, other
great champions of Christendom had driven the Saracens
out of Spain and Portugal, with the exception of the entrenched Moorish kingdom of Granada, but Henry was
the first Christian knight to carry the Reconquest to Africa itself. Even the pope had commended him, and
asked him to take command of the forces of the emperor
Palaeologus, who was holding off the Turks in the east.

Some said the *infante* was angry because his father had
stopped him from going on with his victorious fleet to
capture Gibraltar, the Moors' twin stronghold across the
strait from Ceuta. To win back Gibraltar, King John had
said, was the prerogative of the king of Castile, who
ought not to be deprived of that glory. It was a delicate
political situation, and King John wanted no quarrels
with his fellow monarch.

But Pedro did not think the Prince an angry man; what
the household at Sagres was witnessing was no mere fit
of pique from an overeager young man, but a true and
profound sorrow.

There had been no further sounds from behind the
chapel door for a while. Pedro risked a cautious peek
past the bend of the corridor. Intent on listening, he
failed to hear the footsteps that came up behind him.

"*Malandro!* Scoundrel! What's this?"

He felt himself seized by the scruff of the neck. Sharp
fingers dug in painfully, gave him a shaking, then spun
him around and released him.

It couldn't have been worse. Dom Álvaro stood there,
his pouchy face dark with temper, looking formidable despite the foppish French tunic with dagged sleeves and
painted hose that he affected, though such finery was reserved by law for knights.

"Why are you skulking about, eavesdropping on the
infante?" the seneschal demanded. "So you can carry
tales back to your squalid little fishing village and puff
yourself up with your fellows? Is that it, eh?"

"Please, *o senhor* ..." Pedro tried to explain, but he
could not get his tongue to work.

"Or perhaps you thought you might have a taste of

what princes eat?" Dom Álvaro went on. "Stuff your peasant mouth with gilded fish and honey cakes—as if your cloddish appetite needed tempting!"

He bent to inspect the covered dishes on the tray, and seemed disappointed that everything was intact.

"No ... I swear, *senhor* ..." Pedro found his voice at last. "There were sounds ... I was afraid to go near the door ... I was going to go and get someone...."

"Or perhaps you thought you'd have a little rest!" the seneschal shouted. "Donkey! Lazy lout!"

A rattle of key chains interrupted the tirade. Bartolomé, the old soldier who had fought beside Henry at Ceuta, and before that with Henry's father in the struggle against Castile, and who had subsequently been given a job as the Prince's household constable, was limping down the corridor, shaking his head at the commotion.

"Have a care, master seneschal," he admonished. "That's enough noise to wake the dead. The *infante*'s devotions are not to be disturbed."

Dom Álvaro glared at him. There was no love lost between the two men. The temporary nature of the seneschal's appointment here by the well-meaning crown prince, and his ambiguous status as an official of a greater household, had undermined Bartolomé's authority on his home ground, and the older man resented the dandified newcomer. And Dom Álvaro, for his part, though constrained to tread softly, had nothing but scorn for the old veteran, who was only a knight-villein of simple blood, elevated for his bravery and his military service.

"Devotions?" Dom Álvaro's eyes rolled ceilingward. "A thunderclap wouldn't disturb such devotions!" He turned his fury on a safer target. "And this halfwit here claims to be so much in awe of them that he's afraid to do his job. Pick up that tray, you ninny, and follow me!"

"*Momento.*" Bartolomé raised a leathery paw and turned his battered face toward Pedro. "What about it, lad? What's the trouble?"

With one wary eye on the seneschal, Pedro stammered out his story.

"So?" Bartolomé raised a grizzled eyebrow. "Leave the tray for the moment. I'd better have a look."

He clumped down the corridor with Dom Álvaro and the boy at his back. He paused at the chapel door, but instead of listening at the crack, as Pedro had expected, he raised his eyes to the niche in the wall where Prince Henry's sword hung. It was a magnificent weapon of tempered steel, its gold hilt set with seed pearls. The Prince's mother, Queen Philippa, had given it to him on her deathbed, along with a splinter from the True Cross that she had worn next to her breast in a golden reliquary, and had blessed his crusade against the Moors. He and his brothers had sailed for Ceuta instead of mourning her. Henry had worn the holy relic around his neck, day and night, ever since, and he had been knighted with the sword, after it had tasted Moors' blood, as his mother had stipulated to the king with her dying breath.

Pedro gazed in awe at the mighty blade. The blood of the Moors it had killed had never been wiped off, and as a consequence the unburnished portions of the steel showed flecks of rust at the margin, but in Pedro's eyes that made it all the more terrible a weapon.

Old Bartolomé was not looking at the sword, however. He was looking at the empty place beside it, where the scourge had hung. The scourge, too, was stained with blood, a memento of the harsh vigil that had preceded Henry's knighting.

"*O flagelo,*" Bartolomé said, biting his lip. "He took it inside with him. That's what you heard."

From the chapel's interior came an incoherent rush of words that might have been prayer, then a grunt of effort and a whipcrack. The Prince bellowed once like a bull, then choked it off and resumed his prayers.

"Holy Mother of God," the old soldier whispered, crossing himself. Pedro followed his example, and even Dom Álvaro's choleric face had gone pale.

"Leave him," Bartolomé said, waving the other two away from the door. "This is no business of ours."

"Shouldn't we do something, *senhor*?" Pedro said, speaking out before he remembered his place.

"No, boy, it's between the *infante* and God," Bartolomé

said gruffly. "They'll have to settle it between themselves." He glanced at Dom Álvaro. "Not a word of this to anybody, do you understand? No kitchen gossip."

"No, *o senhor*," Pedro said in a small voice.

Dom Álvaro had regained his hauteur. "It's that English blood of his that he got from his mother," he said. "The English are too pious a race, given to self-mortification and pilgrimages."

It was true that Prince Henry was half English. The queen had been the daughter of John of Gaunt, the duke of Lancaster, who had been John the Bastard's ally in the war against Castile and a claimant himself to the thrones of Castile and León. The Plantagenet blood showed clearly in Henry's long jaw and broad shoulders.

"The queen was a saint," Bartolomé said with a frown. "She brought virtue to the court. She recited the Hours every morning in the English tongue, fasted till she fainted, and on Fridays would speak to nobody until she said her psalter through. The king gave up his mistress for her."

"She brought virtue to the court, all right," the seneschal replied. "She had the king's squire, Affonso, burned at the stake for sleeping with one of her maids of honor."

"Affonso was a young fool," Bartolomé said reluctantly. "The queen gave him every chance to marry the girl, but he defied her. She was a newcomer and a foreigner—she would have become a joke and a nothing forevermore if she hadn't asserted her authority then and there."

"That she did," Dom Álvaro agreed. "And then she went on to marry off half the court to improve their morals. 'You will report to the altar tomorrow morning,' she'd say, and never mind who your bride would turn out to be. Too bad she didn't find a wife for the *infante*. That's what led to all this fasting and prayer and carrying on that's causing so much trouble in this house. He needs a woman, that's all."

The old soldier's hand dropped casually to the hilt of his sword. "Hear me, Dom Álvaro," he said. "I'll have no one showing disrespect to the *infante* in my presence. Prince Henry has pledged his chastity to God. He made a solemn vow as a youth never to marry and to remain celibate, and he's never broken that oath, though the pope offered to release him from it. But if you'd fought with us at Ceuta, you'd know he was a man, *por Deos!*"

The seneschal indulged himself in a brief scowl, then began fussing over the tray on the floor. "All this food going to waste! The cooks outdid themselves, trying to please." He lifted a cover. "Look here, roasted peacock. And gilded lamprey, with real gold leaf in the yellow sauce. And here's a dainty dish—rabbit with cloves, saffron and ginger. And as many preserves as if it were Christmas Eve! It's too fine to distribute to the servants—it will have to be thrown away!"

He dipped his fingers into a silver porringer and sampled a fricassee of doves, smacking his lips loudly.

Bartolomé regarded him stolidly. "If you have no need of young Pedro in the kitchen, I could use his services," he said.

"Oh, take him, take him!" the seneschal said with ill grace. To Pedro he flung: "See that you're here early enough tomorrow to chop the firewood, *moco!*"

Pedro followed the old veteran into the great hall. "What do you want me to do, *o senhor?*" he asked.

It was apparent that Bartolomé had nothing particular in mind. "Oh, you can take some of that armor off the walls and polish it," he said vaguely. "If the Prince finally comes out, it may do him some good to see his trophies from Ceuta sparkling. They've been gathering dust too long. . . ." He stared ruminatively at the Saracen swords and lances, the battered shields and dented helmets, then turned a grizzled head toward Pedro and said almost fiercely, "He needs something to *do*, y'see. That's the trouble."

Pedro worked through the morning with scouring cloth and oil, sitting cross-legged on the floor of the little chamber off the upper gallery. At about sexte, Bartolomé came to check his progress, and stopped to talk. The old soldier was in a reminiscent mood, talking more to himself than to Pedro.

"Ah, you should have seen the Prince, hacking his way past the beach with that great sword of his toward the walls of the city. That was a day! The Prince wanted to be first ashore, but João Goncalves jumped into the water ahead of him, armor and all, up to his waist. The Moors had a champion, a giant who fought naked, who knocked off the visor of Vasco Martin's helmet with a stone, but Vasco ran him through with his lance. The Prince battered his way through the streets, ahead of the main force. Only a handful of us could keep up with him. Garcia Moniz, who had charge of the *infante* when he was a small boy, tried to slow him down. 'You're too far ahead,' he said. 'You're endangering the lives of those around you,' and that was the only thing that stopped his rush. Even so, there was such a swarm of Moors trying to get at Henry that he would have been killed in a side street, without reaching the citadel, if his servant, Vasco Fernandes de Ataide, hadn't caught up with us just in time to protect the Prince's back. Poor Fernandes took a spear through the liver before we were able to fight free." Bartolomé tapped his game leg. "I didn't get this till later that day, when we took Sala ben-Sala's castle."

Pedro, his imagination fired, cried, "I wish I'd been there, o Senhor Bartolomé!"

"You'll have your chance, youngster. The Prince always needs sailors. There were more than a few fisher lads from your own town of Lagos who shipped out with the fleet when we put in there for water and supplies on our way to the Strait. You're almost old enough now. Never fear, with the Prince settling here at the cape and starting his own shipyard, something will turn up. He's only looking for the right enterprise—something grand and worthy of his ambitions." A shadow crossed his face. "If he'll only break out of this black mood of his."

Pedro failed to notice the shadow. "Another crusade against the Moors?" he suggested.

"Perhaps. If the king changes his mind and decides to allow it."

A thought crossed Pedro's mind. "Maybe the Prince is praying for God to give him some sign."

"You're a shrewd lad. You may have hit the nail on the head." Bartolomé sighed. "There were signs and portents aplenty when we went to Ceuta. An eclipse of the sun that June. And a monk of São Domingos had a vision that spread like wildfire through the city—the Holy Virgin giving the king a white-hot sword to defend her with. Even the Moors received signs. One of their holy men had a dream of a lion wearing a gold crown and his three cubs coming from the north and a cloud of bees swarming through the streets of Ceuta."

Impressed, Pedro made an appropriate expression of reverence.

"Of the three brothers, though, it was Prince Henry who distinguished himself the most," the old soldier went on. "Duarte and Pedro are the first to admit that. They wanted the king to knight Henry first, right on the spot, but Henry insisted on order of precedence, so the older brothers were knighted before him, Duarte first, with the swords their mother gave them."

"What valor!" Pedro exclaimed. "What largeness!"

Bartolomé nodded. "The *infante* always sees beyond," he said. "While everybody else had nothing on their minds but looting Ceuta of its riches, he was already thinking about what the victory meant. Ceuta was so wealthy because it was the center of the caravan trade, the meeting place of East and West. But with the city in Christian hands, he knew the caravans would go elsewhere with their gold and silk and spices. He foresaw that Ceuta would dry up—and it has. That's why he's so keen to push on, to go further, and why he's at odds with his father, who's content with how well things turned out and who sees only the risk of more military expeditions."

Pedro was too enthralled to hear more than the first part of what Bartolomé said. "Was Ceuta so rich, then?" he asked breathlessly.

"You can't imagine the luxury the Moors command," the old soldier assured him. "Even the nobles were astonished at the richness of their dwellings. I heard Zurara say—and he's a grandee, a *rico-homem*—that we Portuguese, in comparison with the Moors, live in pigsties. The plunder was beyond belief—carpets from the East, gold vases, jewels, bales of silk. The soldiers fought over sacks of spices, and you could smell the cloves and ginger and cinnamon that were trampled into the mud of the streets."

"Como maravilhoso!" Pedro said in admiration.

"But the Prince says the real wealth is knowledge. Even while the city was being sacked, he spent his time questioning captured Moors about the interior of Africa, about where the kingdom of Prester John might be found, about whether Africa is an island so that a route to the East might be found through a channel—you wouldn't believe the questions he thought to ask! He rescued a Moorish geographer from some soldiers who were going to kill him, and brought him back here to Sagres to make maps."

"They say the sea boils farther south, and that there are magnetic rocks that draw the nails from a ship's planking," Pedro offered. He had spent most of his young life on the water, but he had never been far out of the sight of land.

"Such things may be, *moco*, though educated men no longer believe it. But the Prince has no respect for such tales."

Pedro took a breath and, daring greatly, said, "I heard the *infante* say that he had failed Christ."

The old soldier's face darkened, and for a moment Pedro thought he had presumed too far. Then Bartolomé shook his head and said sadly, "That's only because he's been thwarted in his desire to take Gibraltar and Tangier and thus control the coastline and begin a Christian empire in Africa. He thinks there's nothing left for him to do. That's why he takes those long walks out to the end of the point and stares out into the Sea of Darkness."

Pedro looked down the long gallery to where the Prince endured his lonely agony. "God will show him the way," he said confidently. "I'd follow the Prince anywhere. I'm not afraid of sea monsters."

Bartolomé gave a short bark of laughter. "You're too raw to understand such things, little cub. It's up to God to decide whether or not to vouchsafe the Prince a sign." He tousled the boy's hair. "Come with me, and we'll hang those shields now."

As they crossed the great hall with the load of armor, they heard loud voices coming from the vestibule.

"What's this?" Bartolomé frowned. "I left orders that the *infante* wasn't to be disturbed."

Three dusty, travel-stained men were pushing their way into the great hall, with a page running after, trying to stop them. Two of them were dressed like minor nobility—typical down-at-the-heels *escudieros* in woolen hose and padded tunics, with swords and daggers hanging from their girdles. The third was a sailor in a rough cloak and knit cap, a squat, ugly man with a face like a burl of walnut.

"I know those two," Bartolomé muttered. "Rogues, both of them. Squires of the *infante*, they style themselves, but without a *soldo* to their name. After Ceuta, they took the ships provided by the *infante* and went buccaneering. From the threadbare look of them, they never found a Moorish treasure ship, or if they did, they gambled it all away and lost their ships to boot! The one on the left is João Goncalves. 'Blue Eyes,' they call him—'Zarco.' The other one is Tristão Vaz Teixeira. They've only come here for a handout." Grudgingly, he added, "They fought well enough at Ceuta—I'll give them that."

The page made a last ineffectual attempt to bar the path of the three men, then turned despairingly to Bartolomé and gasped, "I tried to tell them that no one was to enter today, *o senhor*, but they wouldn't listen!"

"That's all right, Nunozinho," Bartolomé said, "I'll take care of it." He turned to the two squires, ignoring the sailor. "Well if it isn't senhores Zarco and Tristão Vaz!" he said. "Where have you been keeping yourselves, gentlemen? We missed you last summer when we were getting up a second fleet to come to the relief of Meneses' garrison at Ceuta! Was that because there's no loot to be taken from a city that's already been conquered? Why are you coming to bother the *infante* Henrique now? Are you hoping to impose upon his generosity?"

The two squires shot glances at each other, and then Zarco contrived a smile that was all charm. "Is that any way to talk to a couple of old comrades-at-arms, Dom Bartolomé? You're as crusty as ever." He looked around at the empty hall, where only a few servants stole around on their errands. "What's going on? The place is like a tomb!"

"The Prince can't be interrupted. He's busy."

"The Prince is always busy. When we heard he'd given up the court and planted himself at Sagres, we expected a beehive. Is something wrong?"

"Nothing that's any of your business. He isn't seeing anybody."

"He'll see us. Morales here has something to tell him that he'll be interested in, haven't you, Morales?" He pushed the sailor forward. "Come on, *amigo*, all we need is a few minutes."

Bartolomé inspected the sailor. "A Spaniard?" he growled. "And as big a rogue as you, I have no doubt. The Prince pays no money for sailors' tales."

Zarco drew himself up, his hand on the hilt of his sword. Pedro could see that he was a well-proportioned man with large, capable hands and muscular thighs that bulged through the mended hose. He looked like a practical man, in contrast to the dreamier, more slenderly built Teixeira. He wore a fine pair of green leather boots that looked as if they had been captured from a Moor. Pedro found him an admirable fellow and couldn't understand what Bartolomé had against him.

"Morales is my pilot and a good one," Zarco said indignantly. "He was a prisoner of the Moors before I rescued him. We haven't come here to beg money from the Prince. All we want is honorable employment. We're mariners, by God, the best there is! If the Prince has any new undertaking in mind, we're the men he needs!"

Bartolomé bit his lip. Pedro could see how troubled he was. "The Prince has no enterprise in mind just now. The country's at peace. There's no work for knights and squires. You're not alone. Everybody's short of cash these days, and you'll just have to make the best of it." He turned to Teixeira. "Dom Tristão, you're a young man with a new family. Go home and find something useful to do in the country."

Teixeira had more fire than Pedro would have given him credit for. He began shouting at Bartolomé.

"*Por Deos*, Zarco said it right! We're not beggars! Who

are you to keep us from the Prince? Let the *infante* decide whether or not he wants to see us!" He cast his gaze around the upper gallery. "Ho, Dom Henrique!" he bawled. "It's your old shipmates from Ceuta, Tristão Vaz and Zarco! We'd like to have a word with you!"

"*Chega, chega*, remember where you are!" Bartolomé sputtered. "Lower your voices! The *infante* can't receive anyone, I tell you! You'll have to leave."

The two squires started arguing with him, their voices louder than ever. The Spanish sailor, Morales, shrank in on himself, looking worried. Tempers flared, and fingers hovered too close to the pommels of weapons. Pedro began to fear that it was going to come to blows, or worse. He stood there with his arms full of helmets and greaves and wondered what he should do.

The creak of a railing made him raise his eyes to the balcony above. The tall figure that had appeared there leaned out over the hall and a deep voice boomed, "*Quem e?* Pray, who's that?"

"Now you've done it!" Bartolomé hissed. "It's Dom Henrique." He lifted his chin. "It's nothing, my lord. Only two gentlemen passing through."

Prince Henry descended to the floor of the great hall and came over to them. He moved gingerly, as if stiff, Pedro thought. The *infante* was a man in his mid-twenties, with a large frame and powerful shoulders, his fair English complexion burnt dark by the sun. He was wearing only a shirt and hose, and as he passed, Pedro could see that the shirt was stuck to his back and that bloodstains showed through the fabric.

The two squires bowed low, and the page made a leg. Pedro shifted his feet, wondering if he ought to put down his heavy load of armor and do the same, but nobody appeared to be paying attention to him.

"You remember us, don't you, *Vossa Excelência?*" Zarco said anxiously. "Your servants, João Goncalves and Tristão Vaz? We were with you at Ceuta."

Prince Henry's face was drawn and haggard from his ordeal, with a three-day growth of stubble showing. His eyes were red-rimmed from lack of sleep, and he must have been weak with hunger. But, Pedro marveled, none of this showed in his manner. From the *infante*'s air of easy command, the stale shirt, hanging halfway to his knees, might have been a princely robe, and his voice when he spoke was entirely natural and pleasant.

"Indeed I do. How could I forget the Zarco who thought of using ships' cannon to make a start at clearing the beaches and supplementing the work of the archers?" He turned to Teixeira and said graciously, "Or the brave Dom Tristão who led the landing party that came to the rescue of Ataide at the sally gate."

If Zarco and Teixeira were surprised at Prince Henry's appearance, they were doing their best not to show it.

"Those were the great days, Dom Henrique," Zarco said. He jabbed Teixeira in the side, and Teixeira enthusiastically nodded agreement.

For an instant Henry's eyes lighted up. But the spark faded, leaving behind only a look of exhaustion and infinite sadness.

"There are no more great deeds left to accomplish, *cavaleiros*," he said. "In Ceuta, Dom Pedro de Meneses holds the Moors at bay well enough on his own; he hardly needed our aid this past summer to repulse the kings of Fez and Granada. When the *Reconquista* comes to Granada and Gibraltar, as it surely must, it will be the king of Castile who gets the glory. And there are no new lands to conquer—" He smiled wanly. "Unless we were to discover the Isles of the Blessed."

A look passed between Zarco and Teixeira. "Dom Henrique, by your leave, we have something strange and marvelous to tell you," Zarco said smoothly. "Perhaps there are still wonders left in the world."

Despite his evident fatigue, a glimmer of interest showed in the Prince's face. "You have my leave," he said.

Zarco grabbed the Spanish sailor by the arm and dragged him over to stand in front of Henry. "This is Juan de Morales, my pilot. He's living proof."

Morales was flustered at being in the Prince's presence. He bowed awkwardly, remembered belatedly to remove his cap and essayed a crooked smile that was full of missing teeth. "Excuse me, Your Excellency," he said in execrable Portuguese. "I'm only a simple man."

"You're a Spaniard, *senhor*?" Henry inquired courteously.

"Yes, Your Excellency, from Seville."

"He's the best pilot I've ever seen," Teixeira interposed. "He knows every rock and headland from here to Safi, before Cape Non. And what's more, he knows how to sail out of sight of land by dead reckoning alone, with nothing more than a compass and the rhumb lines from his portolan chart."

Old Bartolomé snorted. "Is that what you've come to sell? Word must have gotten around fast that the *infante* is collecting *portolani* for his new observatory."

Prince Henry quelled Bartolomé with a glance and spoke encouragingly to Morales. "You're skilled in the use of compass and dividers, then? And, I have no doubt, in the use of the cross-staff?"

Morales looked uncomfortable at the attention he was getting. "Yes, Your Excellency."

"Such talent is rare," the Prince said. "It's one thing to feel your way around a coastline with the help of a copied *portolano*. But *portolani* tell only what is already known. It's better to discover the unknown."

Teixeira seemed about to say something further, but Zarco signaled him to silence. The Prince stared at Morales thoughtfully and went on.

"Tell me, have you ever sailed beyond Cape Non?"

"No, Your Excellency," Morales replied. "It's the farthest point of Africa. That's how it got its name. You know the old saying—'Who sails beyond Not, returns not.'"

A fleeting expression of impatience, even anger, crossed Henry's face. He recovered his amiability with an effort and said, "You're too intelligent a man to believe in the old superstitions. If ships don't return, there must be reasons. You're a skilled navigator. What do you think those reasons could be?"

For a moment Morales looked startled at being spoken to as an equal by royalty. Then, with an obvious pride of craft, he said, "It may be that there is another blunt cape some hundreds of miles below Non, and the two of them form a shallow bight between them. The bight would be open to the wind, which would tend to plaster a ship against the coastline, and at the same time the ocean current, squeezed between Africa and the Canary Islands at that point, would quicken. But the current would lie across the wind and cause swells. A ship caught in such a trap might find it impossible to escape and be dashed to pieces against the rocks."

"So the remedy would be to stand farther out to sea?" Henry prompted.

"Yes, but . . ."

"But our sailors are afraid of sea monsters and don't like to get out of the sight of land, and so they choose to wreck their ships and drown themselves."

"Morales isn't afraid of anything, are you Morales?" Zarco said, coming to the pilot's rescue.

Morales found his tongue again. "God's tooth, I don't fear the Dark Ocean as much as the Moors do! And they're better at reading the stars than we are!"

"Morales was a prisoner of the Moors for eighteen years, and he learned a trick or two from them," Zarco said.

Henry's interest was definitely awakened now. "And how did he come to be in your service, Dom João?" he asked.

"Do you remember when Don Sancho, the youngest son of King Ferdinand of Aragon, died? It was the year after we took Ceuta."

Prince Henry nodded. "He was a pious man. An example."

"That he was," Zarco agreed. "In his will he left a sum of money for the ransom of Christian prisoners in Morocco. Morales was among those ransomed. By chance, Dom Tristão and I were at that time carrying the war to Moorish ships off Tangier—"

"Pirating, you mean," Bartolomé interrupted. "Collecting slaves and booty."

"Doing God's work," Zarco said smoothly. "And we captured the ship that was bringing the prisoners across to Spain. Naturally"—he raised his eyes virtuously to the ceiling of the hall—"we liberated the Christian captives, but I kept Morales, thinking how his skills in navigation might be of benefit to some future cause of yours."

"We're at peace with Castile," Henry admonished the privateer. "You should have released him."

"Oh, Morales is happy to be in my employ," Zarco said. "He serves me of his own free will, don't you, Morales?"

The Spaniard gave a grunt that might have been acquiescence.

"And the tale that he has to tell ought not to reach Castile," Zarco went on. "Castile already lays claim to the Canary Islands, by leave of the pope, and it seems to me that if there are more islands in the Sea of Darkness, they ought to be the property of Portugal."

The gleam in Prince Henry's eyes grew brighter. "Say on," he said.

Morales began haltingly. "It's a tale I heard in the dungeons, Your Honor. The man who first told it was long dead before I was taken prisoner by the Saracens. But the story passed from mouth to mouth, and so was kept alive. It was known to all the prisoners, but more, the old man from whose lips I heard it had himself had it from one of those unfortunates whom the events had befallen more than forty years before...."

He had the full attention of Henry and everyone else within earshot, even Bartolomé. A number of servants were creeping about, pretending to work and lingering as close to the Prince's impromptu audience as they dared. They had come stealing into the great hall on invented errands when Henry's voice had first been heard there, to see for themselves that the *infante* indeed had emerged from his self-imposed isolation, at least for the moment, and that perhaps it wouldn't be necessary to walk on eggs anymore.

"... there was an Englishman named Machin from Bristol, the wool port, and he was in love with a lady of good family named Anna d'Arfet, and she with him," the pilot was saying. "But her parents would have none of it, and they used their influence to have Machin impris-

oned, while they forced the lady's betrothal to a nobleman of more suitable station. . . ."

The pile of armor that Pedro was holding was getting
heavier and heavier. He was strong, but his arms were
beginning to ache, and he was afraid that they were going to give way at any moment. In trying to shift the burden to a more comfortable position, he made a mistake in
balance, and to his horror a helmet and greave from the
top of the pile slid down and fell to the floor with a clatter. He made an ill-advised grab for them and, worse yet,
a teetering buckler followed them with a resounding
clang.

The eyes of the Prince left Morales and fixed on the
hapless Pedro. "What have we here?"

Pedro was too terrified to reply, and Bartolomé did it
for him. "It's young Pedro Costa, one of the kitchen boys,
Dom Henrique. He was helping me to hang some armor."

The prince had been too preoccupied with the pilot's
romantic tale to be aware of Pedro's predicament, but
now he repaired the oversight with a reassuring smile.
"You don't have to stand there like a statue, Pedro. Go
about your work, and don't mind us."

Pedro found enough voice to manage a *"Muito
obrigado, o senhor."* He stooped to pick up the fallen objects and began to stack them up again.

Zarco was annoyed at the interruption, but he was taking care not to show it. Following the Prince's lead, he
threw a scrap of kindness to the boy.

"Well, Pedro of the Coast, you're well named. Do you
know the sea?"

Pedro blushed at the "Da Costa." He wondered if
Zarco was making fun of him. "Y-yes, *senhor,*" he stammered. "My father's a fisherman."

"Many a fisherman fought with us at Ceuta. Would you
like to be a sailor and fight the Moors?"

"More than anything, *senhor,*" Pedro said honestly.

"Well, you look to be a well-set-up lad. When you get
your full growth, come and see me. Perhaps I might take
you on as a cabin boy or a *moço de bordo*. Would you
like that?"

Pedro could hardly believe his luck. "Oh yes, *senhor!*" he said.

Zarco laughed, and turned to Prince Henry. "You see, Dom Henrique, your subjects here in Algarve all have salt water in their veins, thanks to your example. If I'm ever lucky enough to get another ship, I'll make a proper mariner of young Pedro for you."

Teixeira coughed, and Prince Henry's bloodshot gaze swiveled back to Morales. "Proceed," he said. "What of this Englishman, Machin?"

The pilot resumed his romantic tale. "They had to let him out of prison, as there was nothing against him, and with the help of a friend who disguised himself as a groom and gained admittance to the house, he succeeded in carrying his mistress off. And so the lovers eloped, and Machin found a ship out of Bristol to take them to France, out of the reach of her father's vengeance. But on clearing the Bristol Channel they had to round Land's End, and a northeast wind drove them out to sea, far out of sight of land. . . ."

Henry nodded in appreciation of what was every sailor's nightmare. "The northern waters are treacherous. The storms come from nowhere. The inhabitants of the Scilly Islands off Land's End live on the shipwrecks. I'm told they have a shrine to Our Lady where they pray, not that wrecks should happen, but that if they do happen, they should be washed ashore to the benefit of the islanders."

Pedro, perched atop his ladder to hang a shield over the enormous fireplace, paused in his work to hear better. He wasn't alone; some of the other servants were edging unobtrusively closer. Diversions were few and far between in this bleak castle on an isolated cape, and the Spaniard's story, despite his barbarous accent, was better than a troubador's ballad.

Morales had lost his thread at the royal interruption, and Zarco had to prompt him. "Tell him how long they were driven before the storm, *amigo.*"

Tough old bird though he was, the Spaniard reflected a primitive dread in his seamed face as he replied, "For thirteen days they were driven by the tempest, farther and farther into the Dark Ocean, and all the while they lived in terror of falling over the brink of the world. But on the fourteenth day an island appeared in the middle of the ocean, and they were wrecked on its shores. . . ."

"The Fortunate Isles of the legend!" Henry exclaimed. "The Isle of the Saints!"

Morales shrugged. "It was large and well-watered and"—he struggled for the Portuguese words—"*toda madeira*, covered with wood. Like a paradise, they said, but there were no saints there and no people. The woman, Anna, died after five days, and her lover died of grief soon after. The others, the ones who survived the wreck, patched up the ship's boat, and drifted in it to the coast of Africa where, almost dead of privation and thirst, they were taken prisoner by the Moors. The Moors didn't believe their story and neither did many of the other Christian prisoners. But I talked many times, and at length, with the last old man before he died and also had the accounts of his companions from the boat, though changed in the telling by men who were not sailors themselves and so garbled the details—and I believe it rings true, *senhor*. The island of wood must lie farther out to sea than the Canaries and well north of them, or else Machin's ship would have been caught by the Canaries current and carried down the coast of Africa past Cape Non."

Pedro was enthralled by the story, though saddened at the death of the Englishman, Machin, and the woman. He stole a glance at the Prince and saw that he too had been transfixed by the tale, but in a different way. The *infante*'s face was excited rather than sad. It had come alive and lost its tired look. The sorrow that had lain across Henry's broad shoulders seemed miraculously lifted.

Zarco had noticed the change in the Prince, too, and he pressed in at once to make the most of it. "There was a cross, too, big enough to be seen from out at sea," he reminded the pilot.

"Yes," Morales confirmed. "Machin fashioned a cross for his love from one of the big trees, instead of helping to repair the boat, and when he died, his companions carved an inscription for them both."

Henry spoke decisively. "This island must be found again," he said.

Zarco had sense enough to say nothing. The Prince started to pace.

"This is the sign I have been waiting for," Prince Henry said in a voice that had suddenly become vibrant with purpose. "A divine message. You were sent as an answer to my prayers. Otherwise, why would you have come to me on this very day?"

Zarco and Teixeira exchanged a wary glance. This was more than they had bargained for. The Prince did not notice. He continued pacing, the words coming in an ecstatic rush.

"The intentions of God through us, His instruments, are mysterious. At my birth it was foretold by my mother's astrologer that I was meant, first, for great and noble conquests and second, to discover the unknown, that which is hidden from other men. I took it as God's purpose for me that I was meant to extend the Christian faith—to engage in crusades against the Moors, to bring Africa under Christian sway if I could." He frowned. "There has been no Christian bishop of Africa since the fall of Carthage—what an offering to bring to the Lord the conversion of that hidden immensity would be! And, if by pushing farther one could discover the kingdom of Prester John and gain him as an ally, then think of how many souls might be saved!"

To Pedro, balanced on the top rung of the ladder and once more hardly daring to move, it seemed that the *infante* must have had a vision, for otherwise how had the tired face filled out and become illuminated, and how else had that torrent of words burst forth? But why had there been no sign—no blinding light in the room, no voices? Was that how a vision looked to the others present—a starved and exhausted man suddenly bursting with enthusiasm, like a drunk?

"But I have never forgotten the second charge that was given to me," Henry rushed on. "It seems to me that great discoveries may be accomplished only by great

princes, with their wealth and their disinterest in gain,
for no ordinary sailor or merchant would set out on purpose to discover something new—such men do not
dream of navigating except to places where they already
know they can make a profit. And it also seems to me
that great discoveries may be made a little at a time, one
step after another."

He paused to think, and Pedro had to strain to hear his
next words. "Money may surely be found for such a noble purpose. There are the revenues from the Order of
Christ. As they cannot now be spent on a crusade, is it
not incumbent on me as Grand Master to find another
worthy cause for which to use them? And there is the in-
come from the soap monopoly and the fishing rights in
the Algarve. . . ."

He laughed with elation and turned to the two squires.
"It seems that the Lord does not wish me to conquer
Moors for Him at the moment. I may serve him another
way—by attempting the discovery of things unknown
and enlarging men's knowledge. *Senhores*, are you willing to engage in this great work?"

Zarco hooded his eyes to hide the triumph in them.
He nudged Teixeira. With old Bartolomé looking on in
sour disapproval, the pair kneeled at the Prince's feet.

"I swear to you that we desire nothing better than to
serve you, Dom Henrique," Zarco said in a voice throbbing with sincerity.

Impatiently, Henry waved them to their feet. "I wish
you to attempt the discovery of this island, the island that
is *toda madeira*," he said. "Let Castile keep the Canaries
for the time being—a worthless claim that, far from being the Fortunate Isles as they once avowed, are useless
for colonization until someone subdues a lot of naked
savages who stubbornly refuse to be brought to Christ!
We'll do better with our virgin island of wood, to the
profit of God and Portugal." His red-rimmed eyes burned
into them, and he spoke very deliberately. "But if you
cannot find the island, you can satisfy me by following
the coast of Africa just a little farther than is already
known. Are you willing to do that?"

"*Por Deos*, yes!" Zarco roared.

Henry nodded in approval. The corner of his mouth gave a humorous twitch, showing the Prince to be like ordinary men. "You're not afraid of sea unicorns, then, or of the pitch boiling away in the seams and sinking your ship or of sailing to where the ocean runs downhill and the world fades away in vapors and steaming slime?"

"We're not ignorant men!" Teixeira said indignantly.

"Good," said the Prince. "You'll have your ships. I have two vessels on the beach now, being careened for new planking and rudders. They're only *barchas*, with one mast and a single sail—all I can spare at the moment— but they'll be good seaworthy craft when the repairs are complete."

"Your Excellency won't regret this," said Zarco.

Henry turned to the constable. "There are a million things to attend to, Dom Bartolomé," he said. "Will you see to the provisioners—and get our own ovens to baking biscuit? And put a good cooper to work making water casks. And we'll have to find crews."

"As you say, Dom Henrique," Bartolomé responded.

Zarco had been waiting his chance to say something. "Excuse me, Dom Henrique, but those are dangerous waters. We might meet Moorish corsairs. We'll need cannon to defend ourselves."

Prince Henry did not notice Bartolomé's sardonic expression. "The *barchas* are decked forward," he said. "I'll give you one cannon apiece."

"But—" Teixeira began.

"That will be fine, Dom Henrique," Zarco said quickly. "With cannon and crossbow, we can fight off any Moorish corsair we encounter, and if it comes to boarding, there's cold steel." He cleared his throat. "Ah, of course we're entitled to any booty we happen to come across?"

"Yes, yes, of course," the Prince said impatiently. He turned on the page who had followed the two squires in. "Go find my valet, *moco*, and tell him to bring me a fresh *camisa* and doublet. And riding boots." His eyes fell next on Pedro, who was just then starting up the ladder with another shield. "Go to the stables, Pedrozinho, and tell the groom to saddle a horse for me. And one for Dom Bartolomé. We'd better ride to Lagos and wake up those shipwrights. . . ." He turned back to Zarco and said absently, "*Perdão*, Dom João, what did you say just then?"

Zarco placed a large sunburned hand over his heart. "Only that we'll do our best to find your Island of the Blessed, Dom Henrique."

The rest of the day passed in a dazzling blur for Pedro. The Prince was a whirlwind of energy, issuing orders to servants and gentlemen alike, summoning chandlers and craftsmen from the nearby village huddled at the base of the cape and not disdaining to discuss details personally with the lowliest workman. The household staff, after days of hiding in corners like little mice, looked on in amazement at the Prince's miraculous transformation. Pedro made himself so useful after the first errand to the stables that Bartolomé kept him on hand to run messages and help with the petty tasks. The second thing the Prince had him do was to go to the kitchens and fetch him some food.

"Tell them I'm famished, youngster, and don't let that fancy seneschal fuss about with one of those trays full of dainties that he's so proud of," the *infante* said. "Good, simple honest food—that's what I want. Any leftovers that happen to be hanging about will do—a cold joint, some bread. Anything that I can gnaw on without wasting time sitting down to eat. *Pode ir*, off with you now."

The seneschal did not like the message, and made a remark about fisher boys not deciding what princes shall eat, but when Pedro, gathering his courage, reminded him that the Prince was in a hurry, he grumbled a bit and set about rounding up a roast leg of mutton and a few other things—though he could not resist adding a little arrangement of candied fruits.

When the valet arrived, the Prince stripped off his bloody shirt where he stood, dropping it to the floor and putting on the new garments. Shirtless, Henry revealed himself to be broad-chested and powerfully thewed. Pedro goggled in awe and pity at the sight of his poor back, which was ridged and striped with clotted blood, like any galley slave's. But in his rich tunic, with a gold chain and the emblem of the Order of Christ around his neck, and a stately chaperon on his head, the Prince looked every inch the noble, born to command.

Word had spread fast, and by the time the *infante* was ready to depart for the shipyard at Lagos, at least twenty gentlemen were there to accompany him, forming a splendid entourage in fur-trimmed finery and glittering accoutrements. The best part of all was that Pedro got to go, too, scooped up by Bartolomé and riding behind him on the old war horse, Soldado, who was used to carrying twice that weight in armor.

The shipyard showed little activity as Henry's party rode up. The skeleton of a huge carrack stood upright in the sand, supported by timbers and stays, with no more than a half-dozen carpenters and caulkers crawling over the frame to sheath it. In the open sheds past the beach, a few workmen were sawing planks or shaping oak framing timbers with axe and adze. Some ropemakers stood idle outside the long wooden structure that held the rope walk, evidently having decided to quit work for the day.

Pedro, clinging to Bartolomé's thick waist, looked about with lively interest. He could see the two *barchas* that the Prince had mentioned, rolled over near the high-water mark and anchored against the tide by lines running inshore. They looked small next to some of the other vessels that had also been careened for overhaul— broad-beamed *naos*, chunky *frigetas*, a northern-style cog with castles fore and aft. A few workmen were ripping out old planking on one of the *barchas*, but the other was unattended.

What was left of the African fleet, fewer than twenty vessels, rode at anchor in the bay among all the fishing boats, with only skeleton crews or caretakers aboard. Pedro remembered having seen them sail bravely off earlier that year, banners flying, the gilt trim fresh, the decks crowded with armored men. It had been a different story then.

The Prince reined in beside Bartolomé. "I blame myself," he said. "Too long have they been without my direction. You can't expect men to have heart when their lord lacks it."

The arrival of the troop of horsemen had created a stir among the workmen. The pounding of the caulkers' hammers ceased and the coin-earner who had been wheeling a barrow of pitch stopped to gape. Some of the ropemakers who had been starting to leave drifted back. A sawyer climbed out of his pit and ran to get the master shipwright.

The master shipwright came hurrying up, wiping his hands on his apron. Prince Henry swung down to greet him, and Bartolomé followed suit despite his bad leg, though the *fidalgos* remained mounted out of dignity. Pedro slid to the ground and held the two horses without being asked.

The Prince put the master shipwright at ease immediately with a simple "*Boa tarde*, Dom Diogo," and soon the two of them were trading shipbuilding jargon as equals. "I can't put on extra men without taking them away from other projects, Dom Henrique," the wright said. "There's a shortage of certified caulkers and ship's carpenters here—they've all gone up to the Tagus to seek work, and the new trade representative they just elected is making difficulties about admitting more journeymen to the craft brotherhood."

Prince Henry shaded his eyes and scanned the beach. "You'd have to take men off the carrack and that cog you were refurbishing for me?"

"I'm afraid so."

"Do it, then. As to the craft representative, I'll have a talk with him. He won't make difficulties when I'm through. I'll grant an exemption from the *almotacaria* for shipwrights to make wages competitive with the Tagus. Then we can open up the qualifying examinations and get certificates for some of your journeymen, so you can fill the new places."

They moved on to the nearer *barcha*. Dom Diogo sharply ordered the artisans back to work, and the noise of saws and hammers resumed, but Henry wasn't satisfied until, after a flurry of commands and much running back and forth by apprentices, he saw a score of new carpenters swarming over the frames.

Zarco and Teixeira by that time had dismounted and had moved in to join the discussion about the refitting of the two vessels. A number of *fidalgos* had turned their own horses over to servants and were hovering about, taking care not to get tar on their finery. Pedro, leading Soldado and Prince Henry's horse, followed as closely as he dared.

"By the Feast of Saint Vincent?" Dom Diogo was protesting. "And not only replanked but fully decked as well? Impossible! It can't be done! Maybe by the Feast of Saint Brás."

"You can do it, Dom Diogo," the Prince soothed him. "I've seen you accomplish miracles before. If it's a question of still more men, put them on. I'll find the money."

The Prince's driving enthusiasm was contagious, and in short order the master shipwright was making suggestions of his own, suggestions that could only add to his difficulties. "Hmm, as to running with the wind before the beam, I think I could rig a second mast forward with a small lugsail ... that would help in the northerlies off the African coast to sail a few more degrees against the wind."

There were immediate objections from Teixeira. "Who ever heard of such a thing? Next you'll have us fitted with lateen sails like a Moorish galley—and circumcised as well."

"Lugsails are used in the English Channel," Prince Henry interposed mildly, "though mostly by smugglers and privateers to help them get in and out of coves. Perhaps on a voyage of exploration it wouldn't hurt to have some means of beating against the wind."

Zarco became alert. "Yes," he said thoughtfully, "why not? Let's try it. If it doesn't work we can always take down the sail."

Old Bartolomé gave a sardonic smile. "I thought the practices of smugglers and pirates might recommend themselves to you, Senhor Blue Eyes," he said.

"That's enough, Dom Bartolomé," the Prince said. "Dom João has promised to do his best to find Machin's island, and he's entitled to look out for his own interests along the way."

"In that case," Zarco said boldly, "why not *two* cannon for each ship, seeing that they're to be fully decked?"

To Pedro's surprise, Prince Henry did not choose to take the remark as a joke. He pondered the matter with gravity and finally said, "Perhaps the fleet might spare another bronze half-culverin and some balls, though I confess that it's beyond me why a *barcha* needs to be armed like a Venetian war galley."

That settled, they went on to discuss the question of crews. "I can round up most of the lads who sailed with me before," Zarco said, "and as for the rest, there's no shortage of beached sailors in the taverns of Lagos."

Pedro listened, with a sense that it was now or never. Unable to contain himself on this extraordinary day, he burst out, "Excuse me, *senhor*, you said I could apply to you if you ever got a ship."

Five startled pairs of eyes turned in his direction. "By God, the little cockerel speaks!" Zarco laughed.

"He's right," Bartolomé said. "A promise is a promise."

They turned to Prince Henry, who said, "A gentleman should keep his promises, but it's up to you, Dom Bartolomé."

The old soldier chewed his lip. "There's no future for him in the kitchens, now that that stuck-up seneschal from Lisbon has it in for him. He's a good lad, Zarco, strong and willing."

Zarco flashed a smile. "All right, Pedro da Costa. I'll take you aboard as a ship's boy, at wages of ten *libras* for the voyage. If you prove yourself as a seaman, I'll make you a *moço de bordo* for my next voyage."

That was all the attention that they had to spare for a fisher boy, but Pedro was by then hardly aware of what was going on around him, so dizzy was he with his good luck. This morning he had been plain Pedro Costa, a scullion at a day wage; now he had a fine new name, bestowed on him by Zarco, and he was a mariner, serving Prince Henry.

He came out of his daze to hear Zarco and Teixeira arguing about who got what ship, what course they should take, and about the division of booty. Morales, the Spanish navigator, had been taken a little way off by Prince Henry, and the two of them were conversing in low voices and staring southward over the Green Sea of Darkness to where the mysterious bulk of Africa lay over the horizon.

Prince Henry turned again to the two squires, his face edged in red by the setting sun, and they stopped their bickering to give him their full attention.

"It may be that you'll find nothing this time, *senhores*," he said in a voice of such intensity that Pedro thought he must have seen another vision out there. "All I ask is that you go farther. Always a little farther."

January 1419, The Forbidden City

Cheng Ho crossed the vast expanse of the Dragon Pavement and ascended the carved marble steps of the Hall of Supreme Harmony, where the Yung Lo Emperor waited for him. He could feel the eyes of the entire court following his progress. All of those hundreds of silent officials lining the ramps and rails—both the red-hatted Confucian civil servants and the high eunuchs in their gaudy robes—knew why he had been summoned, and his enemies among them were hoping to see the Emperor fly into one of his rages and order him to be beaten to death there in the courtyard.

Cheng Ho did not think it would happen to him. Was he not the Three-Jewel Eunuch and Admiral of the Imperial Treasure Fleet, whose deeds had added to the glory of the reign? But one never could tell. Though the Yung Lo Emperor was not as bad as his father had been, still, in the seventeen years of his rule Cheng Ho had seen even Grand Secretaries and the Shang-shu of the Six Boards publicly stripped, bent, and tied with their foreheads touching the ground and their buttocks presented, to be turned into shapeless pulp by a hundred soldiers wielding wooden rods. When an official received a summons such as the one that had brought Cheng Ho here today, he said good-bye to his family and was congratulated by his colleagues for still being alive afterward.

One by one the palace guards stepped impassively aside as he mounted the stairway to the Dragon Throne, holding aloft their long spiral pennants on gilt lances that were three times the height of a man. One of the younger archers rattled his bundle of arrows as Cheng Ho passed his rank, as if by accident. Cheng Ho kept his face expressionless. He had no illusions about the feelings of these highborn thugs toward him. The blackrobed corps of the notorious Chin-i-wei had grown to almost two hundred thousand during the present reign, and their sinister private prison system now rivaled the prisons maintained by the palace eunuchs and the Board of Punishments. During the brief reign of the previous emperor, the idealistic young nephew whom Yung Lo and the other uncles had deposed, the Chin-i-wei prisons had been ordered closed and their torture instruments destroyed. The palace guards themselves had been severely trimmed. But Yung Lo had reinstated them and had come to rely greatly on their network of spies and informers. Nevertheless, despite their power, the Chin-i-wei were jealous of the eunuchs' special access to the ear of the Emperor, and Cheng Ho had constantly to be on guard against their plots.

The guards were an annoyance, but a crude one. The real rivals to the influence of the eunuchs were the Confucian bureaucrats. Cheng Ho, taking care not to alter the dignified pace of his climb, flicked his eyes toward them. They stood about in small, prescribed, formal groupings within the zigzag marble pens that bordered the ascent to the Dragon Throne, stooped men whose eyesight had been ruined by the necessity for long study. Most of them were not even allowed beyond the first landing, and none but those on the very highest steps, wearing the porcelain placards of exalted rank on their backs, were permitted to address the Emperor directly. It was no wonder that they hated and despised the eunuchs, who as members of the Imperial household had the opportunity to converse with the Emperor daily, who did not have to pass examinations to gain their posts, and who, moreover, were in charge of the flogging of derelict officials.

Envy made them dangerous. It was from the ranks of these Confucian bookworms with their curved spines that the Anti-Maritime Party drew its strength, and it was the party's leader, Hsia Yuan-chi, who though he once had been a proponent of the Starry Fleet, now lost no opportunity to spread poison against the eunuch admiralty and the expense of further exploration.

Cheng Ho kept climbing. He was almost at the top now. It was not till he reached the next to the last step that a golden lance dropped level with his chest, barring his further progress.

He had trouble concealing his excitement. He had been allowed to approach one step higher than even the First Rank officials with their white crane plaques—the Censor, the Ministers of the Six Boards, the Grand Secretary. But there was no time to gloat. He had to perform the kowtow immediately.

Without seeming pause, Cheng Ho fell to his knees and struck the top step with his forehead three times. He repeated the sequence twice more, for the prescribed nine ritual prostrations that made up the kowtow, then raised his eyes as far as he dared toward the Dragon Throne.

The raised dais and carved screen were a writhing mass of gilt dragons, ninety-nine of them, suffused in thick clouds of smoke from bronze incense burners in the shape of cranes and tortoises. The throne itself was concealed in a lacquered cupboard that was six *ch'ih* wide. One of the cupboard doors opened a crack and Cheng Ho heard a rustle of movement within.

"Well, you ball-less wonder," a gruff voice said, "what have you got to say for yourself?"

"In all things I seek only to serve your perfect self, O Heaven's Equal," Cheng Ho replied calmly. He and the Emperor both came from peasant stock and understood each other well enough.

"I hear you've been up to your usual tricks," the Emperor growled. "The Minister of Works is complaining that you've stolen his best craftsmen for your Treasure Ship yards on the Yangtze. And now your effrontery has passed all bounds. You've transferred twenty thousand carpenters and metalworkers that were engaged in the reconstruction of my new northern capital and put them to work under that naval architect of yours, Chin Pi-feng—and without a shred of authorization. When you know that I've declared that Peking will be finished in time for the celebration of the Year of the Dragon, only one year away."

"Forgive this worthless person, O Sublime Hundredth Dragon," Cheng Ho countered. "I was at pains to take only those rough laborers and journeymen who had already completed their tasks in your inspired reconstruction of the glorious Pei capital. The finishing touches are work for the artisans, the sculptors, the tilemakers, the goldworkers, and these are of no use in the building of ships. Those I transferred were only conscripts who were removed from the southern capital sixteen years ago at the start of the grand project, and who now would be only useless mouths to feed or vagabonds threatening the public order if they remained here. They will be happy to rejoin their families in Nanking and will be usefully employed in the Dragon River shipyards."

From within his cupboard the Yung Lo Emperor grumbled, "The work is never finished. As soon as a wall or pavilion goes up, the rubble around it cries for another extension to make the plan more harmonious. Interference could be construed as treason.... Tell me why I should not sentence you to the death of the ten thousand slices."

Sweating, Cheng Ho kept his wits about him. "The work of enhancing Your Perfection's blinding brilliance does not consist only of constructing walls and towers and palaces, as awe-inspiring as these may be. The voyages of the Raft of Stars also spread the news of your grandeur. And by demonstrating your wealth and power, bring the whole world under your sway."

The doors of the cupboard opened a crack farther, and the Emperor said peevishly, "What do we care for the opinions of barbarians? The Middle Kingdom already possesses everything worth having, and we need nothing from outside." There was a shadow of movement as the Emperor heaved his bulk forward. "The Anti-Maritime Party says that your expeditions eat up funds that would be better spent on such things as agricultural support and granaries and water conservation projects, and I tend to agree. Then, too, there's the expense of my encyclopedia. I've got thousands of scholars working on it, and in four years they've already produced more than eleven thousand volumes—a much better return for my money than your curiosities from abroad, don't you think?"

Cheng Ho relaxed a bit. The Emperor was fencing with him for the fun of it, and the Anti-Maritime arguments were familiar ground.

"The wisdom of the esteemed Confucian scholars who oppose the voyages is beyond question," Cheng Ho said slyly. "But it was Hsia Yuan-chi himself, as Minister of the Board of Revenue, who financed the expeditions in the beginning."

There was a grunt of approval at the riposte. The Emperor was getting his sport. The doors opened still wider to provide a glimpse of a yellow robe and a manicured hand draped over a carved armrest. Encouraged, Cheng Ho continued.

"As for my 'curiosities from abroad,' O Perfect One, don't forget they included the long-necked beast from the land of Zanj that the natives called a *girin* or *zurafa*, but that the learned Confucians decided was the legendary chi-lin of good fortune. If you remember, the Board of Rites composed a hymn of praise to it, saying that it proved that Your Majesty's virtue equals that of Heaven, and that it was the harmonious vapors emanating from your luminous self that had caused a chi-lin to appear in the world."

The Emperor rumbled with laughter. "Yes, the Confucians made a tactical error when they fell all over themselves to praise the chi-lin. It was stupid of them. They outmaneuvered themselves. It made it harder for them to criticize your Treasure Fleet expeditions—though they've been making up for lost time ever since."

The cupboard doors flew all the way open, revealing the Emperor fully. Yung Lo had grown somewhat corpulent over the years, but the pointed beard and the complicated mustache with its four waxed spikes were still as black as ever, and there was nothing soft about that dark immoderate face with its bristling eyebrows.

"But *you'll* remember, my fine Eunuch of the Three Jewels of Pious Ejaculation," he said, "that I refused to accept their sycophantic congratulations. I reminded them that we have had good government without chi-lins."

Cheng Ho knew that the moment for his dangerous gamble had arrived. The Emperor, no matter what he said, had always regretted his rejection of the Board of Rites' outrageous flattery. His attack of mock humility had deprived him of a visible symbol of a fortunate reign, the chi-lin myth come to life, and the wonderful beast was going to waste in the palace zoo.

His heart pounding, Cheng Ho gave the prearranged signal—a slight lift of his left shoulder—to the eunuch who was stationed at the back of the hall, who would relay it outside. He had never been so frightened since the day he had reported to the doctor for the operation that had deprived him of his manhood.

At first no one in the hall noticed anything. The court's attention had fixed on the Emperor's person at the moment the cupboard doors had opened to reveal him.

Then a subdued rustle and murmur began at the back of the hall and began to move forward like a slow tide. The Emperor lifted his eyes in annoyance. His expression grew choleric. "What audacity is this?" he demanded.

Cheng Ho allowed himself a single backward glance. So far things were proceeding according to plan. The auspicious beast from beyond the western seas had covered a quarter of the distance to the Dragon Throne, moving along the central aisle that was reserved for the Emperor's palanquin, its long neck rising high above the forest of lances on either side. None of the soldiers had yet moved to interfere with it.

A brave man was leading the chi-lin by its long, bejeweled halter—the eunuch vice admiral Hou Hsien. Hou had weighed the risks and agreed to do it; he had said his prayers and bid farewell to his family that morning, but had not told them why. He looked petrified, but he carried himself well, his head high and his step unfaltering. No soldier, of course, would have dared to harm the lucky animal, but they might have seized the vice admiral and hacked him to death on the spot.

But the moment of danger seemed to have passed.

Already some of the gray-robed scholars were beginning to kowtow to the long-necked creature, and the red
robes were following suit. The chi-lin had passed between two troops of horsemen, disturbing their gold-
saddled mounts, and the troopers were busy trying to
keep the nickering animals under control.

Cheng Ho's eyes lingered on the chi-lin itself for an
extra fraction of a second. It was an extraordinarily beautiful creature, shy and gentle, with long lashes and the
liquid eyes of a fawn. Despite its towering height, it
moved with a spindly grace. It had two knobbed, furry
horns on its forehead, exactly as the legend had foretold,
and its body was a striking pattern of chestnut-red
patches that were so close together that they formed a
fine network of white lines.

Reluctantly, Cheng Ho faced the seething Emperor.
"This is not the chi-lin whose Memorial of Congratulations you refused to accept before, Son of Heaven," he
said quietly. "This is an entirely new chi-lin, even taller
than the first, that arrived only today and was brought to
you immediately, as good luck requires. It was brought
by a Treasure Ship of a subfleet that I left waiting in the
great southern ocean all this time for a rendezvous with
the Zanj ambassadors who were sent back to fetch it, as
an act of further submission by the dark nations to Your
Majesty."

The Emperor's eyes narrowed, and Cheng Ho knew
his life hung in the balance. But Yung Lo was a realist.
He could not afford to turn this propitious moment into
a disaster, in full view of the court.

"You're a clever eunuch," he said grudgingly, "but
that's why I made you my admiral. You've presented me
with a miracle too great to be ignored."

Sweat trickled from under Cheng Ho's pillbox hat
down his round face. He had not saved his life yet. Yung
Lo was a stubborn and vainglorious man who didn't like
to be bested, not even for his own good. Everything depended on the next few moments.

The auspicious beast reached the bottom of the first
landing, where the second-rank bureaucrats were seated
in packed rows, and began to mount the marble steps. A

small hubbub broke out as the scholars competed in expressions of awe and reverence. Those in front dropped to their knees and knocked their heads against the floor.

Now the steady-nerved vice admiral and his gangling charge had arrived at the foot of the Imperial Path—the ramp of dragon scales carved out of a single tremendous block of marble and transported to the Forbidden City at the cost of thousands of lives—that divided the great staircase in two. It would be a sacrilege for the vice admiral to place a foot on it. An officer of the guards woke up and stepped toward him. Hou Hsien dropped the dangling reins and stepped quickly aside, avoiding an incident.

But what was forbidden to men was not forbidden to the chi-lin. The enormous spotted beast began to climb the ramp, its tiny head bobbing. The court held its breath.

From his place on the step beside the reserved central path, Cheng Ho knelt and touched his forehead to the marble. He was still angled toward the throne, so his obeisance could be interpreted as being directed either toward the Emperor or the heaven-sent beast or toward their divine conjunction.

The chi-lin knelt on its forelegs before the throne. Its long neck stretched forward until its chin was resting on the top step next to Cheng Ho's sleeve.

The vast hall exploded with exclamations of amazement. This was a miraculous sign indeed. The sacred chi-lin was kowtowing to the Emperor.

The Emperor was as astonished as everyone else. Speechless, he stroked the waxed spike of a mustache and stared at the odd spectacle in front of him.

The chi-lin nudged Cheng Ho's sleeve. It nuzzled him impatiently, and then its long gray tongue reached into the sleeve and found the tender bamboo shoots that it had been carefully trained to expect there.

Nobody in the hall saw, with Cheng Ho's broad beam in the way, but the Emperor understood at once. Cheng Ho, when he raised his eyes, saw Yung Lo regarding him with a sardonic smile.

From the steps below came the droning voice of the

Minister of Rites, the only official authorized to address the Emperor directly.

"Truly heaven bows before you, Brilliant One. Even the chi-lin genuflects. Your virtue illuminates the world and causes the sun and the moon to follow their courses and a joyous cosmos to produce chi-lins."

The last part of the quote came from the paean that the Emperor had previously refused to accept. If the Emperor recognized it as being secondhand, he gave no sign.

"Get up, eunuch," he said. Then, unexpectedly, he laughed. "It seems that you've outflanked the Anti-Maritime Party again, *San-pao T'ai-chien*," he said, once more using Cheng Ho's honorific. "Those mewling paste-faces will have to pull in their horns for a while."

He turned to the Minister of Rites and said, "The auspicious beast will be placed at the east of the throne. See that a groom is appointed to collect its dung, which may be sold at a good price. You may compose a new Memorial of Congratulations and publish it throughout the land, not omitting the fact that the chi-lin kowtowed to the Son of Heaven and thus certified his abundant virtue. And don't forget to mention that the chi-lins were brought to me by my faithful Grand Admiral of the Raft of Stars, the Three-Jewel Eunuch Cheng Ho."

The Emperor was in high good humor as a cavalryman of the palace guard led the long-necked animal to the east end of the Dragon Throne's terrace, where it stood like a living artifact among all the fortunate cranes and lucky dragons, still munching its bamboo shoots.

"They won't like having to give credit to the Treasure Fleet expeditions," he guffawed, "but they'll have to swallow it. My father instituted capital punishment for those daring to petition against any of his policies. Perhaps I should revive the practice. Though it wouldn't stop them from intriguing behind my back."

"Your Majesty," Cheng Ho stammered. "I don't know how to thank you."

The Emperor turned to the Minister of Revenue, who was standing about with the rest of the board three steps down. "You, son of a turtle, I've authorized a sixth voyage of the Starry Raft. See that no obstacles are placed in the way of its funding."

The minister could not reply, but he kowtowed vigorously.

The Emperor grew thoughtful. He returned his attention to Cheng Ho and said, "Where will these voyages end, *San-pao T'ai-chien*?" he said. "When all this started, at the beginning of my reign, it was thought that we might make the whole world beyond the Central Kingdom our admirers and tributaries. But the world is turning out to be bigger than we supposed. Beyond the nations you've discovered are other nations and beyond them more nations still. Will it never end? Where is the edge of the world?"

"We will discover the edge of the world, Perfect One," Cheng Ho said confidently, "but not yet. There are many wonders out there—and not only chi-lins. I believe that a way may be found around the vast Dark Land in the southern ocean and that there is a sea route to the land of the yellow-hairs who used to come to us before we closed the silk road. When we discover it, you will truly dominate the world."

"And how will you discover such a route?"

Cheng Ho allowed some of the emotion that he kept secret within him to show. "By sailing farther, Brilliant Majesty, always a little farther."

February 1419, The Sea of Darkness

The *barcha* ran with bare poles before the storm, wallowing helplessly in the deep swells. A wall of green water slammed into the starboard side, jolting the ship from stem to stern and sending a cascade of spray over the low gunwales. Morales was doing his best to keep her head up with rudder and sweep, but the savage northeast wind was driving the little vessel like a chip, spinning it around in the current.

The square sail on which they depended had been ripped to shreds days ago, and Zarco had taken in the ingenious little lugsail before they should lose that, too. Sails or no, the treacherous wind had carried the *barcha* far off the African coast and into the Sea of Darkness.

Pedro clung to the stays for dear life and braced himself for the next crash of water. He saw an enormous wave looming high above him, its crest stripped away by the screaming wind. The ship gave a shudder and another curtain of spray drenched him from head to foot.

The stinging salt shower blinded him. When his eyes cleared, he saw Senhor Alves, the *despensero*, making his way toward him along the pitching deck, finding handholds where he could and moving in a crouch.

Alves shouted to make himself heard above the howling wind. "*Oi*, Pedro, has the glass run out?"

"Not yet, *senhor*—there's still a few minutes to go."

Pedro hid his surprise at being asked. Alves himself had remarked more than once that Pedro was the most reliable of the gromets aboard, never failing to turn the glass the moment the sand ran out, singing out the changes in a loud clear voice, and never neglecting to recite the *Pater Noster* and the *Ave Maria* at the assigned hours, unlike some of the other ship's boys, who were sometimes slack in their duties.

"Of course," Alves said by way of apology. He was the kindest of men, and he must have been very distracted. "Cursed if I know what good it does to keep track of the half hours in these seas anyway. All this tossing about hinders the running of the sand, and the saints themselves know how much time went unreckoned on yesterday's dogwatch, when that wicked boy Simao fell asleep. Morales won't find noon again till the weather clears and he can sight the sun."

Pedro listened respectfully. Alves was a gentleman in doublet and hose—one of the select group around Zarco who slept in the lean-to that had been erected aft to serve as a cabin, instead of curling up like a dog on the deck wherever space could be found, like a common mariner. He was older than Zarco's other cronies—Zarco relied on his steadiness. Pedro gathered that Dom Martim, as Alves was called, was in some kind of straitened circumstances and had been trying to recoup his fortunes when Zarco had persuaded him to join the expedition.

The ship plunged and bucked as another mountain of water lifted it high as steeples and dropped it down again into the trough. Bottle-green cliffs rose on either side and rained down an avalanche of spume. A wave sloshed waist high across the deck, carrying loose gear with it. Pedro knew a moment of terror as it threatened to sweep him off his feet, but his death grip on the stays saved him. Then Morales, miraculously, managed to turn the bow toward the sea once more, and Pedro, still coughing and choking, was able to reflect that the little craft would have been swamped if Prince Henry had not wisely insisted that it be fully decked.

Pedro lifted his smarting eyes and saw a jagged gap in the bulwarks, with water pouring through. The remaining bronze cannon had torn loose from its lashings and crashed through the planks and over the side. Already the carpenter and cooper were struggling across the deck with tools and new lengths of planking; the *barcha*'s freeboard was low enough without an additional bite being taken out of it.

"*Oi*, is everyone still here?" Alves shouted.

A confused babble of voices was heard above the storm. The same question was being asked aft, where Zarco, clinging to the sternpost, was conferring with Morales. A tally was taken; no one had been washed overboard this time. When the first cannon had been lost at the beginning of the storm, it had carried an unfortunate gromet with it, and since then two more sailors had been lost.

A sailor began to weep. "We're all going to die," he said. "This wooden whore is going to take us to the bottom with her."

"Quiet, man," Alves ordered. "That's no way to talk."

Another sailor, his voice ragged with hysteria, bleated, "He's right! The Dark Ocean's got us! You can tell from the way we're moving! The water's starting to run downhill now, and it'll get steeper and steeper! We're caught in it, and we'll all be drawn down to hell!"

"Shut up, or I'll have you flogged," Alves snapped at him. He confronted a circle of white, frightened faces and said, "We haven't sunk so far, and we won't. Morales is a good navigator. This accursed wind can't last forever. As soon as he can see a star or two, we'll rig the spare sail and catch a westerly back to land. If we have to, we'll row. Now, back to work. You there, Fontes, you're supposed to be the *calafate*! Go and help the carpenter to make that patch watertight!"

The men were quelled momentarily, but Pedro wondered how long it would last. All the spare sweeps had been broken, and if they lost the last one, there would be no way Morales could keep the ship headed into the sea with rudder alone; he had tried rigging a small headsail, and it had been whipped away by the wind as soon as he got it up. God alone knew how far the *barcha* had been carried out into the Western Ocean; there was no way in these surging waters for Morales to use a log glass and knotted line to estimate the speed of the ship, and if they were caught in a great westerly current, such calculations would be meaningless anyway.

Zarco came forward, his tunic bedraggled and his sodden hose hanging loosely from its points, and he and Alves put their heads together. They spoke in low voices, but Pedro saw a flash of anger from Alves and a quick, meaningless smile from Zarco as he attempted to placate him. When they finished their business, Zarco turned to Pedro with a jovial expression and said, "How's our little *moco de bordo*? Are you minding the glass and keeping the slate as Senhor Alves taught you?"

"Yes, *senhor*," Pedro replied.

"Did you have something to eat today?"

"Yes, *senhor*, thank you very much."

Pedro had breakfasted on a ship's biscuit and some olives before his watch. Nobody aboard had had a hot meal since the storm had started; the little sand-filled firebox was as drenched as everything else aboard, and even if it had not been, a fire in a ship pitching as wildly as this one would not have been allowed.

"Good," Zarco said. "Don't forget your prayers, and you can lead the men in the *Salve Regina* at sunset—if we can figure out when sunset is in this pea soup!"

He nodded encouragingly at the men in the vicinity, and with one hand on the hilt of his sword to keep it from clattering about and the other hand on the gunwale, he groped his way aft again.

Alves stared after the departing back, shaking his head. "He cares more about the loss of the cannon than he does about our plight or the temper of the crew. I told him it was good riddance. Those cursed cannon have brought us nothing but bad luck. We lost a ship's boy because of one of them, and the other lost us our only prize."

Pedro could understand the older man's bitterness at losing the prize. Zarco had tried to intercept an Arab ship traveling along the Tangier coast—a two-masted *boum* with its deck crowded with pilgrims headed for Mecca. Its master had refused to stop, and Zarco, waving off Alves's advice to give him a taste of a few old-fashioned bolts from a crossbow, had decided to provide a demonstration with the cannon. But aim and elevation were difficult to manage in a choppy sea, and the cannon had punched a hole in the Saracen vessel below the waterline. It had sunk quickly in the rough waters, and the passengers who had been jammed topside had drowned before their eyes. It had been a cruel disappointment to the sailors, who had been promised shares; now there would be no slaves, no ransom money, no booty in the form of jewelry and travel money that they might have taken from the pilgrims. A great tragedy, Zarco had said.

"Perhaps Senhor Teixeira escaped being blown out to sea, and will still find a prize on his own when the storm dies down," Pedro suggested. "Then it will be share and share alike, as the *senhores* agreed—if we ever get out of this fix we're in."

Pedro did not want to say what was on everybody's mind—that the fate of the *barcha* commanded by Teixeira could not be known. The two ships had become separated early in the storm, and Teixeira's floundering vessel had not been seen since.

Alves must have been thinking the same thing, but he bit off his words angrily. "Why go pirating at all? Prince Henry would have rewarded us handsomely just for going fifty miles farther down the coast than mariners have gone before—and if we happened to discover his mythical island to boot, we'd be fixed for life."

Alves's words were troubling. Pedro in truth had been

surprised when Zarco had shown no inclination whatsoever to sail southward along the African shore toward Cape Non, after the bold promises he and Teixeira had made to Prince Henry. Zarco hadn't even sailed as far south as Safi. He had simply hung around familiar waters, looking for prey.

But Pedro was unwilling to criticize his benefactor aloud. It was thanks to Zarco that he was a *moco de bordo* and might aspire some day to become an ablebodied mariner. Zarco had even outfitted him out of his own pocket, giving him a seaman's hooded smock and red stocking cap.

The glass saved him from having to reply. His alert eye caught the last few grains of sand running out. He turned the glass, handed the slate to Alves, and lifted his young voice in the gromet's chant:

> *The eighth glass flows out,*
> *The watch is callled,*
> *Blessed be the Mother of God.*
> *More hours will flow,*
> *If God wills it.*

The men stirred reluctantly, unwilling to leave their safe handholds. A bellow from aft got them moving.

"Look lively, you dogs! *Depressa, depressa!* Get going!" Then, in a coaxing tone: "Come on, boys, we're not dead yet. We've all got to do our part."

Silvio, the gromet who was supposed to relieve Pedro, remained curled up in the shelter of a wine cask, too terrified to move. A kick from the boatswain brought him to his feet, and he came scuttling over. Pedro took one look at his drained face and chattering teeth and wondered if he could be trusted.

"Grab hold of those stays," he said. "It's all right. I'll stay with you till the second glass."

The seas became worse, if anything, during the night. A water cask got loose and smashed against the bulwarks, but no one was hurt. Pedro stretched out in the relative shelter of the prow, but the wild pitching of the ship kept him from sleeping; he doubted that anyone was sleeping that night, from the fear of being washed overboard. About every tenth wave seemed to be a big one, rearing high over the masts and drenching them with its spume, but the little ship seemed to ride out the huge swells well enough.

Toward morning the wind seemed to die down a bit. By the dawn watch the swells had flattened out considerably, and Zarco himself led the exhausted crew in the *Pater Noster*. The skies had not cleared, but a bleary light could be seen to the east.

By mid watch, the wind had become tame enough for Morales to raise the small sail. He set its luff so short that it looked overbalanced and proceeded to sail so close that Pedro feared he would come right up into the wind. The sailors became restive when they saw the trend of the ship was westward, away from the rising light that was hidden behind the clouds, but Zarco calmed them down by explaining that Morales, with the uncanny instincts that he had demonstrated so many times before, was taking a tack that would eventually find them a westerly.

The veiled sun stood high in the sky when the lookout cried, *"O terra!"* There was a general rush to the port side. Pedro climbed the shrouds partway to look, but he could see nothing but what might have been the faintest darker patch in the blurred and milky air that surrounded them.

Then the mists parted, the sun burst out like a benediction, and there, sitting in the middle of the sea, was an island with jagged mountain peaks and a long, beautiful golden beach.

"Porto santo!" a sailor sobbed. "Safe harbor!"

Pedro wept unashamedly with the others. It was only necessary to have faith. He wondered if they would find Machin's cross on the beach. He dropped to the deck and found Zarco standing with Alves at the rail, staring out at the sandy bay.

Zarco turned, not really seeing him, and whispered half to himself, "The tale of an island was true after all."

CHAPTER 1

Sandro emerged from the clamorous depths of the Arsenal into bright sunlight. It promised to be a perfect, golden day—just the sort of day to spend at the archery butts with his friends or perhaps simply to laze away with a stroll through the Rialto, capped by a gondola ride past the Borgo Palace for a sweet, surreptitious look toward Giuditta's window in anticipation of tonight's adventure.

"You'll give my regards to your father, Messer Alessandro, and remember to tell him that we'll be ready next week to accept bids on the new lumber contract," said the squat, enormously muscled man at his side, as they stopped at the wooden drawbridge outside the Arsenal sea gate.

"Yes, Ser Ugo," Sandro said, itching to be released now that his errand was completed. Remembering his manners, he added, "Thank you for the hint."

"It's a pleasure doing business with the House of Cavalli," said the barrel-chested foreman. He cast a swift automatic glance around him and yelled at a workman who was trying to slip out of a side entrance. "Hey you, where do you think you're going? The day's hardly begun! And take off that jacket. You know you're supposed to carry it over your shoulder. If you're trying to steal nails, I'll have you flogged round the shipyard!"

Sullenly, the man removed his tunic and shook it out to show there was nothing concealed in it. Then, with an ugly scowl, he went back into the walled confines of the enormous works.

"There was a bad incident last week," Ugo confided to Sandro. "A couple of the *arsenalotti* lay in wait for a paymaster who'd docked them, and killed him with hammers. They escaped to Ravenna, so it's said." He shrugged his tremendous shoulders. "The commissioners are lax about paying the wages on time, and it's the poor man who suffers." He squinted at Sandro. "Your father ought to apply for the payroll contract. The Cavalli bank would clear a good commission, and the thing would be done right. Suggest that to him, won't you?"

"I will," said Sandro hastily, starting to edge away.

He was eager to be gone from this noisy, teeming place with its pervasive smell of gunpowder and boiling pitch. He didn't like his visits here. He could never escape the feeling that some day he would be caught in one of the gunpowder explosions that periodically maimed *arsenalotti* and rocked Venice. The Florentine poet Dante had used the Arsenal as a metaphor for hell, Sandro's old abacus master once had told him; a hundred years earlier, given a visiting dignitary's tour of Venice's enormous state shipyard, Dante had been struck by the spectacle of thousands of toiling men, the clouds of acrid smoke, the din of the forges—the very images of Inferno.

But if the Arsenal were hell, Sandro couldn't help thinking, then Ugo—dark, hairy, and wide as a door—must be one of its demons. Of course, he amended hastily, that was unfair, because Ugo was a decent sort, a man who had risen by merit from the ranks of *il populi* to become a respected foreman shipwright.

Sandro was not to be released yet. A powerful hand with knuckles of fur closed around his upper arm. "And what of your own plans, Messer Alessandro?" Ugo inquired with a yellow-toothed smile. "You're eighteen this year, aren't you? Of legal age to get an appointment as a bowman of the quarterdeck on one of the state merchant galleys."

"If I can qualify," Sandro said, looking down.

"*If* he can qualify!" Ugo snorted. "Listen to him! I hear you're the best of all the young nobles at the shooting butts!"

"I'm hoping my father will let me sign on with the voyage of the Galley of Beirut this summer," Sandro admitted.

"That's the spirit!" Ugo approved. "Of course he'll agree. It's the best way for a young fellow of good family to get started in business. You'll dine at the captain's table with the older merchants ... they'll show you the ropes, help you get your feet wet. You'll be allowed to load some cargo of your own without paying freight and trade it privately at the ports of call. A young man can clear a hundred ducats or more on a voyage—there are great merchant houses in Venice that began with a nest egg like that. Your own father started out as one of the *balestrieri della popa* on the Barbary run, just to show *his* father he didn't need everything handed to him on a silver platter. That's where I met him. I was one of the common bowmen on that voyage. He was a fine gentleman even as a youth—nothing of the snob about him! We were attacked by Moorish pirates off Tripoli, but we drove them off. Your father's bolt caught the Moorish *aguzino* in the shoulder and threw him off balance; the galley slaves pulled him down and tore him apart. 'Serves him right for flogging Christians,' your father said, but he worried about what would happen to the slaves afterward. That's the kind of man he is...."

Sandro listened politely. He had heard the tale a hundred times before. Finally he made his escape. He paused at the top of the drawbridge to watch a convoy of great galleys rowing out through the channel under an escort of slimmer, more dangerous looking war galleys. They made a fine sight as they glided with furled sails past the glittering facades of the buildings on the Riva, their gilded prows sparkling in the sun, the golden lion of Saint Mark fluttering bravely from their masts, their hundreds of oars rising and falling in unison, like beating wings.

A thrill of pride at being a Venetian went through Sandro as he watched. Venice ruled the known seas. There was no other maritime power to match her. These proud fleets sailed the Barbary Coast unmolested by Moors—indeed Moorish merchants themselves preferred to book passage on these Christian ships because they were reliable and safe. The great galleys sailed on fixed schedules to Tripoli and Tyre to bring back the eastern silks and spices that all Europe craved, past the gates of Constantinople into the Black Sea to fetch cargoes of yellow-haired slaves from beyond the Caucasus, past Gibraltar to Flanders and England to carry cloth and English wool.

Sandro's eye fell on the crimson lining that bordered each galley's bulwarks—the jolly red ponchos of the oarsmen, which they would discard once out of sight of land, to row naked.

That was another thing. Venice's rowers were mostly freemen, except for a few debt slaves working off their sentences. True, they were mostly Dalmatians and waterfront scum rounded up by labor contractors—those dregs of humanity willing to accept pay of a few *piccoli* a day. But they weren't chained to their benches except in port, and in an emergency they could be called upon to help defend the ship. Sandro wrinkled his nose. Let other nations, like Genoa, rely on galley slaves who were never unshackled, not even to relieve themselves. You could smell a Genoese galley coming from a mile away. The Knights of Malta, at least, sank their galleys in shallow water at every opportunity to wash out the filth in the bilges.

The fleet passed the customs house at the end of the point, heading out to sea. Sandro, with a last admiring look, turned and descended the steps to the quay.

He paused for a moment on the embankment, trying to decide which way to go. Anyone noticing him would have seen a tall graceful youth of the nobility, too young for the robe, dressed in bright red hose and a fashionably tight tunic that showed his wide shoulders and slender waist to advantage. Being under twenty-five, Sandro was required to wear the *calar stola*, the strip of blue cloth hanging from his shoulder, but like any self-respecting youth, he kept it rolled up and thrown over his arm. His belt, with a few inexpensive jewels, cost well below the twenty-five-ducat legal limit for his age group; the Cavallis were not a showy family.

The smell of salt water decided him not to cut across the grounds of Saint Martin's and take his usual shortcut to the Rialto through back streets and canals. Instead he meandered toward the waterfront. He formed a vague plan of following the Riva to Saint Mark's Piazza, loitering there awhile in hopes of bumping into someone he knew and exchanging the day's gossip, then strolling along the shop-lined Merceria to the Rialto Bridge to join the well-dressed throngs swarming along the Grand Canal.

The rundown district behind this part of the waterfront was another world. Sandro walked quickly to get past the rotting warehouses, the smell of the fish market, the dank warrens where the sailors of a hundred nations sought out cheap taverns and cheaper whores while they were in port.

The waterfront itself was more interesting. A clean sea breeze swept away the smell of the garbage clogging the narrower canals at low tide. Respectable merchants promenaded here, sometimes with their wives or mistresses, to enjoy the exotic spectacle of ships from every corner of the world moored at dockside and turning the lagoon into a forest of masts, or to stop at an open-air *trattoria* for a seafood snack and a glass of wine.

He stopped idly to watch a waterfront slave auction. The auctioneer had set up his block in an open space fronting the docks, under an awning of striped canvas bearing a faded and indecipherable coat of arms.

The buying and selling of slaves in the city's center was prohibited by a fifty-year-old ordinance, but the market had simply been moved to the quays. The business was too lucrative to be stopped by the pronouncements of moralists, who objected to the traffic in Greeks and other Christians or by the occasional halfhearted spasm of petty regulations from the Senate. Venice enjoyed a favored position in the immensely profitable trade, thanks to its access to the major sources of supply in the Black Sea and the Sea of Azov. Only Genoa, with its own Black Sea trading posts, was in a position to compete for the blond Slavs and Circassians who were so much in demand throughout Italy.

Quite a large crowd had gathered in the impromptu square formed by the widening of the embankment at dockside and the inset buildings opposite. They overflowed the steps leading down to the jetty and were jammed up against the walls and pillars of the facing arcade. The serious buyers, close to the platform, were dealers, there to bid on entire lots for resale. Then there were the individual buyers—businessmen in sober black robes, well-to-do *cittadini*, priests shopping for their superiors—hoping to snap up a bargain in a household servant or a Circassian beauty. Conspicuous by their multicolored finery were small packs of young bloods, there to ogle naked women and enjoy the sport of egging one another on to atrocious behavior. And finally there were those who, like Sandro, had nothing better to do.

On the block at the moment were four pale but otherwise healthy-looking men who were evidently being sold as a unit. They were chained together at the ankles and were stripped, as the law required, to warn the potential buyer of any defects. Their wheat-colored hair and snub noses proclaimed them to be from somewhere beyond the mouth of the Don, probably snatched up by Mongol raiders and brought to the slave market at Tana. If they were Christianized at all, they would be of the Eastern rite, which made them infidels, so that was all right. They looked too savage to make good household servants. Probably they would end up as a work gang on a Venetian sugar plantation on Cyprus or Crete.

"I have a bid of forty ducats," the auctioneer was saying in an aggrieved tone of voice. "Who'll make it fifty?" He was a brawny man with a chewed-up ear and a hideous scar running down the side of his face—testimony to the hazards of his profession.

No one took him up on it. The last bidder, a saturnine

citizen in a dove-gray cloak, grinned in anticipation of his bargain and said something to one of the hard-looking flunkies he had brought with him.

"Come, good *messeri*," the auctioneer wheedled. "Forty ducats would hardly buy you a quartet of donkeys. Here we have four fine, strong fellows, well broken to the lash, who'll give you years of labor. At ten ducats the man, you're paying less apiece than you'd lay out in a year's wages for a housemaid."

The pimple-faced popinjay standing in front of Sandro snickered and made a sotto voce remark that got a laugh from his friends. Sandro looked them over enviously. From the colors of their striped silk tights and the patterns of gold embroidery and jewels on their doublets, they were members of the *Immortali*, one of the clubs of the *Compagnia della Calza*—the Company of the Hose. Sandro longed to join—he was old enough now—but he had never been asked, and if he had been, his father would doubtless have forbidden it. "Strutting peacocks who ought to be hung between the pillars for violating the sumptuary laws," was about the mildest pronouncement he had ever made about the young men of the *Compagnia*.

The gorgeously dressed youth with the bad complexion caught Sandro staring and whispered to his companions, drawing another laugh. Red-faced, Sandro returned his attention to the platform.

Another bidder, with the permission of the desperate auctioneer, had climbed the platform, and was feeling the arms and thighs of the yellow-haired men, who stirred restively, like nervous horses. The new bidder was not impressed. "Forty-five ducats," he said indifferently.

The man in the gray cloak was infuriated at seeing his bargain fade away. "Fifty ducats!" he snapped.

The auctioneer's face lit up. "That's more like it," he said. "Who'll make it sixty?"

The new bid had broken the logjam, and in the end, the four Russians went for eighty ducats. The auctioneer, mopping his brow, went on to the next lot.

This sale promised livelier entertainment, and the crowd became more attentive. A pair of Circassian girls,

ve, hold, sell,
_____ ____ _____ inrent, and do with in
tuity whatsoever may please him, and no man may
gainsay him. What man among you will know the privilege of training these two beauties to work in harness, gentlemen? The bids start at two hundred ducats. . . ."

Sandro was impressed. Two hundred ducats was a princely sum—more than the annual salary of the admiral of the Arsenal. The auctioneer's glib patter went on. At Sandro's left, a middle-class merchant who had probably come to the auction with nothing more on his mind than obtaining a little girl to do kitchen work, licked his lips and began fingering the coins in his purse, doing sums in his head.

"That merchandise isn't for you, *ser cittadino*," laughed one of the supercilious young men of the *Immortali*. "It'll go to a cardinal, at least."

"*Che diavolo!*" simpered the pimply fop in front of Sandro. "They're mares fit for the Doge himself, *il vecchio stallóne!*"

The others chortled at the sally. It was a swipe at the

ish life of a st...
galley. The women, lik...
Moslem harems, with a wink and a nod from the a...
ities. And there was little hope of escape; all the world
cooperated in returning runaways, who then could be
charged with theft for stealing themselves from their
masters.

There were no household slaves in the *Cà di Cavalli*;
Sandro's father refused to permit it and declined even to
dabble in the business for profit, though all of his competitors did. Sandro's pleasure in the beautiful morning
diminished as his upbringing began to take hold.

The pimpled dandy named Orazio, on the alert for
someone else to bait, caught Sandro's troubled expression.

He nudged one of his fellows. "Looking's free," he
said. "But there are those who don't even like to do that."

The other, who couldn't have been more than a year or
two older than Sandro, replied, "*Che peccato!* Perhaps
he's not yet ready for a gallop."

That brought more laughs all around, and then the

stocking-club rowdies fastened all their attention on the platform, where the auctioneer was prodding the sobbing Circassians with the butt of his coiled whip, lifting their breasts with it for a more provocative display of the merchandise.

Sandro, his face still burning, dropped his eyes to the foot of the platform where the next lot of slaves huddled, waiting their turn on the block.

He found no solace there for his conscience. Instead of Tatars, Moors, or Slavs, he found a large number of people who from their features and remaining rags of clothing seemed to be Greek. Probably the poor wretches had been removed by raiders from some remote island in the Aegean.

Even the pope, who maintained diplomatic relations with Emperor Palaeologus of Constantinople, held Greeks to be Christians of a sort—though the slave traders conveniently ignored the distinction; after all, Constantinople had once been profitably sacked by Crusaders at the urging of Venice.

The Greeks were mostly women and children, though one old man, almost worthless, had somehow survived the hold of the slave ship. The auctioneer's assistants were going among them, stripping them of their tattered garments in preparation for the next round of bidding.

Sandro's eyes fell on a beautiful young woman who looked like one of the classic statues that Venice had plundered from the shores of the Aegean to decorate its palaces and public buildings. She had a wide smooth brow, a straight nose, skin like alabaster, black brows, and thick black hair. Unlike the others, she held her head high, so that Sandro could see a length of white throat. She was about Sandro's age, not old enough to be the mother of the small boy she was comforting, so he was most likely her little brother.

Two of the auctioneer's assistants reached her, and while one pulled the little boy away from her, the other started roughly to peel off her drab garments. When she tried to elude him, he fetched her a loud slap in the face and with one powerful motion ripped her dress down the front. He did not use the whip he carried coiled under his arm; the auctioneer would not have wanted him to mark her body before a sale.

Her body, too, was as white and unblemished as marble. Sandro's impression of a carved Venus was enhanced by the instant when, in the classical pose, one hand flew to shield her groin and the other, inadequately, to cover a breast, before the impatient flunky jerked her arms behind her back and bound her wrists together.

A moment later, as her eyes rolled in despair, searching an impossible escape, her frantic gaze met Sandro's. For some reason their eyes locked, and he fancied he could see an animal pleading in hers.

Sandro averted his eyes in shame. His pleasure in the morning was now entirely gone, but he was not yet ready to make up his mind to leave.

He devoted himself for the moment to watching the crowd. There were two bidders left for the Circassian pair; the others had dropped out after a few feeble challenges that never got very far above the auctioneer's floor. One was a fat banker named Cresco, whom Sandro knew by sight, and who was reputed to be immensely rich and of irregular habits. The other was a tall hooded man in a priest's robes, wearing a mask—procurer for some powerful ecclesiastic, possibly even a cardinal, as the stocking-club youth had suggested.

"Six hundred ducats!" the auctioneer bawled out in response to a sign made by the prelate's masked agent. "Do I hear seven hundred?"

The crowd held its breath. The wholesale dealers remained silent. Their profits depended on a sensible turnover of merchandise at a fair markup, not gambling for the occasional rich man's toy. And perhaps, too, they knew who His Eminence was and didn't want to get in trouble with him.

"Six hundred and fifty!" shouted the banker, getting a little purple in the face.

Sandro's eyes wandered through the crowd, picking out faces. He stopped at a lean pallid visage whose beetling black brows gave its owner an angry look. It was his older brother, Maffeo.

Maffeo was talking to a thick-bodied, brutish-looking

individual with a broken nose—a man named Falco, who was well known around the waterfront. Falco claimed to be a labor contractor whose business was rounding up oarsmen for the galleys on commission. But everybody knew that he was factor for one of the big Moslem firms in Alexandria that transshipped Venetian slaves.

Sandro was familiar with Falco's unsavory reputation. Many a drunken Dalmatian wharf rat, it was said, woke up with a hangover, chained to an oar, with his wages in Falco's pocket. If he tried to complain, he was told that he had drunk up his advance. Selling Christians to Moslems was a more serious matter, but somehow Falco got away with it. It was whispered about that Falco and his crew of bravos were available to do illegal favors in the dark of the night for respectable bankers and merchants and that he had even been employed thus by members of the Council of Ten.

Maffeo had his head close to Falco's, talking earnestly. Falco shook his head, making a gesture toward Maffeo's purse. Maffeo scowled and launched into some kind of explanation that involved the spreading of his fingers several times to indicate a sum.

What was Maffeo doing in such company? Sandro wrinkled his brow in perplexity. Their father would not approve of any dealings with a slave trafficker. The profligate Maffeo, always in need of money, had a number of times urged the elder Cavalli to get into the lucrative business, until he was forbidden to bring up the subject again.

Maffeo seemed to have given in on a point; at least his hand went reluctantly to his purse. He darted a quick look around the crowd as he did so, and the brothers' eyes met. Maffeo gave a start of recognition and at once disappeared into the crowd.

The slave dealer had not failed to follow the direction of Maffeo's gaze, and he fixed the still-gaping Sandro with a long and chilling stare.

Sandro turned away to watch the auction again. The Circassian girls had been knocked down for eight hundred gold ducats to the agent of the anonymous prelate. A snap of the fingers from the masked priest sufficed to get them draped once more with their rags, and they were being led away by his servants.

The Greeks were up next. They were going to be sold as a group. The marble-faced girl and the one or two other young women who might have been regarded as choice merchandise were not taken apart to be sold separately, as Sandro had expected. Perhaps the auctioneer wanted to get this lot off his hands as quickly as possible, before there was trouble with the authorities, and he reckoned that the inclusion of the more valuable items would sweeten the price of the whole.

"What am I bid, *messeri*?" chanted the auctioneer. "Here's a fine lot for quick turnover, a guaranteed profit for some shrewd buyer. Nurses and seamstresses, housemaids and cooks—and a few little pearls thrown in with the rest! See you here porters and boatmen and little boys whom you may shape as you will. And scorn not the old men, for there are craftsmen among them."

Sandro stole another look at his alabaster maiden. She stood dumbly, like an animal, her hands bound behind her, seemingly dazed. The boy was not with her; he had been herded to one side with a group of naked children, the youngest of them toddlers of only four or five.

"Come, come, *messeri*," the auctioneer wheedled. "Will you pass up the chance of sure profit. Do I hear twelve hundred ducats for the lot?"

The wholesale dealers fell to scrapping like dogs over a bone. It soon became apparent to Sandro that Falco was bidding more aggressively than the rest. One by one they dropped out. It was obvious that Falco was intimidating the lily-livered among them with a scowl or a gesture. They must have had some reason to fear him; the slave dealers were all ruffians, with their own hired thugs to back them up.

The Company of the Hose was acting up again. "Housemaids and seamstresses, my foot!" said one of them. "They'll all end up in Alexandria, earmarked for some fat pasha's harem. The Turks aren't particular. Eight or eighty, it's all the same to them, as long as they can get their *gid* into a Christian *apertura*."

He was answered by a round of lewd laughter. "Falco

will break them all in first with that bull's tool of his," said another, "and then sell them all as convent virgins."

"As for the boys," sniggered another of the *Immortali*, "once they've had a little operation, they'll make proper Saracen pages."

The image of the Greek girl's small brother came to Sandro, and he found himself clenching his fists.

"I have fifteen hundred ducats," the auctioneer was saying. "Come, good gentlemen, a bargain's a bargain, but there's such a thing as fair."

It was between Falco and one other wholesale dealer now, a jowly man in a red skullcap.

From his place by the pillars, Falco bellowed, "Fifteen hundred and twenty-five!" and glared at his rival.

The other dealer shrugged. Triumphantly, Falco pushed through the crowd to claim his prize without waiting for the auctioneer to go through the formality of accepting the bid. A small group of his bully boys followed him, swaggering young toughs in cheap finery.

"Look at the specimen in front with the body like cream," said the pimple-faced stocking-club companion, Orazio. "She might be a lady, the way she's stayed out of the sun. Perhaps we could pay Falco to have a go at her before he sends her on. I hear he does that sometimes."

"Christian or heretic, they're the same where it counts," said another of the *Compagnia*, licking his lips.

Sandro could contain himself no longer. "*Che sporcizia!*" he exclaimed. "For shame!"

Orazio turned around and regarded him lazily. "What have we here?" he drawled. "A little upstart who needs a lesson?"

"It's the infidel lover, Orazio," said one of the other fops. "The one who doesn't like to look."

Sandro didn't like the look of flushed excitement on their faces. Two of the *Immortali* had begun to circle around behind him through the crowd. Sandro knew all about bullies. Their purpose was to seize him by the arms and hold him for Orazio's "lesson." People began to move out of the way, getting clear of the impending scuffle.

Sandro was unarmed. Orazio and his friends carried

daggers, he could be sure, but that didn't worry him. They would hardly dare to use them, in view of the stern penalties.

There was no sense in waiting for a ritual exchange of insults. He was going to get a beating, that was certain, but at least he could give this pimply weasel something to remember him by—and maybe one or two of his friends if he were lucky.

While they were still gloating about how helpless he was in their trap, he swung his fist as hard as he could at Orazio's blemished face. He felt a crunch, and had the satisfaction of seeing blood spurt from Orazio's nose. Without wasting time, he swung his other hand in an arc and gave the bleeding dandy a box on the ear.

He whirled in time to see the next fop groping ineffectually for him. He had caught them by surprise, but that wouldn't last more than another second or two. He pushed the other in the chest with both hands and saw him go sprawling in the filth of the quay. Then he himself got a blow behind the shoulder from someone, and another in the ribs. Two of the stocking-club companions grabbed his arms from behind, and thrash around as he would, he could not shake them off.

Orazio was standing before him, trembling. Thick gobs of blood were dripping from his nose and spoiling his jeweled and embroidered jacket. The jewels might be washed and resewn, but he would never wear the doublet again. "You'll pay for that!" he cried in a shrill voice, and began hitting Sandro.

He was too enraged to do real damage. The rain of blows fell at random, hurting but not yet doing serious injury. Sandro struggled, throwing the youths who held him off balance, and twisted to keep blows from landing too squarely on his face. As soon as he had a clear shot, he kicked Orazio in the groin.

Orazio staggered backward, doubled up. His face had gone white, making the purple scars stand out more, and he was cradling his injured parts, on the verge of being sick.

Another of the *Immortali*, a curly-haired fellow with puffed shirting showing through the slashed sleeves of his doublet, stepped into the breach and drove his fist into Sandro's belly. This one knew how to hit. The engulfing pain turned him stupid, and before he could do anything to evade it, an enormous swat caught him in the face, making his head ring.

Before a third blow could land, a limping Orazio pushed Sandro's assailant aside. "Out of my way!" he snarled. He had a knife in his hand, a thin Florentine dagger with a jeweled hilt.

"Get the watch!" someone in the crowd shouted. People in the immediate vicinity scattered to be well out of the way.

Sobbing, Orazio slashed at Sandro. His breath back by this time, Sandro struggled furiously in his captors' grip, and the knife, which had been aimed at his chest, ripped through the sleeve of his doublet and slid past his shoulder.

Orazio raised the dagger for another blow, but there were shouts of *"I custodi!"* at the back of the crowd and the sound of running feet. Orazio's friends pulled him away from Sandro, and the Company of the Hose ran off as fast as their pointed red shoes would carry them.

Sandro hesitated only a moment. The watchmen of the *Capo di Contrada*, slowed down by their armor, were ploughing their way through the crowd toward him, their pikes held high. He was innocent, but who could tell what might happen once you got caught in the toils of the Council of Forty? Someone might even be found to swear that *he* had been the one with the dagger. Prudently, he took to his heels. "Run for it, young fellow!" somebody shouted encouragingly after him.

The *custodi* rattled after him, but he had a good head start, and they gave up when they saw him reach the mouth of one of the narrow, twisting alleys that fronted the Arsenal seaway leading down to the quay.

He kept going until he had crossed the next canal and lost himself in the maze of the San Giorgio district. He stopped in a narrow thoroughfare between two houses to inspect himself. His doublet was spotted with Orazio's blood, and probably some of his own as well. His sleeve was ripped down, and what his face looked like, he did not care to imagine. He screwed around his features, and from the feel of it he had at least the beginning of a bruise under his eye.

A walk through the Rialto was out of the question now. His main concern was to get back to the Cavalli palace and change his clothes before he could be seen by his father.

He didn't feel much like an outing now anyway. The last sight he'd seen as he made his escape from the quay with the *custodi* pounding at his heels was still vivid in his memory. He'd had to run past the auction block and the slave pens, and he'd caught sight of the auctioneer making out the bill of sale to Falco for the Greek lot. The brawny contractor was standing in front of the table, picking his teeth, his eyes assessing the merchandise he'd just acquired. The girl whom Sandro had gotten into the fight over was standing like a pillar just behind the auctioneer's shoulder, her face a study in grief. Nobody had bothered to cover her. Her hands were still tied behind her back, and the little boy she'd been taking care of remained tied to a string of preternaturally silent children who stared with big eyes while Falco's bravos rounded them up.

Falco had looked up sharply as Sandro ran past and gazed thoughtfully after him, the splinter of wood he'd been using as a toothpick dangling loosely from his lower lip. But the Greek girl, lost in her own misery, had not raised her eyes at the diversion.

He dabbed with his handkerchief at the cut on his lip. He would have liked to have hired a gondola, but he wasn't allowed much pocket money. With a sigh, he set off at a brisk walk toward the *Cà' Cavalli*.

CHAPTER 2

From the land side, the Cavalli palace was a pile of gilded marble boxes rising from overgrown gardens. Beyond, the Grand Canal shimmered through a narrow slice of sky. Peering down the side channel that separated his home from the adjoining *palazzo*, Sandro could see the Cavalli gondola bobbing at its striped mooring pole, and old Lorenzo, the boatman, dozing on his bench against the palace wall.

Evidently his father had not yet left for the Cavalli warehouse. That was unusual. Usually he was off to work bright and early. But when he had sent Sandro off on the errand to the Arsenal that morning, he had not looked well.

Sandro listened for sounds from the house. All was quiet. Perhaps he could still get to his rooms unobserved. Nevertheless, he squared his shoulders and walked through the garden openly. Cavallis did not skulk.

His first hurdle was Bruno, the night watchman. But it was no trick to get past Bruno, whose habits were as regular as the chimes of Saint Mark's. At this hour, after his night's vigil, he would be napping in his little alcove off the rear portico, and though he boasted that he slept with one eye open, all you had to do was take a detour around him.

Sandro peeped around a gilded column and saw Bruno
sprawled on his pallet, his mouth gaping wide open,
snoring loudly. Bruno was a hulking, lantern-jawed man
from Istria, who had been with the family for more than
twenty years. He was so deep in sleep that Sandro didn't
bother to skirt the alcove, but marched right past him.
Bruno stirred and mumbled, but didn't open his eyes.

Sandro could hear the sound of activity from the
ground-floor kitchens, where Monna Tessa would be
fussing over the preparations for morning dinner. Jacopo,
the majordomo, would be somewhere upstairs at this
hour, supervising the cleaning, pleased to leave the domestic chores in Monna Tessa's competent hands.

Whistling silently to himself, Sandro strode toward the
wide marble staircase that spilled its giant's treads into
the center of the drafty downstairs hall. He was halfway
there when Monna Tessa came bustling through the
kitchen, shooing a maid ahead of her on some errand.

"Ah, èccole, Master Alessandro ..." she began, then
caught sight of his torn tunic and bleeding lip. "What
have you been up to?" she clucked. "Fighting in the
streets, like a common *bimbo* ... or are you going to try
to tell me that you fell off a scaffold at the Arsenal?"

Sandro endured the scolding stoically. Monna Tessa
would never believe he had grown up. It was she who
had taken over the responsibility of raising him properly
after his mother had died; Cristina Cavalli, frail and
lovely, had not long survived the birth of Sandro's little
sister, Agnese. Monna Tessa had come with the young
bride to the Cavalli household as a green maid, scarcely
out of childhood. Even at that age, however, she had
proved to have such a sensible head on her shoulders
that she was soon promoted to housekeeping duties. She
and the new bride had learned the running of a great
household together, and, quite naturally, Monna Tessa
had kept things going after her mistress's death. She was
now a handsome woman of forty, with a fine figure and
a square, open face. She had never married, though she
had no shortage of suitors, saying that she had family
enough in the Cavallis and in the servants under her
care.

"... and look in on your father, but don't let him see you looking like that!" she finished.

"I will, Monna Tessa," he promised. He'd be lucky, he thought, to get past his father unobserved after this tirade in the open hallway.

She bit her lip. "He's a little under the weather today. I'm cooking him a capon for his dinner, with the raisin and sumach sauce he likes, and truffles. Will you stay to join him?"

"Yes, Monna Tessa."

"*Bène*," she said.

The scolding forgotten, she bestowed a smile of affection on him. She had long ago despaired of Maffeo—although she would never be brought to admit it—and the flood of maternal warmth had been diverted to Sandro. Her favorite, though, was little Agnese. Quiet and frail, with the start of an attenuated beauty like her mother's, Agnese was a ghostly reminder for the entire household of the departed Cristina.

She turned around and saw the maidservant waiting for her. "What are you hovering about for, little goose? Get going!"

Sandro climbed the stairs to the second floor, hardly aware of the greatness of the Cavalli past that surrounded him. He had grown up on these glorious frecoes of the lives of the apostles with the modest likenesses of former Cavallis tucked among them, on the pious and instructive martyrdoms of the saints, on the stiff ancestral paintings and portrait busts. On the landing, however, he paused to admire the one that had always appealed to him as a child—a ferocious Massacre of the Innocents that had been commissioned by his great-grandfather from the shop of a painter called Master Angelus.

He thought he had negotiated the landing successfully, and was on the verge of continuing up the broad staircase to his own apartment on the third floor, when he heard his father's voice calling from the big square second-floor salon.

"Sandro, is that you? I'm in here."

Resigning himself with a sigh to being questioned, Sandro said, "Yes, Father, I'm coming."

Girolamo Cavalli, dressed in a plain black robe, sat at a table in front of the huge carved fireplace, his head turned toward the balconied window that overlooked the Grand Canal. A sparkle of sunlight on water was reflected on the high ceiling, giving the salon an aquatic look. At the elder Cavalli's elbow was a pile of account books that he had been working on.

He looked up as Sandro entered, and in that unguarded moment, Sandro—with Monna Tessa's remark still fresh in his mind to counter the inobservance of youth—saw a face of clay.

But the familiar, firm lines of Girolamo Cavalli's countenance reasserted themselves, and he was once again the father Sandro had always known, a man of gentle authority, durable and solid as a rock.

"*Che cosa?* What happened to you?" he exclaimed as his eyes lit on Sandro's disarray.

Unwillingly, Sandro explained how he had gotten into the fight at the slave auction, leaving out only the fact that he had seen Maffeo there. He expected a lecture, so his father's next words surprised him.

"I don't condone your brawling in public," Girolamo began sternly, "but you were right to have felt as you did, and I'm proud of you for it. This traffic in human beings is shameful, and I don't mean only the enslavement of our fellow Christians. Let the Genoans get their hands dirty if they must, but it's demeaning for citizens of the great Republic of Venice, those of noble blood most of all, to deal in that filth." He shook his head in disgust. "It was the labor shortage after the plague that made the business boom again, after it had been dying out nicely. The Council should put a stop to it once and for all!"

"The enslavement of Moors as well, Father?"

Girolamo Cavalli stroked his broad chin thoughtfully. "Why not?" he said at last. "The world would be a better place for it."

"But the Moors are our enemies. They take Christians every chance they get and sell them as slaves!"

"We also do business with them and they with us, and certain rules are observed on both sides. The soldan of Egypt doesn't imprison the crews of the Venetian galleys

that put into Alexandria to land cargo and load pepper
and cotton. And we grant protection to the Moorish passengers that ride our galleys—so much so that we sent a
war fleet to Rhodes to free the Moorish prisoners who
had been kidnapped from our ships by those cursed
Knights of Saint John. By such displays of good faith we
Venetians maintain our commercial relations with the
Moslems. Never forget, Sandro, that these so-called enemies are our only portal to the goods of the Orient."

"And yet," Sandro ventured respectfully, "there are
those who say it's an act of virtue to cheat a Moor. Signor
Borgo—"

His father snorted. "Don't talk to me of Ser Borgo.
He's one of those who'd cut his own throat for profit—
but the rest of us end up doing the bleeding in the long
run."

Sandro made a strategic retreat. Now was not the time
to bring up the subject of Giuditta del Borgo and his romantic intentions toward her. He had thought he was being clever, going round the bush like this—but it
suddenly didn't seem to be such a good idea with his father in his present mood. Later, perhaps, he could try
again. The House of Cavalli and the House of Borgo
were bitter commercial rivals, it was true, but his father
couldn't hold that against Giuditta. And from a practical
point of view an alliance between the two great houses
could only be to the advantage of both.

But his father had not yet finished with the topic.

"Even among the *longhi*, Sandro, there are greedy
sorts of men who'll do anything for money. But long families or short families, old money or upstarts, they begin
by selling their fellow Christians to the Moors and end
by trading arms and munitions that will only be used
against Christian nations—as when Prince Henry of Portugal faced Venetian bombards at Ceuta. What's the
sense of that, I ask you? There's plenty of profit in spices
and other eastern luxuries. Honorable men ought to be
satisfied with this."

"Yes, Father," Sandro said, lowering his eyes.

"There are honorable men on both sides. Do you remember Yakub al-Khalid?"

"Of course," Sandro said, surprised at the question. "You entrusted me with some of the correspondence with his firm in Tunis when I was only fourteen. He died soon after that, but I had to write to his son, Ahmed ibn-Yakub, only last month to straighten out some detail about a shipment of tinware."

The encounter with the tall, dignified Arab merchant was one of the bright spots of Sandro's childhood memory—a magical adventure, never to be forgotten. It had been less than a year after his mother had died. His father, though distracted, had had to sail to Barbary to attend personally to a silver bullion transaction in which he had sunk far too much of the firm's assets. Agnese was in the care of a reliable wet nurse, and Maffeo, a surly fifteen-year-old, had been entrusted to the Cavalli head clerk, Ippolito, to be instructed in the basics of the business. But Sandro, then seven and making good progress both with his reading master and his master of the abacus, could be spared. Perhaps it had been unwise of Girolamo to take a small boy with him on a long and arduous voyage in hostile waters, but, still not recovered from his bereavement, he wanted the company of his flesh and blood. And an armed Venetian convoy was reasonably safe from Barbary pirates.

Yakub had made much of the small boy, given him sweets while he talked business with Girolamo, found the time to show him some of the wonders of Barbary, including a caged ape wearing a red jacket and a chained lion that guarded his counting house, and even patiently taught him a few words of Arabic.

"Learn well, *ya* Alessandro," he had said with a laugh. "It will give you a competitive advantage to speak the language of the Prophet. You are your father's son, and one day, if Allah wills it, you will inherit the business."

Sandro was too young to be shocked by infidel blasphemy, but he was old enough to detect nonsense. He knew the business would be inherited by Maffeo, as the elder son, though he would receive enough of a patrimony to keep him as a Venetian gentleman and perhaps strike out on a venture of his own, and though he might improve his fortunes a notch by working for Maffeo.

When the galleys had been loaded and it was time to sail from Tunis, *sidi* Yakub, as Sandro had learned to call him, had showered the little boy with presents. There was a pair of green leather boots in the Moorish fashion and a little scimitar with curved writing on the blade and a beautifully carved toy Arab ship of varnished wood, with sails of yellow silk. Sandro had heard Yakub and his father talking on the quarterdeck while he was supposed to be asleep under the stern canopy. "It's hard for a child that age to lose his mother, *ya* Girolamo," the Arab merchant was saying. "A mother is the ship's mast—isn't that how one of your Venetian proverbs puts it? You should get married again, my old friend." His father had said something indistinct, and *sidi* Yakub had replied with a sigh, "So be it. But he's a smart boy, and he'll grow up to be the pleasure of your old age, *inch'allah*. You should give him an equal share in the business."

The little Arab ship, with its perfectly rigged miniature lateen sails, had been lost in the canal that summer when a puff of wind had blown it out of reach, and Sandro himself had almost taken a dunk when he had leaned over too far trying to retrieve it, but the child-size green boots and the scimitar were still on a shelf in his rooms, where he could see them. Some of the Arabic words had stuck with him, too; useful words like *fil-fil*, pepper; *harir*, silk; *kam*, how much; and *minfadlak*, please.

His father was speaking to him. "I've been criticized for getting along too well with the Moors—some say it's suspicious. But treat a man fairly, I say, and he'll treat you fairly. Yakub was a good friend, and his sons have always dealt honestly with me." He shook his head. "Do you know that a denunciation of me was placed in the lion's mouth?"

"What?" Sandro could hardly believe his ears. The denunciation boxes in the form of lions' heads were scattered at strategic spots throughout Venice, and people were encouraged to place secret accusations of treason, malfeasance, or tax evasion in them. But how anyone could doubt his father's loyalty or honesty was beyond Sandro.

"Yes," Girolamo said evenly, "it must have been one of

my competitors—one who *doesn't* get along well with the Moors because he cheats them." He gave a thin smile. "I was called before the *Inquisitori di Stato* of the Council of Ten, but the inquisitors soon saw there was nothing to it and dismissed the charges. We can be thankful that such proceedings are conducted secretly so that no rumors went flying around the Rialto. There are always people who are prepared to believe the worst."

"Infamous!" Sandro exclaimed indignantly. "People who accuse falsely ought to be put to the question themselves!"

Girolamo pushed aside the account books he had been working on. "In this world those who achieve a little success must always be prepared for malice," he said tiredly. "Remember that, Sandro, and never give an inch. Always be true to your principles."

"I promise, Father!" Sandro said passionately.

"And now I have a surprise for you." Girolamo tapped the pile of ledgers with a long forefinger. "Ser Ippolito tells me you've been doing well at your assignments in the counting room. He says that you have a thorough grasp of the double-entry system and that he has no more to teach you. He says he entrusted the preparation of the *cónto saldo* to you and allowed you to close out the ledgers on some of our enterprises, and though he checked your balances well, he found no errors."

Sandro flushed with pleasure. "Thank you, Father."

"I think it's time to entrust you with a more important responsibility. I'm going to send you with the Galley of Flanders in July to conduct our business in England."

"England?" Sandro was stunned. "B-but I thought to ask you to let me sign on this summer as one of the *balestrièri della popa* on the Beirut run. I've always heard you say that sailing as a bowman is the best way for a young man to get a little seasoning. . . ."

"You show good sense beyond your age, Sandro. You're seasoned enough. It doesn't require a high polish to deal with the English. They're a rude and untried race, with much still to learn about trading."

"But England . . ." A growing excitement was mixed with his first dismay at the thought of that strange northern land. "What about our English agent, Messer John Gooddaye?"

"This is too delicate a transaction. It requires family. And besides, Gooddaye is an Englishman, and this piece of business brushes up too close to those savage export laws by which the English try to monopolize all the profit in the wool trade. Let Master Gooddaye sit in his office in London while you take care of the first stages of the deal. I'll give you a letter to him, and afterward he can help you move the necessary funds through a bill of exchange on the Medici branch there."

Sandro's interest quickened. "Is it English wool you're trading for, then?"

His father was pleased at the question. "Not this time, Sandro. For generations wool was the only commodity of value that the English *had* to sell, in exchange for all of the eastern luxuries they've become addicted to. And they've made a good thing of it. English sheep are the finest in the world. Their Merchants of the Staple control the raw material that keeps Bruges and Antwerp and the rest of the weaving towns of the north humming, and since the wool tax is the only reliable source of revenue that the English king has, he cooperates with the staplers to keep the trade sewn up tight for them. But all that's changing. There are fresh winds blowing in England, and as always, it's profit and loss that are making them blow. It's finally begun to dawn on those dunderheads that they can make a profit on selling the finished cloth, too, and there are forward-looking businessmen all over their little island organizing the spinners and weavers and fullers and dyers in their guilds. They're importing renegade master craftsmen from northern Europe to teach them their secrets. And their upstart Company of Merchant Adventurers is beginning to challenge the Genoese in their own waters. Soon they'll be a thorn in our side, too, but for the present—with the Merchants of the Staple and the Merchant Adventurers jousting with one another—the opportunities for us are wide open. Bristol scarlet cloth in particular is acquiring a fine reputation, and even the Moors are willing to pay high prices for it. That's fortunate for us, because Bristol reds are cheaper than the London red if the buyer goes directly to the source, before the Merchant Adventurers get their hands on it. So I've made an arrangement with a mercer of Bristol, a Master Philpot, to take a cargo of his finished cloth, to be paid for with the spices we'll unload at Bruges and Southampton."

Sandro's breath was taken away by the clarity of his father's vision. "That's marvelous, Father. But won't it be dangerous?"

"There are no flies on Master Philpot. He's an important man in Bristol, with many contacts. He's arranged to furnish us with a license to bypass the Calais Staple and bought us a safe-conduct. It was well worth the outlay. There'll be more profit for him, and for us as well."

"But the Galley of Flanders doesn't put in at Bristol—only London and Southampton. The customs officials there will be ready to pounce. And you can't transfer cargo at Bruges or Antwerp either—the English cloth-makers are anathema to them."

Girolamo looked at his son with pride. "As I said before, Sandro, you have a good head on your shoulders. I want you to hire or, better yet, buy a cog in Bristol and sail with our cargo. You can lay off Dover, in the narrow part of the Channel, and join up with the Galley of Flanders on its way home."

"Buy a cog?" Sandro gulped.

His father smiled. "It's time for the House of Cavalli to start a fleet of its own, instead of always leasing space on great galleys at the state auctions or, still worse, being cheated by these villainous captains of private vessels whose only thought is how to overload cargo, make unauthorized stops, carry illegal pilgrims, and otherwise evade state regulations."

"I don't know anything about round ships, Father," Sandro said. His voice must have shown some of his disdain for the wallowing, broad-beamed vessels used by northerners, which, as a proper Venetian chauvinist, he associated with the dull, stolid Germans of the Hanseatic League, sailing with their cargoes of salt herring or whatever else pleased their joyless customers in the icy Baltic waters that they ruled.

"You'll have plenty of time to learn about them on the outward voyage," his father said sharply. "I'll expect you to ask questions of the *capitanio* of the Galley of Flanders, who is Messer Garzoni, a friend of mine, and who is well versed in the sailing qualities of round ships, since he's commanded more than one of them taken as prizes from Genoa. And, since the galley will spend at least three months in London or Southampton and not leave until spring, when the sheep are clipped, you'll have plenty of time to hang around the Bristol waterfront as well, looking for bargains and finding someone who can supply expert advice. They say that King Henry is thinking of selling off his fleet now that he no longer needs it against the French, and the glut in ships will make them cheap." He gave Sandro a hard stare. "And if you can't judge ships, judge people. You're your father's son, after all. Is the sailing master reliable or shifty? What's his reputation? His record?"

"I'm sorry, Father."

Girolamo softened. "Don't turn up your nose at round ships, Sandro. They're the wave of the future. They may be slower and less predictable than rowed galleys, but they can carry more cargo, and they're better suited for sailing in the open sea. That's going to be more and more important as commerce expands and sailors gradually lose their fear of the Ocean of Darkness . . . the English sail all the way to Iceland, and so does the Hanse when it's worth their while. Round ships are not only cheap to build, they're cheaper to operate. They only need a normal crew to handle the rigging—not a hundred and seventy half-starved wretches straining at the oars."

Seeing the doubtful look that remained on Sandro's face, he added, "Don't worry, we'll have a few galleys in our little fleet as well, but they'll be rowed by freemen."

"Father . . ." Sandro floundered. "I hardly know what to say. . . ."

"Come, come, don't look so dumbfounded. It's no more than you deserve." He smiled broadly. "Well, what do you say? How does it feel to be a fully accredited representative of the firm and the captain of its first ship?"

Sandro struggled for a reply. "Father, this is a great

honor ... but shouldn't Maffeo be the one to go? It's his prerogative. He's the oldest."

His father's expression clouded over. "Maffeo will have to change his ways before I'd chance entrusting him with a mission of this importance," he said harshly. "He needs to settle down to his responsibilities."

Sandro felt as if he were walking on eggs. "But ... he'll be offended. . . ."

He knew all too well the depths of resentment to which his brother was capable of descending. He had never forgotten the fits of temper when Maffeo found that Sandro had been entrusted with the Tunis correspondence—though Maffeo had previously shown no interest in the affairs of the firm. He wanted no further quarrels with his older brother.

"Perhaps this will wake him up, then," his father said coldly. "He's twenty-five now—old enough to take his rightful seat in the Great Council and wear the robes of state that his blood entitles him to. I had great hopes for him once."

Sandro sensed that his father wanted to tell him something further, but discretion won out and Girolamo clamped his jaw firmly shut.

He attempted a last feeble objection. "*Padre mìo*, I don't know the English tongue. . . ."

"There are always stranded English pilgrims hanging about the Piazza San Marco trying to beg passage home. Find one who can teach you the rudiments and act as your interpreter in England—choose a learned one, a friar or a scholar. Tell him we'll pay his fare on the Galley of Flanders and give him a bonus to boot if he'll accompany you to Bristol. Be careful not to be taken in by a rogue."

"But—"

"Enough. I have decided."

He passed a hand tiredly across his face; the firm lines of his mouth sagged for a moment, and then he recovered himself. Sandro moved to withdraw, but his father said, "Stay a moment."

Downstairs, someone cursed at a servant and footsteps stomped up the marble staircase. They stopped outside the salon, and a moment later Maffeo, his cloak thrown back to reveal a rich doublet and fancy hose, entered.

"I looked for you in the warehouse but you weren't there. . . ." he began, and then he saw Sandro. He gave him a fierce look and a warning nod, the meaning of which was clear; Sandro was not to mention seeing him at the slave auction with Falco.

Sandro shrunk a little. He was not looking forward to the moment when Maffeo would find out about the trip to England. But he gave the barest return nod to show Maffeo that his secret was safe.

"I'm glad you thought to stop in at the warehouse," Girolamo said dryly. "There's much there for you to do. You still haven't finished the work on the pepper transaction, and that has to be settled before next month or we lose our advantage. Why did you leave there so soon?"

"That donkey Ippolito refused to give me an advance on my personal account," Maffeo fumed. "He says I'm too far overdrawn already. By God, he needs a thrashing to show him who's master and who's servant! He said I'd have to see you about it."

He glared at nothing in particular.

"Ippolito's served the family faithfully for many years," Girolamo said mildly. "He's the most scrupulous of accountants. We couldn't run the business without him."

"Well, what about it?"

"One can't keep dipping into a pool without drying it up. A businessman can't afford to get into bad habits. A ladleful soon becomes a bucketful. Ippolito is right. He needs to be supported if he's to do his job properly. I won't countermand him. You'll have to manage your own affairs better, that's all."

Maffeo stormed out. Sandro could hear him raging all the way down the stairs. The door to the water entrance slammed; Maffeo must have kept a hired gondola waiting there.

Girolamo sighed. He turned to Sandro and said, "I have something more to tell you, Alessandro. I've drawn up a new will. The notary will have it today for my signature. I've made arrangements to leave equal shares in the *Casa di Cavalli* to you and Maffeo, but you're to have operational control."

The spacious salon seemed to press in on Sandro with the weight of the world. "To put me above the firstborn," he whispered. "Father, this is unheard of."

Girolamo Cavalli's face was as bleak as Sandro had ever seen it. "I don't want the House of Cavalli run into the ground after I'm gone, nor its honor tarnished. And you needn't be so concerned about your brother. Given his character, this will be in his own best interest as well. You'll end up doing the work. But the money will keep coming in. At least Maffeo won't end up with the *Barnabotti*, an out-at-the-elbows pretender selling his vote and begging for favors from the Council."

"Father . . ."

"And if you're worried about Maffeo being publicly humiliated, the two Cavalli brothers will be equal partners as far as the world is concerned. He can continue to strut about for our friends and customers. The inner workings of the bank and trading company are nobody's business. Except that I've arranged with Ippolito that, in the important things, you'll pull the strings." He frowned. "And there's Agnese to consider. I've provided for an ample dowry for her, but dowries have a habit of melting away in the wrong hands. You'll look after her interests, won't you, Sandro?"

"Of course, Father. But all this is far in the future. You'll live to see Agnese married and to see your grandchildren grow up, too."

Some of the bleakness in Girolamo's face melted away. "Yes, yes, Sandro, don't worry—I expect I will, if that's God's intention. A bit of dyspepsia can make a philosopher out of a man."

"Have you told Maffeo yet?"

"No. I'll tell him when he comes back. Perhaps he'll have cooled off somewhat by then."

Sandro was thankful that he would not be there tonight. He hoped that Maffeo would stay away until he was gone.

"I'd better change this doublet. I'll join you in a little while for dinner. Monna Tessa's outdone herself."

"*Bène*. If Maffeo came home to eat more often, he wouldn't need so much money. Well, he'll have nothing to jingle in that fine jeweled purse of his for the next month or so, so perhaps we'll see more of him."

The prospect of more Maffeo, in the current circumstances, filled Sandro with dismay, but he managed a smile and a "*Va benissimo!*" as he departed.

After he had changed his ruined doublet and washed the caked blood from his lip, he looked in on Agnese.

"Good morning, *piccola*. What are you doing?"

She was sitting by the window overlooking the garden, practicing her letters, her small, delicate face grave with concentration. Girolamo Cavalli believed that girls as well as boys should be taught to read and do sums and otherwise learn about the world, and at age eleven Agnese had gone through a procession of reading masters, abacus masters, music and drawing masters, and an astronomy and Latin master for good measure, as well as being taught embroidery and the other skills of her sex.

"Oh, Sandro . . ." She turned to him with a quick sunny smile and caught sight of his bruises. Her hand flew to her lips. "Your face . . . are you hurt?"

"It's nothing, little one. *Non è niente*. Just a stupid fight."

She put down her slate and flew to his arms. She felt like a bundle of sticks, feather light. "Your poor lip!" she cried. "It's all puffed up! How will you go serenading tonight?"

He held her out at arm's length, conscious of her fragility. "Oho! Listen to the fluff! Everyone's taken in because she's so quiet, but she sees and hears everything, like a little cat!" He squeezed her hands and frowned. "What's this? Why are your hands so cold? I'll call Ser Jacopo and have him make a fire in here."

"He says this chimney can't be used. A bird built a nest in it, and when he got a boy to clean it a few days ago, he cracked the chimney down where it's hard to get at. He says he'll have it reconstructed this summer."

"Then he'll have to keep a warming pan filled with coals for you." A thought struck him. "Still better, we'll have you moved to a nice, sunny front apartment, facing the canal. The one on the end that's been closed up since ..." He bypassed the rest of the sentence; the apartment had been their mother's. "Anyway, we can have it cleared out for you."

She wrinkled her nose. "It's too big and grand for me. Besides, Maffeo wants to move in there. He spoke to Jacopo about it the other day. He says he needs more space."

"Maffeo can stay where he is," Sandro growled. "He's got the best rooms on the third floor already."

"Please, Sandro, don't make a bother. I like it here, looking out over the garden."

"It's too damp in here without a fireplace, and it's getting worse." He sniffed the air. "I can smell the mildew starting. We've got to look after you, *carissima*. Don't forget the bad cough you had all winter."

"Oh, *fandonie*! The doctor says I'm better. He makes me drink that awful-tasting stuff!"

"Don't you want to have a view of the canal, and see all the traffic and everything that's going on?"

"I'd rather watch the birds in the garden. It's nice and quiet and peaceful there. The canal's noisy and dirty."

He teased her. "Besides, how will your suitor serenade you in a gondola unless you're facing the canal?"

She smiled at him impishly. "*You* can serenade me tonight, Sandro."

"One doesn't serenade one's sister. Don't be a goose."

"Who is it you're going to tonight, Sandro? Is it Giuditta del Borgo?"

"Little spy. How do you know so much?"

She giggled. "I got it out of Lorenzo. He says you told him to wear his best livery and shave and polish all the fittings and use the cloth-of-gold canopy instead of the everyday one. Does Father know?"

"Well, not exactly. But he won't mind. The old canopy's getting worn."

"I've seen the Siora Giuditta in church. She's beautiful. Like an angel."

"Yes," Sandro breathed. "She is."

"Why don't our families get along?"

"It's too hard to explain, *piccola*. It's business."

After a pause, Agnese asked, "Will you get in trouble?"

"No, little one. It's all arranged. Her father and the rest of the family will be out, taking half the staff with them. Some big reception at the Ducal Palace. The *gentildònna* will be alone. Such lackeys as remain behind in the house would hardly dare to attack the gondola of a noble family without the orders of Messer Borgo."

She clapped her hands. "Oh, Sandro, will you tell me all about it afterward?"

"But *cèrto*, little one." He had a second thought. "Well, perhaps not *all*." He hoped for a kiss tonight, if Giuditta could be induced to come down to the water gate.

"*Davvéro?*"

"*Davvéro.*" He slipped his arm into hers. "Come on, *piccola*, I'll take you down to dinner."

Sandro examined himself by the light of a candlestand in the tall mirror of the *sala*. He was no dandy of the *Compagnia*, true, but he thought he cut a fine enough figure in the puffed doublet with the gold chain he had received for his birthday and neat, shoulder-length locks under a red velvet cap with a feather in it.

Now, if only old Lorenzo would take the trouble to shave and refurbish the gondola as he had asked. It was a sober family craft, not at all showy, and the elderly family retainer made a somewhat prosaic boatman, but Sandro was determined to make as dashing an appearance for Giuditta as possible.

He took a few minutes to tune his lute once more, though he knew the damp air of the canal would loosen its strings. He had a good voice, he knew without conceit, and he had been well instructed by his music master in the art of playing the lute and *chitarra*.

Through the open window he could hear other music floating above the night; his would not be the only serenade to be heard in the dark maze of waterways this eve. The voices of a thousand lovers would be raised to their inamorati, the strolling bands of *cantóri di piazzi* would be competing with them, and there would be more music coming from the ballrooms of great houses, their facades lit up like candle racks at church.

Other, less felicitous sounds were coming from the floor below. Sandro paused in tightening the peg of the top string and listened. His father and Maffeo were having an argument. Maffeo had appeared long after the supper hour, in a foul mood, and gone straight to his rooms. Fortunately, Sandro had missed seeing him. But he had heard through his door when Maffeo had been summoned to his father's chambers by a servant.

Sandro gave a final twist to the peg, straightened the feather in his cap, and tiptoed down the great stairs with the pear-shaped instrument slung over his back. The voices grew louder as he passed the closed door of the salon, and he heard his father burst out, "What? You contracted a debt in the Cavalli name with a rogue like that? I won't pay it! I see now that I was right in what I did!"

Lorenzo was leaning on his pole, half-asleep, when Sandro emerged from the palace, but he straightened up, made an attempt to look spruce, and said, "Buona nòtte, Messer Sandro." He had shaved and was wearing his good livery. Things began to look better to Sandro. "Yes, a fine night for an outing," he said.

Lorenzo shoved off. The narrow craft sliced through the black water, making a rippling path of light with the lantern dangling from its prow. Sandro leaned back in the cushions and watched the firefly twinkles of other gondolas around him in the darkness. Overhead, a scattering of stars like fat silver flakes cast a frosted glow over the frilly rooftops of the palaces lining the Grand Canal.

He tested the lute, found that it had stayed in tune well enough, and adjusted a couple of pegs minutely to make sure. How should he begin? The best love songs came from Burgundy; he had painfully learned several of the more popular ones, struggling with the unfamiliar dialect, to the despair of his music master. Experimentally, he strummed a few notes.

> *J'ai encor un tel pâ-té,*
> *Qui n'est mie de lat-té . . .*

He broke off. Was it too high-flown? A little too risqué behind the innocent talk of sharing patés? Perhaps he'd better not risk it. He strummed the instrument again. A simple *canzóne* in Italian, one of the ones making the rounds of the *piazzi*—the "little fruits," as they were called, of love.

The splash of a nearby oar made him self-conscious, and he desisted. Better wait until he could sing his lungs out properly under Giuditta's window.

Suspended patches of gauzy light drifted by on either side—candleglow from scattered windows, delineating the facing banks of palaces. He knew this part of the Grand Canal by heart. That dim row of tall arches reflected in the light of mooring lanterns was the lower level of the Farsetti Palace; the indistinct squarish mass a little farther on was the Grimani Palace; that half-seen peak on the opposite bank was the church of San Silvestro.

A vague bulk loomed ahead, showing a single rectangular blur of light high up.

"There, Lorenzo!" he blurted. "That's the one!"

"I know," grumbled the boatman. "The Ca' Borgo. Just where it always was."

He changed grip on the long oar and sculled the gondola toward a broad flight of marble steps that disappeared into the water. As they drew abreast of the palace, Sandro saw a lantern hung in the deeply inset entranceway, making gargoyle shadows out of all the carved marble gewgaws and statuary that announced the Borgo wealth to the world.

Reversing oar, Lorenzo pulled up and allowed the gondola to drift at a polite distance from the steps. Polite, but also prudent; a gondolier with as long a past as he had was apt to consider the small but not unthinkable hazard of the contents of a chamber pot spilling from an upper window on the head of an unwelcome suitor—and on the innocent head of the boatman who poled him, as well.

Sandro thought he saw a flutter of movement up above, but he could not be sure. He unlimbered his lute and began to sing.

"O rosa bèlla . . ."

It was an English song that had made its way to Italy in translation, and that now was the craze of the *piazzi* and the serious musicians as well. The English had discovered a trick of harmonizing in thirds and sixths instead of fourths and fifths or by the lucky accidents of contrary motion, and it gave their music a sweetness that made the angels weep. Once you got the hang of it, it wasn't hard to pluck a few notes on the lute that harmonized in the English fashion.

Now there was another stir of movement at the window, and this time Sandro was sure. He saw the profile of a woman, a pale bosom, puffed sleeves, and hair spread out in long plaits under a tight-fitting cap.

Sandro redoubled his efforts. *"La Bèlla Dònna, e le compagne elette . . ."*

There was furtive movement at other windows. He was putting on a show for the household servants as well. He didn't care, as long as no surly lackey came down to the landing and shouted for him to go away; it would be hard to maintain his dignity under those circumstances.

"A little closer, *figlio*," he whispered to Lorenzo between songs. The boatman grunted, and with a wary eye on the palace facade, edged the gondola to a point beneath Giuditta's window.

"Venga, venga, donzèlla," he sang. *"Che dònna è gentile è sempre bèlla . . ."*

He caught his breath as she pushed the shutters all the way open and stepped out on the balcony. She made a heart-stopping picture in the soft candlelight, with her cascades of golden hair spilling over her shoulders, a generous display of white breasts stopping where imagination had its job made easy, the low square bodice of her gown edged in pearls, rich satins surrounding her like the petals of a lily. She smiled at him, showing a row of small, perfect teeth.

"Cara mìa!" he said huskily, and then, songs forgotten, he poured out his thoughts to her in a flood of words.

"Ah, *bèllissima . . . che graziósa . . .* I think of you day and night, *madònna mia . . .* I can't live without you," he finally finished, running out of breath.

Her voice, too, trembled with the emotion to be expected from a young, well-brought-up girl of good family who has just been treated to the spectacle of an ardent young swain of the proper station paying court to her from a gondola, laying his heart at her feet in the extravagant parlance of courtly love.

"You shouldn't be here, Sandro. My father will be furious when he hears about it."

"I don't care, *carissima*. I'd brave the furies of hell to be near you."

"You mustn't talk like that, *signore*," she said, as she was expected to. But her voice invited him to go on.

"Together forever, that's our destiny," Sandro declared extravagantly. "*Madònna mìa*, pity me!" He fell back on the borrowed eloquence of one of his songs. "*Cessate di piagarmi, o lasciateme morir!* I'll die!"

"It can never be," she said, falling in with the drama. Your family and mine are enemies. We're doomed, *condannato*!" She savored the word. "*Condannato*," she repeated.

"Ah, *bèlla*, what do our families have to do with us? We'll find a way. And if we don't, we'll run away and live like mice."

This was really going too far. "Control yourself, *signore*." She relented a little. "You can come serenade me again. But be discreet."

"Ah, *alma mìa*, you give me joy. My heart's yours in a little box if you want it!"

Gradually, the flowery rhetoric gave way to the ordinary enthusiastic chatter of youth. Giuditta was no older than Sandro, and she could not sustain the grandiloquent tone for very long either. Soon Sandro was telling her all about his forthcoming trip to England on the Galley of Flanders and his important new responsibilities. It did not occur to him that Gian del Borgo was his father's commercial rival and might gain an advantage from foreknowledge of the Cavalli plans.

But some instinct or trace of family feeling made him refrain from mentioning the dominant position in the firm his father's new will would give him. He would not boast at Maffeo's expense.

"Oh Sandro, what a plum!" she said in a rush. "To go to England all on your own and be entrusted with an important piece of business like that! You'll be a great merchant some day!"

"The only bad thing, *cara*, is that I'll be gone so long. Will you wait for me?"

"From July till the next spring—almost a whole year! It's such a long time!"

"Say you'll wait, *cara mìa*," he begged.

"All right. *Chissà*. Perhaps. But you mustn't expect me to stay locked up and not have fun."

"*Gràzie, madònna.*" He worked up his courage again. "Give me a token—some keepsake I can take to England to remember you by."

"What nerve!"

"Please!"

"Very well." She giggled. Her hands became busy at her hair, and a moment later a glimmering scrap of something came sailing down from the balcony.

Sandro almost fell in the water trying to catch it. He examined his treasure. It was the gold fillet that had bound her hair so tightly under the little cap. He kissed it devoutly and tucked it carefully into the purse at his belt.

"*Mille gràzie!*" he said fervently. "I'll never forget this moment. I promise I'll think of you every day in England. And when I come back, I'll overcome the enmity between our families somehow! I'll win your father over, you'll see! Sooner or later he'll take the mutton from me!"

Carried away for the moment, Sandro could almost believe it—his mind's eye saw, plain as a miniature, a formerly forbidding Gian del Borgo beaming at him and, according to the old Venetian tradition, accepting a symbolic leg of meat in exchange for his daughter. "Dead meat for live meat," so went the formula for the little charade that preceded the formal blessing.

The ripples of a passing gondola full of merrymakers, seen in a pool of light from their lantern, rocked the Cavalli craft off station.

"What are you waiting for, donkey?" jeered a drunken

voice. "Get her under the canopy." A woman's laughter tinkled in the air.

Lorenzo straightened the gondola out with a stroke or two of his paddle. "The young make love, the old get the damp in their bones," he grumbled.

Sandro peered up at the balcony. Was the mood broken? He had been about to try to coax Giuditta down to the landing; now she would put it down to that fool's suggestion.

But no, she was still leaning expectantly over the balustrade.

"*Carissima,*" he said, striving for the right courtly words. "You're so far away. Like an angel above me. Why don't you come downstairs so I can see you more closely?"

"*Non posso,*" she said, but with a coy pantomime of indecision, she went back inside. There was an interminable wait, and then, from behind the window, he heard two female voices having a whispered altercation. He groaned. Just his luck—it would be Giuditta's duenna, some poor female relation whose sinecure in the Borgo household depended on her keeping Giuditta out of trouble. But Giuditta was no meek lamb. The voices were raised, became shrill, and then there was a cowed murmur from the older woman. A door slammed angrily.

An eternity later the arched door to the boat landing opened. And then, like a blessed miracle, Giuditta appeared, the light of the recessed lantern throwing a blurred golden halo around her hair.

"Row me over there," Sandro hissed at Lorenzo.

The old boatman pushed at his oar with a grunt, and the gondola edged toward the flight of marble steps. Sandro, taking care not to rock the boat, struck a pose, kneeling on one knee, his hat held over his heart, the lute laid aside.

Then, out of the surrounding darkness, a lantern appeared. Sandro heard the splash of an oar, saw the dim outline of an approaching gondola—a hired one from the plain look of its beak.

"Messer Sandro, Messer Sandro!" a voice called. The

passenger had spotted the Cavalli crest, and the black craft was skimming purposefully toward him.

Sandro cursed under his breath. Who among his acquaintances knew he was here? He had told none of his friends. Some prankster must have wormed it out of one of the servants who knew about it from Lorenzo, and was here to give him a ragging.

He turned to give the interloper a piece of his mind. In the gleam of the bow lantern as the other craft drew abreast he saw Cavalli livery and recognized Bruno's shovel chin.

"Messer Sandro, come home," the watchman said in a voice hoarse with strain. "Your father's dead."

CHAPTER 3

Monna Tessa met him at the door, weeping. "It must have happened before midnight. The candles had burned out in their sockets, but he hadn't gone to bed. He was sitting in the chair with the tall back. He must have tried to get up to reach the bell rope. Jacopo found him face down on the floor with his arm stretched out. Bruno was making his rounds, and he woke Jacopo up right away."

"Where is he now?"

"In his room. Jacopo is seeing to having him laid out. There's a priest with him. A priest was sent for right away." She wailed, her square teeth bared in a primitive grimace of pain. "He gave him extreme unction, as well as he could, but who's to say how long he'd been dead?"

Sandro started for the stairs. He stopped with his hand on the rail. "Where's Maffeo?"

She wrung her hands. "He went out, Ser Alessandro. After the disputa with your father. No one knows where."

"Send Betto, Piero—whoever can be spared—out to look for him. Comb the city—all his usual haunts." The scene that morning by the slave quay came to him. "Tell them to try the waterfront dives at the east end of the Riva."

"Yes, Ser Alessandro."

"What . . ." His voice shook, but he got it under control. "What about Agnese?"

"She's in her room. She knows. I sent one of the maids to stay with her. Marcolina—she's fond of her."

"*Gràzie*. I'll look in on her in a moment. Will you go to her when you can?"

"Yes." There was a new outburst of weeping, and she mopped at her eyes with her apron. "Oh, what's to become of the poor thing?"

He took a damp hand and squeezed it, then turned and took the steps two at a time. His father's room smelled of candles and incense. Jacopo, the majordomo, stood in a long straight robe and silk cap, giving instructions to two women of the household and one whom Sandro did not know. A priest with a long face and tufted eyebrows sat in a corner, mumbling prayers. Jacopo broke off talking to the women when Sandro came in and hurried over to him.

"Messer Alessandro! Thank heaven you're here! It's a terrible thing! I knew he wasn't feeling well these last few days, but he put it down to indigestion. He drove himself too hard. He was going through the books all day as if salvation depended on it. The notary came to see him, and the lawyer. There were papers scattered all over the floor. I gathered them up and saved them. . . ."

"Later, Jacopo. I want to see him now."

"It's not very pleasant. There hasn't been time to wash him, arrange his features. I was going through all that now with the *femmine*. We'll find someone here to keep the vigil tonight, but for tomorrow night I'll hire a professional—"

"Fine, fine." Sandro shook him off and went to the bed. The priest lurched to his feet, to stand by his side.

"Great riches mean only more to leave behind," he said sententiously. "Who has most, leaves most. We take with us only our sins to the judgment." His breath smelled of garlic.

"Thank you, *padre*," Sandro said absently. He wondered if the man had been paid. He'd give him something later.

His father's face was twisted, as Jacopo had warned;

the mouth wore a lopsided grimace that might have been
alarm or disbelief, the lid of one eye was pulled back to
show a dusty pupil, staring wide. Sandro picked up a
stiffening hand and kissed it, the tears running, while the
priest and the majordomo looked on and the women, out
of respect, stopped their whispering.

Afterward he went in to see Agnese. Marcolina lowered her eyes and dropped him a curtsy, then left the
room; she was a country girl with wide hips, large
breasts, and a coarse honest face, who had been in the
house only a few years but whom everybody liked.

Sandro sat on the edge of the bed and Agnese flung
her arms about him. "Oh, Sandro," she sobbed, clinging
to him, "they won't let me see him."

"There, there, *siròcchia mìa*, you'll see him tomorrow,
in his best clothes, looking peaceful. He goes to God."

"Marcolina says that devils fly around in the air, waiting to catch a soul on its way to heaven, but that if your
last words were of God, they can't touch you."

"Don't worry about it, *piccola*. I'm sure he thought of
God at the last."

"But he was having such a terrible fight with Maffeo.
They shouted at each other. And then there was an awful
sound, and they stopped shouting, and Maffeo ran down
the stairs and left by the back way."

"*Non si preoccupi*, little one. Whatever Father said in
anger, they wouldn't have been his last words."

She fluttered in his arms. He could feel her thin
shoulderblades, like the bones of a bird. "I wish Maffeo
would come back."

"I sent the footmen to look for him. They'll find him
soon."

"Will Maffeo be our father now?"

He was startled. "No, little one."

"Where did he go?"

"I wish I knew."

The shutters were drawn for the night at the Sign of
the Goat, but the regular patrons still lingered over their
wine under the flickering light of the smoky oil lamps

that held the unwelcome dawn at bay. The one-eyed proprietor, who went by the name of Luca the Squint, regularly paid the *Capo* of the district for the privilege of
being free from visits by the nightwatch patrols, and was
also reputed to have come to some kind of arrangement
with one of the *Cattaveri*—the officials who were supposed to see to the protection of the hordes of tourists
who used Venice as the jumping-off place for pilgrimages
to the Holy Land.

The rough benches were occupied by a fine assort-
ment of waterfront riffraff, back-alley *bravi* who did dirty
work for the wealthy, pimps, touts, and tricksters, with a
scattering of foreign sailors who had gained entry, and
who soon would be plucked clean by whores, cutpurses,
and confidence men. A large round table in the corner
had been taken over by a band of Piedmontese merce-
naries who had been left unemployed by Venice's victory
over Sigismund of Hungary in the war for control of the
Dalmatian coast and who had pawned most of their armor, by the scruffy look of them. In another dark corner
a shifty-eyed agent for one of the pilgrim galleys, his
banner leaning against the wall, sat with his gull—a
ruddy-faced Englishman in a monk's robe, whom he had
somehow pried away from the Piazza and its watchful official guides.

But the place also had its aristocrats—*bravi* with important reputations, fences, Lombards, a crooked lawyer
or two, shady businessmen of various sorts. The sort of
men you didn't bother at their tables unless you were invited to sit down with them.

One of these was Ser Falco, the labor contractor. He
was sitting at one of the good tables, in a secluded alcove, with a man in black who looked like a crow, and a
scowling young dandy in velvet.

"Traitors!" the dandy was saying. "A traitor of a father
and a traitor of a brother!"

Falco said, "Keep your voice down. You've drunk too
much wine tonight." He turned to the man in black.
"What do you say, *Zio*?"

The other replied in a rusty, scratchy voice. "The

young gentleman is learning the lessons of life. To wit. The first pain is betrayal, the first joy, revenge."

"He plotted all along to steal my patrimony," Maffeo burst out. "The sniveling little dissembler! They thought they had it all worked out between them. But by God, what a lawyer does with a pen can be undone with a knife. I'm cleverer than both of them. And I'll have the House of Cavalli at the end!"

"Calm yourself, young gentleman," the man in black said.

Falco ran a thumb around the rim of his glass. "There's been much talk of money. But I haven't seen any."

"There'll be plenty of money." Maffeo glared. "Don't worry about money."

"It's my business to worry about money," said the black crow.

Maffeo flushed.

Falco leaned forward. "The risks are great. Do you know the penalties in such cases? Even a thief stealing to the value of twenty *soldi* loses his eyes and his right hand. For you, they'd burn your innards in front of your face before hanging the rest of you from a window of the Ducal Palace."

"Let my brother worry about being hung from a window of the Ducal Palace," Maffeo said. He took a swallow of wine.

The crow cackled. "That's the way, young gentleman."

"Well?" Maffeo demanded. "You were full of big talk. What about it?"

Falco sighed. The three of them fell silent while Luca the Squint came with a pitcher to refill their glasses. When he left, Falco gave Maffeo a shrug and beckoned to two of the *bravi* who sat dicing at a table in back. They got up quickly, flattered to be noticed, and came swaggering over.

"It's got to go off smoothly," Maffeo said, suddenly anxious. "Remember, you said you could bring it off smoothly."

The man in black stood up with a scraping of chair legs. "Excuse me, *messeri*," he said. "I'll be off now. I'm no part of this."

• • •

The great of Venice began to arrive by the first light of dawn. The first to come was the brother of the Doge, Lionardo Mocenigo, who was one of the Ducal Councillors. While not as old as his brother, he still got around with difficulty, and it was a singular mark of respect that the old man struggled from the gilded chair in his gondola and puffed up the stairs to the *sala* where Girolamo Cavalli's body lay in state.

"A profound loss," he said to Sandro as he turned to go. "I can tell you in confidence that the Council later today will vote the sum of three hundred ducats for frescoes to tell the story of his life."

"Thank you, Your Excellency," Sandro said. "Will you stay and take some refreshments?"

Sandro felt light-headed. He had been up all night with Jacopo, seeing to arrangements for the three-day vigil and the procession by land and water that would follow; a messenger had been sent to Saint Mark's, and the bells had tolled in the hour before dawn, but word had gotten around quickly enough without that. Maffeo, providentially, had arrived shortly before then, in a restrained and somber mood, eyes inflamed, lids drooping. He had viewed his father's corpse and said little; his reticence was put down to grief by Sandro. Then he had gone up and thrown himself on his bed for an hour, and had shown up just as the Doge's brother arrived.

"You are thoughtful, *messire*," Lionardo Mocenigo said, casting an indifferent glance at the lavish funeral feast that Monna Tessa had laid out; she had provided an impressive spread even before the markets opened and now was in the kitchen, adding to it. "But at my age, a few roasted chestnuts and a half a glass of wine is sufficient fare in the morning."

Maffeo, without seeming to push Sandro aside, had managed to interpose himself between Lionardo and his brother. "And how is His Serenity, the Doge?" he said smoothly.

"He is well, Messer Maffeo," the old man replied. "Though the jackals nip at his heels in anticipation of the post. That vapid braggart Foscari is the worst; he's trying to spend his way into the office, and if he's elected, he'll spend Venice into bankruptcy. Messer Doge is determined that he will not succeed him."

"I'm sure His Serenity has many useful years left before Venice need think about electing another Doge," Maffeo said.

Sandro could not help but raise an eyebrow at Maffeo's unctuous tone. Maffeo, he knew, was a vocal partisan of Francesco Foscari who, through the offices he had garnered to himself—chief of the *Quarantia*, a *capo* of the Ten, procurator of San Marco—had made himself immensely popular by distribution of the public funds.

Lionardo grunted his appreciation. "War and debt, that's what a Foscari dogeship would mean." He wagged a finger in Maffeo's face. "When are you going to take your seat in the Council, Ser Maffeo? We have need of clear heads like yours."

"Soon, Your Excellency, soon."

"Don't wait too long. It's up to you to represent the Cavalli name now."

He swept down the broad staircase to his waiting gondola, followed by a swarm of attendants in splendid robes.

"Maffeo . . ." Sandro said hesitantly. "We haven't talked."

"Talk? What's there to talk about? On a day like today, the talk's of eternity." He nodded toward the funeral buffet, where the priest who had attended Girolamo, a chicken leg in one hand and a slice of meat pie in the other, stood talking to a fellow priest from Saint Mark's. "If you want to discuss repentance, there's the fellow to talk to."

"I haven't done anything to repent of."

"Haven't you? Then you're different from the rest of us, little brother." Maffeo looked away and became busy greeting new arrivals. "Ah, Messer Arrigo, how gracious of you to come," he said to the tight-lipped man climbing the steps with a flunky at his shoulder; it was the *capo* of the parish, whose goodwill determined the size of one's assessment for forced loans and who could, if he chose, look the other way when it came to enforcing the regulations for the carrying of weapons. A good man to know.

They kept arriving all day—the Ducal Councillors, the three heads of the Forty who with the Councillors constituted the *Signoria*, Senators, the ministers of the *Savii Grandi*. The great merchants who had been Girolamo Cavalli's colleagues and competitors came to pay their respects, including Messer Borgo, who was effusive to Maffeo, short with Sandro—as if he had something to say, but thought it not the place. And there was a mingling of less-exalted folk, too: customers and clients, agents and suppliers, tradesmen, employees from the bank and the warehouse.

The concentration of Venice's wealthiest and most powerful was too tempting for politicians to resist, and several of those whose names were bruited about as worthy successors to Messer the Doge Mocenigo took the opportunity to pay a call, though some of them had hardly known Girolamo Cavalli. There was Marino Caravello, doddering and decrepit, but not yet slaked of a thirst for honors. Maffeo was barely polite to him, his eyes wandering around the room while the venerable aspirant meandered through one of his interminable stories. There was Francesco Bembo, blind in one eye and walking with a limp, but spry nevertheless. And Antonio Contarini, who needed money too badly because of his great swarm of children, to which his wife added a new mouth to feed every year. Captain-General Badoer, whose family had contributed seven Doges to the Republic, sent word that his military duties kept him away, but that he would pay a call tomorrow; and Loredan, the young naval hero who had beaten the Turks at Gallipoli four years earlier, and who boasted of having slaughtered all the pilots and navigators among his prisoners to deprive the infidel of their future services, stayed only briefly in order to avoid an encounter with his archrival, Francesco Foscari.

Foscari himself arrived about midday, for maximum effect. He swept in with a cloud of attendants and began immediately to greet people, smiling and waving, on his way to the bier.

Sandro was a little in awe of the famous politician, who, still in his forties, had set Venice on its ear and earned the hostility of the Doge. Foscari was a splendid figure in a robe of cloth-of-gold, a jeweled ring on every finger, and a red velvet bonnet whose shape, perhaps deliberately, suggested the ducal miter. His face, though, with its wide nostrils and the pads of fat that made slits of his eyes when he smiled, was down-to-earth, practical, and shrewd. The Doge had said publicly of him, "He sets fire to things but is careful not to burn his own fingers."

Foscari stopped to exchange a few words with a seedy aristocrat in darned hose—one of the unfortunate *Barnabotti* who had a title and a vote and not much else. "Of course a dowry can be found for your daughter Enrichetta," Foscari assured the man. "Saint Mark's has a fund for just such worthy causes."

He arrived at the bier with his face arranged in a mask of sorrow and sympathy. "Life goes on," he said sententiously. "Yes, yes, life goes on, do what we will, and the House of Cavalli will continue to play an influential role in the affairs of the Republic. Have you young gentlemen given thought to what the future may hold if the Senate can be persuaded to break off our entangling alliance with Milan and instead enter into a treaty of mutual assistance with Florence?"

Sandro had heard his father say that the pact with Milan was necessary in case of further aggression by Hungary and that it would be a mistake to ally the Republic with Milan's enemy, Florence. Doge Mocenigo had been adroitly fending off the diplomatic overtures from Florence's ambassadors.

"The Doge says that we've got to maintain our friendship with Milan as long as the possibility exists of new trouble from King Sigismund. . . ." Sandro began.

Foscari smiled at him condescendingly. "Hungary is well beaten," he said. "We don't need Milan any more." He turned to Maffeo. "And what do *you* say, Ser Maffeo?"

"Oh, I agree with you, Ser Francesco," Maffeo replied swiftly. "New ideas are needed. Venice has been run for too long by fossils."

He steered Foscari away from the bier and departed

arm in arm with him, talking politics. A circle of people, attracted by the procurator's magnetism, started to grow, moving with them. Sandro shrugged and turned his attention to greeting newcomers. A delegation of the warehouse employees, led by Ippolito, was standing about uncertainly, feeling out of place in the grandeur of the company, and Sandro was anxious to make them feel at home.

"Come over to the table and have something," he said, after they had assured him of their sympathy, and one elderly employee, embarrassingly, had broken down and begun to weep, telling Sandro that his father had been, *"Un santo, Messer Alessandro, un santo!"*

The *sala* was full of people now who, having done their duty, were enjoying the wake as a social occasion. On every side, Sandro heard gossip, jokes, anecdotes about his father, reminiscences about other notables, other deaths.

"Do you remember when the Pisani bank failed? Three of his clients died that very week, and the Ten decided to look into the matter."

The speaker was a portly man with a large purple nose, one of the Balbi brothers. The Balbi were at the center of everything and had ties with the Medici in Florence.

"Yes, but one of the deaths was a drowning accident," another merchant reminded him. "He was wearing full armor, and he slipped from a gangplank while boarding. He sank like a rock. It was in front of a score of witnesses. And besides, it was a plague year. There were many deaths."

"Yes, yes, but of the other two deaths, one had been put down to a heart attack, and it was noticed by a mourner that the corpse had a peculiar smell from the mouth, so . . ."

"That was medication. You're talking about Paolo Orso. He was a hypochondriac. He dosed himself with every nostrum he could get some quack to prescribe: rhubarb syrups for constipation, borage for phlegm, preparations of sage against the tertian fever, theriaca against the plague—"

"They examined the servants under torture," the Balbi cut in impatiently, "and sure enough, one of them suddenly remembered that he had seen one of Orso's customers, a wool trader who stood to benefit by the wiping out of his debt, steal up by the back way to see the dead man earlier. When the other servants were put on the rack and confronted with this, they, too, accused the man. . . ."

That started a round of talk about the art of poisoning, particularly as it was practiced in wicked cities like Rome and Florence. Sandro could see where the talk was going, so he moved quickly to put a stop to it.

"My father died of heart stoppage," he said in a carrying voice to the nearest person at hand. "His physician, Maestro Luzzatto, confirmed it this morning. Father tried to keep it to himself, but he hadn't been in the best health for some time, and he'd been thinking a lot about the future lately. . . . Besides, Maffeo was the last person to be with him. No poisoner could have gotten to him with his son there."

Maffeo, standing a few feet away, seemed to lose color in the face and took a drink of wine. Sandro could have bit his tongue at having touched what must be a sore spot; probably Maffeo was reproaching himself for having left their father alone.

The purple-nosed Balbi was still making rumbles in his chest. "Examine the servants, that's what I always say, examine the servants."

Foscari, surrounded by his claque, put on a helpful face. "Beg pardon, but what did your father have for dinner yesterday?"

Confused at the question, Sandro stammered, "Why . . . capon, with a red sauce, and mushrooms . . . it was supervised personally by Monna Tessa."

"Ah, mushrooms," Foscari said with a significant nod.

"What . . . why are you asking?"

"Perhaps," Foscari said with a smile, "this Monna Tessa ought to be put to the question."

"But . . . but . . ." Sandro sputtered, "Monna Tessa is a part of the family. She's devoted to all of us and to my father especially."

He looked to Maffeo for help, but Maffeo had turned away and was taking another sip of wine.

"The innocent have nothing to fear," Foscari said blandly.

Maffeo turned around. "She's very thick with my father's clerk, Ippolito. All the money runs through his hands. He's been named one of the executors of my father's estate."

"Ah, I see," Foscari said.

There were murmurs all around. "Perhaps this Ippolito ought to be put to the question, too," said the purple-nosed man.

Sandro listened in disbelief. Maffeo's behavior had stunned him to the point of speechlessness. He decided he could only stir things up by making an issue of it. After his father's will was read, he would be in charge. He stood back and listened. Foscari could not stay on any subject long, and soon he was holding forth on the necessity of deficit spending to stimulate Venice's economy; it would bring in more money in the long run, he averred. Balbi and the others listened as if mesmerized. Sandro breathed a sigh of relief.

The long day finally came to an end. The last talkative stragglers expressed their parting condolences, and Sandro watched the bobbing lanterns of their departing gondolas from a balcony window. The hired vigil keeper had arrived and had taken his all-night position at the foot of the bier. Sandro refused an offer of a bedtime cup from Monna Tessa and told her to get some sleep. Tomorrow would be a trying day. Maffeo was nowhere in sight, and the doors to his apartment were shut. Sandro yawned and swayed. He felt as if he were in a dream, standing on an unfamiliar shore, watching a gulf widen and the shore that had held his other life depart.

On his way to his bed, he stopped to look in on Agnese. She was fitfully asleep, the bedclothes tangled, her thin childish face pale and streaked with tears. She whimpered in her sleep when he straightened out the blankets. He blew out the candle and went to his rooms.

•   •   •

The next two days passed strangely. Sandro played his part as if on a stage, seeing himself from outside himself as a little distant figure in mummer's costume, going through the prescribed rituals of pomp and ceremony. The Senate had decreed a public funeral for Girolamo Cavalli, with all the obsequies that entailed, and the deputations from the guilds and confraternities that would be a part of it had to be dealt with. He conferred with Ippolito on costs: food, wax, trappings and banners for the church, torches, the hiring of boatmen. The mourning garments alone came to more than a thousand ducats—long hooded cloaks of the best quality for the family and servants, shorter unlined cloaks for friends and the employees of the Cavalli enterprises. Ippolito, who had always been so tight about doling out the firm's money, said nothing; he bit his lip and portioned out the ducats as necessary, sending each purse with a company page boy to Jacopo or Monna Tessa or whoever else had to disburse it.

Maffeo remained coldly distant to Sandro through it all. They appeared together at the required ceremonies and stood shoulder to shoulder in greeting the various delegations, but out of the public eye, Maffeo was little help. It was left to Sandro to try to comfort Agnese and to see to the thousand practical details that had to be attended to.

On the last day, at sunset, Sandro, with the rest of the twenty pallbearers, helped shoulder his father's funeral litter and bear it to the black-draped barge that waited at the foot of the landing. Girolamo was dressed in his finest robes and wore a sword at his side so that all Venice could see him for the man of consequence that he had been. The canal behind the funeral barge was clogged with the craft of deputations from the confraternities and the city's artisans, including a sizable flotilla from the Arsenal. The banks of the canal burned with the torches of those who had gathered to view the waterborne cortege and then to proceed on foot to Saint Mark's, chanting hymns and prayers. Torches, too, were held aloft in the barks and gondolas, making a bright streak across the night. A portative organ in the funeral fleet struck a deep chord, and voices rose in chorus over the waters. Slowly, the floating procession wound its way through the canals, a serpent with a backbone of fire.

Disembarking at the Piazzetta landing, the water parade joined up with the street marchers. A halt was called in the middle of the Piazza, and the pallbearers set down the open litter while the oldest member of the *Signoria* delivered a funeral oration. Within the basilica of Saint Mark's a requiem was performed, to the thundering accompaniment of the two organs that were the wonder of Europe.

Weary to the bone, Sandro slumped in his pew and somehow got through the rest of it. It would be all over tomorrow. His father's body would lie in state before the high altar through the night and in the morning would be interred in the family tomb. The reading of the will would be in the afternoon; he would face Maffeo's wrath, and then, when things had had time to blow over, he could begin to stitch the Cavalli family and the Cavalli business back together again.

While the great church emptied out, the family was whisked into the sacristy to give them privacy from the departing crush. While they waited, Sandro and Maffeo were offered the use of the Doge's own chapel for their private devotions. Maffeo seemed impatient to be off as soon as possible, but it was an offer he could hardly refuse in the midst of all the well-meaning clerics. With Sandro, he followed the sacristan up an enclosed flight of stairs to a treasure house of a room under one of the domes. Agnese, enfolded by Monna Tessa and asleep on her feet, stayed behind, ignored by the priests who kept popping in and out.

Sandro, oblivious of the enclosing splendor, knelt at the Doge's altar and lost himself in prayer, in a way he had not been able to do during all the crowded public ceremonies. After a while some flicker of light or movement in the encrusting ornamentation caught his eye, and he realized that the Doge had a peephole through which he could look down on the nave below. He slid it open all the way, and found himself peering into the enormous twilight cave he had just left. The crowds were gone, as if by an act of magic, leaving only a few scattered solitary worshipers and loiterers at the shrines. He could see his father plainly at the far end, a tiny recumbent doll in stiff robes, surrounded by gold angels. In a way, it was like being alone with him for the last time. Sandro bowed his head and recited the *Miserere*. He was not aware of it when Maffeo got up and left.

Some time later, a touch on his shoulder brought him back to awareness. It was the sacristan.

"They sent me to tell you that your boatman is waiting."

"In a moment."

Sandro realized that he did not want to go just yet. He started to tell the sacristan that the others should leave without him, but the man had gone. A few minutes later Maffeo came into the room, his funeral robe over his arm.

"Are you coming?"

"No, I'll stay here a while. I can hire a gondola at the Piazzetta."

"Suit yourself."

Maffeo turned and left. Sandro lingered at his prayers. He did not know how long he had knelt there; he must have dozed off for a few seconds, still kneeling, and he woke up with a start. Below, through the peephole, the enormous transept was empty, though a lone figure still knelt in the shadows of the north aisle.

He went downstairs and through the sacristy. No one was there. He left through a side door and walked toward the boat landing. A rising mist shrouded the Piazzetta, and no stars were visible. He groped his way toward the mooring place for the gondolas. A few were always available for hire at any hour.

A shadowy form appeared beside him. "Signor, at your service."

He followed the boatman to a gondola that was moored a little apart, past the pillars of execution. He stepped down into the gondola with a helping hand from the boatman and settled himself in the cushions.

The man pushed off without a word, and the grouped domes of Saint Mark's vanished into fog. After some minutes Sandro realized that he had forgotten to tell the boatman where to go, but the gondola was heading toward the mouth of the Grand Canal anyway. "The Ca' Cavalli," he said sleepily.

"*Sì, signore,*" the boatman said behind him.

Sandro took off his funeral cloak and folded it on the seat beside him. The lantern hanging on the beak of the gondola made rings in the mist but didn't do much to penetrate it. Nebulous shapes slipped by in the haze, wearing their own halos suspended before them, and the warning calls of other gondoliers came out of the fog.

He shivered without the cloak but at the same time wanted only, for this quarter of an hour, to feel the salt air on his skin, to sense the eternal Adriatic in which this ancient ship of a city floated. In some way he had laid aside with the cloak, however briefly, the weight of this new life full of responsibilities that pressed in on him and was still free, back in the hallucination of youth, when all things are possible and one need not be stifled by the life of detail which chained other people.

The sketch of a palace drifted by in the wall of mist, and Sandro was seized by a pang of longing that made his breath come short. He could not say what it was he longed for, but he knew that he had to catch a glimpse of Giuditta and exchange a few words with her.

"Stop at the Borgo Palace," he told the boatman. "Just lay off in front of the right-hand balconies."

The boatman did not reply for a moment. Then he said, "*Sì signore.*"

The Borgo Palace was dark, an oblong blur rising out of vapor. Even the boat lantern had been extinguished; the household must have gone to bed long ago. Sandro wished he had some pebbles to throw at the window. He stood up in the thwarts and called Giuditta's name in a hoarse whisper. He could only hope that she was not asleep, that she would be keyed to hear her name coming from the night.

He tried again, louder. "Giuditta, *cara*, it's me, Sandro." Surely she would be awake, thinking of him on this night. Her father had been part of the funeral cortege; all the great merchants of Venice had attended, paying honors to one of their own.

A casement opened above. A male voice said, "Go away."

"Giuditta, I love you!" Sandro called desperately. If Giuditta hadn't been awake before, the disturbance might have roused her from sleep.

"Go away," the voice repeated. It wasn't even Messer Borgo; it was some servant. Stung by the ignominy of it, Sandro shouted out his message one more time. The window closed firmly.

"All right," he told the boatman. "Take me home."

The man rowed in silence. After an interval the Cavalli Palace loomed out of the fog, but the boatman did not steer for the water gate. Instead, he turned the prow of the gondola toward the weed-infested side canal. Sandro started to say something but changed his mind. The boatman probably assumed that he didn't want to disturb the household at this hour, and he was right. It would be better to creep in through the back garden; if he happened to wake up Bruno while going through, at least he could get past quietly, without Bruno clanking through the whole downstairs.

He paid off the boatman and scrambled for a foothold on the old stone flight that led through the garden. The trees and the broken brick walls cast deeper shadows in the gloom. He had taken no more than a few steps when a pair of black-cloaked figures emerged from the darkness on either side of him. Their quick, purposeful movements showed that they were up to no good.

Sandro groped for a sword that wasn't there. He didn't even have a knife. He flung his bundled-up cloak at one of the footpads and dodged the outstretched hand of the other, while opening his mouth to shout "thief." A night patrol might be within earshot, and the knowledge of that, plus the distraction of seeing Bruno come running out with his pike, might frighten this pair of thugs off.

But before he could cry out, there was a scrape of footsteps on the path behind him and a jarring blow on the back of the head that spun him around and turned the world blank.

He slipped down into oblivion. Somewhere in a pulsing red blindness he felt his knees cave in, strong hands grab him. Then the world dribbled away to nothing.

He woke in a sack. It was a woolsack, scratchy with hair and stiff with the grease of the fells it once had contained. His arms and legs were bound and numb.

He lay still a moment. His head throbbed painfully. It was hard to breathe in the suffocating darkness of the sack, and for an awful moment he thought he was going to be sick. He fought the feeling successfully, then tried to get some sense of his surroundings. There was a rocking motion, and he could hear some of the familiar night sounds of the Grand Canal around him. He was on the water. In a gondola, by the feel of it. The gondolier had been in on it. He was surprised to find himself still alive. It had been something more than a simple robbery.

He struggled to sit up in the sack. A hand pushed him down roughly, and man cursed.

"He's moving around."

"You'd better give him a little tap."

A hand ran over him, feeling for the shape of his head through the coarse fabric. It found the position it wanted, and a thumb and fingers dug in tight to hold his head steady. Then, out of nowhere, a white flash of lightning exploded in his skull and shrank immediately to a bright dot that disappeared, taking him with it.

CHAPTER 4

This time he woke in a dungeon. He was stapled to a wall by about a foot of chain welded to his ankle, and he was fettered hand and foot. A filthy gray light filtered through an iron grate above, giving him just enough illumination to see by.

Someone had propped his head against the wall, or he would have drowned. He was sitting in about eight inches of water that covered the stone floor and swirled about the thick oak door at the other side of the room. The water felt warm, scummy. Bits of straw and worse floated on its surface. His nose told him the water was salt; wherever he was, he was below the level of the canal, and the high tide must seep through the foundations.

Sandro tried to move his head, and winced at the pain. His neck was stiff with the damp and the unnatural angle at which it had been twisted, and the back of his head felt as if someone had poured liquid fire into it.

He pulled himself to his feet with a rattle of his chains. His clothes were a sodden mess, uncomfortable against his skin. He ached in every joint. He could get his hands about a foot apart, his feet far enough apart to hobble if he had not been fastened to the wall. Experimentally he pulled at the ankle chain. It held firm.

Where could he be? His first thought was that he had

ben arrested by the Gentlemen of the Night. Perhaps they had tracked him down after the fight at the slave quay. He had never supposed that the watch would knock people over the head without speaking to them first and giving them a chance to go along quietly, but who could tell how they did things? His second thought was that he was in even more serious trouble—that he had been abducted by the triumvirs of the Council of Ten. They did things in secret. People just disappeared. Later, you might find their bodies hanging upside down between the red columns in the Piazzetta. But it would start, so he had always heard, when an officer of the Three tapped the accused on the shoulder and said, according to formula, "Their Excellencies would like to see you." And then, if an absolute majority of the Ten did not vote for condemnation for four ballots running, the accused was set free. That was what had happened to his father when he had been denounced.

"Hey, anyone!" he shouted. "Come and open the door! Someone talk to me!"

His voice rang off the damp walls. The blocks of stone looked at least two feet thick. A voice wouldn't carry through them. And he couldn't hear anything from outside, either. He might be anywhere.

He took inventory of his surroundings. This place had been used to hold prisoners before. There were iron staples at intervals around the lower wall, some with lengths of chain and leg cuffs still trailing from them. A covered wooden bucket stood just within reach; if he wanted to use it, he could just about stretch far enough to jockey it to him. There was also a heavy wooden bench a little farther away. But he would have to lie at full length in the swampy water in order to drag it toward him.

A rat swam from somewhere, making a V-shaped wave. It spotted him and turned a sleek head in his direction to study him, treading water. He splashed and yelled to frighten it and, unhurriedly, it dived out of sight, perhaps to find some underwater escape hole; at least it did not reappear.

Sandro's stomach turned in revulsion. Sooner or

later—especially if it were not now high tide outside and the water rose farther—it was going to be necessary for him to get the bench over to him. But not yet.

The water, in fact, drained off during the next few hours, leaving slimy little pools in every depression of the worn stone floor. Sandro, pulling his chain taut and straining with all his might, managed to move the crude bench against the wall and sit down on it. He tried shouting a few more times, but nothing happened.

The dingy shaft of light from overhead lengthened and began to retract again. Sandro could only guess at the position of the sun but thought his cell might be facing east. The dungeons under the Doge's palace, the infamous *pozzi*, or "wells," so named because the prisoners stood in water, were also on the east side, facing the side canal that set off the Palace and Saint Mark's. The torture chambers and the Inquisitor's chamber would be conveniently nearby, for quick justice, and somewhere up above would be another set of cells—the *piombi*, or "leads"—where prisoners not fortunate enough merely to be submerged in water and gloom were instead roasted under the eaves, where the lead sheathing turned their tiny cages into little furnaces. Only last year a number of the poor wretches had in actuality been roasted to death when a fire broke out under the wooden cupolas of the church and spread, flooding the Piazzetta and the Molo with molten lead.

At the thought, Sandro gave way to despair. He shouted again: "For the love of God will someone come and tell me why I'm here?"

The door creaked open, and for a moment Sandro, his heart beating wildly, thought someone had come in answer to his calls. But the creature who sidled into the cell, bearing a cheap pottery bowl in either hand, showed no inclination to speak to him.

"Where is this place?" Sandro asked. "Is this the prison?"

His visitor put the bowls down on the floor, well out of Sandro's reach. He was a hunchback, hardly larger than a child, with a gnarled face that was mostly nose, hands like twisted claws, and short bowed legs that were wrapped in rags under a coarse woolen smock.

"Answer me!" Sandro demanded with a hauteur he did not feel.

The hunchback gave him a sidelong look from under his cowl. The crabbed face showed no expression. He made an urgent gesture indicating that Sandro was to move back against the wall, as far as he was able.

Instead, Sandro lunged to the extent of his chain. The twisted little man scuttled backward with surprising agility. He gestured again.

Sandro understood that he would not be given the bowls unless he cooperated. He was not interested in food, though he had not eaten since the previous day, but one of the bowls contained water, and the long morning had left him parched. With a shrug, he retreated. The little man crept forward, keeping a wary eye on Sandro, and pushed the bowls along the floor toward him. As soon as he judged that they were within reach, he sprang backward like a feral creature. He'd been a bit too hasty; the water sloshed, and some of it spilled.

"Wait!" Sandro cried. "Don't go! What's your name? Who are you? Does anybody know I'm here?"

The gnome moved sideways to the door, his eyes never leaving Sandro's face. He scurried through, and the door closed with a thud. Sandro could hear the slam of a heavy bolt.

He went to examine the bowls. First he lifted the one with the water with his bound hands, careful not to spill it, and took a long greedy drink. Then he picked up the other one. There was a gluey mass the size of a fist in it, and after a moment he identified a mess of beans, boiled to mush. With it was a jagged half-moon of the kind of hard biscuit that was fed to sailors and galley oarsmen. He forced himself to eat a few mouthfuls of the tasteless, sticky glop, picking it up with his fingers, and broke off a piece of the ship's biscuit. Then, losing his appetite, he set the bowl down again.

"Dear God," he prayed. "Get me out of this."

By now, his father would be buried, interred in a place of honor in the wall of the parish church—not ferried to the isle of the dead like ordinary people. Perhaps at this moment everyone was gathered for the reading of the will—Ippolito and the other executors, the *buonomini* whom the Republic would require to be present in the case of a public figure with such a fortune, Maffeo, Agnese, the uncles, Jacopo and Monna Tessa and others of the household staff who were considered part of *la famiglia*, his father's partners over the years in the ever-changing web of joint enterprises that sustained the great merchant houses like the Ca' Cavalli.

His heart raced at the pictures his mind formed. They would all be wondering why he was not there. And Giuditta, who must have heard him being chased off last night! What would they all be thinking of him right now?

A small flurry of movement at his feet made him jump. The rat was there at the bowls. It seized the crescent of hardtack in its sharp little teeth and scampered away with it. It sat down across the cell and began to nibble at its prize, knowing it had nothing to fear from Sandro. He had nothing to throw at it but one of the bowls. It regarded him through beady imperturbable eyes. *"Fuòri!"* he told it. "Go away!" He wept.

He could measure time only by the creeping progress of the bar of light across the floor, the periods of darkness, the rise and fall with the tides of the water on the floor, the visits of the gnarled little jailer. He was fed once a day, as near as he could judge. The hunchback never spoke to him. Sandro cajoled and pleaded, trying to prolong the visits, but the little man's only response was to shrink away from him, then motion him backward to the limit of his chain while he inched the bowls into the zone of safety. Sandro put on a show of docility. Perhaps he succeeded in lulling his skittish captor. By the third day, Sandro could stand it no longer. He backed up tamely as usual. His keeper, with the usual sidelong glance, pushed the bowls one at a time along the floor to him, his twisted body poised for flight. But this time he was a little careless, and perhaps he pushed the bowls an inch too far. Sandro leapt. The chain jerked at his ankle and he fell flat on his face, but he had the little man's scrawny wrist in his grasp.

The gnome mewled with terror. It was not a normal sound, such as a person would make, but a high, gargling, animal noise. He struggled and twisted, but Sandro, despite three days of starvation and inactivity, was stronger. He caught the man's other wrist and drew him closer. The hunchback tried to bite him, but Sandro gave him a shaking and he desisted.

"Now you're going to talk, damn you!" he said through gritted teeth, and then paused at his new dilemma. He could hold the creature as long as he had strength, but there was no way to force him to set him free. The iron cuffs were forged to his wrists and ankles, not locked; those keys dangling from the dwarf's waist were for doors, not chains. There was no possible way to threaten the man to fetch a chisel and hammer; the instant he let him go, he would simply scuttle out of reach again. All he had succeeded in doing, Sandro realized ruefully, was to spill his supper.

"At least you'll talk!" he grunted, shaking the little man like a terrier with a rat. He was rewarded only by a series of bubbling squeals from somewhere in the other's scraggy throat.

"Let poor Berto go," said a voice from the door. "He can't answer you."

Startled, Sandro relaxed his grip, and the hunchback broke free and scrambled out of reach.

Sandro looked up and saw a sallow, long-nosed man swathed in a black cloak and long hood with a point. With his yellowish beak and skinny legs, he resembled a crow.

"Why not?" Sandro said.

"He lost his tongue long ago. He was a glassblower, and he violated the law about revealing trade secrets to foreigners. But they let him live; it wasn't treason, only overtalkativeness."

The newcomer seemed to have a little trouble talking himself. His voice sounded husky, strained, like a rusty hinge. He spoke with a Lombard accent.

"Who are you?"

The Lombard cocked his head. "Well, young gentleman, that's neither here nor there. The question is, who are you?"

"You know who I am."

The other cackled. "Suppose you tell me. Who do you think you are?"

Sandro drew himself up as much as the chains would allow. He was conscious of his bedraggled appearance: the soggy clothes, the filth that encrusted him, the matted hair, the thin stubble starting on his face. But by God, he was better than a sniveling weasel of a turnkey and a Lombard bloodsucker!

"I'm Alessandro Cavalli, a son of the House of Cavalli." He remembered the will. "The *head* of the House of Cavalli!"

The man in black shook his head in amusement. "No, young gentleman, you're mistaken. You're not those things anymore. You're as low as it's possible to get. Lower than a slave, without even a slave's civil rights. In fact, you're not even a person anymore."

"What are you talking about?"

The Lombard savored his words. "You've been sentenced in absentia by the Council of Ten. For parricide, among other things. And the theft of your brother's inheritance. Offenses against the honor of the Venetian state, as specified in the codes contained in the *Promissione al Maleficio*."

Sandro reeled as if from a blow. He felt as if the blood had drained from his head. His vision darkened and narrowed, so that there was only the crowlike figure standing at the end of a long tunnel. "It's a lie," he whispered.

"It must be true, young gentleman," the Lombard said. "The denunciation was placed in the *bocca del leone*, the lion's mouth, and their Excellencies voted to condemn you after the most serious deliberation."

Sandro's vision was beginning to return. "Who?" he croaked. "Who would denounce me?"

"Who indeed?" the Lombard replied. "The little messages put in the denunciation box are rarely signed."

"I want to talk to the Councillors," Sandro said hoarsely. "I never had a chance to defend myself."

"Well, now, young gentleman," the crow said with mock concern, "if I were you, I'd want to leave well enough alone. You're lucky. If the Council had got its hands on you, you would have been put to the torture and sung any tune and then have suffered the penalty reserved for parricides—the flesh torn from your body with hot pincers, castration, disembowelment, and even then not death until the crowd had its fill."

"I don't understand. The men who abducted me ..."

"Were only *bravi*, such as may be hired by anyone, including, on occasion, the Council of Ten itself. The minions of the Ten went to arrest you two nights ago, after you failed to appear at the reading of your father's will, and found that you had already disappeared—fled in the fear of having your guilt discovered, it was decided."

Sandro was hardly able to speak. "I'm not in the Doge's prison, then?"

"Goodness no, young sir. A certain profit may still be made from you."

"I demand that you release me immediately." Sandro forced his voice to be firm, with the authority of his class. "You Lombard leech! You have no right to keep me here. You're the one who has to worry about the *Promissione al Maleficio*. You'll be flogged between the pillars for this. What's your name? What are you in this?"

"Someone to whom a great deal of money is owed." The Lombard gave a dry chuckle. "And who will be repaid many times over. My debtor's interests would be served simply by tying your feet to a block of stone and dropping you in the lagoon after dark, but he's in no position to insist on anything. And perhaps he wouldn't have the stomach for it; you never can tell when these popinjays are liable to lose their nerve. No, my young gentleman, the interests of all parties will be served just as well if you're silenced another way—disposed of in such fashion that you'll never trouble us again."

He bent to give an order to the hunchback. The little man, with a jittery look at Sandro, nodded and exited crabwise through the thick door.

Ice ran down Sandro's spine. "What are you going to do?"

"Do?" The Lombard spread his hands under the black cloak, giving the impression of flapping wings. "I'm going to do you a favor. I've already bargained for your life. And now I'm going to give you a warning. Don't insist on your identity."

"I won't rest till I see you punished," Sandro said recklessly.

"Young gentleman, young gentleman!" The Lombard shook his head. "There's no appeal from a sentence of the Ten. Even the son of the Doge Venier died in the *pozzi*, with his father unable to save him. For that matter, the Ten once sentenced a Doge to death—Marin Faliero, who grabbed for too much power—and had him beheaded on the spot. Do you think their Excellencies are going to admit that they made a mistake with *you*? No, my young friend. Where you're going, there'll be no one to listen to you. But if by some miracle you ever got to so much as speak your name within the hearing of Venetian authority, you'd be brought back to suffer the penalty I mentioned."

Sandro wept with rage. "What wickedness!" He struggled to pull his chains free and get at the Lombard, but all he succeeded in doing was to pull the skin off his ankle and set it bleeding.

"Not so anxious, young sir," the Lombard said. He spat with sudden malice. "You'll be out of here soon enough. And then perhaps you'll wish you were back here!"

He was left alone for an hour in the dark. The last shreds of dingy gray light faded and plunged the cell into the pitch black of his last three nights. The little humpbacked glassblower, Berto, did not return to refill his spilled water or to replace the overturned bowl of beans that lay somewhere beyond his groping fingers. He heard little cautious scrabbling sounds that told him the rat had returned and then a chittering and a scrape of ceramic against stone as it tried to right the bowl. There was more than one rat this time, by the sound of the chittering.

He heard a rattle of iron, and the door swung open. A

broad, powerful man came in, holding a fish-oil lamp. Two shadowy shapes were behind him, one of them holding implements of some sort.

With astonishment, Sandro recognized the broken-nosed face revealed by the lamp's smoky yellow light. "Ser Falco!" he cried. "What's the meaning of this?"

Falco paid him no attention. He walked over to Sandro in a businesslike way and gave the lamp to one of his henchmen to hold. Impatiently, he motioned the other to hand him the tools. They were a hammer and chisel.

He bent and positioned Sandro's leg in a strong grip, like a man shoeing a horse. "Hold still," he said.

He swung the hammer against the chisel in a casual swipe that sent a shock through Sandro's leg and parted the link that held him to the wall. Sandro stumbled, and an arm as hard as wood caught him.

"*Avanti.*" The two *bravi*, one on either side, hustled Sandro along. The ankle chain kept tripping him until he learned the trick of shuffling to match the play in the fetters. A short flight of stone steps presented more of a problem, but the two thugs half-lifted him at each tread and kept him propped upright.

They pushed him through a low door into the night air. After the fetid atmosphere of his cell, it felt marvelous. Sandro took deep breaths. The stars were out, huge and brilliant, in a narrow slot overhead. He was standing on a stone wharf, facing a ribbon of greasy water between old warehouses.

"Get him out of sight," Falco hissed.

They heaved Sandro into the foresheets of a flat-bottomed *battèlo* tied up at the wharf and threw a stinking tarpaulin over him. Sandro felt the boat rock as they got in. There was movement as they settled themselves on the thwarts and cast off; then someone was rowing with strong, economical strokes.

"Where are you taking me?" Sandro said from under the canvas.

"Shut up, you." Someone kicked at him. It caught him in the ribs and drove the breath out of him.

He could tell from the feel of the swell and the change in the sound of the oars that they were heading out into the lagoon. When they were far enough out they let him come out from under the tarpaulin and breathe fresh air.

Hundreds of ships rode at anchor out here, crowding the stars with a latticework of masts and bare yards. A scattering of small craft still nursed at their sides, left half-loaded till morning, and there was still some desultory gondola traffic, rolling drunken sailors home.

Falco shipped oars while he lit a lantern, then sat down to row again. "You're a useless pair," he said to the *bravi*. "If one could row with a stiletto, we'd be there by now."

"Let the *galeòtto* row," one of them said.

The other one sniggered.

"Shut up," Falco said.

He worked his way through the anchored fleet, heading for its fringes. Sandro could see that most of the ships here on the outskirts were foreign—some fat Dutch cogs and Hanseatic traders, far from their territory; a long, low Spanish galley; a Portuguese *barcha* that was hardly more than an open boat; an English carrack with a high castle in the stern. There were even a few Genoese ships, broad-beamed merchantmen huddled together for company; they were allowed under the present treaty, but they wouldn't want to linger in Venetian waters long.

His nose told him he was approaching a slave galley. The excrement of a hundred or more chained men who were never allowed to relieve themselves over the sides created a permanent miasma around such vessels, no matter how often the ship was sluiced out between voyages.

"Ahoy!" Falco called. He stood up between the thwarts, holding his lantern aloft.

He got an answering hail from the poop. A figure with a lantern appeared on the balcony of the castle's second story, where the captain's cabin would have been on a Venetian great galley. The *battèlo* bumped the vessel's overhanging flank, and sailors worked by moonlight to lower a narrow gangplank into the water.

Sandro drank in as much detail as he could from his vantage point in the sheets. The galley was a large two-masted vessel with a wicked-looking battering ram in the shape of a dragon's head projecting from its prow. The tall poop was draped like a pavilion in scalloped curtains embroidered with an unfamiliar coat of arms, but the two stern flagpoles were bare and anonymous.

"Up there, you," one of the *bravi* growled.

Sandro scrambled up the gangplank. It was almost vertical, with ladderlike rungs, so he was able to use his shackled hands to help him climb. Otherwise, with his feet hampered by the chain, he never would have made it. Even so, there was a terrifying moment when he slipped and thought he was going to plunge into the water below, weighted down by his fetters. But Falco, coming up behind him, seized him with one immensely powerful hand and set him right again.

"No you don't," he rumbled. "Not till I get paid."

Sandro looked down the length of the galley at row after row of naked backs, sitting three to a bench, on either side of a narrow catwalk. The smell was worse up here on deck. Most of the men were hunched over in sleep, and those who were awake were too exhausted or apathetic to turn their heads to watch the activity at the poop.

A large squarish man with a short beard climbed down from the castle, holding a lantern. From his bearing and his rich costume, Sandro took him to be the captain.

"I've got another jailbird for you, Messer Capitano," Falco said. "As I promised."

"Let's have a look," said the captain. "I could use three more. Two of my *condannati* died during the night, and one of the replacements doesn't look too good. These prison turds don't last."

He spoke in a foreign dialect that was almost unintelligible to Sandro. After a moment he placed it as Genoan; this galley was escort to the Genoese round ships. Sandro told himself that he should not be surprised. A man like Falco, who supplied illegal slaves to the Moors, would not hesitate to deal with Venice's traditional enemy.

"Sorry," Falco said. "My last shipment of *condannati* is already gone to Tunis. This is all I had left."

The Genoan shined his light on Sandro. He frowned when he saw the ruins of what had once been an expensive shirt and hose. "What have we here? A gentleman? Let's see his hands." He grabbed a fettered wrist and forced Sandro's hands into view. "These hands have never done work."

"He'll toughen up," Falco said. "I know your *aguzzino* will give him loving attention. Where's the price we agreed on?"

Grumbling, the captain counted out coins from a purse. "What's his name?" he asked.

"He doesn't have a name," Falco said. He turned an ursine grin on Sandro. "Do you, *galeòtto*?"

Sandro lunged at Falco, swinging his wrist chains. Someone behind him knocked him to the deck with a club.

"Some of them don't learn," the captain said dolefully. "Chain him to the Turk. That will give him a fast start at his lessons. And in the morning, thirty lashes."

Two sailors dragged Sandro down the length of the catwalk. A sweating blacksmith, working with sledgehammer, tongs, and a charcoal brazier, fastened his chains to a bench, next to an enormous man whose shaved head retained the tuft of hair that marked him as a Turkish prisoner of war. His back was raw meat. The Turk gave Sandro a stare of pure hate; the other man on the bench avoided looking at him at all.

The blacksmith worked in nervous haste, casting frequent sidelong glances at the Turk. Sandro looked up at the catwalk and saw the *aguzzino* there with his whip. A crossbowman stood beside him with his weapon pointed at the Turk. The Turk's huge bunched muscles twitched. "Try something," the *aguzzino* said pleasantly.

The blacksmith finished his job and scrambled back to the safety of the catwalk. "We'll shave his head in the morning," the *aguzzino* said. "In the meantime, you can strip him."

The Turk reached over with his manacled arms and ripped Sandro's shirt down the back. Sandro was too startled to resist. "Good," said the *aguzzino*. "We don't want anything getting in the way of the whip. You can keep it if you want. A bit of cloth's always useful, eh?"

With a contemptuous return gaze, the Turk tossed the

scraps of Sandro's shirt overboard. The *aguzzino* laughed.
"Come on," he said to the crossbowman, and they walked
away.

Sandro stared dumbly at his new chains, at the
footbrace and the scarred backs of the galley slaves in
front of him that now comprised his entire world. The
Turk was looking him over, his jaw working. Sandro's
other benchmate, an elongated man who was all gristle,
after a quick look to make sure that the *aguzzino* and his
whip were out of earshot and another glance at the Turk
for permission to break silence, spoke for the first time.

"A gentleman, did they say?" he whispered in a voice
full of malice. "One of the *signori* of the quarterdeck who
think they're the lords of creation? Well now you're down
among the galley slaves. They take those chains off on
the day you die."

CHAPTER 5

"Stop that boy!" the constable's voice bawled from the crowded lane behind him.

A busybody's hand snatched at him, but Tom wriggled free and raced for the mouth of an alley ahead. He flung a look over his shoulder as he ran and saw the constable, fat and wheezing and waving a truncheon, with Master Philpot puffing along behind him, his skinny shanks exposed by his flying robes. But Tom, small and wiry, was agile as an eel, and they had no hope of catching up with him unless he tripped, or unless one of the good citizens of Bristol interfered.

He dodged past a pig rooting in the lane and ducked under the legs of a file of packhorses loaded with bales of cloth for the Italian galleys at Southampton. The horses shied and whinnied, and the man who was leading them cursed at Tom.

"Watch where ye're going, ye screwd young ninny!"

He flicked his whip at Tom's scrawny shoulders, but Tom danced easily out of reach and kept running.

There was an astonished bumpkin still to get past—an apple-cheeked countryman swinging twin tubs of butter from a shoulder yoke—and then Tom reached the safety of the alley. He skipped ahead adroitly to avoid the contents of a slop jar that a servant girl tried to empty on him from an upstairs window, and then he was darting like a trout through a narrow twisting maze where the overhanging upper stories of the houses blocked off the sky.

He emerged into Fish Lane, whistling and acting as nonchalant as his fifteen starveling years and poor clothes would let him. He was only a weaver's son, the youngest of Jack Giles's brood of hungry offspring, but he liked to think that seven years of apprenticeship to one of the most prosperous mercers of Bristol had given him a certain town polish.

He had come out by the Key, near the church of Saint Stephen. The masts of oceangoing ships rose thickly above the jumbled rooftops, leaning at crazy angles because low tide had left them grounded. The Key Head and the Frome Bridge lay to his right, and across the imprisoned river were the docks of Saint Augustine's Back. To his left was another sprawl of rooftops, and beyond them another forest of masts, where more ships were tied up along Saint Nicholas's Back on the Avon.

The open sea was miles away, where the Avon emptied into the Severn estuary, but from anywhere in Bristol you had only to lift your eyes to the skyline to be reminded that this was England's second busiest seaport, rivaled only by great London itself. The treacherous river passage, through a narrow gorge where the tides rose as high as forty feet, also served to keep the town safe from the pirates that plagued the Channel ports. And Bristol's favored position, directly on the western ocean, gave it an advantage over London and Southampton in the Spanish and Portuguese trade.

Tom never tired of the grand sight of the masts that hemmed Bristol in. Whenever he could escape Master Philpot's watchful eye, he liked to sneak down to the waterfront to look at the ships—the wine ships from Spain, the fish ships from faraway Iceland, the wool ships loading their sacks and bales for the continent, the sleek Genoese galleys and the foreign gabble of their sailors—"Janneys," the people of Bristol called them. Especially, Tom liked to creep round to the taverns and, if he were not thrown out, to eavesdrop on the fantastic tales told by sailors—tales of sea monsters and pirates and strange ports and people. He could not count the times he had been dragged back to Master Philpot's and given a sound beating for deserting his chores. The memory of it made Tom wary; the waterfront was the first place they'd look for him today. And today would be more than a beating.

He doubled back along Corn Street, between the two rivers, toward the market cross at High Street, to lose himself in the crowds. Next to the bustling activity of the docks he liked the color and excitement of the marketplace, with its limitless possibilities for entertainment. Sometimes there was a traveling mountebank, there to peddle nostrums and amaze the people with his magic tricks, or a juggler or a rope dancer.

He slowed to a saunter. A crowd was gathered over by the arches, past the market stalls. He could hear jeers and the sound of merriment. He walked over to see what was going on.

A thief had been nailed by his ear to a cartwheel. He was a gangling fellow in motley, with a foolish grin on his face. They'd given him a knife, and he held it in his hand as if it were a poisonous serpent.

"Go on, thou swikele hinny!" someone taunted him. "If ye mean to do it, then make it snel!"

The thief raised the knife tentatively, then lowered it again. He still hadn't nerved himself to the deed. The authorities had given him the choice of determining the length of his own sentence. All he had to do was to cut off his ear. Then he could pay his fine and leave town, promising never to return.

Some small boys who had been hanging around a pieman's stand decided to help him along. One of them picked up a lump of horse manure and flung it at the thief's head. Unable to dodge, he caught it on the cheek. The impact made him flinch, and he dropped the knife. Pleased with the reaction they had got, the urchins began pelting him. The crowd roared at his dilemma: with his ear fastened to the cartwheel, the thief not only was unable to avoid his tormenters, but was unable even to stoop to retrieve the knife and set himself free.

It was his previous heckler, a florid man in guild livery,

who put a stop to the sport. He chased the boys away and, with a sarcastic bow, picked up the knife and handed it back to the unfortunate prisoner. "How now, sir goodfellawe," he said. "Will you have back your key?"

The crowd laughed at this sally. The thief smiled sheepishly but again was unable to decide. Hoots and catcalls came from the crowd.

It was not a mountebank or a rope dancer, but it was something to watch. Tom forgot his own predicament for the moment and waited to see what would happen.

"He took a goose, so they say," said a large woman next to him. "Those that steal, come to dool. A tachut ear's too good for him. If I had my way, they'd drag him at a horse's tail to the scaffold, as a lesson to those who wraken honest folk!"

Tom's vivid imagination immediately changed the complexion of the scene before him. It was no longer a quarter-hour's simple entertainment. He looked at the thief's sweating, befuddled face and saw his own there. His mind's eye painted a dreadful picture of the punishments meted out to more serious offenders, like the murderer he had once seen who had been dragged on a hurdle all the way down Broad Street while the executioners trotting alongside poked at all his tender parts with hot irons, then delivered to the scaffold to be hanged, drawn, unmanned, and quartered. And the Lollards. They burned Lollards, he had heard, though he had never seen a burning.

"And that goes for fornicators and adulterers and all those who do balle!" the woman proclaimed self-righteously, her face growing red and angry at some remembered injury.

Tom moved unobtrusively away from her. He had been trying not to think about what might lay in store for him if he were caught. If the penalty for merely stealing a goose was having your ear nailed to a cartwheel, then the magistrates would surely deal with his case most severely—especially when an important man like Master Philpot was making the complaint.

If only Mistress Eglantine had not come upon him in the countinghouse that day!

He allowed himself a moment of bitterness. Apprentice—that's what he was supposed to be. That's what Master Philpot had promised seven years ago when he had come to the weaver's cottage in Redcliffe and offered to take him off his father's hands. Tom had been only eight years old, the baby of the family, and his mother had wept when she gave him over. But there were too many mouths in Jack Giles's home and not enough places for them. Tom's oldest brother, Wat, had been apprenticed to an enterprising fuller who leased one of the new water-powered fulling mills farther up the Frome and was the pride and hope of his parents. Three brothers had found employment with guildsmen of Bristol and Redcliffe and could look forward to being given certificates of their own and admitted to the mysteries as soon as they passed the guild tests. But the other boys could not be placed—Jack had not reciprocated by taking boys from other Redcliffe families into his overcrowded household. And of the four girls, two were still at home. One of Tom's brothers—poor sweet Hal—worked when he could as a shearer, another had run away to sea, and the others hired themselves out as best they were able. Jack had apprenticed two of the older boys to himself—though there was scarcely enough work to keep one pair of hands busy at his loom.

Times were hard in the weavers' suburb of Redcliffe, despite the general prosperity. The water mills with their never-tiring trip-hammers had drawn the fullers out of town—a mill with a fixed rent of fifteen shillings could be subleased for as much as sixty-six shillings, to the profit of all—and with the departure of the fullers, a good share of the business that had once gone to the weavers of Redcliffe had been spread through the countryside. And then there were the new entrepreneurs like Master Philpot, who kept looms working in their own halls and gave out work to the cottages more and more grudgingly. The weavers regularly petitioned the town fathers to end the pernicious practice, but rich men like Master Philpot ran the Guild Merchant—the governing body that controlled the craft guilds—for their own ben-

efit, while the powerless weavers were expressly barred
from membership.

And finally there was increasing competition from the
swarms of journeymen weavers roaming the countryside—feckless fellows, many of them Lollards who used
their status as itinerant laborers as a cover to spread their
false doctrines. They gave the weavers of Redcliffe a bad
name—though there were freethinkers in Redcliffe too,
God knew. The town authorities were less than diligent
about rooting out heresy among them, unless one of
them created a scandal by preaching openly. They moved
on so frequently that it was scarce worth the trouble of
racking them, and they provided a convenient source of
cheap labor for such as Master Philpot.

"The mercers and the clothiers are turning us into
their hired swinkeres," Jack Giles had said that day, shaking his grizzled head as he looked round the shabby cottage at his underfed progeny. "Once I was a freeman,
buying my own wool at my own price from the spinners
and selling it to the fullers, who sold it to the dyers. Now
it's Master Philpot's wool, delivered to our doorstep and
taken away again, and I glad to get it."

It had been a large order that day, one that would feed
the family for many a week. It had been too large, appar-
ently, for Master Philpot's own looms to handle, and the
great man had come personally to oversee the distribution of the spun wool among a number of the cottages of
Redcliffe.

He had lingered no longer in the Giles cottage than
was necessary, holding a perfumed handkerchief to his
nose against the smoke rising from the central hearth,
but as he turned to go, his eye chanced to fall on Tom,
who was sitting quietly in a corner, playing with a broken
shuttle.

"What, yet another idle sprat to feed, Goodman Giles?
Can no employment be found for him?"

Tom's mother rushed to his defense. "He's only a
barne, Master Philpot. Time enough still to put him to
propre swink."

"He's a bright lad," Jack Giles said apologetically. "He

makes himself useful around here. When I can find a place for him, I'll have him bound."

Master Philpot had looked down his nose at Tom. "He's not much, I trow. But I could put him to some use."

"He'll not be some stable grub!" Tom's mother had said. Her voice got fainter after her first spirited outburst. "He has it in him to make something of himself some day."

"Quiet, woman," said Jack Giles. "What was it ye had in mind, Master Philpot?"

"We'll see what the boy can do. There are many possibilities for a wight young lad with a quick mind and a strong back."

"You see?" said Jack. "What better opportunity could little Tom have than to be taken under the wing of a considerable man like Master Philpot?" He drew the mercer over to a corner, and they spoke in low voices. Tom saw the wide eyes of his sisters and brothers upon him. Jack Giles bobbed his head to Master Philpot. He said, "I'll have him at your place first thing in the morning, scrubbed and willing."

After Master Philpot left, Tom's mother said, "Well, what did he promise?"

"Promise?" Jack cried, almost angrily. "What do you want from the ferrest gentleman of Bristol? A paper drawn up at law?" His tone softened and turned pleading. "Tom's a barne no longer. He's of an age to be bound. Do you want him to stand at the market cross every morning for the rest of his life, waiting for the chance at a day's hire? When the time comes, Master Philpot can place him at his own gyse with a nod to the right guild warden. In the meantime, he'll have the chance to learn the way of things in a great household and to earn his keep."

"I thought he could wait a little longer. Until Wat could commend him to the fuller."

"And how long will that be? And will the fuller's affairs continue to grow apace, with others clamoring for water leases? And in the meantime, how much bread must Tom eat?"

"His keep," she said bitterly. "That's all you care about."

"Yes, his keep!" he flared again. "And that's no small thing."

They made much of Tom that night. His mother put honey in his oatmeal and gave him a doucette, to the envy of the other children. His father stood him in front of his knee and explained. "The world's opened up for you, Tom. Of course, you cannot hope to become a mercer or a draper yourself—that's not for the likes of us. It's not the same as being apprenticed to a crafts master and learning a trade. The merchants of these great companies do not work with their hands. Rather they make Sir Penny work for them. And it takes a great many Sir Pennies to set up in trade as a member of a company. But if you serve Master Philpot well and faithfully, he can grease your way into the mysteries that are beholden to him. You might even become a dyer or a tucker—how would you like that? A dyer can be a rich man, with a fine house and servants."

His father spoke without looking at him directly. There was a haunted urgency in his exhortations. Tom could tell that Jack Giles was anxious to be rid of him.

He rubbed his eyes and yawned and after a bit was released. He climbed to the loft and found his corner and pretended to sleep. In the night he heard his mother crying and the urgent whispers to his father.

In the morning they took away the loose sloppe that he had worn as a child and dressed him in a coat of falding passed down from his older brothers. They crossed the river to Bristol over a spacious bridge with houses on either side and a church with a steeple that soared to heaven at the end of it. The streets were full of sailors and people in queer foreign costume. Tom saw a sailor with a bright green bird that talked on his shoulder and another with a monkey on a chain. They passed a tremendous hall, as great as a church, with a checkered front and mullioned windows as tall as trees, that Tom's father explained was the hall of the Merchants of the Staple.

He was deposited at the doorstep of the grandest

house he had ever seen. Its front was carved timbers with plaster between, and it boasted enormous many-paned windows that overhung the street. His father knocked, and a servant in finer clothing than was worn by proud franklins in Redcliffe answered the door.

"Remember, Tom, be hende and obey Master Philpot and his goodwyfe in all things," his father called after him as the servant took him inside and closed the door.

In all the years that followed, the promised vista of a proper apprenticeship never opened before him. There were weavers aplenty to come and sit before the looms in Master Philpot's hall, and he kept his own brewer and baker as well. And, Tom soon learned, Master Philpot paid the ground rent of two of the fulling mills on the Frome and leased them at exhorbitant cost to tuckers who were little more than his lackeys. But the weavers were mostly vagabonds who stayed a few weeks and left or scurvy fellows from the town whose feast fee to the guild master and wardens was paid by Master Philpot himself. The brewer and baker chased Tom from their domains, and his only contact with the fullers was to carry Master Philpot's instructions to them as he got old enough to be trusted with messages. He was never taken properly in hand and taught a craft in such wise that he might somewhen appear before the master and be enfranchised. It soon became apparent to Tom that he was naught but a slavey.

He worked in the scullery and stable yard, doing the meanest chores that were scorned even by the lowest servants, emptied chamber pots, fetched and carried, and—when the looms were busiest—sat with the other boys whom Master Philpot brought in by the day to pick wool. He was given no new clothes as the law required for apprentices, but wore hand-me-downs and shoddy. He never sat down at table with the journeymen and the louts who were styled "apprentices," to share their middling fare, but dined scantily on kitchen scraps and what he could steal from the buttery. He was always hungry, and he was beaten frequently—for daydreaming, for stealing, for being impertinent or raffe, for laziness, for spoiling work, or on the general principle that it was good for boys to be beaten. Tom took the beatings in stride—even the apprentices and journeymen were beaten—but he could not abide the hunger that his growing body screamed at him.

But he had been quick to grasp things, and as he grew older he also grew cleverer at making himself useful—just long enough and at his own choosing—to avoid a cuff or a beating.

He grew tired of being bullied by the young louts with whom he picked wool. There was an overgrown, whey-faced hinny named Snayth who pinched him or pulled his hair when the journeyman in charge wasn't looking, or addled his pickings and got him into trouble. Tom make it known to the journeymen's skeveyne that he knew how to work the heddles; he had often sat in Jack Giles's lap while Jack was working, and on slow and rainy days Jack had let him help. Soon he was allowed to assist when an apprentice was missing or when a journeyman went outside to piss. It got him more jabs and pinches from Snayth and the other picking boys for a while, but more often it got him out of picking entirely. Before long he was taking his place regularly among the websters when he wasn't wanted elsewhere.

He became as adept as a clerk or scrivener at reading, too. As a weaver's son he had been entitled to attend the grammar school of Saint Mary Redcliffe from his seventh year, and he already knew his letters and the numbers. There was always a Lollard with a clandestine Bible passing through Master Philpot's workroom, most of them overjoyed to find an eager young lad with a few letters who was willing to listen while together they traced out the lines of Bible tales together. Tom loved the stories in the Lollard Bible, which was written in English, the way ordinary people talked—exciting stories, like Samson and Joseph's coat and the whore of Babylon. Once he was caught and whipped, and the Lollard was taken away by the constables, and he was more careful after that.

He took to hanging around the countinghouse when Master Philpot was away, and the countour, a kindly man named Dudley, tolerated him. When Dudley found that he knew his letters, he helped him to improve his reading and writing. There were always plenty of things to read in the countinghouse. Tom pestered the clerk to let him read the letters from faraway places like London and Bruges and Calais, where the Merchants of the Staple and the Company of Mercers maintained branches. The dry correspondence about prices and merchandise and shipping arrangements was always enlivened by gossip. Still better were the news letters from Venice and Flanders, which the merchants copied out and exchanged. The news letters were almost as good as the Bible, with their marvelous tales of murders and pirate battles, great marriages, alchemists offering to turn lead into gold, witch burnings, the doings of King Henry in France, where he still lingered. Tom learned scraps of French and Latin from the letters—he already had picked up some Spanish gabble from the wine-ship sailors during his expeditions to the waterfront.

He was not as good at numbering as he was at reading, but Dudley patiently instructed him until he could do well enough. Eventually he was a help to Dudley as well as a nuisance—he could copy out letters in a fair hand, look up entries in the heavy books so that Dudley did not have to leave his stool, painstakingly add up columns of figures to present Dudley with subtotals. He was caught at it one day when Master Philpot returned without warning from a meeting with the mayor. Tom expected to be punished, but to his surprise, Master Philpot merely stood there with a sour, thoughtful expression, stroking his long chin, while Dudley stammered out an explanation.

"Mayhap the boy can be useful," he had said finally. "You can send him to Saint Nicholas's Back on the morrow to check the bills of lading on the cargo of tin and red cloths. Use him as you must. It will save the hiring of another clerk." He turned on Tom with a scowl and said, "But see you that you don't use your clerking as an excuse for neglecting your other chores."

One of Tom's chores was to tend to Master Philpot's night stool first thing in the morning. He was expected to bring a basin of water and a towel and a supply of cheap cloths and to empty the pot in the cesspit afterward. The merchant and his wife slept naked, and neither of them paid him any more attention than if he had been a spaniel. If Mistress Eglantine were still abed when he returned with the scrubbed stool, she would often send him to fetch and carry for her—bring her ale and bread from the kitchen or do her some other small service. But she hardly looked in his direction when she gave her orders, thinking it done because she had said it.

But one day when he was about fourteen, and Master Philpot had left for the morning, she looked at Tom as if she had never seen him before. He had grown into a fair enough lad, with hair like straw and eyes of the brightest blue and fine straight limbs, though his bones jutted through too little flesh.

"Put that down," she said, "and come over here by me, Tom. What meed calls, that you must be in such a hurry to leave? S'trouth, you're an unketh lad. Can you not talk?"

She was sitting up in the great bed, holding the coverlets to her with one hand. She was a milky, freckled woman with russet hair, who had become more ample in the years since Tom had been in the house. She was twenty years younger than her husband, but of late she had begun to wrinkle a bit at the neck, and a network of fine cracks showed at the corners of her eyes.

Tom became wary. No good could come of any sort of attention, he had learned. "I must be to the brewery, lady, to fetch ale for the journeymen," he said.

"They can wait," she said. "Come sit down here and have a word with your mistress." She patted the bed next to her.

He stood awkwardly, not knowing what to say, until she reached out a pale arm to pull him down beside her. "Can you not say something nice?" she said. "I have heard that you are a learned lad." She was breathing quickly, and there was a kind of discontent about her. Tom slept in a corner of the scullery, not under the rafters with the apprentices to share their horseplay and japery, but he had heard their sly jokes about Mistress Eglantine. " 'Tis soth," one pimply fellow scarcely older than Tom had snickered. "Madame scabbard has an eye to weigh the bob under a carl's hose when old softsword's away." "She'll not weigh *thy* bob, thou babelavaunte," another had scoffed. "A crowing jangeller like thee, who tells all." A third apprentice said knowingly, "Lucky will be the leman who's in her favor when the old skinflint dies, for she'll want a pliant make who'll leave her the governance of the house and business."

She took Tom's rough hand and placed it under the coverlet on her breast. "Do you not find me fair?" she whispered. Tom shivered and held himself still, and she felt beneath his smock and said, "You've grown, Tom of Redcliffe. You're under the yard no longer, but have reached a man's estate."

He gasped at her touch. She drew him to her. Tom had the wit to kick off his shoes. "Be you bold," she breathed.

There were a half-dozen encounters in the next year, usually in the bedchamber, but once behind the buttery screen and once in a storeroom. Tom gathered that he filled in between the transient journeymen because she thought him safe; she feared the wagging tongues of the apprentices under the eaves and would have nothing to do with them.

He had not been admitted to her favor since Eastertide. He had been barred from the bedchamber since a new servant girl had taken over the morning chore. Tom reckoned that Mistress Eglantine had grown tired of him, and he was both sorry and relieved.

He had been working alone in the countinghouse that morning. Dudley, the countour, was away for the day, settling with the weavers of Redcliffe. Tom had been left to sweep up.

He was surprised when Mistress Eglantine came in. He had never seen her in the countinghouse before. She looked swiftly both ways down the passage and closed the door softly behind her.

"Well, Tom, you've been neglecting me," she said coyly. "Have you found some younger burd?"

"Mistress, I . . ." he began.

She raised a finger to her lips. "Say nothing. He's gone for an hour, at least. He's at the mayor's court."

She kissed him and let him fondle her, and then, gasping like a fish, she lay on the floor and hitched up her skirts. "Quickly, quickly, my stout boy!" she puffed.

When he had finished with her, she pushed him away and struggled to a sitting position. He had barely time to pull up his breeks when the door opened and Master Philpot came in.

"What's this?" he said. "What's this?"

Mistress Eglantine screamed. She scrambled to her feet and cried, "Save me, my love! Oh, the gynne rascal! He enticed me in here and tried to wrek balle!"

Tom did not wait to see the merchant's reaction. Holding up his breeks with one hand, he skinned past the wavering Master Philpot and streaked out the door. He almost bowled over an apprentice coming through with an armload of bolts, then shot past and into the street.

He ran, fastening his breeks as he went. Master Philpot came out the door behind him, shouting, "Constable! Constable of the ward!"

It was just Tom's luck that Constable Drury, the bane of his growing years, was rounding the corner at that moment. Tom heard the sound of pounding feet and the detested voice shouting, "Stop, stop, you young scapegrace!" Tom did not pause. He whipped round the next bend and fled.

And now here he was, watching a poor fellow with his ear nailed to a wheel and waiting for the long arm of the law to catch up with him.

The thief now was feeling with his left hand for the position of the nail. He didn't want to lose any more of his ear than necessary. He raised the knife. His knees were shaking and his lips were moving in prayer. Tom leaned forward with the rest of the crowd. This was what they had been waiting for.

"There he is!"

With dismay, Tom saw Master Philpot and the constable bearing down on him through the crowd. He started running again.

Behind him, the crowd cheered. The thief had finally screwed up his courage. Tom felt cheated. After all, he had missed the moment. Why couldn't Master Philpot and the constable have shown up a minute later? He kept running until he lost them again.

He kept to the alleys and bystreets. He was getting hungry and he hadn't a farthing in his pocket. Where could he go?

He stopped to think it out, sitting on a doorstep. Shortly no place in Bristol would be healthy for him. He couldn't leave town by the High Street Bridge; Master Philpot and the constable stood in the way. Perhaps he could steal away by the Frome Bridge. But there'd be someone waiting for him there, too. There had been time for a runner to be sent to the ward constable. Master Philpot and Drury were searching through Bristol for him, and they'd leave word wherever they stopped.

If only he could reach Redcliffe ahead of the summoner they'd be sure to send after him there. He had not seen his parents for years, though he sometimes saw poor Hal or one of the other boys standing by the market cross early of a morning and asked after them. Perhaps Jack Giles might have a penny or two to spare for him, and he could join a party of pilgrims on the road and tag along with them toward Canterbury. That would get him safely across country and bring him close to London. London was a place where a person could lose himself.

Or perhaps he could claim sanctuary at Saint Stephen's on the Key. Tom was fuzzy about how one went about claiming sanctuary. You threw yourself on the altar, so he gathered. Then you sent for the chief magistrate. That would be Mayor Canynges. You confessed and took an oath of exile. Then, dressed in a shirt and holding a candle, you went to the waterfront and waded in up to your neck, calling, "Passage, for the love of God!"

Tom shook himself back to reality with a rueful smile. He could imagine a nobody like himself, a half-grown bound boy, sending for the mayor of Bristol, and having a constable like Drury respecting his right not to be dragged from the church. Or a kindly shipmaster taking him on board for free. He had seen the way the shipowners of Bristol squeezed the pilgrims every spring, taking all their money and packing them shoulder to shoulder and hip to hip in the hold to sail to the Holy Land or to closer shrines, like Saint James of Compostela in Spain.

But the thought sent his restless feet once more toward Saint Augustine's Back and the Key. Master Philpot would already have searched that haunt of his and now would be turning his attention to the docks at Saint Nicholas's Back. Perhaps the Key would be safe for him for an hour or two.

He wandered through the quay among the bales of fells and the wool-stuffed sacks that were piled there. A convoy of wool ships was tied up at the landing, riding on the high tide that surged between the banks. They were almost loaded. They would have to leave within the hour if they didn't want to lose the tide. Sweating men wrestled the remaining sacks and bales to the cranes and cranked them to the decks, where other men lashed them in place.

Tom stopped a sailor out of old habit and asked him where the ships were sailing.

"Where would they be sailing but to Calais?" the sailor said. "To be parceled out to the spinners of Bruges and Antwerp and thereabouts and sold back to us English as the coats on our backs." He winked at Tom. "Get ye to Bruges some day, young fellow, and find ye a spinning girl. They have a wondrous motion."

Out of the corner of his eye, Tom saw Master Philpot and the constable emerge from Fish Lane. They had come back to the Key after all. They hadn't seen him yet. He darted to a stack of bales and ducked behind it.

When he dared look out, they were halfway to his hiding place. They had stopped an alongshoreman to make inquiry. Tom saw the man shake his head and return to his loading. The two of them walked farther along. Tom saw them heading toward the sailor he had talked to.

No one was watching. The cranemaster nearest him was bent over a bale, knotting a broken cord. The deck of the ship opposite was empty, except for two men with their backs to him, making rope partitions for the piles of woolsacks. Tom broke from cover and dashed down the stone steps of the quay, to hurl himself over the rail of the ship and roll to the foot of a stack of bales.

He froze, still as a rabbit. No one had noticed him. He crawled between the bales and buried himself deeply among the bulging sacks of wool.

He was not discovered till nightfall. The ship had negotiated the long passage through the green countryside and come safely through the rocky gorge where the tidal currents ate unwary vessels. They must be well out into the Bristol Channel; Tom could see nothing on either side but what looked like open sea.

He took a deep satisfying breath of the fresh salt air— the air that had come to him in Bristol in whiffets and vagrant sea breezes. It promised to be a clear night, and the stars were coming out overhead, one by one. Tom stretched and cracked, his limbs stiff from their long immobility.

"Well, what have we here?" a gruff voice said behind him.

A sailor hauled Tom out from between the woolsacks and gave him a shaking. He was taken before the captain, a square-bearded man in splendid particolored hose.

"Please, master, I'll work as hard as ever you've seen," Tom said, wriggling free of the sailor's grip. "I'm strong, and I can read and number . . . and . . . and do all sorts of things."

"Shall I throw this mop overboard?" the sailor growled.

The captain appeared to ponder the matter. "We're short a boy," he said with a wink. "Let's see if he works as well as he boasts."

CHAPTER 6

"Needles and thread," her mother sighed. "That's what a woman's life is, needles and thread."

Inês gave a small smile to show she had heard, but she kept her eyes on her work. This was to be a fine padded doublet for her father, part of the pair of clothes he would wear to go to Sagres, where he was to appear at Prince Henry's court, and it had to be perfect. Her nimble fingers continued to fly, almost of themselves, never missing a stitch.

"We sew for our men so that they may go out in the world," her mother grumbled fondly, "and a million stitches measure out our days."

She was embroidering the shirt that would go with the doublet, a high-collared *alcândora* of the sort that lately had come into fashion in Lisbon. The fabrics had been very expensive—a red-dyed English wool from Bristol for the doublet and mantle, the finest imported Flemish linen for the shirt—and a good share of the family's resources had been invested in them. Six yards of cloth were required for the mantle alone; cutting the pattern so as not to waste any had been a nerve-wracking ordeal. Inês and her mother could not afford mistakes.

"I don't mind, *Mamãe*," Inês said. "I like to sew."

She was proud of her needlework. It was as good as

her mother's, all the older women said, and her mother
had tacitly agreed when she had entrusted Inês with the
important job of making the doublet. It was exciting to
see her father's suit taking shape before her eyes from
bolts of fabric. It made her feel a part of the great world
of men and affairs.

Senhora Alves continued her refrain. "But your father
must look his best—like a *rico-homem*. Everything in
this life is appearances. The worst thing you can do is to
look *indigente*. Those who need money are never the
ones who get it, while those who don't need it have their
purses filled for them. It's not as if the Alves blood wasn't
good—it's better than this Zarco's."

"Senhor Goncalves?"

"That's how well respected he is, that everybody calls
him by a nickname." She bit her lip. "The Alves have always been *infancões*—not your run-of-the-mill *escudieros*
like this Zarco and his friend Teixeira. It's not your father's fault that there's no money in the land."

"Father doesn't have to impress Senhor Goncalves,"
Inês replied with all the spirit of her fifteen years. "Senhor Goncalves holds him in the highest regard. He told
me so himself. When he and the other landowners
around here banded together to rid the district of that
nest of bandits, it was Father who they chose to lead
them. He said he was impressed with Father's good
sense and his way with men, and that's why he asked
him to sail with him as *despensero* on that voyage where
they were blown out to sea and discovered the island."

"And when, pray tell, *minha filha*, did you have a private conversation with Senhor Blue Eyes?" Dona Beatriz
said, stopping her work and fixing Inês with a severe expression.

"Oh *Mamãe!*" Inês said, blushing. "It was outdoors in
plain sight, when Father was showing Senhor Zar . . .
Goncalves and Senhor Teixeira the fig orchard, and Maria was with me the whole time."

"Ah, Maria. And since when is a lazy *desmazelada* of a
servant girl a proper chaperone for a young lady of your
standing?"

"Oh *Mamãe* . . ."

"Or perhaps you think that the family of Dom Martim Alves e de Aragão can afford to be lax in its standards and allow you to go about like the daughters of certain of the country squires in this neighborhood, who think they're living nobly because they can afford a horse and an usher and mutton on the table."

She broke off her recitation with a shake of her head that made her tall headdress wobble and applied herself resolutely to her needlework. Inês, eyes downcast, did the same. She knew what her mother forbore to say. She had heard it all too often in her young life. The Alves family circumstances were much reduced these days. They were down to a handful of household servants—a woman for the kitchen, a maid, a little Moorish slave, a man who worked indoors and who could also handle an axe and a pruning hook. Dom Martim still kept the horse and the weapons that made him a *cavaleiro*, but Inês and her mother knew this was a luxury that strained the family finances.

The devaluation of money and the breakdown of the social order after King John's revolution had fallen hard on old-fashioned gentlemen like Martim Alves. With the disappearance of the bound peasants he had to depend increasingly on landless *lavadores* hired for wages instead of the obligatory labor of serfs to get in his own crops. At the same time, his sharecroppers and few remaining fixed-fee tenants were too poor to feed themselves, let alone pay the rents in currency.

Once things had been better. Even Inês was not too young to remember. The house had been brilliant at night with wax candles, not the miserable tallow dips they used so sparingly now. There had been a dozen servants to attend to their every need, and a majordomo to manage them smoothly. The table had groaned with delicacies—meats and pastries and conserves prepared with expensive eastern spices—and the Alves hospitality was famous for miles around.

Zarco's expedition, under the patronage of Prince Henry, had seemed at first to offer a way to recoup the Alves family fortunes. The smooth-talking squire, himself in financial difficulties, had painted such a glowing picture that Dom Martim had scraped together every *soldo* he could lay his hands on to go shares with him and Teixeira.

And the gamble had at first seemed to pay off better than anyone had dared hope. An island had been discovered where no island was supposed to be—a little paradise they had named Porto Santo. Prince Henry had been overjoyed. He had proposed to Zarco and Teixeira that they colonize the island immediately—he would foot the bill. King John, his father, had concurred. It was important to get the jump on Castile, before his Spanish cousin could become interested. The pope had already granted Castile title to the Canaries, and John the Bastard wanted no new Spanish outposts off the coast of Africa.

So Inês's father had sailed back to Porto Santo with Zarco and Teixeira in a three-ship fleet laden with seeds, tools, and servants to build houses and plant a crop. Other gentlemen, sensing impending fortunes to be made, had clamored to go along. Wives and families, Senhor Alves had explained, would be sent for as soon as they had things going.

The unceasing rhythm of Inês's flashing needle slowed as she remembered. Her mother had been terrified of the idea. To venture out into the Ocean of Darkness looking for a speck—how could the sailors be so sure they'd find it again? Her father had tried to explain how the Spanish pilot, Morales, had drawn a chart with something called rhumb lines, but it sounded like black magic. Inês had been less apprehensive than her mother. She adored her father, and if he said it could be done, he must know what he was talking about. Didn't men know all sorts of things? Even her mother had finally been won over by the force of Dom Martim's conviction, and for a little while before his second departure the atmosphere at home had seemed brighter, gayer, full of hope.

"The Prince thinks the place might make a good sugar plantation," her father had said. "The climate's similar to Sicily. Whatever happens, we can expect further largesse from him. There'll be land grants, the creation of new hereditary titles." He teased Dona Beatriz. "How would you like to be the Countess of Sugar?"

And then he had sailed off in Zarco's little cockleshell of a ship with the other gentlemen and all the farming implements, promising to return in a year or two with the foundation of their fortune.

Who could have foreseen the disaster that had followed? The paradise had turned into a hell. All their hopes had been shattered. The ships had crept into port at Faro without fanfare. Zarco was afraid to face Prince Henry. The *infante*'s Sacred Haven would have to be abandoned.

And all because of a rabbit.

Inês stifled a sigh. Her inattention had caused her to drop a stitch. Lips pursed, she set about to repair the error. She stole a look at her mother to see if she had noticed, but Dona Beatriz, still stewing about society's injustices, was about to come to a second boil.

"And certain people who hold themselves above your father just because they've lately gotten their hands on a few *cruzados* ought to remember where they were not too long ago and show a little gratitude. Your father was generous to his in-laws when we were well off. He came to the rescue of Dom Rodrigo when the whole tribe of them was plunged into debt and in danger of losing everything! You'd think he could help us now—especially when we don't know where your dowry's going to come from. But no, we get nothing from him but pompous sermons! I say it even though he is the husband of my sister."

Inês found it hard to imagine her aunt and uncle as poor relations. That had been before she was born. They lived so grandly now, like the higher nobility. It made her feel quite small and insignificant to visit them. Her cousins, Helena and Miranda, were dressed like little princesses, in *cottes* and *houppelandes* of velvet and brocade, and had maidservants of their own to follow them about and pick up after them.

"Don't worry, *Mamãe*," she said. "It doesn't matter about a dowry. I don't care if I ever get married."

"What a thing to say! I've never heard such nonsense.

How do you expect to find a husband if you don't have a proper dowry? Who would want you? And not to care about getting a husband! You're already fifteen years old. Do you want to end as a spinster?"

"There are those who marry for love, *Mamãe*. Without a *dote*. Perhaps someone will come along."

"You're a daydreamer, my girl. You get too many notions from songs and romances, *Cantigas de amor* have nothing to do with real life."

"But—"

"Don't tell me about it. Some knight comes from nowhere and a silly girl runs off with him and they live on pink clouds forever! Those songs are written by men, and they're meant to turn a poor girl's head. Some rogue tells her they'll say a few words in a field and have a marriage *a furto*, without a priest or witnesses, and when the time comes when he wants to get rid of her, nothing can be proved. It was a mistake to let you have that songbook. I'll speak to your father about it."

Inês blushed. Her mother had described exactly the story of so many of the poems in the treasured *cancionero* her father had bought for her at great expense when she began her music lessons. The lovers always seemed to live free as birds, without any mention of practical difficulties. The scribe who had copied the book had been unusually talented, and the beautiful little scenes he had painted to illuminate the text were a feast for the imagination; Inês could lose herself in the pages by the hour.

"I'm sorry, *Mamãe*."

Her mother relented. "That's all right, *preciosa*, a girl's entitled to dream. I had my dreams too. As for the dowry, your father will manage somehow. You're very pretty—and very accomplished with your embroidery and your music—and we'll find a fine husband for you, one not too old, who'll make you happy."

"Thank you, *Mamãe*."

Dona Beatriz's plump face assumed a wistful expression. "You make a pretty picture when you play and sing, and I know it pleases your father."

She returned to her sewing, frowning with concentration and pulling the thread through at each stitch with quick, emphatic movements. The two of them worked in companionable silence through the next hour. Then Inês tied off the thread and put the doublet aside.

"I'm finished, *Mamãe*. I only have to do the trimming and the buttons on the sleeves."

"Let me see."

Shyly but proudly, Inês held up the doublet. Her mother nodded in approval. "A fine job, *querida*," she said. "See, you already know how to clothe a husband."

Dom Martim returned shortly thereafter, looking discouraged. He'd been making the rounds of his holdings with the foreman he'd left in charge, checking up on how things stood after his year's absence. He set down a basket of eggs and a wicker-cushioned carboy of wine that someone must have given him in lieu of a rent and dusted off his boots.

His tired eyes lit up when he saw the suit that was laid out for him. "*Maravilhoso!*" he exclaimed. "I'll be the best-dressed man at court." He beamed fondly at them. "Was ever before a man so fortunate in his wife and daughter?"

"Must you leave in the morning?" Dona Beatriz said.

"Yes. It's two days' hard riding. We don't dare delay. Word may have gotten back to the *infante* already."

Dona Beatriz noted his troubled expression. "He can't blame you. How was anyone to know?"

He shook his head. "It was that fool Perestrello. We never should have taken him along with us. But what could we do? He was foisted on us by young Prince John. This Dom Bartolomeu Perestrello's one of his favorite gentlemen at court, well versed in all the finer points of etiquette, but not the sort of companion you'd want to help you carve an empire out of a wilderness. When he heard about the island, he thought it would be a fine adventure to come along and be a colonist. It was a lark to him. And it didn't exactly bother him that King John and Prince Henry were so keen on the project. Well, I can't blame him for that. After all, the other *fidalgos* we took along thought they were getting in on a good thing, too. But most of them were practical men, with heads on their shoulders. I don't think Perestrello ever tied a vine in his life. His contribution was to bring along some livestock—a rabbit in a cage that some friend gave him as a good-bye gift."

"Don't upset yourself again, *senhor*," Dona Beatriz said.

Dom Martim's color was rising. "The accursed rabbit was pregnant. And when we got to the island, the idiot released it. 'Go on, little bunny,' he said. 'Go forth and multiply.' "

"Please *senhor*, remember yourself," Dona Beatriz implored, with a significant glance toward Inês.

"Eh, what?" Dom Martim's manner changed. The red faded from his face, and his sense of humor returned. "We all know that if there's one thing rabbits do, it's to multiply," he joshed his wife. He winked at Inês. "Isn't that so, miss? You're grown up now, but you were raised as a country girl. Remember those rabbits you had when you were little?"

"Yes, *Pai*," Inês said with a tolerant smile for her mother.

"We had to keep enlarging the hutch, didn't we? And keep separating them."

She giggled at the memory. "Yes."

"You're incorrigible, Dom Martim," Dona Beatriz said. But there was a smile on her face, too.

Dom Martim put his hand on Inês's arm. "Your little daughter has more sense than a *fidalgo* from Lisbon, madame," he said. "Porto Santo was a Garden of Eden— but without snakes. And without cats, dogs, foxes, wolves—without any of the natural enemies of rabbits, in fact. So they raised families. And the families raised families. And the families of the families raised families. They ate everything in sight—the grass, the leaves, the bark of the trees. And in the spring, they ate our crops— every shoot and every stem—as soon as they came up. We planted a second crop and they ate that, too. It wasn't possible to keep the rabbits' numbers down. We trapped them, shot them, clubbed them till our arms were weary. But the more rabbits we killed, the more were born." He chewed at his lip. "It will never be possible to grow any sort of crop on Porto Santo. We brought back a load of

timber—the rabbits killed enough trees—and resin from
the dragon's blood trees we found there, but that will
hardly defray expenses."

"The island must be good for something," said Dona
Beatriz. "The *infante* said it was the answer to his
prayers."

"No, nothing!" Dom Martim burst out savagely. He got
himself under control again. "There's no reason for the
infante to pour good money after bad."

Dona Beatriz's lip trembled as she counted up the cost
to her family. Inês saw her eyes stray to the new cloak
and doublet of English cloth. "Let Senhor Perestrello
take the blame then," her mother said.

Her father laughed bitterly. "We left him behind with
the laborers. He hadn't the stomach to face the *infante*. It
would serve him right if we didn't go back for him. He'll
be a good deal thinner by the time we retrieve him, I'll
tell you that! I hope he's thoroughly sick of his bunny-
rabbit diet by now—I know I am! We ate rabbit stew,
rabbit pie, rabbit hash, fricasseed rabbit, rabbit pudding
. . . it's a wonder I haven't grown long ears and nose
whiskers!"

Inês smiled uncertainly. She didn't know if she was
supposed to laugh or put on a long face. Her mother
stepped into the breach quickly. "It will be all right,
esposo meu. Haven't we always managed?"

"One more toss of the dice, *querida*," he said soberly.
"That's all we can afford. It all depends on how well
Zarco can fix Prince Henry's attention."

"That Zarco!" Dona Beatriz said, compressing her lips.

"He had his head together with Morales when I left
them this morning. They were talking about clouds."

"Clouds?"

Dom Martim walked over to his new doublet and ran
the fabric through his fingers. "Zarco's a rogue, I admit,"
he said. "But he's sharper than any mountebank. He'll
pull something out of his hat. And it won't be a rabbit."

Prince Henry was unsympathetic. "If you don't like
your island," he said, "then find a better one."

His words and manner were mild, but Dom Martim Alves, standing on the sidelines, could see his long Lancastrian jaw working with emotion. The *infante* was angry—angrier than Dom Martim ever cared to see royalty—and the entire household trembled in apprehension.

But Zarco was not at all intimidated. "We tried, Dom Henrique," he protested. "Find me an island, you said. And we found you one. Settle it, you said, and we gave up our families and sailed into the Ocean of Darkness and worked like *lavradores*—the *fidalgos* alongside the servants. But we were defeated. Just as in a war, sometimes you have to retreat."

"Defeated by rabbits!"

Zarco shrugged. "We would have preferred to be defeated by Moors, *Vossa Excelência*, but God sends us our enemies."

Prince Henry was not amused. He got up from his seat on the dais and began to pace. "This Porto Santo was to be a stepping stone into the unknown. How are we to venture into the Sea of Darkness if we're halted at the first step?"

"By my faith, Dom Henrique," Zarco said unctuously, "we want nothing more than to see your great project go forward, but there's nothing to be done. This plague of rabbits—"

"Enough!" Henry's voice was like the crack of a whip. "I don't want to hear another word about your rabbits!"

A page crossing in front of Dom Martim flinched at the Prince's wrath and almost dropped his salver. The gentlemen standing around the hall shifted their feet and looked uncomfortable. Zarco shrank a little, but stood his ground.

"I only await Your Excellency's orders," he said, meeting the Prince's eyes and holding them in challenge.

Dom Martim, waiting with some of his shipmates from the ill-fated expedition, was thankful that it was Zarco on the griddle and not himself. He exchanged a glance with young Gonzalo Ayres Ferreira, one of Zarco's well-born cronies from Faro. Ferreira had set out with high hopes. He wanted to found a noble line on the island, he had confided to Dom Martim, and would name his first son Adam and his first daughter Eve. He hadn't wanted to give up and had urged Zarco to stay and fight it out another season.

"The *infante* pinned his hopes on us," Ferreira whispered. "See how the work went forward while we were gone."

Dom Martim's eyes roved around the hall. The Prince's new residence was still incomplete, with blocks of dressed stone for the outer wall still piled outside by the cliff's edge. Priority had been given to finishing the observatory, a circular building overlooking the tossing waves below. There were also barracks, stables, storehouses for naval supplies, classrooms for what was going to be a school of navigation, a new chapel dedicated to Our Lady, and—so far—about a score of dwellings to house the inhabitants of what would become the Prince's town, the Vila do Infante. The Genoese had gotten wind of what was going on here, on the bleak promontory that formed Europe's southwest corner, and had tried to buy it for a Genoese outpost. But the Prince had refused their offer. Whoever commanded Sagres Point would have a crow's nest in the Ocean of Darkness itself. To the south lay Africa, to the north England, and to the west— Dom Martim made an interior grimace—so far, an island overrun with rabbits.

"Is it true that there was a quarrel?" the Prince was saying. "That blood was shed?"

"I see that someone has come running to Your Excellency with tales," growled Zarco.

"Is it true?"

"Perhaps Tristão Vaz and I twitted poor Perestrello too much. We shouldn't have goaded him that far about the ... about what happened. Words were said, yes. And daggers were drawn." He added magnanimously, "But it was only a scratch."

Zarco was too clever by half, Dom Martim couldn't help thinking. He shook off blame like a duck shakes off water. It had been Perestrello's blood that had been shed, not his or Teixeira's—though it was true that it had been a mere plinking of the fleshy part of the arm. Afterward there had been a drinking bout and reconciliation. Perestrello was too conscious of his fault to hold a grudge.

There were thunderclouds on the *infante*'s brow. "Senhor Perestrello did not return with you?"

"No, Your Excellency. He stayed behind with the servants, to try to salvage what they could. We'll send a ship back for them. If one can be refitted." He cocked his head in a question, but the Prince did not respond. "They hoped to have a load of timber and dragon's blood ready to defray their passage," he added.

"I'll be very anxious to see Senhor Perestrello," the Prince said grimly.

"Don't be too hard on him, Dom Henrique. He didn't mean to ruin your colony. It was only a mistake."

"Senhor Perestrello will have to accept the consequences of his mistake."

Zarco swallowed. "Consequences?"

"I'm going to make him governor of the island. I'll send him back with a load of cattle—I'll take the expense on myself. If there's not enough forage for cattle, he can try raising goats. One way or another, I'll see Porto Santo settled by Portuguese, not by Castilians or anybody else."

For once, Zarco was at a loss. "But Dom Henrique, where does that leave me? And these other *fidalgos*? After a year of backbreaking work—nothing."

"You said you did not want the island, did you not?"

"Yes, but—"

"Then you'll not be burdened with it."

Zarco gulped. Dom Martim could see that his mind was working furiously. From somewhere, Zarco dredged up a smile of total unconcern. "It was a small island anyway," he said. "Not the island of wood foretold in the story of the Englishman, Machin, that Morales heard in prison."

"No," the Prince said, his broad brow furrowing as he tried to fathom what Zarco was leading up to.

"There are trees on Porto Santo, true, but nothing like the dense forests that were described. And we found no giant cross, like the one Machin was supposed to have fashioned."

The *infante* was frowning now.

"And yet the story seemed so convincing in all its details," Zarco went on. "As if the island of *madeira* really existed somewhere at that latitude." He appeared to hesitate, then said with seeming reluctance, "Of course there's the matter of the cloud. . . ."

"Cloud? What cloud?" Prince Henry said.

Zarco took his time about answering. "From the south coast of Porto Santo, we always saw a distant cloud on the horizon. Always in the same place—not something that could be explained by passing weather conditions." He looked over at the attending *cavaleiros* and raised his voice. "Isn't that so, Tristão Vaz?"

"Yes, yes, Dom João," Teixeira responded. "Nothing more than a dark line on the horizon, really. But always in the same place."

"Morales thought it might be a sign of land," Zarco continued. "A fog bank, like one that would naturally hang over a wooded island when the sea breezes hit it. We often wondered about it."

An extraordinary change came over the Prince's expression. His color became high in a visible flush of excitement, and his eyes glittered with sudden speculation. But none of this showed in his voice, which remained sober and rational. "There's no point in wondering. The thing to do is to go there and find out about it."

Zarco gave a broad, willing smile. "Find a better island, you said before, Dom Henrique," he offered blandly.

"Yes . . . a better island. You mustn't delay."

"I'll have to have funds to outfit the ships again," Zarco said, becoming brisk. "And see if I can persuade some of these gentlemen to sail with me again."

Dom Martim had faced bandits, pirates, Moors, and storms at sea and never had any trouble with his knees. But now he felt his knees go weak under the fine hose he had donned that morning for the audience. He pulled himself straight, reminding himself of what a fine figure he must cut in the scarlet doublet and cape his wife and daughter had made for him and tried not to betray his relief. It seemed that life was offering him another chance after all.

"I'll give the orders at the shipyard," Prince Henry said. "Come, let's not delay." He strode to the door without bothering to dismiss the audience or waiting to see if he would be followed.

"What a bore!" her cousin Helena said. "Isn't there anything to *do* here?"

"We could play a game of *curre-curre*," Inês offered. "Or I could get out the throwing rings and we could play *conca*."

"Guessing games," Helena sniffed. "Quoits. Children's games! Oh, it's so *dull* here! Why don't you live in town?"

Helena was a year older than Inês and very polished. Inês thought she was perfection itself, with her smooth, pretty face, her honey-colored hair that was so exquisitely braided and coiled without a strand out of place, her fur-trimmed *houppelande* and steeple-shaped hennin with fine veils trailing from it. The only feature that might have been improved was her nose, which was as thin as a blade and a little crooked.

"Yes, it's so dull!" echoed Miranda. She was several years younger than her sister: a miniature version of a lady in her tall hennin and green velvet *houppelande* with long trailing sleeves. Beneath the elaborate costume she was as thin as a slat and fidgety. Inês thought she was a brat.

But she tried to be nice to her. "You had fun playing *conca* last time you were here," she said.

"I was just a *child* then," Miranda said scornfully. *"Uma pequina crianca."* She looked at her sister for support. "Who wants to play outside and get your hems and your shoes all dusty? Besides, it's too hot!"

Inês could sympathize with her there. She didn't see how her cousins could bear the June heat in their fur-trimmed finery and with the hanging veils of their hennins wrapped around their throats. There were unladylike beads of perspiration on Helena's upper lip, which she tried surreptitiously to wipe away with a corner of her veil.

It was the second day of their visit. The entire Da Cunha family had appeared, unannounced, at the dinner hour the previous morning, with a retinue of servants who had to be fed and for whom bedding had to be found. Mecia, the cook, and Maria, the maid, had scurried around trying to scrape together a feast that would be worthy of Dom Martim's notable in-laws, and Dona Beatriz had slipped a *libra* from the household money she had been left with to Nuno, the general handyman, and told him to go quickly to the butcher and the woman in the village who sold pies.

Dom Rodrigo, a mustachioed vision of splendor in camlet hose and sable-lined riding cloak, had announced that they were there to pay a brief call and offer Dona Beatriz the comfort of her sister's company during the absence of her husband. It was inconvenient to absent himself from his own household for any length of time, he harumphed, but they might manage to stay a week or two.

It was not quite clear how he had learned of Dom Martim's second departure. Prince Henry had slapped a seal of government secrecy over the expedition—after the discovery of Porto Santo, Venetian secret agents had been caught trying to bribe Portuguese chartmakers for the latitude—and Dom Martim had warned his wife and the servants to tell nobody. But in so large an enterprise, with so many people involved, it was hard to keep the lid on. However Dom Rodrigo had come by his knowledge, it was clear that he had come to his sister-in-law's home to try to sniff out whatever information he could about this rumored gold mine in the sea, and poor Dona Beatriz, unable to evade his questions, had told him everything she knew—about the disaster of the rabbits and about the search for a better, larger island.

Once he had wormed what he could out of Dona Beatriz and the servants, Dom Rodrigo seemed to have lost interest in being sociable. He had made himself scarce, and, drawing on previous acquaintances in the district, had gone off hunting with some of the local bloods. An overburdened Dona Beatriz, trying to cater to her demanding sister, Dona Florbella, and at the same time having to run a household with strange lackeys roaming all over the place and devouring her substance, had no time to spare for children. It was left to Inês to entertain her cousins. By now she was at her wit's end.

"You play the clavichordium, don't you?" she said in desperation. "We could play a duet."

The newfangled stringed invention, imported from Spain, where it was known as an *exchiquiera*, was gaining favor as a ladies' instrument, since it could be played by pressing keys, like an organ. Inês knew from her father's dry remarks that Dom Rodrigo made a point of being up-to-date in all things and would have been piqued at the thought that anyone might get ahead of his daughters musically.

"Oh, yes, my father got me an expensive one, with an ivory lid and cherubs painted on it," Helena said.

She condescendingly allowed Inês to lead her to the instrument and commented unfavorably on its plainness and much-used appearance.

"Do you want to play descant or firmus?" Inês asked politely.

"What?"

Inês thought she'd better give the easy part to Helena. The cantus firmus could be played with one finger.

"Play the *Salve Regina*," she suggested. "I'll do the top part."

Helena seated herself beside Inês at the little keyboard, looking poised and superior, but it was soon apparent that she had no talent for music. She couldn't keep the simplest sort of time, and she kept hitting wrong notes.

"This is no fun," she said. "Let's do something else."

"Look, Helena," Miranda piped up. "What's this?"

She had found Inês's precious *cancionero*, and was dangling it open by the soft leather cover so that the binding was in danger of cracking.

"Careful—don't handle it like that," Inês said. "Lay it flat on the table."

"What is it?"

"It's a songbook." Inês managed to pry it gently from Miranda's grimy little hands and get it placed on the table, next to the clavichordium. "See, these are the words, and these little marks tell you what notes to sing."

She couldn't keep the note of pride out of her voice. This was no cheap copy, stitched together from separate quires scribbled in haste by underpaid scribes, but an *exemplar* from which such copies were made. It was a treasure such as might belong to a prince or be found in a monastery library chained to a desk, and it belonged to her personally.

Helena looked at it disdainfully. "My father has a library of *twenty* books," she informed Inês with a toss of her her head. "Almost as many as the bishop has. He keeps them together on a shelf, and no one can touch them. They have fancier covers than this one, too."

Miranda was turning pages with a rattling abandon that made Inês wince. "It has little pictures in it, Helena. Oh, look, here's a knight and a lady riding away together on a horse."

"Don't touch the pictures with your fingers, Miranda," Inês admonished gently. "Turn the pages by the edges."

"I'll touch them if I want to," Miranda said crossly. "You can't tell me what to do. Daddy says you're only a poor relation."

She flipped the page over vehemently, rumpling the stiff parchment. Inês stifled an outcry. "I'll tell you what," she said, trying to distract her cousin, "let's all sing a song together. Here's a pretty one—'You went, my love, today.' Here, let me give you the tune."

It drew a stare of incomprehension from Miranda, who did not bother to follow Inês's pointing finger. After a moment of bafflement, Inês realized that her little cousin didn't know how to read. She turned for help to Helena, who was frowning off into space, and saw that she couldn't read either.

What was more, neither of them was embarrassed or discomfited in the slightest degree. In fact, they were looking at Inês with something like scorn. "Our father says it's not seemly for a woman to learn to read," Helena said loftily. "He says that for girls, a cushion and embroidery is the best book."

Miranda, to Inês's relief, lost interest in the *cancionero* and pushed it aside. "This is stupid," she said. "Don't you have anything else to show us?"

"I could show you some of my embroidery," Inês said, using the opening that Helena had given her. "I just finished helping Mamãe sew a pair of clothes for my father. What are you working on now?"

Though she had not observed either of her cousins sewing since their arrival, it was axiomatic that a girl always had some piece of work in hand—if not clothing or linens for the household, then a showpiece of some kind. If their current projects were too large and unwieldy, it was possible they would have left them home, but in that case they would have brought along something smaller and more portable to keep themselves busy. Perhaps, thought Inês, the sisters had not yet unpacked their embroidery.

"I'm cross-stitching a border on a handkerchief," Miranda said. "All the fine Italian ladies have handkerchiefs now, and Mother says we ought to carry them too."

Inês tried not to show her surprise. It was simple work for an eleven-year-old—more suitable for a beginner of four or five. At Miranda's age, she had been making all her own clothes.

Helena was slower to reply. When she did, it was with suitable hauteur. "Oh, I'm embroidering a cushion for my trousseau. My mother's making a big fuss about it. I have my maid work on it at night so I can show some progress." She gave a malicious stare. "*You* don't have a maid, do you?"

"There's Maria . . ."

"The domestic who does the housework here? I mean a lady's maid of your own."

"No."

"And you and your mother actually make your father's *clothes*?"

"Well . . . yes."

Inês didn't know why she was being defensive. That was the way in most families.

"*We* have a seamstress for the ordinary needlework," Helena said, looking down her long nose. "But Father uses a master tailor for his doublets and hose."

"Helena," Miranda whined. "I want to see."

"Oh, all right," Helena snapped, turning to Inês. "I suppose you can show us your embroidery."

She was not greatly impressed by the bright counterpane on which Inês had expended so much labor or the embroidered bed curtains and pillows. As a last resort, Inês opened up her clothing chest.

"You don't have many dresses, do you?" Helena said.

Miranda had dived into the chest and was pawing through her things. "Ooh, what's this?" she cried.

"Let me see that!" Helena said, snatching it from her.

Miranda had come up with a veil for a *crespina* that Inês had made as an exercise some time before. It was embroidered in the Luccan fashion with gold thread that her mother had entrusted her with when she deemed that Inês's skill had developed sufficiently and bordered with a treasured scrap of Flemish lace left over from a piece that Dom Martim had bought for his wife in better days. Inês had nothing imposing enough in her wardrobe to be worthy of it, but it had seemed a shame not to use the gold thread and lace in something sumptuous.

"I thought I might be able to wear it some day," Inês said shyly. "Maybe for my wedding."

"This lace is too good for the things you have here. Where did you get it?"

"It . . . it came from Bruges."

"Well it's certainly wasted on you. Look, Miranda, wouldn't it go well with the silk toque of mine from Italy?"

She draped it over her towering headdress and did a pirouette for her sister's benefit.

It made Inês uneasy to see Helena posing with the veil. When somebody admired something as extravagantly as that, it was only good manners to offer it to them. Equally, it was good manners to refuse when the item was some treasured object. Of course, Helena would decline so munificent a gift. But still, Inês was torn with anxiety as she opened her mouth to make the offer.

She was saved by the arrival of one of the Da Cunha servants. He spoke directly to Helena, insolently ignoring Inês's presence.

"Dom Rodrigo has returned from the hunt, *senhorita*. He's ordered an early supper. He wishes you and Senhorita Miranda to join him at table directly."

"Did he bring us anything, Felippe?" said Miranda.

The fellow winked, a liberty he should have known better than to take in front of someone outside the immediate family. "Maybe he did, miss."

Miranda gave a squeal. "Come on, Helena! I'll bet it's bracelets! He promised me a silver bracelet if he got to town!"

Helena tossed the veil in the general direction of the open chest, and the two girls followed the varlet out. Inês picked up the veil, folded it, and stowed it carefully away. She didn't bother to lock the chest; if a thief ever broke into the house, he'd be looking for jewels and plate, not an armload of far-from-costly girl's clothing.

From downstairs she could hear loud voices, the yapping of dogs, the jangle of equipment, and the stamp of boots. Dom Rodrigo and his retainers, still flushed from the chase, were milling about the hall.

Inês could imagine what a frantic scene must be taking place in the kitchen as Mecia and Maria raced around trying to get some sort of a meal on the table at least an hour earlier than they had expected. The size of the meal that was required made it harder. The evening before, Dom Rodrigo had made known his displeasure at the fact that supper had been limited to three courses and side dishes, though dinner that morning had been enormous. Most households, even noble ones, confined themselves to one or two courses for supper when the earlier meal was large. An embarrassed Dona Beatriz, worriedly counting the dwindling household funds that Dom Martim had left her, had ordered Mecia to ignore the sumptuary laws thereafter—or to evade them by combining separate courses of meats, fowls, and sweets in an English "great pie."

Mecia had risen to the challenge and, from what Inês had seen in the kitchen that afternoon, was whipping up miracles. Still, there was no way to hurry the roast or the poultry or the sauces, and Mecia was going to have to temporize by serving the impatient houseguests soup, fried fish patties, warmed-over game pies, and such ready-made delicacies as vegetable jams and pork jelly.

When Inês, a few minutes later, made her way to the hall, she found that Dom Rodrigo and his family were already seated at the long table, twiddling their thumbs. A squire and a priest were seated with them, and a few of the ranking retainers—cheeky fellows in gaudy livery— had been placed below the salt, but the rest of his troupe of servants had been placed at a trestle table that Nuno had set up farther down the hall, to enjoy one another's company and feast on the leftovers.

At the moment Dom Rodrigo was making do with a goblet of wine and some fish patties that Nuno must have fetched from the baker in the village. He was sitting well back in his chair, his legs stretched out. He had not bothered to remove his hunting boots and spurs. His crossbow and lance leaned against the near wall. The carcasses of a boar and two fallow deer had been dumped at the end of the hall, for all to see, and there was a pile of dead birds, as yet unplucked. Mecia was going to have to deal with all these later.

"Well, *senhorita*," he called out with great joviality, you've kept us waiting." He inclined his head toward Dona Beatriz. "You should teach your daughter better manners, madame."

Meekly, Inês took her place.

"You see how I'm fobbed off at my brother-in-law's table, *Padre* Domingos," Dom Rodrigo sighed to the priest, gesturing at the fish patties. "When I've risked my life to supply his larder." He nodded toward the corpse of the boar.

"By God, that was a thrust, sir," the squire said. "I thought I was a goner when the beast veered toward me, still going with three quarrels sticking out of him. But the honor of the kill is yours."

"We'll have fresh pork for dinner in the morning," Dom Rodrigo said, still in high good humor. "If these lazy servants can be made to do some work."

Maria and Nuno, looking harried, were bustling back and forth setting *escudelas* of soup before the guests. Nuno went back to the kitchen, and, with the help of a sullen page boy he had pressed into service, distributed round manchets of bread to Dom Rodrigo's retinue to serve as their trenchers.

"You really should have more servants, and ushers to attend the table," Dona Florbella said to her sister. "You don't live properly here." She was a sallow, stringy woman with a large jaw. There was no family resemblance between her and Dona Beatriz.

Dona Beatriz smiled wanly.

"*Mãe*, I don't like these wooden plates," whined Miranda. "Why don't they have silver, like us?"

"That's enough," her father said. "Dom Martim lays out what he can afford." He gave Dona Beatriz the smile of a shark. "Poor Dom Martim never was a practical man," he said to her. "Chivalry, that's what he's given his thought to all his life. That doesn't help you get ahead in the world. I can't tell you all the times he's ignored my good advice. And where's it gotten him, I ask you that? Just look around you. But perhaps that will change now, eh? This new interest of Prince Henry's. There may be money in it. The Prince is an odd one, there's no denying that, but he commands the resources to change fortunes—his incomes from the Order of Christ and his dukedom, the tuna monopoly in the Algarve, the fishery tithe, the soap and dye franchises granted by his father. I understand that he's created Dom Bartolomeu Perestrello the governor of this new island of his, with hereditary privileges."

He paused to give Dona Beatriz a shrewd glance, and the expression on her face confirmed it.

"But nothing like that yet for Dom Martim, am I right?" he went on. "Never mind. If this new expedition succeeds, it may be the making of him. And in that case,

Dom Martim can do no better than to put himself in my hands. Perhaps I might get in on it with him. I'm over-extended as it is, and the demands on my time are many—but anything to help a relative, eh?"

He turned his attention to the oysters that Nuno set before him, and by the time he finished them, there was a dish of lamprey eel, lightly sauteed with coriander, parsley, and onion. In the kitchen Mecia was borrowing time by sending out the dishes that didn't require much preparation. The squire and the priest fell in heartily, but the two girls pushed their dishes aside, making faces.

Dom Rodrigo worked his way through the courses steadily, while holding forth on the deficiencies of the service, the lack of imported spices in the sauces, and the inferiority of the wine. At last the roast could be delayed no longer, and Nuno wheeled it in on a cart. Dom Rodrigo frowned at the sight of the steaming vegetables that surrounded it.

"What's this? Cabbages and broadbeans? Turnips and greens? Does your cook take me for a peasant? What insult is this? Meat and fowl are the proper things to set before a guest!"

Dona Beatriz tried to placate him. "Dom Martim always likes to have a few vegetables as an accompaniment to the roast. He trained the cook that way. He says that vegetables are why peasants rarely have scurvy or night blindness. But they're on the platter only for flavor— ignore them, *faz favor*, Dom Rodrigo."

Grumbling, he accepted her apology. But his face darkened anew when the roast was carved, and he saw the juicy pink slices.

"It's underdone! Fit only for the dogs! This is really too much. This is what comes of hiring a country woman as a cook instead of having a decent kitchen staff."

Inês shriveled in her seat. She longed to spring to Mecia's defense. It wasn't poor Mecia's fault; Dom Rodrigo was the one who had insisted on sitting down to supper early, when the roast still had more than an hour to go.

But her mother was falling all over herself to apologize.

"Forgive it, Dom Rodrigo. I'll have a word with her. It won't happen again."

Dona Florbella sniffed. "I don't see why you must live in such a provincial manner. And after the dowry you brought to Dom Martim!"

"Dom Martim should borrow on his property, and live in a grander style," said Dom Rodrigo. "It doesn't pay to niggle. I'm not ashamed to say that that's what *I* did in order to get my affairs underway. By my faith, I'm tempted to give him an advance myself against his rents."

Inês saw that her mother was becoming flustered at the turn the conversation had taken. Money and its management was not a fit topic for women. It was awfully hard to understand. She remembered hearing her father fume about the sums that Dom Rodrigo had never repaid to him; those must have been some of the loans to which Dom Rodrigo had just alluded. "And now's the time we could use it," her father had said when he thought she was out of earshot. But he had been too proud to go to Dom Rodrigo and ask. That was what puzzled Inês now. If Dom Rodrigo still owed her father money, why was he talking about giving a loan instead of paying back what he had borrowed?

"Perhaps you ought to talk to Dom Martim when he returns," Dona Beatriz said nervously.

"Nonsense. You're the sister of my wife, after all. I feel obligated to do what I can. We needn't stand on legal ceremony in such a matter. It makes no difference that the wife doesn't hold her husband's property. As a man of honor, Dom Martim would feel bound to acknowledge a small debt contracted by his wife during his absence so that she and his daughter could exist."

"No ... I ... really ..." Dona Beatriz said in a faint voice. She started to fan herself furiously.

"We'll talk of it tomorrow. In the meantime, I can ask around a bit when I'm out hunting. Have a look at some of the tenancies."

"Don't you think I know how pinched you are for money?" Dona Florbella said disapprovingly to her sister. "At the rate you're spending, you won't have a *soldo* in the house by next month."

Dom Rodrigo waved aside the slice of beef that Maria was trying to tender to him. "Take it away. Give it to the servants. You can fry me a venison steak from one of those fine stags I brought."

Inês was glad when supper was finally over. Her aunt and uncle had been supercilious and condescending all through the meal, and her mother had seemed to grow smaller and smaller. The one kind word she had received from Dona Florbella was a compliment on her embroidery. "Do you mean to say that Inês embroidered this tablecloth all by herself? *Que linda!* It's an heirloom! I wish I had a girl like that around the house. Helena, Miranda, look what your cousin's done. Why can't you apply yourselves like that?" But then her cousins had sulked, and it had become very unpleasant at the table. Matters hadn't been helped when Dona Beatriz had responded by insisting that Dona Florbella accept the tablecloth as a gift. *"Esta às ordens,"* she had said self-effacingly, and the two girls had gone into a fit of petulance. "I don't see what's so special about that," Helena had flung out. "Wait till we get home and I show you the veil I made."

After Dom Rodrigo and his brood had departed for the comfort of the chambers that had been reserved for them, Inês loitered a while in the hall, watching as the servants fed their gravy-soaked trenchers to the dogs and the tables were dismantled until the morrow. Nuno and Maria gathered up all the dishes, and especially the spoons, so they wouldn't be stolen, then Nuno got two stout fellows to help him drag the boar's carcass to the scullery so he could butcher it. By that time Dom Rodrigo's servants were beginning to lay claim to the warm corners in the kitchen and hall that they had chosen to sleep in, though the servants of the Alves household still had many hours of work ahead of them.

"Boa noite, Mecia," Inês said to the cook. "Everything was very good."

"Good night, child," Mecia said. She was a large, ruddy woman, strong as a man, who had buried two husbands. She shook her kerchiefed head. "Don't you listen to what those two little snips say. You're worth a hundred of them, and they wouldn't be where they are if your father hadn't set *their* father on his feet that time he got himself into trouble. They're only social-climbing little snobs."

"I won't have you talk about my relations that way in front of me, Mecia," Inês said as sternly as she was able, spoiling it with a blush.

"All right, little miss. Have it your way. But you shouldn't let yourself be walked on." She paused in her plucking of the partridges to glower at a Da Cunha lackey who had started to spread an armload of rushes from the hall in the corner warmed by the oven. "Hey you with the bandy legs, stay out of there! That's my spot!"

On her way to her room, Inês passed Helena on the stairs. Helena seemed in a rush, her face averted and one hand hidden under her *houppelande* as if pressing something to herself. It was the fashionable pose for sophisticated young women, even maidens and brides—a sort of pseudo-pregnancy that was sometimes augmented by pads of cotton to make the stomach protrude more—though Dona Beatriz had never allowed Inês to assume the style. Inês admired her cousin's modishness. "Were you looking for me?" she asked, but Helena only mumbled something and hurried past her.

Inês closed the door behind her, glad to be alone. She put the candle she was carrying in its niche and knelt beside the bed to say her prayers. With a yawn, she removed her clothes, carefully folding each garment in turn, and went to put her chemise and gown in the chest, where the heavy lid would help to press out wrinkles.

The chest needed to be straightened out after the way Miranda had rummaged through it. Inês smoothed things over, and then suddenly realized that the *crespina* veil, with its edging of Flemish lace, was missing. She thought she remembered putting it on top before going down to supper.

She went all through the contents of the chest, at first carefully, layer by layer, and then in a panic. But the veil was gone.

CHAPTER 7

"Quick, kill the little bastard!" yelled Perestrello, and his manservant, startled into action, swung his hoe. But the blade whacked into bare earth, and the rabbit scampered off.

Zarco, hands on hips, watched the bobbing white tail recede. When the rabbit reached the edge of the field, it sat down and turned, ears aloft and nose twitching, to look at the men from a safe distance.

"Nothing's changed since we left, eh, Dom Bartolomeu?" Zarco said sardonically. "Except that the rabbits are getting bolder."

Perestrello cursed. "We thought we'd try one more crop with our last seeds. But the little devils strip away everything green as soon as it comes up."

Pedro, trudging up the steep path from the beach with a sack of grain on his shoulder, stopped behind Zarco and waited to be told what to do. He didn't like what he saw. Even in the short time they had been away, the settlement had deteriorated. No progress had been made on the cluster of shanties and lean-tos that served as shelter. Nothing remained within a wide swath around them except scrub vegetation, and Perestrello had demolished what part of the landscape the rabbits hadn't eaten by cutting down every tree in sight.

The last year had filled Pedro out. He had reached the full stature of a man and had to shave two or three times a week. The backbreaking work had given him thick, knotted upper arms and big wrists. Zarco had lived up to his promise and promoted him to *moco de bordo*—ordinary seaman.

Shifting his load, he turned his head to look down at the beach. There, at least, Porto Santo was still beautiful. The wide golden sands stretched on for miles, and the sparkling blue waters looked clean and inviting—not at all like a boundary of the Green Sea of Darkness with all its unknown terrors. The three ships of the expedition rode easily at anchor in the shallow bay, their sails reefed and their gilded rails gleaming in the bright sunlight.

Senhor Alves, stripped to his shirt like everybody else, was coming up the path with three more of the crewmen, who were staggering under the weight of heavy sacks, and Senhor Alves himself, though a gentleman, had not shirked carrying a sack as well.

"Where do you want these, Dom Bartolomeu?" Alves asked. His face was gray—this was work for younger men.

"Oh, stack them over there in that shed, I suppose," Perestrello replied. "At least it has a door on it."

"Wasn't it nice of us to bring you fresh supplies, Dom Bartolomeu?" Zarco said. "Now you can hang on another season—with enough flour for your rabbit pie."

"I'd rather stay on in purgatory," Perestrello growled. "As soon as I get the lumber and dragon's blood loaded, I'm sailing."

"Oh, you can't do that," Zarco said. "Prince Henry has every confidence that you can make something of the place." He grinned, enjoying himself. "Oh, didn't I tell you? You're captain of the island. Congratulations."

"He can't do that to me!" Perestrello sputtered. "Didn't you tell him how things stood here? It's a hopeless struggle. It will always be a hopeless struggle."

"You'll have to tell him yourself, when you go to fetch your wife and family. Don't look so down in the mouth. The Prince is prepared to give you enough support so that you don't starve. He's sending you a herd of cattle and some convicts to work the place."

"What've you got up your sleeve? You sold him on some other scheme, didn't you?"

Zarco only grinned at him infuriatingly.

Pedro unloaded his sack of grain with the others and followed Senhor Alves out of the shed. The older man was breathing hard and had put a hand to his side as if he had a stitch in it. Pedro would have liked to have asked if he wanted to sit down for a minute, but that would have been an unheard-of presumption for an ordinary seaman.

But Zarco, turning from Perestrello, had noticed Alves's perspiring forehead and lack of color. "Dom Martim, you shouldn't be carrying those heavy loads. Let the boys do it—they're young enough not to mind. Besides, you're my second officer. It's beneath your dignity to work like a mule."

"Nonsense, there's much work to be done in little time. I don't mind pitching in. The faster we work, the sooner we can raise anchor. Anyway, it encourages the men." His color was returning. He smiled at Pedro. "Isn't that so, Pedrozinho?"

"What, *senhor*?"

"That you enjoy seeing your *despensero* working like a mule?"

"No, *senhor*. I mean yes, *senhor*."

Zarco laughed. "It's true we've got a lot to do before we sail on." He squinted at the piles of timber that Perestrello had accumulated in his absence. "For a start, we can saw some of that lumber into planks and build a couple of longboats."

Perestrello became protective of his logs. "What do we need longboats for?"

Zarco did not answer directly. His eyes were fixed on the southern horizon, where a long low cloud sat like a skimming of cream.

"Tell me, Dom Bartolomeu," he said, "has the cloud stayed in that same position all the time we were away?"

"Yes—when the weather was clear enough to see it." He became irritated. "What are you up to, anyway?"

"There's nothing for us here, Dom Bartolomeu. We're packing it in. You're the captain, and good luck to you. You can have our shares for all they're worth now. Isn't that right, Dom Martim?"

"This place will drain away money, not spew it forth, for a long time to come," Alves agreed bitterly.

"So we might as well chase clouds, eh, my friend?" Zarco said. He showed a row of white teeth to Perestrello. "You can stay here, Dom Bartolomeu, and be king of the rabbits."

The cloud thickened and spread as they approached, and though the sea remained calm and the wind steady from the north, they were sailing blind. Pedro could feel the humid air around him, heavy and warm, as if God had put on a kettle.

And now there was something new. Pedro, braced against the quarter-rudder, could feel the ship begin to lift and fall in a different way, as the long ocean swell gave way to a choppier motion.

The Spanish pilot, Morales, standing next to him, felt it, too. He looked at Pedro, but said nothing. He wasn't going to spill anything until he was absolutely sure, not with the crew acting so edgy.

They had sailed before dawn. Perestrello hadn't bothered to get up to see them off. He was still miffed at Zarco. The expedition had stayed for eight days on Porto Santo while water casks were filled, gear was mended, and the two boats were built by the ships' carpenters and a half-dozen assistants they had pressed into service. The eager newcomers Zarco and Teixeira had brought with them—ambitious *fidalgos* like Ruy Paes and Gonzalo Ayres—were a reproach to Perestrello's blasted hopes, while the old hands like Alves hadn't forgiven Perestrello his pregnant rabbit; and Zarco had not refrained from rubbing it in.

The eight-day stay had given time for friction to arise between the two factions. The Perestrello camp, resentful of the perpetual hard labor that they seemed to have been condemned to, started rumors out of spite—rumors calculated to take the starch out of mariners who were about to sail once more into the unknown. Monsters had been sighted in the sea; the white cloud was steam; Porto Santo was the last outpost in the Ocean of Darkness, and those who went farther would be swallowed up. Zarco did his best to squelch all this rubbish—hadn't most of them sailed with him before, and hadn't he proved by the discovery of this very island that all the stories about the Dark Ocean were nothing but old wives' tales? But the ancient superstitions that lurked under the surface in every seafaring man had been awakened.

Matters hadn't been helped when they had been becalmed, and an easy day's sail had stretched into two, giving the sailors' imaginations more time to work. The disappearance of the reliable wind from the north was a sign, the older salts said. There was open muttering among the men now, despite the return of the northerly breeze, and the *fidalgos* sharing the aft deck shelter with Zarco kept their swords well loosened in their scabbards.

Pedro, working the tiller under the direction of Morales, stole a glance at the little scene taking place a few feet away.

"Well, what do you want, man?" Zarco snapped. "Speak up!"

The unfortunate sailor who had been chosen by his fellows to speak for them shuffled his feet.

"Well?"

"The sea's beginning to boil here, *senhor*. It's the beginning of the end of the ocean. We . . . that is, the men . . . want you to turn back."

"What, turn back, you ninny, just because of a little foam in the water?"

The *fidalgos* gathered around Zarco grew restive. "It's mutiny," Ruy Paes said. "Say the word and I'll run this dog through."

"Shut up," Zarco said. He hadn't taken his eyes off the sailor, and now he said in a more conciliatory tone, "You're an intelligent man, Ramos. You've sailed with me all those leagues from Sagres, and we made landfall just where Morales said we would. Why are you getting cold feet now?"

Paes turned away, offended. A couple of the other *fi-dalgos* scowled to show that they didn't approve of Zarco's leniency.

The sailor licked his lips. "It's well known that it gets hotter as you go south. Men are burnt black when they venture there—the proof's the black slaves the Moors bring back from the African interior. Beyond these latitudes, the sea boils away, leaving nothing but a salty swamp that breeds serpents big enough to swallow a ship whole."

"Man, man," Zarco said, shaking his head. "We've come barely ten leagues from Porto Santo. We're in the same latitude as the Holy Land, and pilgrims go there all the time. I promise you that you won't turn black."

The sailor stood his ground, head lowered stubbornly, his feet planted apart to balance him against the rolling of the ship. The motion was more pronounced, as though the sea was trying to shrug them off, and even the most landlubberly of the *fidalgos* could not fail to notice it now. The second dawn was arriving. Pedro stared off into a brightening predawn blur at wisps of vapor and imagined he could see a vast looming shape there, a columnar creature rising high above the ship, ready to gulp it down. But Senhor Alves had told him there was nothing to fear, and he trusted Senhor Alves.

"It's boiling, I tell you," Ramos muttered. "You can see it."

He lifted his head, and at that moment Pedro heard what he must have heard then: a faint, dull, booming roar.

"Aloft, *moco*," Morales said peremptorily. He shouldered Pedro aside and took the rudder from him.

Pedro sprang to the mainmast—the *barcha* had sprouted a new mizzen in Prince Henry's shipyard to hold the new oddly lopsided lugsail that the Prince's shipwright had contrived for making tacking easier—and shinnied up the pole.

At first there was nothing but the black ocean around him and the pitching wooden tub below, looking absurdly small. Then as his eyes adjusted for distance, he found the source of the bubbling froth that had unnerved the sailors. It was a line of white surf that lay like a scarf across the water, delineating the invisible shore that must lie beyond.

"*Surfe adiante!*" he yelled to the little figures on deck. The dots of faces turned upward to him and he stretched an arm to point toward the breakers.

With the skirt of breakers as a clue for the eye, and with a sliver of rising sun beginning to dissipate the fog bank ever so slightly, it was possible for the mind to grasp the spectral shapes suggested in the mist. What Pedro now saw was a steep mountainous bulk sloping precipitously down to the sea.

"*Terra!*" he called. "*Terra firme!*"

Morales ordered the mainsail lowered to kill headway, and with rudder and a push from the small auxiliary sail, the ship came about. Zarco was not going to risk encountering submerged reefs in the dark.

"The fog's thinner toward the east," Zarco said to Morales. "Let's try our luck in that direction." Pedro, back at the tiller, followed Morales's instructions and steered a course parallel to the emerging shore.

The land that was now throwing off its veils was lush with thick green forests that marched down tall mountainsides to the sea. Tropical flowers made a riot of color. The morning was loud with birdsong. The crystal sparkle of a mountain stream threaded its way through the luxuriant growth to the beach below.

"It's larger than Porto Santo," Zarco said. "Much larger."

"And richer," said one of the *fidalgos*, his voice shaky with excitement. "Look at all that timber. There's wealth beyond measure in those forests."

Up forward, the sailors were laughing and chattering. One of them was dancing on a plank in a clear space they had made for him, while they slapped time on their legs and sang a hornpipe.

"Well watered, too, by the look of it," Ruy Paes said, his belligerence forgotten. "By all the saints, who would have thought there was this much land in the empty ocean?"

Martim Alves stood a little apart from the others, looking shoreward. Pedro could guess what he was thinking. For the younger men Prince Henry's "better island" represented a chance to make their fortunes. For Alves it was a chance to save himself. Despite the fine new suit of clothes Alves had worn when he had arrived at Sagres, Pedro gathered that the failure of the colonization attempt at Porto Santo had left him desperately in debt.

Morales spoke, breaking his usual reticence in the presence of Zarco's band of gentlemen. "This is the one," he said with utter certainty. "This is Machin's island that I heard about when I was a prisoner of the Moors. The *ilha de madeira*—the isle of wood."

"That's what we'll call it, then," Zarco said. "Madeira."

In an hour or two the fog was completely gone. The two converted *barchas* of the little fleet sailed east along a verdant shore, which proved to be a long, low-lying point that Zarco dubbed Ponta de San Lourenco. He rounded the point and, with the wind abeam, spent the better part of the day poking along the island's southern shore.

Here the tilting landscape was even more pronounced. He came to a high land covered with wood from shore to mountaintop. He discovered four fine rivers along with a wide blue bay whose shores were covered with fennel, which prompted Zarco to christen it Funchal. It was there that Pedro learned the reason for Zarco's insistence on building the longboats.

"Not easy to penetrate the interior through those thick forests," Zarco said in a little conference at the stern with Alves, Paes, Ayres, and Morales. "We'll split up tomorrow and take the longboats up some of those streams as far as we can go."

But Zarco was not a man who liked to wait. One of the rivers, with a broad mouth emptying into an inlet, was too tempting, and while Teixeira stood offshore in the other *barcha*, Zarco had Morales work his vessel in with lugsail and oars. There he disturbed a pack of seals, who fled at the approach of the ship into a cavern at the foot of the rocks.

"Sea wolves," Zarco said, watching them slip off the rocks where they had been basking and swim away. "A sign of the richness of the waters here. *Camara dos Lobos*, that's what we'll call this den of wolves, eh, Morales?"

Morales was getting nervous about taking the *barcha* in so far. Pedro bent his back to the oars along with the others, and they rowed the ship back out to sea.

By now the sky was growing dark again, and the sailors were showing signs of returning jitters. The southern shore began to angle to the northwest, and Morales was forced to haul in more and more closely as the lugsail lost the beam wind, and its leading edge began to flutter with each small maneuver. To the sailors this was a clear indication that the ocean wanted them to turn back.

A few miles farther on the struggling ships reached a tall, forbidding headland whose brow still wore clouds. There were no beaches on which a landing could be made—only sheer bluff rising directly from the seas. The almost vertical face of the cape blotted out the declining sun and cast a shadow over the waters that was felt by the men in the *barchas* as a chill. There was no way to guess what might be found on the other side of that grim barrier. The sailors begged Zarco to turn back to Funchal. He gave in to them gracefully, seeing that it was so late in the day.

He named it the Cape of Turning. Morales made the entry on his chart. The ships anchored for the night in the Bay of Funchal.

In the morning they went ashore. Zarco took formal possession of the island in the name of King John of Portugal, Prince Henry, and the Order of Christ. Pedro stood with the others, his head bowed.

"We'll erect a cross," Zarco said. He pointed to the westward arm of the bay. "There, where it can be seen both from sea and from land." His arm swept over the meadow of fennel. "There'll be a city on this spot one day."

He began to give orders. To Gonzalo Ayres he said, "Take some soldiers with you and go inland. See if you can get up one of those mountains and have a look round. Bring back botanical samples, and look for wild-life."

"No rabbits allowed here, eh, Dom João?" said one of the *fidalgos* with a laugh.

Zarco was not amused. "Dom Álvaro," he said to Affonso. "Take one of the longboats and work your way westward along the shore. Row up one of those rivers we sailed past, and see how far upstream you can get. See if you can bag some birds. And collect wood samples; let's see what varieties of timber we have here."

Pedro, to his great delight, was chosen to go in the other longboat with Senhor Alves and Ruy Paes. "Double back to the east toward San Lourenco Point," Zarco told the gentlemen. "Explore the coast in that direction. We didn't have a chance to see much yesterday morning in the fog."

There were eight men to row and one to handle the steering oar—almost half the *barcha*'s complement. The longboat's stubby mast remained unstepped, and the sail stayed folded under the aft thwarts; Paes intended to follow the shoreline closely, and as a man who was more comfortable on dry land, he mistrusted fancy sailing.

Pedro had expected to be asked to man the sweep—his strength and skill as a helmsman had earned him Morales's trust in that post despite his youth—but Paes positioned him as one of the starboard oars. "You're a fisher boy, aren't you?" Paes said with hardly a glance at him. "You ought to be used to rowing." Senhor Alves looked as if he was about to say something, but he changed his mind.

Pedro bent his back to the oar, keeping time with the others, and the longboat shot forward into the blue waters of Funchal Bay. An hour's hard rowing took them to the eastern arm of the bay, and Paes let them ship oars and rest awhile as he and Alves surveyed the shoreline.

"Listen to the birds, Dom Ruy," Alves said. "They haven't been disturbed by man since time began. This is truly an Eden."

As if to emphasize his words, there was a huge explosion of birds from the point, and the sky was filled with wheeling gray shapes.

"Jackdaws," pronounced Paes, listening to the raucous cries.

"We'll name this discovery Jackdaw Point," Alves said, doing an imitation of Zarco.

Paes did not smile. He took his prerogatives as head of the little scouting expedition seriously. "We'll have to exterminate them," he said with a frown. "Or they'll be at the grain."

"God's tax," said Alves. "A little grain in exchange for the company of birds."

"Birds like that are worth nothing. They're not even good to eat." Paes turned away to indicate that the discussion was ended.

The longboat rounded the point and turned its bow north by northeast. The sea became choppier now that they were out of the protection of the bay. Pedro felt the breeze in his face and thought the sail could be rigged to provide some headway and take the strain off the rowers, but he did not know how to make the suggestion to Senhor Paes. It would have been easy with Senhor Alves; he always listened.

He stole a glance at Alves to see if he, too, had noticed the shift in the breeze, but Alves's expression told him nothing.

Pedro pulled stolidly on his oar, feeling his joints crack. A couple of the other oarsmen had begun to weaken, giving the boat a pronounced yaw to starboard, and he adjusted his stroke accordingly, as did the stronger rowers on his side. But Paes, seeing only what he thought was a slackening of effort, angrily bawled out an order, and the starboard rowers had to pull harder again—letting the yaw be corrected by steering oar alone—to provide the same result with more effort.

Feeling the hot morning sun across his shoulders, Pedro watched the vertical landscape slide by. The beauty of Madeira was breathtaking. The impossible emerald mountains seemed to lean dizzingly over the sea. He flung a glance over his right shoulder as he rowed and saw that the longboat was heading toward the long, low point of land that Zarco had named after San Lourenco.

Far off to starboard he could see some smaller islands, lying flat in the sea.

Alves called the islands to Paes's attention.

"More land to divide up," he said. "They're not big enough to settle, but they'll be good enough for grazing cattle. An island makes a good pen, with the sea for a fence." He chuckled good-naturedly. "On Madeira, we'll have to lead our cattle around on leashes, like dogs, to keep them from falling into the ocean."

They were still too busy staring out to sea at the low islands to keep track of the shoreline when the longboat pulled past a shoulder of land that concealed a river mouth, so it was the helmsman who first sighted the cross.

"*Uma cruz, senhores!*" he cried, forgetting himself in his excitement. "*Uma cruz, para bombordo!*"

An exclamation of wonder burst from Paes's lips, and then a sharp intake of breath from Alves, and a moment later the boat was drifting idly, its oars forgotten, as everyone turned to gawk in the direction the helmsman had indicated.

Pedro, his oar trailing in the water along with the rest, stared in awe. It came to him that he was the only one there who had been present in the hall in Sagres when Morales had told the astonishing story of Machin and his cross to an exhausted and despairing Prince Henry. Even Alves and Paes must have heard it secondhand from Zarco or Teixeira later. It had been a remote marvel to Pedro then, like a story of a saint's miracles. To see it now, as something real in the sunlight, casting a long shadow down the beach into the water, produced an emotion that was indescribable.

It must have been more than fifty feet high. It had been fashioned from a giant tree growing above the beach—something tall and straight like an ironwood—that had had all its branches trimmed. A spar made from another tree trunk must have been hoisted by block and tackle to form the crossbar. Sailors would know how to do that.

"Zarco won't have to erect a cross," Alves said. "There's one already here."

•   •   •

The sailors stood in a semicircle on the black-pebbled beach, their caps in their hands and their heads bowed in respect, while Alves conducted a service. The longboat was drawn up on the beach, out of reach of the tide. The graves of the lovers, badly overgrown, had been found not far from the foot of the cross, and farther back in the underbrush was the weather-beaten ruin of a shanty that Machin must have built for Anna and himself.

Each of the sailors, without prompting, had placed a stone on the graves when they landed. Paes had been about to order that crosses of lashed branches be placed at the heads of the graves as markers, but Alves had pointed out that the castaways already had a memorial, one that could be seen far out to sea.

"The Englishman did the job himself," he said, shrugging a shoulder toward the gigantic cross that overshadowed them. "The only reason we missed seeing it yesterday after rounding the point was the fog."

It could be seen that an attempt had been made to square off the cross at the base—a long undertaking for one man with an adze, if that's what he'd had—but Machin hadn't gotten very far before he died. His shipmates had not bothered to finish the job, but they had provided an epitaph, carving it deep in the wood to resist the inroads of time. It was in Latin, the common language of literate men, and Alves translated it aloud for the benefit of the sailors:

"Here came Machin, an Englishman, driven by the tempest, and here lies buried Anna d'Arfet, a woman who was with him."

The sailors shuffled their bare feet and crossed themselves or surreptitiously murmured one of the old forbidden charms of the Roman gods. The church had never been able to completely stamp out the singing of Januaries or the whitewashing of doors in the name of Janus, especially among common folk, and Pedro, though a good Christian, saw nothing contradictory about the practice.

One of the older salts volunteered to make garlands for

the graves, another pagan survival, and Paes, in all innocence, gave his permission.

Alves was unusually somber after the service. Pedro came upon him sitting under a tree, staring out to sea. Paes had taken two of the sailors and gone to have a look farther up the river, and the rest had been freed for an hour or two to frolic as they liked. Pedro could hear the voices of men at play coming from the woods and from down the beach.

"Ah, Pedro," Alves said, looking up. "Not having a romp with the others?"

"No, *senhor*."

"Why not?"

"I . . . I wanted time to think quietly by myself."

"Think about Machin?"

"Yes, *senhor*." Pedro nodded his head vigorously. "That's it exactly."

Alves seemed to know what he meant. "Yes, it makes you think, doesn't it? This man who lived so long ago, in a time when none of us were born, reaching out across all those years to affect our destinies. He thought he was only sailing to France, and a wind came out of nowhere—and sent him to this island to die. And we're here now because of it. It can't be explained. Fate is strange."

"Not fate, *senhor*." Pedro struggled to express himself. "God's plan, surely."

"God's plan for us to discover these islands?"

Pedro spoke earnestly, forgetting the difference in their stations. "Prince Henry thinks so, *senhor*. I heard him say so."

Alves looked at him in surprise. "You were there when Zarco brought his crackbrained proposal to the Prince?"

"Yes, *senhor*. I was only a *moco de cozinha*. But the *infante* took notice of me, and because of that, Zarco signed me on the first voyage."

"And do you think that was God's plan for you, Pedrozinho?" Alves said gently.

Pedro hesitated, but he could find no trap in the question. "I don't know, *senhor*. Who could know such a thing?"

"Who indeed? But maybe there's a reason all the same for your being here now, *filho*. Perhaps it's your destiny to be a discoverer." He sat up straighter against the trunk of the tree and suddenly made a face.

"Are you all right, *senhor*?"

"I'm fine. It must be the dinner we made of the long-boat rations. My digestion isn't up to that pickled swill anymore." He made an effort to smile through a face that was sweaty with pain. "Exploration's for young stomachs, eh, Pedro? You'll go on for a good many years to come. I have a daughter about your age. Did you know that?"

"No, *senhor*."

Alves's breathing gradually eased. He looked up at the enormous cross. "Machin must have loved his Anna very much to have refused to leave the island with the others."

"Maybe he died before he could change his mind."

"Maybe."

"If he *had* left with the others, he'd only have been captured by the Moors."

"God's plan again?"

Pedro flushed. "I don't know, *senhor*."

Alves looked up at the cross again. "Perhaps love is everything, after all." He sighed. "It's not for us to worry about God's intentions. In the meantime, there's work to do."

"Let me help you, *senhor*."

Alves struggled to his feet, at the cost of another spasm of pain. "I'll be all right." He leaned on Pedro's arm. "I can't afford to slack off—an old dog like me has to show he's worth his salt. Paes will be back soon, and there are still plenty of hours left in the day for exploring the north shore."

His eyes swept the two graves, piled with stones and garlanded with fresh flowers. "Machin's strivings are over, at least," he said. "He's earned his rest."

"You can see the outline of the entire island from the top of the mountains," Gonzalo Ayres reported. In the firelight he looked close to exhaustion from the long day spent scrambling around the interior, and his hands and face were covered with bramble scratches. At that, he wasn't as spent as the soldiers, who had worn light armor at his insistence. "Here," he said, "I've drawn you a sketch."

He handed over a much-reused scrap of parchment on which new lines had been traced over someone's faded Latin scribbles. Zarco took it closer to the fire and held it judiciously up to the flickering light. "Excellent, Dom Gonzalo," he said in approval. "We'll compare it with the *portolani* that Morales made from the sea approach and try to arrive at an accurate rendering of the coastline."

A dozen blazing bonfires, heaped high with Madeira's abundant wood, made circles of ruddy light on the gravel beach. The companies of the two ships were sprawled around them, too stuffed to move. The monotonous sea rations had been supplemented tonight by roasted fowl— all one could eat. The hunting parties sent out by Zarco had come back with every kind of bird imaginable, from nesting seabirds the size of geese that had been too unwary of man to flee the spears and crossbows, to magpies and larks from the uplands, netted or shot with hardly any trouble. Scores of the spitted carcasses were still charring over the flames, going to waste because nobody wanted to bother to remove them; there would be more hunting parties tomorrow.

"The peak behind us commands the entire bay," Ayres said. "It's as steep as it looks. I could see you all plainly from up there—you looked like fleas."

"Fleas, is it?" belched one of the *fidalgos*. "If so, we're the only fleas on the island. Have you noticed, gentlemen, how we've stopped scratching since we left the ship? These are indeed the Blessed Isles."

Zarco stared at Ayres thoughtfully. "We'll put a cannon up there," he decided. "In case the Castilians come round, with their claims and their papal decrees, we'll show them who owns this island, their patent on the Canaries notwithstanding."

"The range is too great for one of our half-culverines," objected Teixeira, sitting on a water cask and nibbling on

a magpie wing. "The balls will just roll down the mountainside."

"It doesn't matter," Zarco said. "The cannon's there to
bark, not bite. We only need it for effect—to make anybody else think twice if they come. The *infante* would
have our hides if we got his father into a war with Spain
again."

Another of the *fidalgos* protested, "But Dom João, it'll
be a hellish job to get a cannon up that mountainside,
and once it's up, it stays. We might need it on the voyage
home, in case we run into any Moors."

Zarco flashed a smile. "Forget all that. We don't need
to capture Moorish prizes anymore. We've got our prize.
It's a whole province to lord it over, *amigos*."

"For you, maybe," grumbled the *fidalgo*. "You and
Teixeira will be the ones to be named captains of the island, if anyone is."

"I won't forget my comrades," Zarco assured him. He
turned to Ruy Paes. "And I must say I'm pleased with
what you've told me about your reconnaissance to the
north, Dom Ruy. The spot where the Englishman erected the cross has a good harbor, you say?"

"Yes. Not as good as the harbor here at Funchal, but it
will make a good place for a settlement."

Zarco chewed the thought around. "We'll name it
Machico, in the Englishman's honor," he said. "That's
only proper." He turned to Teixeira. "Is that all right with
you, Tristão Vaz? If our island of wood is to have a double captaincy, Machin's bay might serve as one of the
capitals."

"Sounds all right," Teixeira said. "What about the three
desert islands that lie opposite?"

"They'd go with the northern captaincy, naturally."

A couple of the *cavaleiros* sitting around the fire
looked disgruntled at the blithe manner in which Zarco
and Teixeira were dividing up a property to which they
had not yet been granted title, but nobody said anything.

"What does Alves have to say about the anchorage
there? I'd be interested to hear his opinion. Has anyone
seen him?"

Paes glowered, clearly thinking that his opinion ought to be enough.

"He was talking to that sailor over there a little while ago," someone said. "Hey, *moco!*"

Pedro, who had been standing deferentially outside the circle of firelight waiting for an opportunity to interrupt, stepped forward.

"Excuse me, *senhores*, he said he wanted to turn in early," Pedro told them. "He sent me with his apologies for not joining you."

He wished that he could have let Zarco know that Senhor Alves was not feeling well—that he was moving like a man with broken joints and that he had not wanted to eat anything—but he could not take it upon himself to say anything. Senhor Alves had specifically instructed him to say only that he was tired, and it was no business of a *moco de bordo* what gentlemen chose to tell one another. Senhor Alves had his reasons; he was too proud to want sympathy, and perhaps he was afraid he'd be left out of things if Zarco thought he wasn't fit.

"I don't wonder that he's tired after the day that he and Paes put in," Zarco said. "Thank you, Pedro. Take Senhor Alves a cup of wine with my compliments, if he's still awake."

"*Sim, senhor,*" Pedro said.

After Pedro left, Zarco turned to the others with a shrug and said, "Alves isn't a young man anymore. He pushed himself too hard."

Paes crunched the remains of a lark and wiped his mouth on the back of his hand. "Everyone has to pull his own weight," he said.

Zarco dismissed the matter from his mind. "Now, as to getting the cannon up the mountain, gentlemen. Any volunteers?"

In the morning, Senhor Alves looked fine. The night's sleep seemed to have refreshed him. His complexion was ruddy, and he had a ravenous appetite for breakfast—far better an appetite, in fact, that some of the other gentlemen, who had trouble facing food after the way they had imbibed the night before. He feasted on salt fish and hardtack, with half a cup of wine to wash it down, and Pedro brought him some cold fowl that he had saved from the fires of the previous night before it had charred away to nothing.

"Son Pedro," he said, popping a last tiny morsel in his mouth, "you're a paragon. That's just what I need to conquer the day." He wiped off his hands on the beach pebbles. "Now, what's going on this morning?"

Pedro told him of the plans to haul a cannon all the way to the top of the mountain that Gonzalo Ayres had named Terreiro da Luta because of the struggle it had been to climb it. "He doesn't want to go back right away, especially with a cannon. Nobody else is anxious to volunteer either."

"Is that so? It makes a nice problem, doesn't it? Block and tackle borrowed from one of the ships, I should think. There's certainly no shortage of trees to anchor it to, all the way up the mountain, by stages. And we could rig up some sort of harness-and-sling arrangement for carrying it over relatively level ground. It would take about thirty men, I think."

He stood up and smoothed down his doublet. "Come on, Pedro, *filho.*"

"Where, *senhor?*"

"First I want to have a talk with Gonzalo Ayres. He can give me some tips about where to find the smoothest track. Then I'll try to wheedle Morales out of some of the ship's tackle. So Ayres wants to rest today, eh? What about you, Pedrozinho?"

"I'm with you, *senhor.*"

"Ready ... get a grip ... lift!" Alves bellowed.

The sailors grunted in unison, and the bottle-shaped cannon rose a foot off the ground in its slings. They trotted forward with the gun swaying between them, ten men to a side. Zarco had told Alves that he could spare only twenty men, not the thirty that Alves had asked for.

Pedro, staggering along with the rest, felt the strain of his share of a half ton of bronze. The corded sinews of his arms were stretched to the limit and seemed ready to give way. But just when he thought he couldn't last one more step, Alves, with nice timing, shouted, "All right, lads, let it down easy and take a rest."

They lowered the half-culverin to the ground, panting. Gratefully, Pedro dropped where he stood. The perspiration poured down him in great rivulets. It was a hot day, and they were stripped to the waist. He couldn't imagine how Ayres's soldiers had managed in their armor, even without carrying a cannon.

He looked over at Alves. The older man was bearing up well, though his rank condemned him to shirt and doublet. He had elected to carry the powder, wads, sponges, rods and other equipment himself—the balls, thank God, wouldn't be needed for firing off a few demonstration rounds when the gun was in place—and along with his sword, crossbow, and bolts, it all added up to a considerable burden.

Alves allowed them ten minutes to refresh themselves by the rocky stream that ran parallel to their path here. Then, with grunts and groans, they settled the ropes of the cradle across their shoulders again. The ground was beginning to rise more steeply, and after a few more twenty-yard lunges forward with their deadweight of metal, it was obvious that they had taken it as far as it would go.

"All right, lads, it's the block and tackle from here on," Alves said. He sent two of them back to retrieve the skid that they had dragged along with them, stage by stage. It was little more than a flat wooden sledge with an upturned prow that he had inveigled the ship's carpenter into hammering together for him, but it would slide more easily than the hooped tube of the cannon, and there were no projections to catch on anything.

Pedro and another sailor slung the heavy wooden sheaves over their shoulders and began to uncoil the hundred and fifty feet of good rope that Morales had been so loath to part with. Alves went up ahead with them to select a pair of trees to fasten a yoke to.

"These two, I think." He squinted backward along the

unreeled line. "We've got a straight haul of about fifty feet here."

Foot by foot, they hauled the cannon up the mountainside. It was more like working a ship this way, and by closing his eyes as he pulled on the rope with the others, Pedro could imagine that he was raising a yard.

But the work went slowly. The tackle had to be rigged a hundred times—two hundred times—and on some pulls where the wooded slope was denser, they could manage a clear haul of only twenty or thirty feet at a time. Alves had been clever to think of a yoke—it meant that the gun didn't have to be jockied around an obstructing tree at the end of each short haul—but it was still a backbreaking business.

And then there were the places where the gun had to be hoisted over a sheer ledge. A couple of the sailors would have to be sent ahead, to scramble around the obstacle and find a way to the top. Then they had to locate a likely pair of stout trees whose thick lower branches gave a few feet of overhang and secure the tackle in place. There would be two fewer pairs of arms to heave on the ropes—just when more were needed because of the greater strain—because a pair of men had to be left below to steady the cannon with guy ropes passed through the trunnions to keep it from swaying too dangerously on the way up. Then the sailors above, pulling like draft animals, would dig in their heels and walk backward, a step at a time, praying that the ropes would hold and that no one would slip, as the dangling gun barrel rose inch by agonizing inch.

More than once, Alves, seeing the unsupported weight get the better of them, would drop his crossbow and equipment and come to help them heave on the ropes. Then, as the cannon swayed above the lip of the precipice and someone hastened to secure it with a hitch around the bole of a tree, like as not he would hurry forward with the others to help swing the dangling barrel over the edge.

The sailors, though naturally wary at seeing a *cavaleiro* pitch in like any *lavrador*, soon lost their suspicions— Alves had always been popular with the men on

shipboard—and took to calling him affectionately Tio
Martim among themselves, with no loss of respect.

But for Pedro, seeing Alves grow shorter and shorter
of breath with each traverse and seeing his color grow
pasty, it became a matter of concern. He did his best to
hurry to Alves's side and try to take some of the strain of
the rope on himself. But there was no way for him to
suggest to Alves that he take it easy—and certainly no
way he could offer to carry a gentleman's weapons for
him.

Only a couple of hours of daylight remained when
they reached the top of Struggle Mountain, as Ayres had
named it; Alves, though unwilling to order a halt on his
own account, had unbent to the extent of giving the men
longer and longer rest breaks as the way grew rougher
and their stamina ran out. You could see that he was worried about the lateness of the hour; it would be a nightmare to attempt to blunder down the mountainside in
the dark. They could not afford to loiter. But first, they
would have to signal their success with a couple of cannon shots.

The gun's carriage would have to come up the mountain another day—it would be child's play compared to
the job they'd already done. Alves set about to improvise
a way to brace the gun for firing.

"That fallen tree trunk over there, boys. The great big
one. Move it into a better position."

All the lifting and tugging and prying of twenty men
could not shift the fallen giant.

"So much the better," Alves said. "We know it will
make a steady carriage for us, at any rate. We'll fire it
from here. Get to work with your knives and hack out a
groove to lay the barrel in."

Half a dozen blades flew to the task, and in a remark-
ably short time there was a long trough scraped out of
the topside of the log. A pair of stubby grooves were
added at right angles on either side to accommodate the
projecting trunnions, and, with much grunting effort, the
gun was laid in its hollow with the end of the muzzle
projecting a few inches out of the stump. The flare of the
muzzle, along with the embedded trunnions, would ab-

sorb much of the kick, but Alves made sure the gun barrel was wedged in as tightly as possible with stones and dead branches. As an added precaution he lashed the barrel firmly in place with a fifty-foot length of rope.

He dabbed at his drenched forehead with his sleeve. "Better stand well back, *mocos*," he said.

There were no gunners among them, but Senhor Alves could turn his hand to anything. Pedro, at a safe distance with the others, waited while Alves prepared the charge.

From the peak of Terreiro da Luta, as Ayres had said, the figures on the beach were mere mites. Pedro could make out the blackened spots where the bonfires had been, and the bleached squares of tarpaulins that had been turned into rude tents. The two *barchas* rode peacefully at anchor in the sapphire waters of the bay, while a longboat, its tiny oars whipping up a twin white streak that trailed behind it, ferried supplies ashore. Pedro smiled; everybody down there was going to get a surprise in a minute.

Alves had finished ramming home the final wad that trapped the powder. He laid the rod aside and busied himself with his flint box.

"Look to your ears, *mocos*," he warned as he applied a smoldering piece of tow to the touch hole and prepared to leap back.

Pedro covered his ears and squeezed his eyes shut. There was a tremendous clap that would have deafened him, and then he took away his hands in time to hear the sailors cheering. He raised his own voice to join them and turned to smile at Senhor Alves, but the cheers were dying out as all of them took in the sight of Alves's crumpled body lying sprawled to one side of the cannon.

For one crazy moment he thought that Alves had been shot or that the cannon had exploded and killed him, but then he could see that Alves had simply collapsed. He rushed to Alves's side with a couple of the others, while the rest of the sailors milled around, afraid to approach.

Alves was still breathing, though his mouth hung open and his eyes stared, unseeing. Pedro knelt and raised his head.

"Senhor Alves, are you all right?"

Alves was trying to say something, the terror of death in his face. He looked greenish, already like a corpse. Pedro leaned closer to try to hear.

Alves turned his head blindly. "Father in your hands," he whispered, and stopped breathing.

They buried Alves the next day, at the westward arm of the bay where Zarco had wanted to erect a cross. The cross was nothing like the scale of Machin's, but it was made from a pair of good-sized tree trunks and could be seen from the sea, as Alves would have wished.

"Madeira's second cross," murmured Zarco before turning to the assembled crews of the two ships to conduct the service. The sailors, in a great droning chorus, sang the familiar *Salve Regina*, just as if it had been the closing prayer of a day at sea, and for once they managed to stay together. Pedro sang with tears in his eyes. He hoped that Alves's last words had saved him from the fires of hell, though no priest had been present to hear them. He wondered if he, too, would have the presence of mind to utter the words of salvation when his time came.

Alves's body had been left on the peak of Struggle Mountain all night; it would have been impossible to carry it down the slope before the fall of darkness. Pedro had volunteered to stay with it in vigil. The other sailors, in fear of the demons that always swarmed about when someone died, hoping to snatch a soul from the angel who carried it aloft in a napkin, had lost no time in scrambling down the mountain while it was still daylight. At dawn, Zarco had sent a litter party to bring Alves back.

"*Requiem aeternam dona ei, Domine . . .*" Zarco did the best he could, stumbling over whatever words he could remember from the funeral mass, with others chiming in to supply a word or two when he faltered. "We made a mistake, not to bring a priest," he said when it was over. "Next time we'll have one."

"Ha, once you're established as governor, you'll have your own bishop," one of the *fidalgos* said jovially.

Alves's body was lowered into a shallow grave that had been lined with flowers by some of the sailors. He had been clad in his finest clothing, a doublet of red English wool. The grave was filled in and covered with stones. The sailors drifted away. Pedro loitered at the grave, not able to grasp that there was nothing left to do.

The *fidalgos* were clustered thickly around Zarco. "He was a good man," someone said. "Too bad he had to die, with riches almost within his grasp."

"Poor Alves," Zarco said. "I was going to give him a choice piece of property over by Camara dos Lobos." He shook his head sorrowfully. "Tomorrow we'll redistribute the shares. I don't want to think about it today."

The letter had been a month in transit, according to the wandering friar who delivered it. He had it, so he said, from a pilgrim, who had it from a jongleur, who had it from a pedlar, and it had been to the tomb of Saint James and back.

Dona Beatriz paid him a *soldo*—and then gave him three more after he swore he had paid the pilgrim two *soldos* for it—and sent him to the kitchen to be fed. She turned the letter over in her hands. It was weighty and important looking, with an impressive seal. Dona Beatriz could sometimes recognize words by sight, but there was nothing on the outside of the letter that was familiar except the name Alves.

She could hear Inês singing upstairs—the sound of the clavichordium was too faint to carry this far—and called to her to come down. How lucky it was to have a learned daughter!

Inês came running down the stairs at once, her face still happy and flushed from the pleasure of making music. Dona Beatriz thought how pretty she looked with her smooth oval face framed on either side by the coiled braids of jet-black hair that peeped from the margins of her coif and her small neat figure. Inês, she realized with mingled pride and reluctance, was a young woman now, not her little girl. It was hard to be stern with her sometimes, but there were only so many years to set a child on the right path, and a mother owed direction to her daughter.

"It's a letter," Dona Beatriz said, thrusting the cylinder with its blob of wax at her. "It may be from your father. Open it, child, quickly!"

Inês pried the seal loose with her thumbnail and unrolled a cautious inch of parchment. "That's not Father's hand," she said. "It's not like him to use a scribe." Her eyes widened. "It's from Lisbon."

Dona Beatriz could feel her heart fluttering, like a bird trying to escape. "Not from Sagres? Perhaps . . . perhaps they were blown off course, and had to make landfall further north. That must be it."

"The King's court is at Lisbon," Inês said, her eyes shining with excitement. "Father said that Zarco—I mean Senhor Goncalves—told him that if the discovery were of monumental importance, they would be presented at court to King John to receive the royal patent directly."

"What does it say, *filha*? Hurry!"

Inês unwound the tube of parchment further. "It's written in ordinary speech, not Latin, *Mamãe*. It's from a monk at the monastery of Vila do Conde, one of the scribes there, who says he wrote it at the request of Dom João Goncalves, the new"—she frowned—"the new hereditary count of Camara dos Lobos—"

"Chamber of the Wolves? What's that?"

"I don't know." Inês unrolled the scroll all the way. Her face suddenly blanched and she gave a little cry.

"What is it?" Dona Beatriz said, feeling faint.

"*Mamãe*," Inêz gasped. "He says that *Pai* is dead."

Dom Rodrigo came from Alémtejo as soon as he heard to help set things in order. He arrived alone with only a squire and a page boy to attend him, covered with the dust of the road, and, hardly pausing to rest, ensconced himself in the hall and began poring over the household accounts and contracts of emphyteusis by which Dom Martim had collected his rents. He soon had poor Mecia in tears, and he dismissed Nuno, accusing him of stealing. He summoned Jorge, the *abegão* who had been serving as Dom Martim's bailiff, and interviewed him minutely; the man left two hours later, swearing under his breath.

When he finished, he rode into town to call on the *Juiz de Fora* who served as magistrate for the district in the absence of the *Ouvidor*, the crown judge. He was on familiar terms with the *Juiz de Fora*, who was one of his boon hunting companions from previous visits. "You're lucky I'm so thick with him," he told Dona Beatriz. "It will help alleviate things."

"Alleviate things?" Dona Beatriz's hand flew to her bosom. "What do you mean?"

"Don't worry. You can be sure I'll do my best for the sister of my wife. But Dom Martim was not provident." He gave her a steely look. "Unless you don't want me to try?"

"No ... please don't take offense, Dom Rodrigo. I'm very grateful to you."

"Very well, then," he said with cold dignity.

All in all, he stayed three days, spending most of his time hobnobbing with the *poderosos*, the important ones, of the district. When he was through, there were many papers for Dona Beatriz to sign with her mark before a notary.

"It's sad, sad," he said, shaking his head. "Dom Martim was also a debtor to me, though we won't talk of that now. Perhaps I can realize some small part of the loss out of this ruin."

He departed on a day of tears. Mecia and Maria were weeping, their few belongings packed up in kerchiefs, and coming round to say their incoherent good-byes to Dona Beatriz, who was also weeping. "*Adeus, adeus*, Senhorita Inês," Mecia sobbed, smothering Inês in a pillowy embrace. "Oh, that I should see this day!"

"I don't understand," Inês said after they left. "Why do they have to go?"

"We can't stay either, *querida*," her mother said. Her voice broke. "The constable will be here tomorrow to take everything away. I'm sorry, I tried to save your clavichordium, but I couldn't."

"But why, *Mamãe*?"

"The house belongs to someone else. Dom Rodrigo explained it to me. It's to be rented to a *poderoso* from town for a hunting estate."

"Where will we go, *Mamãe*? Are we to live in a convent?"

Her mother shook her head. "No . . . I have nothing to give the sisters, child. You have no dowry for Christ."

Inês could not take in the enormity of it. "Then what's going to become of us?"

Dona Beatriz's face was a blur of dissolution. "I'll ask my sister to take us in. Dom Rodrigo won't refuse."

CHAPTER 8

Tom of Bristol sauntered past the fruiterer's stall, whistling innocently and staring around like any country oaf at the tall spires that poked up above the tiled rooftops of Bruges. A moment later, he had an apple under his jerkin, with no one the wiser.

He skipped lightfootedly ahead, past another row of market stalls, before retrieving his prize and taking a bite. Munching happily, he continued his stroll through the marketplace. Jongvrouw Mathilde fed him well enough, but there was still an inch or two of growth left to him, and he was always hungry.

"Begone, Tom," she said to him this morning. "Mijnheer van den Vondel comes today, and he must not find you. Come back after the last work bell."

Tom hardly needed urging. The three sisters were kinder to him than anybody had ever been in his short life except for his mother—they had taken him in when he was in rags and with nothing in his stomach for two days—but there was nothing for him to do in their neat, precise house during working hours. They would not allow him to help with their spinning—it would not be seemly, they said, for him to do a woman's work—and there were only so many chores he could find to do around the house. As a foreigner, he could find no work in Bruges; he had tried lining up with the day laborers at the bridge that was used for a hiring mart, but the Flemish workers had driven him off with blows and kicks. He had even applied to his fellow countrymen at the Bruges branch of the Merchants of the Staple, but the governor, speaking in a London dialect that Tom could hardly understand, had explained to him that they would not be allowed to hire him, either.

The world had seemed wider and more obliging when he had left the wool ship in Calais with his wages in his pocket and a not too threadbare outfit from the slop chest on his back. The captain had tried to sign him on for the voyage back, saying that Tom had proved himself a good lad, but returning to Bristol was the last thing in Tom's plans. He was in foreign lands now, the foreign lands he had dreamed about when he was a slavey, and he itched to see the world.

Calais was interesting enough, but it was English territory and dominated by the wool trade, and it began to remind Tom too much of Bristol, with its royal officers walking around with their noses in the air and the knots of self-important businessmen standing about at every corner talking about wool prices and due bills in their loud English voices. The Staple town's inns and stalls had eaten up his poor wages too quickly, and he had been caught filching a hen from a market coop. He'd gotten away by the skin of his teeth, throwing the hen back at its owner in a flurry of feathers, but as the market warden knew his face and liked him little, he thought it healthier to leave Calais behind him.

So he'd set out on foot for Bruges, only a week's walk away and the site of a wondrous fair, according to the cartmen. He'd slept under hedges, stolen leeks and turnips from fields along the way, and—braving the unknown penalties of a strange land—stoned birds, snared rabbits, and poached trout bare-handed, as any good Redcliffe lad knew how to do.

He'd reached Bruges not in a week, but a month later, in rags and very hungry and too late for the Saint John fair. Bruges was a marvel: a city of canals and bridges and great buildings of dripping stone enclosed by high walls and watchtowers. Tom had gotten himself past the watchman at the city gate by choosing the right moment to help a cartman with his load of wool and walking in the lee of the oxen. Once inside Bruges he'd found it was not so easy to steal under the vigilant eyes of the city patrolmen—hound-beaters, they called them: red-faced apoplectic men armed with heavy clubs. He had begun to starve then and had taken the risk of begging, though he was whole—a "sturdy beggar," as the law would have called him in England. Screened by the surrounding bustle of the immense cobbled square in front of the Cloth Hall, he stopped a gray-cloaked spinster—a slender young woman who was shouldering an enormous bundle of wool, and said in the best Flemish he could muster after a month in the Lowlands, *"Ik heb honger, Mevrouw . . . Kunt mij helpen . . ."*

"Skaam ew," she said sternly. "You ought to be ashamed." And then her eyes took in his rags and general emaciation, and softened with pity. *"Hier,"* she said, fumbling in her purse and handing him a groat.

He was unlucky. A beefy man with a badge pinned to his tunic had his upper arm in a powerful grip before he knew it, and said, *"Nou, dan gaan we maar!"*

The spinster must have had a kind heart, or at least didn't want to be responsible for getting Tom whipped, because she said instantly to the patrolman, "You're mistaken, *meneer*. The boy isn't begging. I asked him if he wanted to earn a groat by helping me with my bundle."

The patrolman let go of Tom's arm reluctantly. "Be careful, *jongedame*," he said in a surly tone. "It doesn't pay to get mixed up with trash like this." He turned to Tom and growled, "And you, *jong*, you watch your step!"

He walked off, swinging his club.

"Thank you," Tom stammered. *"Hartelijk dank."*

"Niets te danken." She eyed him critically, then said, "Very well, then. Come along." And turned her back.

He hefted the woolsack to his shoulder and followed her. She must have been sturdy despite her slenderness, because Tom found the weight of the sack all that he could manage, even allowing for the fact that he did not have his full strength. He hurried to keep up with her, down the stone streets and across the bridges until she stopped at a narrow house, compressed by its neighbors and fighting for its individuality with brightly painted shutters and geraniums in window boxes.

"Ik woon hier," she said, and when he was slow to understand, she motioned him impatiently in after her.

Inside, sunlight spilled through mullioned windows to a checkered floor, sparse furniture, a round mirror that made a tiny curved image of Tom, and a vivid geometric rug draped over a straightbacked bench. Two women in pale gowns and white caps sat at creaking wheels, spinning; a third wheel remained idle. Tom stood gaping. The spokes whirled in such a blur and the strands wound themselves so fast around the slim rods that it was dizzying; in Redcliffe, the women span with distaff and spindle, and it struck Tom all at once how far England was behind the cloth towns of Flanders still, and how much Master Philpot would have given to have these women teach their secrets.

The woman he had followed hung up her cloak on a peg next to the curved mirror, and Tom saw that she was dressed identically to the others. They looked as alike as three eggs, too, with their smooth, round faces and snub Flemish noses and flaxen hair, though all were of different ages. The two spinning women studied Tom serenely, saying not a word and never stopping their wheels.

"You can put the wool down over there," said his rescuer. "Come with me, and I'll give you something to eat."

She took him to a blue-tiled kitchen and set bread, cheese, salt herring, and pickled cabbage before him, together with a mug of the brew the Flemings called *biere*—something like ale, with some bitter herb added to it, but not as robust as honest English ale. She clucked when she saw how ravenously he was eating and cut a thick slice of ham for him from a hanging larder with more bread, then doled out a bowl of some thick pudding.

When at last he slowed down, she asked him his name. "Tom, is it?" she said, pronouncing it *Toom,* "and an English *van* Bristol? Well, Tom of Bristol, how is it that you came here?"

He stumbled through an explanation in his halting
Flanders dialect, augmented by trade French, which every true Fleming loathed but understood since their
country was owned by the duke of Burgundy, and it was
the language of their masters from the count of Flanders
on down. He found that she even had a smattering of
English—ordinary working people were intensely pro-
English, since their livelihood depended on the English
wool trade. When it came to that, even the upper classes,
despite their pro-French bias, had perceived what side
their bread was buttered on after the duke of Burgundy
had allied himself with Henry of England in the war
against France that had just concluded. Tom gathered
from the street rumors of the last few months that King
Henry had married Catherine, the daughter of the van-
quished Charles of France, who had been forced to dis-
inherit the dauphin and legally adopt his new English
son-in-law as heir to the French throne. The pale ghost
of France was now ruled, in essence, by an English-
Burgundian partnership, and things English had never
been so popular in Flanders.

When he finished, with a lame excuse for having accosted her in front of the Cloth Hall, she looked at him
severely and said, "So, Tom, it is not so good for an apprentice to run away, is it? See where it got you."

"It got me here," he said gallantly. "To speak with *een
mooi jongedame*."

She blushed. "Oh, so he is glib, is he?"

He pushed the empty plate away and stood up.
"*Bedankt, Mevrouw*," he said. "*Het was goed*."

"And where is it that you go now, Tom of Bristol?" she
said. "Back to the hound-beaters?"

It was his turn to blush. "I'll be fine."

"Wait here. You can't go like that. I'll give you some
clothes. They were our father's. And I'll give you
some food to take with you."

She was gone a long time, and Tom poked around the
kitchen and an adjoining pantry, not to steal anything but
to marvel at the neatness of this Flemish house, where
there was a prescribed place for even the smallest object.

When she returned, she had a bundle of old clothes

that she thrust unceremoniously at him. "You can put them on in there. They'll be too big for you, that can't be helped, but you can fold back the hose, and we can take a tuck and a stitch here and there in the other things." She looked him up and down until he grew uncomfortable and then said offhandedly, "I've talked to my sisters, and they've agreed that you can stay here tonight."

That was how it began. He'd expected a corner of the storeroom and at best a pile of straw that first night, like any stray dog, until he realized that it seemed to be taken for granted by all concerned that he would share one of the big feather beds upstairs with the sister who had taken him in. Her name, he learned, was Mathilde. When he crawled under the puffy coverlet with her, still wondering if he ought to have retained his shirt, he found that she was naked, too, as honest folk were in their own beds. She turned to face him and pressed an admonitory finger to his lips. But she herself was noisy when she found her first release, and he could hear two sets of giggles from the surrounding darkness.

The older sisters were named Margriet and Marian, and they scarcely spoke to him during the daylight hours. When he expressed uneasiness about the giggles to Mathilde, she said, "*Shhh,*" then whispered, "And why shouldn't I? They have their young men, too, when they wish." The word she used for young man was one he hadn't heard before—*kerel*—and it seemed to carry overtones of a lover or suitor.

The three sisters were *femmes soles*, the same name by which such independent female workers were known in England. They belonged to the spinners' guild, which in Bruges was dominated by women, just as in London the silkwomen ran their own trade. There had been a brother once, a weaver like their father, and with their mother, who was a washer and carder, the house had been a beehive of industry in which the whole family prospered.

But their father had died in an outbreak of plague, and their mother, declining rapidly after that, had followed him two years later. The brother, restless, had gone to try his luck in Ghent, or so he said, and there had fallen in with the disaffected weavers of that rebellious city, which

had risen against the count of Flanders and his foreign
overlords more than once and thrown off its shackles for
a time. But the propertied classes by now were thoroughly frightened by their dangerous citizenry and
clamped down hard on any sign of dissent or heresy. And
so Mathilde's brother had been arrested with some suspicious companions as a member of the "White Hoods,"
a militant group taking its name from the old Ghent people's militia, and a probable Hussite—which, Tom gathered, was the same thing as a Lollard. Whether he was
either was open to question, but he was hanged all the
same.

The heavy loom had never been dismantled and still
sat, gathering dust, in the sisters' loft. Tom, with little to
do with his time, got it into working order and surprised
the sisters one day with a sample of cloth he had made.
"I can earn my way," he offered. "If some of the weaving
is done here as well as the spinning, it will bring more
money into the house, as before."

But the sisters were not pleased, as he had expected.
They were terrified when they saw how much thread he
had used. A spinster could be excommunicated for wasting yarn, Mathilde explained. Mijnheer van den Vondel
and the other putter-outers had obtained a letter from
the bishop threatening such a penalty for women who
did not know their place.

"But your father was a weaver and so was your
brother," Tom expostulated. "Why can't you hire an apprentice and keep some of the money under your own
roof? It would even be to the advantage of your Mijnheer
van den Vondel, because after delivering wool to you he
could take cloth directly to the fuller."

If the problem, he thought, was that they were too
timid to let him weave on the sly, as he had done for
Master Philpot, that ought to take care of it.

"No, no, you don't understand," Mathilde had replied.
"*Ja*, it's true that a widow can be admitted to her husband's guild, just as in England, and then give the guild
membership to her second husband. A widow can even
hire an apprentice. But our mother never applied to the
meister after our father died because our brother was al-

ready working at the craft, and even if she had, that couldn't be transferred to a daughter. No, no, Tom, we are only spinsters."

Tom, remembering how Master Philpot had manipulated the guild master to serve his own ends, asked if they might get Mijnheer van den Vodel to intervene on their behalf in return for having his palm greased with a portion of what the apprentice brought in.

Mathilde laughed bitterly. "And for what? He already has his weavers under his thumb. He claims debts that no one owes and sends his men around to collect them, and there is no one to say no to him. Only last week he summoned a poor widow to his house and told her that her husband had died owing him a hundred and sixty guilder, even though her husband himself had told her just before he died that he had cleared his debt at the last accounting and owed Mijnheer van den Vondel no more than thirty guilder for the last delivery of thread, which he had already woven into cloth and on which she would realize a profit of eight guilder when she sold it back to Mijnheer van den Vondel. The poor woman had to sell her house to pay him, and then he claimed a further debt of seventy guilder for the last delivery of thread. He doesn't pay what he himself owes to the workers, and the magistrates uphold him. One woman who kept complaining had her tongue cut out."

"Your Mijnheer van den Vondel sounds like a fine rogue," Tom said. "They can't all be that bad. Why don't you work for another putter-outer?"

She blanched in fear at the suggestion. "You don't know what you're saying."

"You're free, aren't you? You're a *femme sole* in good standing with the guild."

She shook her head sadly. "You're very nice, Tom. But nobody would dare to go up against Mijnheer van den Vondel. We'd never get any more work. It's better to have at least something. When he dies, perhaps, we can join with the other workers and sue his estate for what he's cheated us of. That's done, sometimes. By my accounting, he owes my sisters and me eighty pounds for underpayment over the years. It would be nice to get it some day."

"You'll be an old woman by then."

"It must be the same in England."

He thought it over. "Yes. We haven't learned to regulate ourselves as you do, with the work bells four times a day, but in every country there are those who do the work and those like Mijnheer van den Vondel and Master Philpot who let Sir Penny work for them."

"Sir Penny?"

He laughed, and sang the carol his father had taught him as he played between his knees at the loom:

> Sir Penny is an hardy knyght,
> Penny is mekyl of myght,
> In euery cuntre qwer he goo . . .

He explained the words to her and she said, "Yes, the weavers here sing songs like that, too." She was silent for a moment, perhaps remembering her brother, then said, "But they're afraid of us, you know. The first time the French sent their knights against us, it was like a crusade. The knights were so anxious to slaughter us that they swept their own foot soldiers and crossbowmen aside and charged the citizens in full armor. But they didn't reckon on the canals. The canals stopped their charges, and the men and horses tumbled in the water, too heavy to get up, and the people speared them like trout. They stripped the corpses afterward, and seven hundred golden spurs were hung up in the church to celebrate the victory. It took them eighty years to get even." She shuddered. "I wasn't born yet, but Margriet and Marian were. Father told us stories of how the knights chased people across the fields, dragged them out of their cellars and the churches, and butchered them till the streets ran with blood."

Tom nodded in understanding. "Yes, the common people of England rose up once—it must have been nigh the same year your folk were punished by the knights. My father told us stories, too. The peasants were led by Wat Tyler and Jack Straw and the priest John Ball. They preached that no man should be held in bondage to another, and that villeins and gentlemen should be equal, and were called Lollards for that. They marched on London town, hanging lawyers as they went, and the king met with them and agreed to send charters granting freedom all through the towns of England, and so they were gulled. But then the lord mayor of London struck down Wat Tyler with his dagger, and the charters were recovered, and things went back to the way they had been before. Seven thousand peasants were hanged, so they say, and John Ball was drawn and quartered. The jurors themselves were hanged if they failed to find the peasants guilty."

She touched his hand. "So you see," she said. "It shows one mustn't hope for too much."

"No," he replied fiercely. "It shows one must hope for everything."

"They'll never let go their grip, the van den Vondels," she said sadly.

She would not discuss it further. Tom left it at that. Mathilde was right. The order of things never changed for people like her or Jack Giles, mired in one place. He had no right to meddle in her livelihood. She knew she would have to make the best of her life in Bruges, Van den Vondel and all. Most people never felt the pull of other places. Tom found that hard to comprehend. That was how to find change. It waited, always, beyond the familiar horizon. All you had to do was to pick up and leave.

He could do it right now, he realized. Right this minute, if he wanted. He glanced down at himself in the fine new suit Mathilde had sewn for him out of her father's recut garments. The close-woven Flemish cloth was sturdy enough for travel; he was better dressed for the road than when he'd fled England. And he had a few coins in his pocket. Mathilde had pressed a silver groat into his hand when he'd left that morning, and he'd only spent a penny of it so far.

Tom shook off the thought. He couldn't desert Mathilde without a word. She had been troubled when she had sent him off for the day—she was afraid of Van den Vondel's visit, but she wouldn't say why. She had pushed Tom out the door with a kiss and said only, "Don't get caught by the curfew. But don't come back before the vespers bell. I'll save you some supper."

He lifted his head as the bells of terce sounded from all the towers in Bruges. The clamor filled the sky, then died away. The morning was half gone. Only three more hours of it remained until the sober folk of Bruges could lay aside their work and pause for dinner. Tom's own lack of purpose chafed at him. The novelty of Bruges had long since exhausted itself for him. Life had become too easy; he had ceased to use his wits to survive. Dissatisfied with himself, he hurried on with no more than a perfunctory glance at sights that were becoming stale to him.

Head down, he crossed the Place de la Bourse, where all the bankers and merchants got together in the morning to make deals and test the day's news for advantage. As was usual at this hour, the square was filled with noisy clumps of gowned men shouting prices back and forth, and here and there voices were boisterously raised in quarrels as well. The Hôtel des Bourses, a sawtoothed building of three stories, still displayed on its angular facade the coat of arms bearing three purses—bourses—of the Van der Bourse who had started it all.

Hemming in the building on either side were the bulkier edifices of the Genoese and the Florentines, with their spires and battlements. There was a branch of the Medici bank here as well; the Italians were well entrenched in Bruges, and got the lion's share of the business.

Tom kept walking. The merchants of the Hanse maintained their shops and offices a little farther on, and beyond were the special streets that confined the Danish, Norwegian, Portuguese, and Spanish traders. He quickened his pace. However gray Bruges had become in Tom's eyes, he could still find scraps of color in the foreign enclaves.

The Spanish concession in particular was interesting. One of the grandees kept a pair of Moorish slaves as linkboys, and Tom had struck up an acquaintance with them in the fragmented Spanish he had learned from the wine sailors at the Bristol docks. Their faces were as black as char, and their heads were wrapped in towering silk cocoons. Tom had never seen so fine a sight. He could generally get up a game of dice with them and trade tales if their master wasn't using their services. He didn't believe half of what they told him about the wealth and power of the Moorish kingdom of Granada, where they had lived before being captured, and believed still less of what they had to say about the fabulous lands to the east, but the stories were marvelous to hear. He had to be careful, though, not to get caught by their master, a Señor de Covarrubias. The *señor* was touchy about Englishmen, having lost a wool ship to English pirates. It was his own fault for having failed to get a letter of safe conduct from the Merchants of the Staple at Calais, which would have cost him a good deal less than the wool he had lost. Señor Covarrubias, however, failed to see it that way, and Tom took care to stay out of his sight.

Lost in his thoughts, Tom at first didn't pay attention to the commotion that was starting in the square of the Bourse. Then someone ran past him, and he glanced up. The little clots of bargaining merchants were breaking up, their members dispersing, and as the ripple of movement spread—from a focal point where a horseman was gesticulating excitedly—the square began to empty. At the same time, bells began to ring through the city, at first one or two, then increasing numbers of them. Tom recognized the deep tones of the Cloth Hall bell, answered by the ponderous clang of the bells of the Town Hall, a distinctive duet that was gradually submerged in the general pealing from the churches and guildhalls.

It wasn't only the Bourse traders who were now streaming through the streets. Half of Bruges was pouring out of the houses and shops and hurrying toward the north gates of the city. Those who could were traveling by water as well. As Tom reached the bridge that crossed the nearest canal, he saw people pushing off in rowboats. A merchant's barge, painted and canopied, made its stately way, propelled by eight sweating servants in livery.

He reached out and plucked at the sleeve of a man in

an apron, with the blue fingers of a dyer, who was charging past with the mob.

"*Ik moet weg, meneer* ... where's everyone rushing to?"

The man shook him off. "The Galley of Flanders is here! They were sighted off Sluys an hour ago!"

The dyer disappeared into the hurrying throng. Tom stood listening for a moment and heard a far-off cannon. It was the harbor gun. A moment later the salute was answered by a faint cannon shot that must have come from the Venetians, then another and another. Tom counted five in all; five galleys, no fewer, were pulling into the harbor at Sluys!

Tom caught his breath. He had never seen one of the legendary great galleys of Venice. The Galley of Flanders, as their annual convoy north was called, never stopped at Bristol. It always laid over at London or Southampton on the English leg of its trip. Tom had grown up with the sight of the galleys of the Janneys and the Spaniards and other nations—stinking outhouses rowed by chained convicts—but it was agreed by all seafaring men that these were mere imitations that could not bear comparison with the proud Venetian fleet.

What was he waiting for? He plunged joyfully into the river of human traffic heading for Sluys, his boredom forgotten.

There was a holiday spirit in the crowd. Tom let himself be carried along by the thick flow that filled the roads, dodging around those who could not keep up. The harbor was only a few miles away, but not everybody's legs were as young as his. He managed to hitch several rides on the tails of wagons until he was kicked off, and once, in the carnival atmosphere that prevailed, he was invited to ride on a scow where some jolly craftsmen and a number of agreeable maidens in rumpled work gowns were having a floating picnic on the way to Sluys. But it was slow going, with the men taking inebriated turns at the rowing and frequent stops along the banks for horseplay, and Tom became too impatient of their progress to stay with them.

He arrived at the deepwater port just as the bells of

sexte were ringing, footsore but happy. The crush of people was enormous at the waterside, and was made worse by the swarms of vendors and entertainers who had come to work the crowd. Tom pushed his way through the wedged bodies, trying to get a close look. Above the wall of heads he could see the tremendous yards of the Venetian galleys tilted against the sky, the furled sails draped in brightly striped festoons. He could not believe the size of the yards, the longest he'd ever seen, or understand how it was possible to hoist so great a weight aloft. The upper ends of the slanting yards, higher than the mainmasts they were hung from, were being used to fly enormous silk pennants forty or fifty feet long. The device on the pennants was a winged lion in gold, the emblem, he supposed, of the Venetian Republic.

Tom could hear music coming from the anchored ships—pipes and brass instruments, a thrilling sound. The Venetians did things up with pomp and ceremony. The customs officials were already aboard, Tom imagined, but the music couldn't be for them. The *capitanio* of the fleet must be entertaining a delegation of town dignitaries and the really important men of Bruges. As always in this world, the men at the top got first crack at everything good, and the lesser merchants would pick over the leavings during the weeks ahead, when these vast floating warehouses were tied up at the docks. But in the case of the Galley of Flanders, even the leavings amounted to an incredible treasure trove—a million gold ducats' worth, Tom had heard.

He struggled forward. A juggler in motley had set up his act on top of a pile of hogsheads—the only few feet of clear space he could find for a stage—and was extracting a few small coins from his immediate audience, but Tom had no eyes for him. He shouldered his way through the jam of onlookers and won to the edge of the stone quay.

Now he could see the great galleys in all their splendor. They had anchored a little way out, and a swarm of skiffs and other small craft was already bumping at their flanks, manned by vendors trying to sell food and wine to the oarsmen or by people who hoped to do a little unofficial trading with individual members of the crew.

The vessels were three-masted, all with those huge slanting yards that carried the dipping triangular sails that galleys mounted instead of square ones, as the round ships of the north did. But, of course, they weren't dependent on sails. The real motive power was those banks of shipped oars, standing out like bristles on either side, and the two hundred or so oarsmen in each ship who pulled their guts out. A Venetian galley never had to wait for the wind; it could sail on a fixed schedule. On the other hand, accustomed as they were to their enclosed southern sea, they made timid sailors, hugging the land during the day and putting in at night. In fact, Tom had once been told by a Janney sailor, it was against the law for a Venetian to sail at night.

He drank in the sight of the five sleek shapes in the harbor. Rising from each gilded stern was a three-storied castle, covered with a rich canopy embroidered in thread of gold with a noble coat of arms. Tom gasped at the amount of cloth that was required for each such tent; surely the Venetians must be wealthy beyond all measure. The long catwalk that ran between the two rows of oarsmen's benches displayed the private treasure chests of the nobles aboard; the bulk of the cargo would be below decks. He could see two of the nobles strolling along the catwalk now, small figures in stiff robes, but the rowers were hidden by a rampart.

"Look at them crowding round, like kittens waiting to suck," said a coarse voice next to him.

Tom looked around and saw a lard-faced fellow with a gap between his two front teeth, pointing at the flotilla of rowboats that were nosing up to the galleys.

"You'd have the whores out there, too, peddling their goods, if those horny bastards on the rowing benches had oars long enough to reach them," the lardy one went on.

His companion, another ill-laced lout of the type the Flemings called *grauw* or *boor*, laughed at the witticism. "They'll dip their oars soon enough, Joost," he said. "As soon as their *schipper* starts handing out shore leaves. And then, by God, there'll be a thousand of those Venetian *hooploopers* filling the brothels of Bruges and Sluys, crowding out the regular customers like us."

Joost scowled. "What's keeping Meester High-and-Mighty Coornhert? If I'm going to have to row him out there, I don't want to wait around all day. I've got a slut waiting for me at Damme, and she won't keep forever."

"Maybe he's gone back to take the edge off that fat wife of his," the *boor* snickered. "She likes a two-handed job, and he doesn't dare to leave her alone too long."

"He's gone back to get more bribe money, that's what. He's made a private arrangement with one of those blue-blooded thieves of a crossbowman, but it almost fell through last year because he didn't bring enough ready cash with him. These Venetians believe in what they hear clinking."

He leaned out over the quay to have a look at the few remaining skiffs that were tied up there. Tom followed his gaze to a boat that was moored on the other side of the wooden jetty that projected out from the quay at this point. He could just make out a foot or two of its stern, bobbing in the tide. Several large bundles were lying in the stern sheets, as if stowed awaiting someone's return.

"No sign of him?" asked the friend.

"No. If I didn't need the job I'd shove off and let the old pisser try to row himself."

Tom didn't see what Joost was grousing about. As for himself, he would have given anything for the chance to have a closer look at the galleys. His eyes ran along the quay to appraise the handful of tethered rowboats. A couple of them were half filled with water, in need of bailing before they could be used. But two or three were in good condition. All, however, lacked oars.

Tom sighed. If it hadn't been for the missing oars, he would not have hesitated to borrow one of the boats, though doubtless that sort of borrowing was as much frowned upon in Bruges as it was in Bristol—even treated as theft, if the owner were cranky. He could have scrambled aboard and pushed off before any possible owner watching from the quay—or even anyone who knew who the boat belonged to—could have reacted, and then taken care to return the craft to some relatively un-

tenanted stretch of the bank and scurry off before anyone
could ask questions. But the only boat with oars in it—he
could see the blades projecting out over the stern—was
the one that belonged to Meester Coornhert, with his
goods already stowed aboard, and he had a feeling that
such an attempt would not be taken lightly. He'd have
these two big bastards pounding right after him, for one
thing, and even if he got away with it, he was sure that
as soon as the sharp-dealing Coornhert arrived, he'd have
the harbor police rowing out after him.

"Here he comes now."

Tom looked out at the wooden jetty and saw the roly-
poly figure of a man in a wide drooping hat and a fur
cloak fastened at the throat with a glint of unmistakable
gold. There was something odd about the silhouette, and
as the man bent to take the painter of the boat, Tom saw
that he had one arm—that was why he needed someone
to row him.

Joost was still leaning out over the water. Tom made
his decision in a flash. He took one nimble step that
placed him squarely behind Joost, shoved hard, and
walked quickly away before it could dawn on anybody
what had happened.

Behind him there was a yelp of surprise followed by a
splash. There were shouts of *"Kijk daar!"* and "What
happened?" and he heard the friend's voice cry, "Help
him! He can't swim!" But there was no indication that
the friend had seen anything, and no one was after Tom.

Tom was down the stone steps of the quay in a
trice—to all intents and purposes the first of those going
to Joost's rescue. But when he reached bottom, he
veered right toward the jetty instead of going left with
the others. A stampede of pounding feet surged past him,
and then there were four or five more splashes as a
number of brave fellows leapt into the water without
pausing to strip off their doublets.

CHAPTER 9

Tom, without appearing to hurry unduly, wasted no time getting to the jetty. The one-armed man was sitting in the stern of the skiff with his bags and boxes, looking about impatiently. Tom saw rich velvets and furs covering bulges and bloat, a gross face on a pyramid of chins.

He dropped lightly into the boat. "Meneer Coornhert?" he said, contriving a sort of bow without rocking the skiff.

"Who are you? Where's Joost?"

"Joost couldn't come. He sent me to row you instead."

The puffy face grew purple. "That good-for-nothing loafer! This is the last time, let me tell you! You can tell him not to bother to come in tomorrow! Well, pick up the oars! What are you waiting for?"

Tom sat without moving. "He said you'd give me a penny."

The choleric face grew darker, if possible. "He did, did he? Well, we'll see when we're finished."

Tom made no move to take the oars. On the other side of the jetty he could hear a confused muddle of voices, shouts of advice. Everybody still seemed to be busy fishing Joost out of the water. There was no urgent need to get under way yet.

Coornhert gave a growl under his breath and extracted

a small coin from his purse. He tossed it to Tom. "There," he said. "All right. *Ga mee.* Let's go."

Tom rowed out past the jetty. He could see what was happening at the quay now. A bedraggled rag doll was propped against the stone wall, and two stout fellows were working the arms like a pump. Tom saw a gush of water come out of the tiny dot of a mouth, like a silver thread, and then the rag doll was throwing off its rescuers and feebly attempting to get to its feet. Another small figure, which Tom recognized as the friend by the cheap russet dye of his doublet, was pointing up at the low parapet Joost had tumbled from, and then people seemed to be looking in every direction.

Meester Coornhert was too fat and stiff to turn his head around all the way. "What's all that noise back there?" he asked.

"Oh, some fool fell in the water and they pulled him out," Tom said. "Probably a drunk."

At Coornhert's instructions, Tom rowed for the flagship of the Venetian fleet. "Go around to the port side," Coornhert ordered. "Then lie to under the gun platform, forward."

It was hard to avoid bumping other skiffs, so thickly were they clustered around the galley. Tom got warned off a couple of times, but most of the warning was done to the competing craft in Coornhert's loud voice. Under the latticelike screen of the shipped oars it was cooler, and with the noonday sun out of his eyes, Tom could see more clearly what was going on here. Some of the oarsmen, naked brutes with shaved heads, a very few of them sprouting curious tufts of hair or bushy mustaches, were lowering baskets on lengths of cord or hauling up groceries they had bought. "None of your lowlandish beer!" one was bellowing in a villainous Italian that Tom had difficulty following despite his dockside familiarity with the Genoese dialect. "A jug of wine—understand? *Vino!*" The Flemish provisioner, whose overloaded skiff had about three inches of freeboard between it and a trip to the bottom of the harbor, shrugged helplessly and kept trying to get the man to pull up a wooden *canneken* with a bung in it. A little farther along, a buxom whore, rowed by a pocky fellow, was leaning back in the thwarts and giving the oarsmen a good look under her skirts. "Remember," she yelled encouragingly to one and all, "go to the sign of the Swan—*de Zwaan!*—and ask for Big Margot! I'll give you the grand tour! *Den grooten tour!*" Joost had been insufficiently sanguine about the commercial instinct. A couple of oarsmen had lowered a rope sling and were trying to coax her into sitting in it, but she was too wary for that. Tom could appreciate her caution. He didn't want to imagine what would happen to a whore if two hundred dangerous animals, who had been deprived of women for so long, ever got one under their benches. She would never have come out of there alive.

"Tie up to the anchor cable and wait," Coornhert said.

Tom looked at him in surprise but did as he was told. Nobody chased them away. After a while a young Venetian noble came along the gun deck and leaned out over the boarding platform. He was the most gorgeously dressed man Tom had ever seen. He wore long, pointed red slippers, curled up at the toes, and his silk hose, resplendent in gold, silver, and pearls, were in different colors for each leg. More pearls were sewn into his doublet, which was slashed to show the sleeves of a silk shirt beneath, and he wore a cocky red hat with a feather in it.

"Well, *Opper-Koopman* Coornhert," he said in good Flemish, "I see you've brought along a lot of unnecessary merchandise. I've come to sell, not to buy."

"Don't be hasty, Messer Lodovico," the merchant replied. "Wait till you see what I've got. Don't worry, you'll take good Flemish gold away with you, but you'll want to take part value for your jewels and glassware with some small items you can sell to the infidels for ten times what you paid for them."

The Venetian sighed. "Very well, then, I'll have a look. But be quick about it. There's an arrogant cock named Maffeo aboard who's greased more palms than I have, and my time is limited. The *capitanio*'s in his cabin with your *grootenkoopmen* at the moment, but he won't look the other way forever."

Coornhert rose unsteadily to his feet, and for a mo-

ment Tom was afraid that he was going to capsize the
boat. But despite his bulk he got to the anchor cable
surefootedly enough and, to Tom's amazement, began to
climb it one-handed, almost as rapidly as a man with two
arms might have done. The way Coornhert managed it
was to tuck the cable under his armpit, wrap his meaty
forearm around it, clamp it in the crook of his elbow, and
inch his way up with alternate grips of elbow hinge and
hand, while at the same time making a vise of his knees
and heels and pushing. He wriggled up the rope like a
great fat worm, his vast rump heaving, levered himself
over the rail with that single iron arm, and called down
to Tom, "Well, what are you waiting for? Bring up my
goods."

It took Tom a dozen trips up the rope to fetch everything. He stood to one side, forgotten, while the two men
haggled. He could hardly believe that he was actually
aboard one of the great Venetian ships that traveled, it
was said, all the way to Byzantium and fabled Trebizond
as if it were no more than the crossing of a pond.

He looked about his surroundings with lively interest.
The high poop, wearing its immense scalloped stole,
seemed miles away. A few distant figures in brilliant
robes stood around in front of its gilded archways. To get
there you had to travel along a raised catwalk between
the two long wells that contained the rowers' benches. It
must take a brave overseer to walk that narrow platform
on a slave ship, Tom mused, when you were always
within reach of a hand that could grab an ankle and pull
you down to be torn apart by a pack of penned human
beasts; the Venetians, however, prided themselves on using free rowers, who, though lower than the lowest member of the crew, at least were reasonable creatures who in
an emergency could even be trusted with weapons to
help defend the ship.

The benches, Tom saw, were arranged in a herring-
bone pattern. Unlike the galleys of other nations, the Venetian vessels did not allot several men to the same oar.
Instead, each bench seated three rowers, each pulling in-
dependently on his own counterbalanced oar. Tom could
see how the canted benches let them pull in unison with-

out getting in one another's way, and the oars themselves were of staggered lengths. Still, there wasn't much space between the handles, and the Venetians must have worked with marvelous precision to avoid broken hands.

Closer at hand, there were more interesting things to see. Tom inspected a huge bronze cannon, pointed forward over the battering ram, and marveled at the size of the iron balls it threw. There were also smaller cannon poised on the wings of the gun platform, and mounted on the rails of the boarding platform were smaller cannon still, which could swivel either to fire a broadside or add to the forward salvo that must make the sight of a Venetian ship bearing down on them a terrifying thing to pirates. The ram itself was a long murderous beak tipped with a solid bronze lion's head; that would finish the job the cannon had started. No wonder Venetian merchant ships sailed unmolested everywhere.

He had wandered too close to the catwalk. A sineway arm shot up like a snake from the pit, and a fist closed around his ankle. Tom jumped out of his skin.

"Sssst!" Want to buy a necklace?"

Tom stared down at a man with a head like a skull. He was naked except for a pair of canvas breeches, and every rib showed, but his shoulders and arms were enormous, as if he'd been assembled from two different-sized men.

The hand let go, and Tom stooped down. "What have you got?" he asked, his interest awakened.

"*Venga*—come on down and I'll show you. Open house isn't till tomorrow, so you'll get the best choice." It wasn't any particular language—mostly trade Italian with bits and scraps of other tongues—but the man's general meaning was clear enough. The poor bastard must have been used to making himself understood in a hundred ports of call.

When he saw Tom hesitating, he said, "Don't worry, you won't get robbed." The skull grinned disconcertingly. "We get nailed to the mast with a knife for that."

Tom looked over his shoulder and saw Coornhert deep in conversation with the Venetian noble. Mentally keeping a hand on his purse, he lowered himself into the pit.

The stench was overwhelming. Tom saw gnawed bones and other garbage scattered on the planking, remains of the feast brought by the Flemish skiffs on which the rowers had gorged themselves. There was human waste too, lying in corners, that had not yet been washed into the bilge. But the worst smell of all came from the rowers themselves—all the overripe bodies, rotten breaths, and urine-soaked breeches. Tom tried not to gag, then, by breathing shallowly, found that he could stand it.

There was hardly any space for Tom. He was jammed in among the three rowers who occupied the bench. A low footrest, against which he supposed they braced themselves while rowing, made a boundary of sorts between this set of rowers and the next, but he was hemmed in on all sides by unwashed flesh.

A hand plucked at his sleeve. "*Scusi, signore,*" said another human cadaver.

"Back off, Topo, I saw him first," snarled Tom's proprietor. There was a brief clash of wills, and the other oarsman let got of his sleeve. But Tom still felt the rows of eyes on him.

"After you've gone through the Dalmatian's junk, see me, Excellency," said another of the rowers, unintimidated. Tom gave a start; it was the first time in all his life he'd been addressed in such a manner, and for an instant he had trouble relating it to himself.

The Dalmatian, with a glare all around, scrunched down on his knees in the narrow space between bench and foot brace, and came up with a small wooden chest wrapped in a filthy rag. He untied the cord that held the lid down and began laying out small items on the few inches of bench that belonged to him.

"Genuine Venetian glass," he said, holding up a string of colored beads. "Only the glassblowers of Murano have the art, and it's the death penalty for them to emigrate."

Tom gaped at the glittering treasures that spilled forth. Some of the beads looked like pearls, others like rubies. Those that didn't imitate jewels were wrought in fantastic shapes—paper-thin sheets of glass wrapped and molded into tiny shells of rosebuds.

"How much?" he asked, trying to act cool.

"For you, *Messire*, one silver groat."

Tom thought about it and shook his head. With the penny that Coornhert had given him, all he had added up to a groat.

"What else have you got?" he said.

In the end he bought the necklace for Mathilde for four pence. For Margriet and Marian he bought fine brass thimbles, such as any woman would be delighted to have, for only two pennies each. With the four pennies he had left he bought himself a gift—a little Venetian knife in a tooled leather scabbard.

"If they're all as sharp as you, I'll make no profit on this trip," said the Dalmatian, stowing away his little box. But he did not seem displeased.

"How is it that they let you trade?" Tom said. "Aren't you in competition with the big merchants who hire the galleys?"

The oarsman bristled. "We're freemen, same as the crew, same as the bowmen of the quarterdeck, for all their blue blood. *Everybody* does a little trading on his own—even the *capitanio*. You may think we're the scum of the earth, but we've got our rights under Venetian law, same as them! They can't cheat us on our rations— eighteen ounces of biscuit and a bowl of bean soup every day! No kickbacks to the *capitanio*! We can buy our own cheese and wine, without any restrictions!" He glowered. "As for private trading, we're allowed a customs exemption of ten ducats." He clamped his mouth shut as he realized he'd told Tom the value of the merchandise in his trading box.

Tom apologized. "Tell me," he said, "have you gone to the Holy Land?"

"In the Galley of Flanders? No," the Dalmatian said, mollified. "That's the Galley of Beirut. But I could be recruited for one of the other runs at any time. The Galley of Barbary. The Galley of Romania, that goes to Constantinople and Trebizond in the Black Sea."

A plan was forming in Tom's mind. "Do you think . . . that is . . . does the Galley of Flanders ever take passengers back to Venice?"

The oarsman guffawed. "Not the likes of you, lad.

Sometimes the Senate will agree to lease a galley to a king or a great prince, so that he and his entourage can travel to the Holy Land in comfort. But as for the run-of-the-mill pilgrim, he's lucky to buy himself eighteen inches of sleeping space on the deck of a private galley!"

Tom was not to be deterred. "What about working passage? I never heard of a ship that didn't sometimes have to take on a hand in foreign parts."

Now the Dalmatian gave him a glance of pure malice. "Do you hear that, *amici*? This *sciocco* thinks the *capitanio*'s going to reserve him a place on the crew. Well, there are no places, *bimbo*, except on the benches, and I doubt that a scrawny one like you would last. And even if you would, we've still got four rowers in reserve. We've only thrown six bodies overboard so far on this run."

The other oarsmen, who had lost in interest in Tom when they saw that he had no more money to spend, now began to jeer.

"Go home, *seccatore*," said someone from the next bench. It was the rower who'd called him "Excellency." The man gave him a shove in the shoulder that turned him partway around, and then another rower pushed him in the other direction.

Tom gave the roughhouse no time to develop. He twisted out of their reach and, using the bench as a stepping stone, sprang lightly to the gunwale. A couple of reaching hands fell short. Tom could see that, in spite of the Dalmatian's protestation that they were all free rowers, a number of them were chained to their benches. You were free, he guessed, if you volunteered to row to pay off a debt or work off a prison term.

Coornhert and the Venetian nobleman were finishing off their business. "So, Messer Lodovico, you find that those Flemish laces are to your taste? You'll make a good profit on them back home. Every fashionable Venetian lady will want them."

"You won't do so badly yourself on the jewels and the spices," said the Venetian. "You'll make a killing on the pepper—you got it at least ten percent cheaper than the bulk pepper will go for later."

"Yes, and you sold it for ten percent more than you could sell it anywhere but Bruges," Coornhert retorted.

The Venetian's eyes narrowed. "You can send someone around tomorrow to offload it. In the meantime, you owe me a balance of fifty gold ducats."

"I'll pay you in guilder."

"In that case, it's fifty-five."

Coornhert agreed with suspicious alacrity. But he counted out the gold coins with an expression of pain on his pyramidal face.

He turned to Tom. "So there you are? *Kom.* Take that cask. Be careful with it. It's Alexandrian sugar."

Tom was impressed. Alexandrian sugar was worth its weight in gold—worth several times its weight, in fact. He hugged the cask to him as he slid down the anchor rope and stowed it carefully where it wouldn't get wet. It took him only a few more trips shinnying up the cable to collect the rest of the goods; Coornhert was leaving more than he was taking back. The real fruits of the day were probably in his pocket—the portable wealth of jewels.

He saw trouble before he had rowed halfway back to the embankment. The truculent figure of Joost was standing there, arms akimbo and his eyes trained on Coornhert's skiff, with a couple of beefy helpers at his back.

Tom made a futile and foredoomed attempt to change course but gave it up when he saw Joost and his friends moving along the embankment to intercept the skiff. Wherever he landed, they would be waiting.

"What are you doing?" snapped Coornhert. "Put in where the steps are."

Tom pulled on the oars without enthusiasm. Every time he looked over his shoulder, Joost was standing there, getting closer.

"What's that fool Joost shouting?" Coornhert said. "He has some explaining to do."

Tom could make out the words and didn't like what he heard. "Watch out for that footpad, *meneer!* Stand well back—we'll take care of him!"

Tom reached the landing with a final violent pull on

the oars that sent the bow of the skiff grinding on the lowest step. He turned around to find Joost grinning hugely, enjoying the thought of smashing him. As Joost reached for him, Tom stood up quickly, the cask of Alexandrian sugar between his two hands, and thrust it into Joost's outstretched arms.

"Here," he said loudly. "Be careful with the *meneer*'s sugar."

Joost, caught off balance, staggered backward with the cask, not daring to drop it. Tom vaulted over the prow of the skiff and ran past him, staying clear of his two friends. In their eagerness to help with the beating, they had crowded too closely behind Joost, and now he crashed into them, still fighting for balance.

In the meantime, the backward impetus given the skiff when Tom had jumped out of it had sent it sliding off the stone step and out into the water. Coornhert was scrambling forward on his knees and his formidable arm, trying to get to the prow and grab one of the iron rings used for mooring boats.

Tom, running like the wind, felt confident enough for a backward look; he was thirty feet away, and none of these Flemish puddings could run as fast as he could.

He saw Joost finally lose the battle with his center of gravity. The cask slipped from his arms and rolled into the water, where, with a splash and an eruption of bubbles, it began the job of sweetening the harbor. Coornhert gave a wail of anguish and began sculling with one of the oars Tom had left in the tholes. He got close enough to the landing for one of Joost's muscle-bound friends to grab and yank. The friend fell in the water, but Coornhert, with remarkable agility for a man his size, scrambled up the steps and began belaboring Joost with the oar.

By the time any of them remembered Tom, he was out of sight and still running. He slowed down, finally, when he was past the sprawl of warehouses that hid the harbor front and had found the road leading back to Bruges.

He fingered the marvelous possessions in his purse— the glass necklace, the thimbles, the little Venetian knife.

He gave a wide, happy grin. The unpromising day had turned out well after all.

"Bedankt, maat," he said, sliding off the tail of the ox-cart that had carried him the last three miles to the city. He looked up at the dark silhouette of the watchtower bulking against the starry sky. The bells of compline had rung more than a half hour ago; he had heard them from the distance as the ox cart jolted along the rutted road. He could see no lights anywhere along the high walls; Bruges was a city that was dead at night.

"It's past curfew," said the peasant who had given him the lift. "We'll have to stay outside the ramparts till morning."

Suiting action to words, he began spreading straw on the ground for himself. The oxen remained hitched; the heavy cart itself would tether them, with a long pole thrust through its wheels.

"I think I'll just have a look 'round, *maat*," Tom said.

He walked across the bridge and looked up the silvery outline of the thick tower hulking over the gate. "Hel Open up!" he called.

"Go away," said a voice above.

"Hoe last is het?" Tom inquired innocently.

"The gate's closed," the watchman said. *"Dicht!"*

"Have a heart," said Tom. "Just raise it a crack and let me in."

There was a whisper of air past his ear, and a crossbow bolt buried itself with a thud in the oak paling at the side of the bridge.

"Go away, I said."

Tom walked back in the direction he had come from with an itch between his shoulder blades. When he was out of sight of the watchtower, he doubled back and began walking along the bank of the ditch that paralleled the city walls at this point. Bruges had eight gates, and he was under no illusions that he would find a better reception at any of the others. But after twenty years of peace, the city had forgotten that there was more to a fortification than strong gates.

He found what he was looking for about a half-mile
farther on. A stone barge, laden with great blocks the
size of hay wagons, was tied up in front of a place in the
wall where they were erecting another tower. A treadmill
crane had been set up on the wall, looking like some gigantic perching bird with its beak overhanging the barge.
The crane's tremendous hook, big enough to sit in, dan-
gled above an unended granite block, almost low enough
to reach.

Tom scrambled aboard the barge. There was no night
watchman; who would steal a block of stone? The up-
ended slab was neatly trussed up with rope, ready to be
lifted in the morning. Tom untied knots and pulled a
length of rope free. Standing on top of the building
block, he doubled the rope and started casting it, trying
to catch the loop on the hook. He succeeded on his second try. Grasping both sides of the rope and using all his
weight, he pulled on the hook.

On the city walls above, the enormous squirrel cages
of the crane, twenty feet in diameter, creaked and
groaned. Tom was able to pull the hook down about four
feet before one of the safety cogs caught and braked the
wheels to a stop. He tied down the dangling ends of his
rope, climbed to the hook, then hauled himself overhand
to the peak of the crane. He had a look over the dark
rooftops of Bruges, like God's cobblestones with the
spires of churches and commercial buildings sticking up
at the cracks, then walked down the spine of the crane to
one of the slanting roofs that sheltered the treadmill
wheels from rain. He slid down the roof, hung by his fingertips, and dropped to the stone parapet. He found a
flight of steps not too far away and set out through the
unlighted streets.

It wasn't difficult to avoid the night patrols. You could
hear them coming from a block away, calling out to one
another and rapping on suspicious doors with their
sticks. Keeping as much as possible to the back streets,
Tom arrived at Mathilde's door a quarter-hour later.

He expected a scolding or at least a show of hurt for
returning so late, but Mathilde seemed only distracted.
She hardly spoke as she served him the supper she had

kept warm for him in the tiled oven—a fine bird that had unfortunately dried out somewhat and buttered carrots and turnips.

Margriet and Marian had long since gone to bed, and Mathilde had dark rings under her eyes, but Tom kept her up a little longer as he chattered happily about the day's events. She did not laugh, as he expected, when he told her how he had outwitted Joost and the fat merchant, and she had few words of comment even for his description of the way the Venetian noble was dressed, which he thought would interest her. Finally he opened his purse and showed her the bauble he had bought for her.

"It's very nice, Tom," she said as he held the beads out to catch the candlelight. "But you shouldn't have spent good money like that."

She went to put the beads in a porcelain box in the cupboard. "What's the matter, Mathilde?" he said.

She turned around, and the look on her face was terrible. "Oh Tom," she said. "Hold me!"

He stood up and took her in his arms. She began to weep. Between sobs, she told him the whole story. Van den Vondel had come to take away the completed yarn that morning, but he hadn't paid them for it. He had suddenly claimed an unpaid debt of their father's, twelve years old. It was for two hundred guilder, he said, and he had documents to prove it. It was an impossible sum, a disaster. He would take her house for it, and in the meantime he would send his men tomorrow to take the loom and whatever other conveyable property he could find the help satisfy part of the debt.

"He'll leave us the wheels. He said we could spin for him at half price to help pay off what he claims."

"He can't come here and take away your things," Tom said. "He'd have to go to a magistrate and have it done lawfully."

"Mijnheer van den Vondel *is* the law," she said. "Don't you know yet how things are?"

"We'll bar the doors. Don't let him in. We'll go to the magistrate first thing in the morning. You'll take your oath on the holy relics. There's no debt. I don't care what kind of documents he's cooked up. Didn't you tell me that there have been cases where the court decided for the workers? Justice can't be completely one-sided."

"He said ... he said ..." She began to weep again.

"What did he say?"

"He said that I was comely, that I hadn't yet dried up like my sisters. He said the virtue of a *femme sole* wasn't worth anything. He has his pick of any of them, and none dare refuse. He said he'd let us continue to live in the house as long as I gave him pleasure."

"Has he ever ..."

"Me, no. Margriet once, when she was a little girl. He tore her. Mother didn't tell our father about it."

"I won't let it happen!" he cried, pressing her against him.

"*Nee, nee,* Tom," she said gently, stroking his hair. "You can't do anything. You're just a boy and an Englisher. You can't go against a man like that. You'll have to leave. I think he knows about you anyway."

"I'll ..."

"*Shhh,*" she said, pressing a finger against his lips. "It's been very nice, hasn't it? Think of me sometimes, won't you, my English *kerel* with the straw hair that never stays in place?" She smoothed out his hair and eased herself out of his clasp.

"Mathilde ..."

"Take me upstairs, Tom."

They lay in each other's arms all night, not sleeping and not making love. Tom dozed off a little toward dawn. He was awakened, with it still dark outside, by a violent pounding from downstairs.

"*Vlug, vlug!*" a harsh voice was shouting.

Mathilde sat up, clutching the coverlet to herself. "It's Mijnheer van den Vondel!"

Through the doorway Tom could see Marian and Margriet huddled like frightened mice at the balustrade of the stairwell, looking down. Marian, still pulling her gray work gown down over her thick hips, started for the steps.

"Don't open the door!" Tom cried. He reached for his underclothing beneath the pillow and jumped out of bed.

From downstairs came a splintering sound as the oaken bar across the door gave way. The door crashed open, and a broken lock tinkled on the floor.

"Upstairs!" came Van den Vondel's voice. "You two start taking the loom down. I'll have a look around and see if our little *femmes soles* have anything else worth taking."

Tom had his doublet on and his hose half laced by the time Van den Vondel and his henchmen clumped up the stairs. The cloth dealer was large and square, with oily black hair hanging in curls and a little goatee making a black wedge on his broad chin. His lackeys were a pair of hulking, thick-bodied bruisers with small unintelligent eyes.

"*Zoo, wat is?*" Van den Vondel said, his eyes lighting on Tom. "Have you taken to robbing the cradle, *mevrouw?*"

"Leave him alone," Mathilde said from the bed. "He's going now. He won't be back, I swear it!"

Van den Vondel strode to the bed and ripped the covers off Mathilde. He stood staring down at her naked body, his jowls working.

"Get away from her, you fat pig!" Tom burst out.

Van den Vondel's voice turned to silk. "I'd say we've found a burglar, wouldn't you?" he said to his bruisers. He frowned at Tom's half-fastened hose. "No, a rapist, caught in the act. It's up to us to protect our women workers, wouldn't you say?"

Tom backed away a step, his eyes going from Van den Vondel to the two lackeys. His normal instinct to run was complicated by the presence of Mathilde.

"Give him a permanent beating," said Van den Vondel. "One eye, one ear, one gimpy hand. But first hold him. I'm going to kick his balls in."

The two hirelings made a grab for Tom. Tom's hand flashed to his purse and came out with the little Venetian knife. He slashed at a meaty forearm and sliced it open from elbow to wrist. The lackey screamed, and the other one recoiled, his eyes on the knife.

Van den Vondel cursed. He drew a dagger of substantial length from a jeweled scabbard. "A dead rapist," he grunted, "that we're going to deliver to the watch. Grab him, Hans!"

He lunged with the dagger. Tom was free of Hans by the simple expedient of drawing his blade across the knuckles of the hand that had clutched at him. He stepped sideways, and Van den Vondel's dagger slid past his ribs. Before the merchant could strike again, Tom plunged his knife into the thick gut, with such force that his knuckles struck flesh. Van den Vondel gave a curious sigh and sank to his knees. The dagger clattered to the floor.

"Run, Tom, run!" Mathilde screamed. "Meet me tonight when the *avondglocke* tolls . . . at . . . at the place where we first met!"

Tom was out of the room before Hans, still sucking at his knuckles, and the moaning lackey with his slashed arm could decide to intercept him. The front door was hanging open. He closed it behind him and adjusted his step to not too fast a pace, but one that would get him quickly around a corner. Behind him he could hear, after an interval that must have been designed to let him get clear, the sound of the sisters screaming through a window.

The watch came running in response to the screams— two ample patrolmen with long clubs. They headed, naturally, to the source of the cries, not to the corner where Tom, close against the wall, was fastening the remaining points of his hose and drawing at least one disapproving stare from a passerby. The policemen reached the door just as two bleeding men came running out. They looked at the naked women hanging out the window and promptly grabbed the pair. Hans waved his good hand and tried to explain. One of the policemen, misconstruing the gesture, rapped him on the head with his club. Tom straightened his doublet and walked away.

The air was turning chilly with the approach of evening. Tom shivered in an archway of the Cloth Hall, watching the slantwise shadow of the belfry lengthen across the square, and hoped he was not conspicuous.

The bells signaling the end of the workday had just finished ringing, and the vast structure was disgorging people into the square. Mathilde had chosen their meeting place well. The evening crowd, loitering to chat or to finish up some piece of the day's business before going home to their suppers, would dilute their presence.

He saw her hurrying toward him across the stone pavement, a tall slender figure in a gray cloak. She was carrying a bundle in one hand, and there was something tucked under her arm. He stepped out of the archway as she drew near, and she stopped in front of him.

She looked around before speaking. "He's dead," she said.

Tom turned the thought over in his mind, trying to sort out how he felt. So he was a murderer now. He had killed a man. It was strange that he hadn't meant to, had never wished to. Master Philpot, after some prank or escapade of his, had often called him a scapegrace and predicted that he would end up on the gallows, and now that actuality was hanging over him.

After a moment, he replied, "I'm sorry."

"You can't stay in Bruges. Here, I've brought you a cloak. Winter is coming. And here's a basket of food."

"Thank you."

"And here's some money—what we could scrape together. No, don't argue, take it!"

"You're not in trouble?"

"How could I be? By the time the police got it straightened out that it wasn't those two dunderheads who had killed Mijnheer van den Vondel, it was agreed that he was murdered by a burglar and would-be rapist. The pair of them will testify to that—after all, didn't they hear Mijnheer van den Vondel say it?"

"I'm glad I could do that much for you, at least."

"You did more than that. Now the house will not be taken away from us, and there is no debt of two hundred guilder. And I will not have to sleep with that fat pig, so I thank you for that, Tom of Bristol."

"Well . . . that's good, then."

She nodded. "Yes it is. I'll be working for a new putter-outer—Mijnheer van Tromp. He's already been around to talk to us and some of the other spinners. He's a better man than Mijnheer van den Vondel. He has a name for being fair. He is going to get us together with some of the weavers and dyers and help us in a proceeding against Van den Vondel's estate to recover some of the money he cheated us out of over the years. Now that the *mijnheer* is dead, we're free to do that. Everyone is very happy."

Tom fastened the cloak around his shoulders. There did not seem to be a great deal left to say.

"Do you think that's awful?" She looked at him anxiously.

He thought it over. "No."

She squeezed his hand. "You'd better go. You have to be outside the city gates before curfew."

"I know."

"Where will you go?" She looked wistfully at him.

He thought it over. The Venetian oarsmen had squelched any hope he might have entertained of getting aboard the Galley of Flanders, but he still had his legs.

"I don't know," he said. "The Holy Land or Constantinople, maybe. But first I'll have to walk to Venice."

CHAPTER 10

"He's dead," the *aguzzino* said. "Unchain him."

He tossed a chisel down to the bench. The Turk snatched it out of the air with a hand the size of a mutton roast and waited for the hammer, with a fixed stare for the men on the catwalk and no expression at all on his face.

"Gives you ideas, does it?" the *aguzzino* said with a chuckle. "Not a chance."

He threw the hammer. The Turk caught the spinning handle in his open palm, and his thick fingers closed around it.

Sandro grasped the foot of the corpse with one hand and the chain with the other and spread the links taut for his hulking benchmate. The Turk inserted the heavy iron wedge at the welded junction of the leg-iron and with one well-aimed blow popped it open. His enormous muscles bulging, he pried the cuff far enough apart for Sandro to force the dead man's foot through.

"Poor Poggio," Sandro said, recklessly breaking the rule of silence; it seemed to him that the death of a man, even a galley slave, ought to be worth something. "He was the one who kept telling me that the chains come off on the day you die. He taunted me with it. And now, finally, he's the one who's free."

"Shut up, Venetian!" the *aguzzino* barked from above.

"Just give me an excuse, by God!" The end of the whip dangling from his fist twitched like a cat's tail.

Sandro hunched his shoulders, his brief rebellion quenched. The last cuts on his back hadn't completely healed over yet. It was a bad thing to get a cut laid over a cut; he'd seen men develop gangrene in the wounds after a flogging followed a flogging too soon, and sink so fast that even the *aguzzino*'s cure-all—a third flogging and a sponge soaked with vinegar forced between the teeth—couldn't rouse them to row again. In that case, over the side they went, dead or not.

"Not today, eh?" the *aguzzino* said, sounding disappointed. "All right, throw him overboard."

Wordlessly, the Turk lifted the body by the shoulders and waited for Sandro to take the ankles. Together they hefted the dead man to the rail and, working to the limit of their chains, heaved him over the outrigger that supported the oars. The body, flopping bonelessly, tumbled into the gray sea below.

"The chisel, Turk," the *aguzzino* said. "And the mallet as well, if you please."

The crossbowman beside him lifted his weapon.

Sandro, aware of the contained fury in every line of the Turk's body, held his breath, wondering if this would be the time his formidable benchmate finally snapped and did something stupid, like throwing the hammer at his tormentor's head. But the Turk handed the tools up, meek as a lamb.

"Very good," the *aguzzino* grinned. "Not ready to die yet, are you? Don't go away. We'll find a new helpmate for you right quick."

He turned on his heel and swaggered down the catwalk toward the sterncastle, followed by the crossbowman. He was hardly out of earshot when a chorus of hissing started, in the acquired technique of sotto voce whispering from between almost motionless lips by which the galley slaves communicated.

"*Ssst*, Turk . . ."

It was from a couple of benches away, but it was highly directional. The Turk inclined his shaven head slightly to show he had heard his name.

"You could have at least stripped him before dumping him. The breeches and sweatcloth were in fair condition. I would've given you a tenth of my biscuit tomorrow for that."

The Turk replied without moving his head. "You'd steal your grandmother's winding cloth, Ahmad. He was only a Frank, and a miserable man at that, but those stinking rags were all he owned. He was entitled to take them with him."

"You're crazy, you know that."

"Shut up."

"I only . . ."

"I said shut up. Or I'll tear your sorry head off and feed it to the fish."

The other man ceased in mid whisper, though there was no way the Turk could have reached him.

The exchange had been in Arabic, but Sandro understood it well enough. His childhood exposure to the language on the trading trip with his father on the Galley of Barbary had provided a subsoil, waiting for a seed to take root, and his grasp of the idiom had grown greatly during the two years he had been chained to the Turk, even though the Turk had had little to say to him. Half of the galley slaves were captured Moors, and the constant background of whispered dialogue was one of the few things Sandro's starved senses had to work on.

The Moors, as well as the Genoans, called the big man "the Turk," though Sandro had at first taken him for an Egyptian. Later, putting together dribbles and clues, Sandro concluded that the Turk had indeed passed at least part of his later boyhood in Cairo, but as a slave—a particular kind of slave called a *mamluk*. Sandro's understanding of Arabic word structure had by that time improved sufficiently for him to recognize the verb form denoting "one who is owned," though it was not the usual word for slave. It came from the same root as *malik*, or king—"one who owns others."

A Moor at the bench behind him had tried to explain that the soldan of Egypt and the viceroy of Damascus also were slaves—"like the Turk"—but that made no sense to Sandro, and the Moor, in disgust, had given up on him.

Whatever the distinction, it was clear that the Turk considered himself a man apart. He had nothing but contempt for his Egyptian and Syrian compatriots. *"Da-eef!"* he grunted. It meant weak, soft. He had more respect for the Genoese who ran the ship and for the ferocious qualities of Franks in general. Sandro suspected that some of it rubbed off on himself as a Venetian—a fellow outcast here and a hereditary foe of the Genoese. At least the Turk left him pretty much alone.

The Turk's name was Kara Yusif—Black Joseph, in the parlance of the tribe he'd been snatched from as a boy. He'd been a soldier of sorts, though a slave—trained in the use of sword, mace, battle-ax, and lance since the time he could toddle. The horrific scars on his body showed he'd practiced his profession.

Other than that, Sandro had learned little about his terrifying benchmate in the two years. He gathered that the Turk had been sold by his Egyptian master to someone in Damascus and there had been part of the *mamluk* army that had fought against the Mongol hordes of Tamerlane—fought them, unbelievably, to a standstill, until the city was unaccountably abandoned by the boy soldan of Egypt and his flighty ameers. Damascus had had to surrender to Tamerlane, and though the Turk's body bore the marks of Mongol torture, he had somehow escaped the slaughter of males that had followed—escaped having his head added to the tower of skulls that Tamerlane had built as his victory monument. Roped together with a few hundred other survivors, he had been taken by the Mongols to the slave market at Tana on the Sea of Azov, and that was where the Genoese captain had bought him.

The Turk took pride in the fact that he had been bought cheap. Nobody wanted a dangerous-looking brute like him, his back already crisscrossed with the lash marks that showed he would never make a tractable slave. He wasn't even worth the trouble of gelding. He was good for nothing but the galleys.

"Esmah, listen!" Sandro said. "That was fine, what you said about Poggio." In fact he had been surprised to hear

such thoughts issuing from the mouth of his taciturn companion. "I know he hated me, but I hold no grudge against the dead."

The Turk sank into his usual glowering silence, giving no indication that he had heard. Had there been a red flicker of response from beneath those hooded eyelids? Sandro could not be sure and did not care to press his luck further.

He rested on his oar, taking advantage of the respite while he had it. At the moment the ship was under sail with a stiff following wind, and the rowers had nothing to do. The galley was two days out of Trebizond, with a cargo of alum, metals, silk, and Persian luxuries. There had been a couple of paying passengers too—an old man and his two grandsons, who were under the impression that they were boarding a Venetian state galley. But as they were Moslems, the captain had ordered the old man thrown overboard as soon as they were out of sight of land and the two young men put to work filling vacancies on the oars. The *aguzzini* were breaking them in now.

The galley was headed for Kaffa on the Crimean shore, where Genoa had a fortified trading outpost. There it would pick up furs, hides, wax, honey, and probably a few slaves before sailing home by way of Constantinople and the Holy Land—where, if the captain's luck held, he could take on a partial load of returning pilgrims who didn't know any better than to sail aboard a cargo carrier. It had been a long voyage but so far a profitable one.

He stared eastward toward the coast of Caucasia but could see no land. The captain was steering well clear of the Black Sea coast to avoid attracting the attention of raiders. Those were savage folk yonder, and when Genoese galleys ran aground, they were plundered and the crews enslaved. Not, Sandro thought bitterly, that it would make any difference to him.

He stretched cautiously, feeling the stiffness in his limbs and the sting in his back when he moved. The *aguzzini* doused the rowers with buckets of salt water once a day to maintain a minimum sanitary standard and flush away the worst of the excrement underfoot, but

while the brine toughened up scarred backs, it was agony
after a fresh whipping.

He looked down at his ridged abdomen, pared of the
last ounce of spare flesh, and the knotted bulges of his
forearms. His hands were great horny paws, stiff with
calluses; he could not have played a lute now if one were
thrown to him, though he could have snapped a board in
two. He wondered what two years had done to his face.
Surely the old rosy-cheeked, boyish Sandro was gone.
He sought a clue in the way the other *galeòtti* looked; the
Turk was ageless, a figure carved out of gnarled oak, but
the rest of them had been turned into gaunt, hollow-eyed
apparitions.

"Look alive!" came a hated voice from above. "Here's
your new playmate!"

The *aguzzino* had returned with a scrawny weasel
whom Sandro recognized as one of the "free" replacement rowers—some petty criminal who had volunteered
to exchange his prison sentence for a set term in the
galleys—five years for two was the bargain—and who
had been leased by the state to the captain. He had been
enjoying a vacation for the past two days with his place
being taking by one of the kidnapped grandsons, but the
chronic shortage of rowers had caught up with him again.

"Not with the Turk, *padrone*," he whined. "I beg you."

"Get down there, you whoreson!" the *aguzzino* roared.

The jailbird scrambled down with alacrity. Free rower
or not, he wore leg-irons and carried a length of chain
over his shoulder.

Sandro and the Turk made room for him on the bench.
The *aguzzino* tossed down a heavy iron padlock.

"Go on, louse," the *aguzzino* said. "You know what to
do."

"Have a heart, *padrone* . . . you don't have to chain me."

"By God, are you arguing with me?" the *aguzzino* rumbled.

"I'm doing it, *padrone*, see?" the replacement said
hastily.

He looped the loose end of his fetters around the common chain and snapped the padlock in place. The Turk

looked on in contempt at the sight of a man fastening his own shackles.

"That's the way, Giuseppe," laughed the *aguzzino*. "I'll just keep the key, if you don't mind. I'll unlock you in a year or two—if the Turk and the Venetian don't eat you alive first."

He sauntered off, swinging his lash. The replacement huddled on the bench, making himself as small as possible. He stole a look at the Turk and pulled back from him, then shrank from Sandro, too, giving Sandro some indication of how he must look.

Sandro was moved to pity at the man's obvious terror. "Don't worry, *figlio*," he said. "We won't hurt you."

The Turk's gleaming dome of a head came around and the red-rimmed eyes fixed on Sandro. His face remained the usual stony mask, but he unbent enough to growl, "You're too tenderhearted, Venetian. We've got to make sure this cockroach pulls his weight."

The walls of the fortress rose from the sea, thrusting crenellated towers toward the sky. Sandro could see the tiny figures of crossbowmen on the battlements above, brilliant in Genoese silks. The land rising beyond, which might have been bleak with its background of low scraggly mountains, bloomed with peach and cherry blossoms, and the lavish scent of roses hung over the shore.

Genoa had controlled Kaffa for more than a century. The Crimean stronghold was a terminus for the caravans from the east and north and guarded access to the Sea of Azov through the narrow Kerch Strait. Once, in a brief interval of amity, Genoa had shared Kaffa with Venice as a way of enforcing a boycott against the khan of the Golden Horde at Tana, but that hadn't lasted. The Venetians hadn't been able to resist resuming their profitable direct voyages to Tana, and then fighting had broken out between the Venetian and Genoan trading quarters in Trebizond. Today, ships of either maritime republic were fair game for the other in these hostile waters, despite all treaties and fine statesmanlike speeches by the respective doges, but it was usually the Genoese who got the worst of it.

From where the galley was tied up at the end of a long stone pier that jutted into the sparkling bay, Sandro had a fine overall view of the ancient town behind the port. Aside from a few painted towers and the rooftop gardens of the wealthy, it was a sprawling collection of eastern hovels enclosed by a wooden wall. Still, the wall had been good enough to hold the Tatars at bay all these years. The gates were open, and men and camels could be seen moving in both directions. A large caravan was assembling on the plain beyond; the slight tilt of the plain made it visible as a multitude of moving dots, like swarming ants, and a scattering of patchwork tents where cooking fires sent thin threads of smoke into the sky.

Sandro returned his attention to his bowl of bean soup and oil—the one meal of the day. The captain had been generous. There were a few bits of stringy meat in it that might have been goat; meat was something that happened only a few times a year. Sandro drained the last drop, then licked the bowl to get every fragment.

When he lifted his head, he found Giuseppe, the replacement rower, staring longingly at him. The little Genoese wasn't above licking another man's bowl if he could get away with it, even though his diet was better than theirs. He even got cheese and wine from a pittance that was due him; he had tried at first to gobble it up, but after a hard stare from the Turk, he had learned to share.

"Cheer up, son," Sandro said. "There'll be another bowl tomorrow."

The Genoan flushed. "Your stomach growls as much as ours, Venetian," he said. It had not taken him long to lose his fear of Sandro, though he still did not dare to trifle with the Turk.

A fellow Genoan a couple of benches away lent support. "The Venetian's a dainty eater," he sniggered. "One might think he's dining with his doge."

Sandro did not bother to respond. It was true that he tried not to wolf down his rations immediately, as most of the others did. A man had to have a little pride—not let them turn him into an animal. Despite the hunger clawing at his belly, he always forced himself to eat slowly, pausing from time to time to break off a piece of hoarded biscuit and dip the jaw-breaking morsel in his bowl.

"If Allah wills it," put in one of the Moslems, "perhaps there'll be a kind passenger. Remember the Christian pilgrims we took on that time in Jaffa who took pity on us and passed out some of their fruit after it began to go rotten?"

The Genoan spat. He didn't like Moslems. "There'll be no kind passenger coming aboard today.... I could tell you something if I wanted to...."

The Genoan had been unshackled that morning and taken aft while the captain, who was negotiating with a Kaffa slave dealer for oarsmen to replace dead or moribund *galeòtti*, reassigned his free rowers. Either the deal had not gone through or the captain had underestimated his needs because the Genoan, to his disgust, had been brought back to the bench and chained again after several hours. But while lingering at the sterncastle, he must have had the opportunity to pick up some shore gossip.

"What are you talking about?" Sandro said.

"The Venetian stench in my nostrils. It's suddenly gotten stronger."

He bared blackened gums, enjoying some secret joke at Sandro's expense.

"If you have something to say, say it," Sandro said.

The Genoan's toothless grin suddenly turned into a grimace of pain as the Turk seized his upper arm and squeezed it.

"Yes, you tell us, eh?" the Turk said.

"Finiscila!" the Genoan squealed. The Turk released him and he rubbed his arm. "It's only that the passenger who's coming aboard today is a Venetian. Some rich lord."

"What?" Sandro said. "You must be mistaken."

The weasely little man looked apprehensively at the Turk. "No mistake," he said sullenly. "They're preparing quarters for him now in the poop. He won't have anything but the best. He's bought a tenth of the cargo space, and they're treating him like royalty. He's loading some choice items that came overland from Tana."

Sandro felt a constriction in his chest that made it difficult to breathe. He had not thought about his homeland for a long time; his former life of wealth and privilege seemed like a dream. "A Venetian? What's he doing here, shipping goods through the Genoese? Why isn't he sailing with the Galley of Romania?"

"I don't know," the other said, nursing his arm. "Leave me alone."

"What cargo is he loading?"

"What's it to you, galeòtto? Ow!" Another squeeze from the Turk set him to babbling again. "Silk, I suppose. And slaves. I saw them chalking out spaces for slaves on the cargo deck."

Sandro fell silent. He had already known the answers. The Galley of Romania would not be sailing from Venice on its annual voyage for another couple of months. The unknown merchant would be an unscrupulous trader, getting the jump on his fellow Venetians. Luxury goods could be offloaded somewhere past Constantinople and be transferred to marginally legal Venetian shipping to get it past the customs gauntlet in the Adriatic. Slaves were another matter. They could be transshipped from Crete to evade Venetian import restrictions altogether. Crete was a thriving center for the reshipment of slaves to the Moorish lands and western Europe, and the Genoese captain would be making a stop there.

It was not surprising that a renegade Venetian would be using a Genoese galley to do his dirty work—particularly a shady vessel like this one. Never mind the raids on unprotected Venetian shipping by the Genoese colonies at Kaffa and Tana. Never mind that the Galley of Romania plundered Genoese ships when it caught them in the Sea of Azov. The Genoese traders, like their Venetian counterparts, were from the aristocratic families with capital, apart from the occasional rich cittadino trying to buy his way into the nobility. Class was more important than nationality, and these patrician profiteers flocked together, circumventing their own nations' interests to line their own purses.

"Sssst, Venetian!" came a hiss from another bench. "Maybe your countryman will buy you from the captain and take you home with him."

It was meant maliciously—it came from the Genoese rower who had needled him about his eating habits—but for an incautious moment, Sandro's heart leapt. It was true that passengers took little interest in the stinking galley slaves who rowed them, preferring to stay far astern with the wind behind them—but was it inconceivable that the Venetian might become aware of his existence? That some appeal might be made to him, despite the risk of the *aguzzino*'s lash? The number of families listed in the Book of Gold was limited, and any Venetian, noble or not, would recognize the illustrious name of the House of Cavalli . . . might even look beyond the shaved head and hollow cheeks and recognize Sandro!

Then he slumped over his oar once more. Despair flooded back as the words of the black crow in Falco's dungeon came back to him: He was lucky that the Council of Ten had not got its hands on him. The punishment reserved for parricides was unspeakable. He had been tried and convicted in absentia, and there was no appeal. "Don't insist on your identity," the crow had warned him.

He had taken the Lombard's advice. Even in this floating hell, far from the long arm of the Tribunal, he had kept his name concealed. He would die one day at his oar. But a worse fate awaited him in Venice.

He spat angrily to rid himself of the sour taste of hope. What had he been thinking of? Suppose—the Tribunal's terrible vengeance aside—that he *had* succeeded against all odds in throwing himself at the feet of this double-dealing Venetian who trafficked on the sly with Genoans and other enemies of the state? Then what? An unscrupulous merchant like that would not be overly anxious to bring a galley slave back with him to advertise his misdeeds.

Glumly, he stared shoreward, down the gray length of the stone pier. A line of longshoremen and camels was picking its way toward the galley. The camels were heaped high with bales and boxes. The Venetian's goods were about to be loaded.

For the next several hours the galley resounded with the bawl of overseers, the slap of sandaled feet against deck boards, the raucous complaints of camels at the end of the pier. The slaves came last—women and children, mostly, and Tatars by the look of them. The khan had no objection to selling his own people. In Venice, Tatars were thought to make the best household servants; like dumb animals, they could be trained to a few simple commands, and they got along on less. Sandro supposed it was the same in other cities.

Sandro watched as they were herded down the hatches to the cargo deck below. They were a stoic lot, with little wailing, even from the children. The blacksmiths followed with buckets of glowing coals, and for the next hour there was the sound of hammering on iron and the smell of scorched metal. The cargo deck must have been crowded by now, because there was no room for about a dozen of the slaves. These were chained aft, where a couple of rowers' benches had been removed for the sheep pens. Over the loud protests of the ship's cooks, the pens were squeezed into part of the kitchen space to make more room for the slaves. Even so, it took some clever juggling by the cargo master.

The last of the Venetian's bundles and chests were stowed above deck with the private cargo of the officers and seamen. The cargo master, assisted by a wizened little man in a turban who must have been the Venetian's factor in Kaffa, tagged everything and saw to the stringing of rope enclosures.

"We're riding too low in the water already," Sandro's Genoese oarmate muttered. "The captain's been greedy."

A Tunisian rower on the next bench forward craned his neck around and said in bad Italian, "Are you worried about having to row harder, Christian dog?"

"He'll row as hard as he has to," another Moor laughed. "The Turk will see to that."

"A heavy ship will make it harder for us to get away from Moorish corsairs!" the Genoan flared. "But that's what you Saracen bastards hope for, isn't it? You think you'd be set free. Well, think again! Pirates are always short of galley slaves, and they don't bother looking at a man's *zib* to see if he's circumcised."

"The captain's taking some extra fighting men aboard for the voyage home," said a big Spaniard—a Morisco who had been found out by the Inquisition and sentenced to the galleys; he had been bought for a song by the captain in Sicily. "He's going to join up with two more Genoese galleys past the Horn."

"You don't know what you're talking about," scoffed another rower.

"I do—I heard two of the crossbowmen talking!" the Spaniard protested.

Sandro listened dully. The Mediterranean must be heating up, he thought, for the captain to take such precautions. There had been rumors of a new soldan in Egypt. Perhaps he wouldn't be so lenient about Christian depredations on his shipping as the last one had been. It was always a delicate balance between hostilities and trade. The Genoese captain paid bribes to the soldan's officials at Cairo and Alexandria, but that didn't stop him from behaving like a corsair himself when he caught smaller or less heavily armed Moslem vessels outside of protected waters. On this very voyage, in fact, he'd rammed an Egyptian vessel in the Sicilian strait, put the crew to the sword, and transferred as much cargo as he could from the slowly sinking hulk.

Beside Sandro, the massive body of the Turk shifted on the bench. "Here he comes now, your man from Venice," he grunted.

At the gangplank lowered from the stern pavilion, a man in a flamboyant red cloak was being helped on board by ship's officers. His profile was hidden from view by an extravagant hat that flopped down on one side. Behind him, left to struggle aboard as best they could, came two men in more somber dress.

The Venetian must have been an impatient one, waving aside the captain's amenities, because he did not accompany the officers into the sterncastle. Instead, he must have called for his factor, who shortly thereafter came scurrying out of the hold with the cargo officer close behind him.

Some sort of discussion ensued, with much agitated gesticulating by the factor. The participants were partially concealed from Sandro by a reefed yard that slanted athwart the deck, but he could see the factor's flapping arms and the disembodied hose of the others.

"What are you looking at, *canàglia*?" said a voice from above. "Do you need extra duty, like mending sails?"

A patrolling *aguzzino*, looking for a place to lay his whip, was passing by. Sandro gave him a measured stare, just to keep his self-respect, then made an elaborate show of lounging back and staring between his feet at his footrest. As soon as the *aguzzino* passed, Sandro was once again peering over rows of naked backs and through piles of deck cargo to see what he could see.

The gorgeously dressed Venetian was moving with his small entourage down the central deck to inspect the stowage of his merchandise. He was still too far away for Sandro to hear what he was saying. He stopped at each iron-bound chest to check the locks and made the harried factor search through a thick sheaf of bills of lading for the location of every sack and bale. The cargo master trailed along in offended dignity.

As the party drew nearer, Sandro tensed. No conscious intention formed in his mind. If he thought of doing anything, it was to avert his face in case the Venetian happened to glance his way—though it was hardly conceivable that anyone would notice a filthy galley slave—or, even if by some chance he did, see anything in the hardened and haggard face to connect it with that of some unmarked youth he might have glimpsed two or more years ago on the Rialto or the Piazza San Marco.

A hand touched his arm.

"Don't do it, Venetian," the Turk said softly in Arabic.

Sandro jumped. "Do what, for God's sake?" he said. "I'm not crazy."

It was only then that he realized how tightly drawn he had been—enough so that the Turk could read something reckless in the poised lines of his body.

The hand withdrew. "*Mumtaz.* That's fine then. No good could come of it. It's when they notice us that the trouble begins."

"What's it to you?" Sandro said angrily. "Why don't you take your own advice?"

The Turk bared yellow tusks. It was as close to a smile

as Sandro had ever seen from him. "I think of myself, not you, infidel. I don't want to have to pull for two while you recover from a flogging. It would be worse if you died from it. I'd have to break in some new weakling just when you're starting to measure up."

Their Genoan benchmate darted a suspicious look at them, trying to comprehend what was being said. But the Arabic speakers at the nearby oars started hissing back and forth. The Turk had never before exerted himself to show the least human warmth to anyone. For him to bestow even this qualified endorsement on a rowing partner—a Christian dog, at that—was unheard of. "Can it be," whispered one of the braver ones, "that the Turk's going soft?"

The flurry of whispers suddenly ceased as the Venetian passenger and the group with him approached. "I assure you, Signor Cavalli . . ." the cargo master was saying.

Startled, Sandro snapped his head up and saw Maffeo's face under the foppish Venetian hat.

"Maffeo, is it you?" he cried and leapt to his feet. The chain around his ankle checked his momentum, and he fell sprawling.

The Turk, his expression gone stony again, shrugged and looked away. The Genoan cringed from Sandro, to be as far away from him as possible when the lash came singing down.

Sandro scrambled to his feet, climbing to the top of the bench and pulling at the chain. For a moment he found himself staring directly into his brother's eyes. "Maffeo, don't you know me? It's me, Sandro!"

The shock showed in Maffeo's face. Then he took a step backward. "Who is that man?" he said. "Can't you keep your slaves under control?"

"A thousand apologies, *signore*," the cargo master was saying. "Shall we go on? There's one more bale of yours up forward."

"No, I'll take your word for it. Just have my *rappresentante* check it off." He turned on his heel and walked quickly back to the stern of the ship. After a moment the two more soberly dressed Venetians who had come with him, casting a last perplexed stare at Sandro over their shoulders, followed.

And then the *aguzzino* was on Sandro with all his fury. "You whoreson!" he shouted. "I'm going to kill you!"

The first blow of the whip knocked Sandro flat. He cried out as a streak of fire flashed across his naked back. Blinded by pain, he tried to get up, but the next slashing cut sent him sprawling again. He lay there, unable to move, while the blows rained down. The world turned into a continuous red blur of pain, but Sandro continued to call out Maffeo's name until he lost consciousness.

The sudden shock of a bucket of seawater across his lacerated back lifted Sandro out of blackness into sunlight and raw agony.

"*La teharak*—don't move!" the Turk said. He grabbed Sandro's arms and wrestled him down again. "Here, you, cockroach, hold his wrists."

Sandro found himself forced to a crouching position with his arms draped over the shaft of a shipped oar, his wrists pinioned, and the Turk's heavy paw on the top of his head clamping him down.

"Hold still," the Turk said gruffly. "This is a deep one. The bastard cut you almost to the ribs."

A molten river of anguish poured into Sandro's wounds. He yelled aloud and thrashed around, but he was weak as a kitten, and even the Genoan had no trouble holding him still. The Turk worked quickly, with surprising gentleness and deftness, sponging Sandro's torn back and shoulders. The smell of vinegar and salt was sharp in Sandro's nostrils as he tried to throw himself from side to side, moaning. An eternity later it was over, and Sandro knelt leaning across the oar with his back throbbing and afire.

"Here, drink this. The Genoan cockroach was persuaded that he didn't want to keep it for himself."

The neck of a bottle was forced between Sandro's crusted lips. He gulped down the sour wine eagerly, though it was as close to being vinegar as the stuff that had salved his back.

"You don't have to finish it all," the Genoan complained.

"Shut up, louse," the Turk said.

They let Sandro sit up. Every move was pure anguish. "Thirty-three cuts," the Turk told him. "I've seen men die from fifty. You're lucky the *aguzzino* was too mad to have you tied to the mast where he could get at you more conveniently. He was going to finish the job after you woke up and could feel it, but the captain came down to have a look and told him it was enough. Galley slaves don't come so cheap that he was willing to sacrifice one just to appease a passenger—even one who's paying as much freight as the Venetian."

He looked at Sandro quizzically but didn't say anything further. The Genoan opened his mouth once or twice, but a look at the Turk's closed face made him decide to keep silent. After an interval he worked up the courage to retrieve what was left of the bottle of wine and gulp down the dregs. A buzzing had started at the benches, which the Turk loftily ignored. Sandro caught a whisper in Arabic of *"akhu-uh"*—"his brother"—and knew he had been raving while unconscious. It would be all through the rowers' deck by now.

An inch at a time, he eased himself into a position that seemed to offer the least torment and took in his surroundings. The sun was in his face, hanging at the level of the main yard. He must have been out for hours. He had missed the pomp and ceremony of casting off, the trumpet fanfare, the rowing out of the harbor. The Turk must have pulled for him. The galley was under sail now with a stiff westerly wind behind it. Sandro could see the Crimean shore to starboard, a greenish-gray line that indicated that they were well out to sea, following the coast to its western extremity, where they would pick up the warm westward current that would carry them to the Bosphorus. A galley slave learned the winds and currents well; they were the currency that bought off aching muscles.

He waited through the hot morning for Maffeo to come, fighting off delirium. Once or twice he crumpled, and the Turk hoisted him back to the bench and propped him against the oar.

"He thought I was dead," Sandro said to the Turk's immobile profile. "You could see the surprise in his face. He can't have known that Falco sold me for a galley slave for a little extra money. I'll tell him it doesn't matter anymore. I can't go back—he knows that. The House of Cavalli is his. He's welcome to it. I'm no danger to him now. He can buy me out of this—give me enough money to get me to France or Spain. He's had time to think it over now. I'll tell him he'll never see me again."

The Turk looked at him with something like pity. "He won't come, Venetian. Who do you think asked the *aguzzino* to tie you to the mast and flog you to death?"

Hot tears ran down Sandro's face. He hadn't realized he was still capable of feeling something.

"No!" he cried. "Shut up, you Saracen swine, or I'll kill you!"

The nearby benches went silent as the rowers waited to see what the Turk would do. The Genoan shriveled up into a protective ball to be out of the way of any violence.

The Turk spoke ruminatively, as if he were talking to himself. "In Damascus, after the soldan and his ameers deserted us to run back to Cairo, we fought on without commanders. We fought Tamerlane to a draw and had only to wait him out. And then we were betrayed a second time. Tamerlane took by words and cunning what he could not take by force. He parleyed with the *qadhi* Ibrahim and the leading citizens. He promised that if they opened the gates of the city to him, no one would be harmed, provided they raised a fund of a million gold dinars for him and accepted a Mongol governor. When his troops were inside the city, he made the *qadhi* sign a bond for ten million dinars. Then he gave Damascus to his troops to plunder. They picked it bare. The men were killed slowly for the sport of the Mongols. They were hung head down over fires . . . sliced to pieces a little at a time . . . tied to posts and used as targets for horsemen. To add spice to the sport, the wives and daughters of the victims were brought to the public squares to be raped before their dying eyes." The Turk's face remained expressionless. "I was a young man, a sergeant of ten. I had a wife and a baby daughter in Damascus. The baby was torn in half in a Mongol contest of strength. My wife did not survive the first fifty soldiers. They grew annoyed at my silence. A Mongol trooper ran me through with a lance. They thought I was dead and lost interest. They left me hanging there. I did not move all day. In the night I let myself down. I worked the lance head free and plugged the flow of blood, and bound myself. The bodies were piled in heaps by then. I found a hole to crawl to and hid there the next five days. By then the Mongols were picking the bones of the city. They began to regret wasting so much plunder. They rounded up all the men and women they could find who could still walk and roped them together to be sold as slaves. The smallest children and the babies were to be left behind to die when the city was set on fire. The Mongols did not think I was worth taking, but when they pricked me with spears, I walked. They took me along out of curiosity to see how long I would last. I walked behind Mongol horses all the way to Kaffa. Hate kept me alive."

The Turk's stunning tale penetrated even the black curtain of despair that had blotted out the world for Sandro. The general history of the Turk had been known more or less throughout the benches—his bill of sale, after all, had represented him as one of the *mamluk* defenders of Damascus, and there were few secrets on a galley—but not the details.

"Hate for the Mongols?" Sandro asked, moved to pity in spite of himself.

"No, hate for the Egyptians and the Damascans."

"Listen, Turk, I . . ."

"Shut up, Venetian. You're stupid. I told you not to do it. I'd punish you myself, but I'd rather have you row sooner. You've got too many bruises already."

In mid afternoon the breeze began to fail. The big triangular sails emptied and fell slack. The *aguzzini* began running along the catwalk to prepare the slaves for rowing. "Get those oars in the water, you bastards! Look alive now!" There was a preliminary tattoo on the drum that would give them the rhythm when they got started.

The Turk reached across and placed Sandro's mangled hands on the shaft of the oar. "Listen," he said. "Keep your hands there and let the oar take some of your weight. Try to look as if you're rowing. It will hurt. Can you do it?"

"I . . . I think so. But not if we have to stand and fall back to pull harder."

The *aguzzino* who had whipped Sandro to insensibility came by to have a look. "Can he row?" he said.

"He can row," the Turk replied.

The *aguzzino* laughed. "You'll see to it, won't you, infidel?" he said.

Sandro gritted his teeth against the agony that sitting straight caused him. The *aguzzino* turned to him.

"And you, Venetian scum. I don't care if you think you're the *pope*'s brother. Here, you're my meat."

Sandro started to growl a reply, but at that moment the Turk suddenly let the oar drop an inch and the words became a gasp of pain.

The *aguzzino* chewed a splinter and waited. When nothing further was forthcoming, he said, "Cat got your tongue? Your fellow countryman's still trying to convince the *capitanio* that you committed an act of mutiny and that he'd better execute you now as an example to the other *galeotti*." He spat out the splinter. "Row well, Venetian, and maybe we won't feed you to the fishes yet. . . ."

The drumbeats started. The *aguzzino* stayed to watch the first stroke, and then he was off to take up his duties. Above, barefoot sailors were reefing the big sails. The oars dipped and rose in unison, and the huge vessel sliced through the blue waters.

For Sandro, though he could not exert the same muscle power as his straining companions, each straightening of his back brought a fiery reminder of his condition. At that, he thought, he was lucky that this was not a Venetian state galley, where the oarsmen rowed *alla sensile*—each man to a single oar, in banks of three—instead of *al scaloccio*, three men to an oar. He would never have been able to keep up this pretense otherwise.

"Put your back into it, you Genoese cockroach!" the Turk rumbled. "You've got to take up some of the slack."

And for a few strokes the Genoan would heave a little

harder. But it was obvious that it was the Turk who was doing most of the work of compensating for Sandro.

"*Shukran* . . ." Sandro said hesitantly. "Thanks, Turk. . . ."

The Turk whirled on him in a fury. "Piss on your thanks, Venetian! You're still a stupid piece of dung! You were about to invite that strutting dog to use the whip on you again, weren't you? You haven't learned a thing."

Stung, Sandro retreated to his private climate of pain. Each rise and fall of the oar he was leaning on was excruciating. But after a while, as the pain became predictable, it also became supportable. Though it got no better, in some strange way he was able to put himself—a lightheaded and distant Sandro—above it. Cautiously, he began to test his strength on the oar. Soon—though he was by no means pulling his weight—he was making a definite contribution. The Turk looked at him once but said nothing.

The Genoan felt it, too, and started to slack off, until a threat from the Turk renewed his former pitch of effort.

By the time the *aguzzino* made his rounds again, things looked almost normal, though it was only the Turk's bonecracking exertion, taking part of the load off Sandro, that made it possible. The *aguzzino* grunted and went away.

Sandro rowed blindly, a dull fury rising in him. What the *aguzzino* had said to him might have been a lie, calculated to provoke him to action, but he did not think so. The bile rose in his throat. In his mind he could feel his strong rower's fingers closing around his brother's throat . . . could see Maffeo's sullen face turning black.

"Yes, I've learned," he hissed *galeòtto*-fashion through clenched teeth. "I'll kill him one day. Somehow I'll find a way."

"You're starting to hate, Venetian," the Turk said. "That's good. It will keep you alive."

By the time the ship docked at Constantinople, Sandro's back had healed. His questing fingers could feel the deep grooves and hard ridges the knotted cords had left. He did not have to imagine what they looked like; he had seen them often enough on other men. The marks on the Turk were worse—a regular gridwork of raised flesh with deep valleys at the intersections—but they were old. The Turk had not been flogged—really flogged, not counting the occasional cut or two from an *aguzzino* forcing the pace in an emergency—for years. Looking at the Turk, Sandro knew he would carry his own scars to the grave. Even if by some unimaginable miracle he were released and took his place in the world of men again, anyone looking at his naked back would know he had once been a *galeòtto*.

It had been an uneventful trip across the Black Sea to the Bosphorus. It was not yet the season for the heavily armed Venetian state galleys, and the Genoan merchantman was well-enough equipped with cannon and crossbowmen to deal with casual raiders like itself. The serious corsairs, both Christian and Moslem, mostly prowled the well-traveled seas beyond the Dardanelles.

They lay over at Constantinople for only four days, anchored under the thousand-year-old seawalls and mighty towers of Byzantium, while the overcrowded hold of the ship was further stuffed with cargo. A few of Maffeo's slaves had died below deck during the voyage from Kaffa, but Maffeo made no effort to take advantage of the extra space that he still had a lease on; the Genoese captain gave him partial recompense and took on some additional bales of silk and gold thread.

"The Cavalli firm has an agent in Constantinople," Sandro confided to the Turk's unresponsive profile, "but I don't think he even let him know he was here, in case word got back to the *bailo*."

The agent, Carlo Cappello, served a number of Venetian clients, and was a gossip. The *bailo*, the head of the Venetian trading colony in Constantinople, was directly responsible to the *Signoria*, and Maffeo would not want to attract the attention of the Council of Ten to his dealings with the Genoese.

Maffeo did make a few forays ashore, muffled in a black cloak, to sample the Byzantine nightlife, but he stayed aboard during business hours. Sandro caught sight of him from time to time, attending the thrice-daily religious services at the sterncastle or going to dine at the captain's table with the young nobles from among the officers and crossbowmen.

But a distant glimpse was all Sandro got; Maffeo never again ventured beyond the privileged boundaries of the poop deck.

"If I could get loose for five minutes, that's all it would take," Sandro brooded aloud. He spoke in Arabic for the Turk's benefit. The Genoan, he was sure, carried tales during the intervals when he was unshackled, trying to curry favor, but understood no Arabic beyond the usual few overworked obscenities. "I could get to the sterncastle before anyone realized what was happening and break his neck before they could stop me."

He did not care that the Turk failed to respond—that he feigned not to hear. He knew the Turk was listening anyway. He had to vent the consuming bitterness that was gnawing at his vitals or die, and the Turk, more than anyone else, would know what he meant.

He spun out his musings, knowing they were only daydreams.

"It's not impossible. It could happen that we got a new permanent benchmate, and I might grab the hammer and strike off my shackles and bowl the *aguzzino* over. Or I could steal a file—once I saw the ship's carpenter carelessly leave his toolbox almost within reach of the benches. Or it might happen that they'd need a work party for some emergency that came up and themselves strike the shackles of a few of us to work under guard. I could bide my time...."

The Genoan was dozing after the midday ration of bean soup and hardtack, but some of the nearby Arabic-speakers were following Sandro's fantasies for their entertainment value.

"You've got sunstroke, infidel," jeered one of them. "No one's ever gotten loose. The thing can't be done."

"You don't have the stomach to kill a brother—if he is a brother, dog of an unbeliever," another Moor baited him. "That's why you talk about it. You can only talk."

"Even if such a thing were possible, you'd only die for it, *Maseehiyeen*," cautioned another. "They'd peel you to the bone in front of us."

"It would be worth it!" Sandro flared, then fell into black silence.

Later that night, when the rowers slept, the Turk leaned across the supine form of the Genoan and said in a low-keyed whisper meant for Sandro alone "They were right, Venetian. You'd never reach him. And then you'd die for nothing."

Sandro held up a bunched handful of chain and shook it at the Turk. "What's this but a death? I'd just as soon get it over with."

"Forget it, Venetian."

"*Ya salehm!*" Sandro said in mock amazement. "Did I hear that? Are you turning soft, *Turkeeya*, like the Egyptians you profess to hate so much? Aren't you the one who told me to hate?"

The Turk did not reply, but he did not turn away as he usually did. Sandro could hear his heavy breathing.

"You know how I could do it, don't you?" Sandro said. "You've figured out a way. You could get loose yourself any time you want to. But you're waiting till the time is right—maybe till we're close enough to a Moorish shore for you to swim for it. And you don't want me to spoil it for you."

"Shut up, Venetian," the big man said uneasily.

Sandro drew a breath. "I was right, then."

"Shut up, I said, or I'll snap your neck."

"No, you won't. You don't want to draw attention to yourself. They might look at your chains and notice something. Is that it?"

The Turk's enormous hands flexed. Sandro stared unflinchingly into his face from only a foot away. A bright crescent of moon, hanging above the great dome of Saint Sophia beyond the seawalls, drew silver outlines on all the ridges of the Turk's battered face. Sandro could see the cords of his neck quiver.

"You're afraid." Sandro taunted him deliberately. "You've been a slave so long you're afraid to be free. That's why you haven't gotten yourself loose yet. It's not that you're afraid you'll die in the attempt. You're afraid you'll succeed."

"I'm not afraid, Venetian."

Somewhere in the dark a rower moaned in his sleep. "Mother . . ." he cried in Arabic.

Sandro and the Turk froze. When all was quiet again, Sandro whispered, "Help me, Turk."

"I'd be helping you to die, Venetian."

Sandro felt a tingle of excitement. Until now he had not been sure, but the Turk's surly words were an admission.

"That's my business. What do you care? You can even use it as a diversion. I'll work things out with you beforehand."

The Turk rubbed his shovel chin with a chained paw, but said nothing in response.

"I swear I'll be patient," Sandro pressed him. "I'll wait for a good time . . . arrange it so that you're not implicated. What is it? You have a file that you've hidden, is that it? Or a piece of hacksaw blade?"

"There's no file, Venetian."

The Turk tried to turn away, but Sandro held him. The Turk's upper arm was like a carved piece of oak, with no give to the flesh.

"Tell me, or I swear I'll give you away. You can't afford to have the *aguzzino* examine your chain, can you? You've been working at it for a long time in secret. One pull and the weak place comes apart. You slip overboard in the middle of the night and swim for shore or a Moorish ship and hope a crossbowman doesn't get you."

In spite of himself, Sandro felt his hand on the Turk's shoulder tremble. It was not easy to blackmail a man who has bided his time for twenty years. He was inviting the Turk to strangle him some night in his sleep. But he had to take the gamble.

The misery was plain in the Turk's voice when he spoke. "I can't swim, Venetian. So you're mistaken."

He shrugged off Sandro's grip and retreated to his end of the bench.

The Genoan stirred. "Can't a man sleep?" he complained.

Sandro waited until he heard the Genoan's snores again. "We're not finished, Turk," he said.

CHAPTER 11

In the morning the galley sailed from Constantinople. Once past the tremendous chain that guarded the Golden Horn, with the walls and towers of the Genoese colony at Pera behind them, they were fair game for Venetian warships. The emperor Manuel II Palaeologus, heir to a shrinking Byzantine empire that now was reduced to little more than Constantinople itself, enforced an uneasy truce in his own territorial waters, but here, beyond the emperor's feeble reach, the Genoese were on their own.

With lookouts posted in the upper rigging to keep a sharp eye peeled for unfriendly sails, the galley proceeded westward under both wind and oars, making all possible speed to get through the Sea of Marmara quickly.

The rowers worked to exhaustion. But extra rations of cheese and wine kept up their strength. There was even meat in their bean soup again, despite the expense. The whips of the *aguzzini* cracked, touching up laggards. Even the Turk, pulling mightily, took a small cut or two. Sandro escaped with a few light flicks that seared like the devil, which was the overseers' intention, but that did not open up old stripes to the point of disabling him.

The captain allowed them a rest after the galley negotiated the narrow constriction of the Dardenelles without incident. The Turkish fortress at Gallipoli allowed them to pass without firing a shot. Only a few years ago the Turks and Venetians had fought a terrible sea battle here, but the new sultan, Murad II, seemed inclined to let Christian shipping pass unmolested while he slowly built up his presence here and further crowded the diminishing empire of Manuel Palaeologus.

The Aegean was a Venetian pond, but there was more sea room here, and the captain continued to let the oarsmen conserve their strength. The arrangements he had made at Constantinople proved accurate, and the ship picked up the promised Genoese convoy in the waters north of the isle of Lesbos.

The fleet consisted of three round ships escorted by another galley. The captain grumbled a little, according to the sailors' gossip overheard by the rowers: "They need our protection more than we need theirs." Still, as the captain admitted, there was safety in numbers, and the round ships, though slow and clumsy, carried cannon of their own.

The greater part of the day was devoted to an exchange of captains' courtesies. The visiting back and forth and the festivities lasted well into the night. A great banquet was held at the galley's poop, with music and dancing. The entertainment was provided by musicians drawn from all five ships. Sandro could have wept at the sweetness of the sounds of the viols and pipes as they came floating through the night air, playing the old familiar dances and *canzóni*. The whole facade of the sterncastle was ablaze with torches and candles, like a ball in the old days, and Sandro was able to pick out Maffeo, splendid in velvets and silks, as he danced a slow *pavána* with the Genoese noblemen.

In the morning the five ships lifted anchor and sailed south, to thread their way through the Greek islands toward Crete. Rowing was light with the Aegean currents carrying them along, and the big lateen sails did most of the work. Rations grew skimpy again, but Sandro did not care. He could not have distinguished hunger from the gnawing in his guts as he thought of Maffeo, sitting at his ease in the sterncastle.

It was a week later, as the ships sailed past the southern tip of the Peloponnesus into Mediterranean waters, when the Turk spoke to Sandro.

He waited until the middle of the night, when the Genoan huddled asleep on the bench between them, and no sound came from the surrounding darkness except snores and the whimpers of bad dreams. Sandro was half asleep himself, his head rolling on his chest, lulled by the rocking of the ship and the creak of the masts. A sensed bulk leaning over him made his eyes fly open, and he thought for a moment that the Turk had decided to kill him after all.

Before he could move to defend himself, a stone hand clamped his wrist and the Turk spoke an inch from his ear, too low for anyone to hear.

"All right, Venetian. I'll help you."

It was a diamond. The Turk had kept it hidden on his person or within his body for four years. It had spilled unnoticed from a treasure chest stowed on deck by a careless merchant and rolled toward the scuppers, where the Turk had palmed it. As quick and deft as he had been, he had been seen by one of his benchmates. The man had tried to steal it from him in the night, and the Turk had killed him by smashing his head once against the lead-weighted handle of the oar.

He had almost died himself for that. He had been sentenced to a hundred lashes, and the only thing that had saved him from receiving two hundred, which would certainly have killed him, was the fact that no other galley slave could be found who would say that he saw the Turk kill the man.

As it was, a hundred lashes was usually considered a death sentence for those who received them. There were sometimes survivors, but they were rarely good for anything again. Before the flogging the Turk managed to hide the diamond by swallowing it. Three days later, half delirious from pain and loss of blood, his back torn to ribbons, he had retrieved the diamond from his excrement.

It was the last serious flogging he ever got. He had something to live for now. Though he was still not a man to be crossed, it was noticed and whispered about that his behavior had suddenly improved—that he no longer sought to provoke punishment, as formerly. The *aguzzino* who had administered the flogging boasted that he had tamed the Turk.

A diamond was better than a file. He could never have concealed a file from the *aguzzini* or his benchmates for any length of time. He kept the diamond knotted in a tuck of his breechclout when he wanted to get at it easily; more often he concealed it in his rectum. In an emergency—if he had reason to fear a body search or another flogging, or if a fever threatened to send him off his head—he could always swallow it again. He had done that twice since the first time.

He told the story to Sandro over the next few nights, a few economical whispers at a time, whenever they could get their heads together without drawing attention. From the bare outline Sandro was able to fill in the gaps.

"One scratch at a time," the Turk said. "Find the same place by touch. Only use your wrist. Let your arm hang down as if it were resting by your ankle, and don't move it."

The Turk had worked on the same weak place in the same link for the last two years, until the minute gap was deep enough for him to pull it apart with one mighty twist. He had tested it, then bent it together again. He had retrieved every crumb of metal that had flaked off so that not even the tiniest clue remained of his labors.

Knowing what to look for, Sandro could detect the spot by daylight. It was only a hairline, filled in with a paste the Turk made of anything handy—a fragment of bean mush from his ration, spittle, his own excrement. The salvaged crumbs of metal had been kneaded into the paste, so that there was a glint of iron to fool the eye. But the smear of human waste—not unusual on the ankle chains of the rowers—would discourage close inspection by an *aguzzino*.

The Turk doled out the diamond to Sandro a few hours at a time, in a quick exchange with their hands under the bench or in a jostling confusion that distracted the attention of the Genoan with a shove or a bump. Sandro never made the mistake of trying to keep the stone longer than he was supposed to have it. Once every few days the Turk would find an excuse to grope around in the vicinity of the footrest—ostentatiously scratching a foot or retrieving a fallen crumb of biscuit—and, brushing the chain as if by accident, check Sandro's progress with a thumbnail.

"You stop when I say," he informed Sandro. "Leave it so that only I can pull it apart. I decide. I do it for you when the right time comes. . . ."

"Agreed," Sandro said.

He worked steadily, night after night, fighting sleep, until his wrist gave out from the small repetitive movement and his forearm became a knot of agony. He was working against time now, as the galley drew closer to Malta. There would be a trading stop at Malta, then Tunis—whose ruler still tolerated Genoese and Venetian merchantmen despite a growing exasperation over the depredations of Frankish pirates. Once through the strait of Sicily, on the last leg of the voyage home to Genoa, Sandro's opportunity would be lost forever. Maffeo, he was sure, would disembark at Tunis with the last of his cargo and take passage back to Venice on a Venetian ship with his illegal profits in his pockets.

Tunis, he had concluded, was where the Turk intended to make his own move. There would be no more opportunities for him either once the galley entered the Tyrrhenian Sea on its way up the coast of Italy. If he could not swim, as he claimed, he would have to make his escape in a port. In Tunis he would not have to run very far. The rampaging Knights of Saint John had recently seized several Moorish passengers from a Venetian ship on the high seas. And though Venice had gotten them freed after threatening the Knights with military force, the king of Tunis was in a boil. He would never return an escaped Moslem slave to a Christian captain.

Finally, with Malta's rocky shore disappearing behind

them, there came a night when Sandro thought he felt
the link give fractionally. He had not thought that the
minute scratching sounds he was making were audible,
but the Turk must have sensed that they had stopped. In
an instant he was groping past the ankles of the sleeping
Genoan and testing Sandro's work with the ball of his
thumb.

"That's enough," the Turk said. "You give back the
stone now."

The storm struck in the narrow part of the strait, when
the little fleet was halfway between Tunis and Sicily's
western tip. Until now they had hugged Sicily's coast for
protection, keeping distance between themselves and the
island of Pantelleria in the strait because of the corsairs'
bases that infested the strategic and disputed speck of
land, but now the dangers of Moorish waters had to be
faced. So the galley was out of sight of land when the
weather abruptly changed.

One moment the sky was clear and blue, the water
sparkling. Then, without warning, the sky at once began
to turn dark. In a quarter hour the sun was hidden from
view.

The Turk lifted his big head and sniffed the air like a
mastiff. "*Kibeer,*" he said, "a big one," and returned to the
rhythm of rowing without missing a beat.

Sandro looked around, too. There was a brittleness in
the air; that must have been what the Turk was sniffing
at. The feel of the ship under him was different, too; the
hull was lifting and falling in a new and heavy swell.

"Here it comes now," the Turk said. "It's in a hurry."

He had lifted his head again to point the direction, and
Sandro followed his gaze. From the hidden coast of Africa to the southwest came a dark mass of cloud, rushing
across the water with incredible swiftness. Sandro saw a
bright twig of lightning leap through it, as if something
had opened the cloud a crack and revealed the radiance
inside.

The sailors were rushing back and forth on deck while
officers bawled orders. A dozen men scrambled into the

rigging to furl the sails. Sandro could feel the first edge of wind hit him, laden with warm droplets of water.

The helmsman was frantically trying to bring the ship about before the full force of the storm struck. A wild-eyed *aguzzino* raced down the catwalk, swinging his whip indiscriminately at the starboard rowers and screaming, "Back water, back water!" in an attempt to use the oars to help swing the ship around.

It was too late. The big sail caught the wind from the wrong side. It gave a mighty slap and spun around on its yard. Sandro saw the hapless men in the rigging flung outward, arms and legs flailing. Canvas flew into the wind in shreds. The raking spar swept more men off the deck, and then there was a huge crack as the mast snapped.

The ship gave a shudder and heeled over. Sandro was sure it would capsize. Rope ends from the torn rigging whipped back and forth, and the falling spar crushed a bench of rowers before trailing over the side with its tatters of sail.

Sailors with axes, clinging like flies to the tilted deck, hacked at ropes, cutting loose the trailing spar. The smaller sail went flapping into the wind like an enormous bat, but its spar was saved. A wall of water slammed into Sandro, taking his breath away. But then the ship righted itself, gushing water and wallowing heavily in the swell.

Coughing water, blinded by salt spray, Sandro felt the lash curl around his ribs. He looked up to see an *aguzzino* laying about him blindly. The howling wind tore away the sound of his voice, but his mouth formed the words, "Row, you bastards!"

The surviving oarsmen pulled for all they were worth, trying to keep the prow of the crippled galley headed into the wind. The ship pitched and rolled violently, picking its head up with difficulty after each plunge. A crash of waves kept the deck awash.

By morning the storm had blown itself out. The rowers lay exhausted over their oars. Their efforts had saved the ship.

The sun rose over a flat, calm sea. The sky was a brilliant blue, washed clean by rain. The ship floated low in the water, helpless and alone. There was not a sign of the other galley or the three round ships anywhere.

Sandro looked around at the other benches. He could see half a dozen dead bodies from where he sat—hit by debris, drowned in a few inches of water when they pitched forward and were unable to rise, or perhaps some hearts had simply burst. But their chains had prevented them from being washed overboard.

The sailors had fared worse. Sandro had seen a dozen of them being pitched into the sea in the terrible moment when the boom had jibed and the mast had snapped. More must have been lost afterward. Sandro could see no more than twenty seamen on deck—not enough to hoist the spare sail on the surviving yard. He could see several of them clambering around overhead, sorting out the damaged rigging.

"They'll need oarsmen to raise the yard," the Turk said softly. "Unless they can get some of those lady-handed crossbowmen to haul on a rope."

The ranks of the crossbowmen were depleted, too, from what Sandro could tell. The captain had them drawn up in front of the castle, giving them orders, and Sandro could count no more than fifteen. The mate had the weapons chest open, handing out bows and bolts to a few volunteers among the nobleman.

"They'd better get that sail up, or we row all the way to Tunis," Sandro said.

The *aguzzini* passed out wine and biscuit as a reward for the long, hard pull. Sandro stretched his sore body and took a gulp of the sour stuff.

"First they have to pump out the ship, *maseehiyeen*," one of the Moors said. "We must have opened some of our seams during the night."

Sandro nodded. He could feel how heavily the ship was sitting in the water; but they did not seem to be sinking, for which he thanked God.

An excited cry came from aloft. "Sail ho!"

Sandro could not see it at first. Then he spotted it coming up over the horizon: the tiny yellow crescent of a lateen sail, close-hauled against the wind and bellied out, coming toward them.

"That's no Christian ship," the Genoan muttered.

The captain had come to the same conclusion. He sent the crossbowmen and the cannoneers scurrying to their posts, then supervised the passing out of swords and pikes to passengers and members of the crew.

"Get some sail up!" the sailing master shouted at the foot of the undamaged mast, looking up at the sailors perched on the naked spar. But it was impossible to do anything quickly. The lines were a hopeless tangle, the yard would have to be lowered for the spare sail to be bent to it, and there were too few sailors for the job.

The drum started a ragged beat. "Row, damn you, row!" the chief *aguzzino* roared. The worn-out men at the benches, with groans and sobs, took up their oars again.

With the first stroke Sandro saw that it was hopeless. The waterlogged ship lumbered in the waves, too heavy to make much progress. The whips cracked down and the rowers begged for mercy. But hours of pumping were needed to make the galley seaworthy again.

The yellow sail grew. The Moslem rowers did not dare to cheer, but one of them leaned forward and whispered venomously, "We'll soon be freemen. And then we'll take our revenge on the infidel dogs who enslaved us."

A shiver went down Sandro's spine. The stories were told, like bedtime tales to comfort a child, when the *aguzzino* wasn't around: A Spanish captain, facing attack by an enemy galley, had been felled by his own steersman and thrown to the rowers. They had passed him from bench to bench, each taking a bite, until he was dead.

Beside Sandro, the Genoan moaned. "Get hold of yourself," Sandro said. "It's probably only a trader—a *boum* or a *baghla*. Even if they find us dead in the water, they'd be insane to attack us."

But as the other ship drew closer, the rise and fall of oars could be plainly seen. It was closing the gap too swiftly for it to be driven by sails alone.

"No, Venetian, it's a galley," the Turk said. "A fighting ship, and a large one."

"A corsair!" the Moslem behind Sandro crowed.

Sandro knew he was right. Barbary pirates were active in the area. They were disowned by the soldan and by the theoretically dependent rulers of Tunis and Tripoli, but they had no trouble unloading their booty in port.

"Don't celebrate yet," Sandro told him. "He's got to close with us first. When he sees how big we are and how many armed men we have, he may decide to look for easier prey."

A whip snapped across his shoulders. "Save your breath for rowing, *canàglia*," an *aguzzino* bellowed.

Sandro pulled with the rest. The injured ship moved sluggishly. At the mizzenmast the sailors had at last succeeded in lowering the spar, but even if they got the one sail hoisted, it wasn't going to make much difference.

At that moment a party of armed men came jostling down the catwalk on their way to the fighting platform forward, where the ram projected. Passengers were pressed into service. One of them was Maffeo, looking white-faced. He was carrying a crossbow and a quiver of bolts. His fine clothes were bedraggled, and he had a large bruise on his forehead, as if he had fallen or been struck by a piece of flying debris during the storm.

It was too much for Sandro. A blind rage boiled up in him, darkening his vision and making the veins of his forehead swell. He forgot that he had agreed to wait until the Turk released him, forgot that he was not strong enough to wrench free the half-severed link by himself.

With an animal howl he abandoned the oar and grasped the chain in his two hands. Bent into an arch, he strained until the cords of his body stood out and the overdeveloped muscles of his arms and shoulders popped. Under the brief concentrated tension the metal gave with a sudden jerk. The Turk had not realized just how strong two years of rowing had made him. Neither had he.

He sprang like a released bow and scrambled for the catwalk. Too late, a startled Turk snatched at a trailing length of chain. Sandro bowled over an armed volunteer who was in his way—one of the somber Venetians who had accompanied Maffeo—and bore Maffeo with him to the deck.

He might have killed Maffeo then and there if he had got his hands around his neck immediately, but, sobbing and blinded by tears, he wasted time by hammering fruitlessly at him, doing no real harm, as if they had been small boys again having a fight. When at last his hands closed around Maffeo's throat, Maffeo's frightened face swam at him in a blur, making him falter.

"Sandro, please . . ." his brother croaked, and the use of his name brought a gush of hot tears that stayed his encircling fingers for another second.

Then it was too late. The armed men were pawing at him, punching him, dragging him off Maffeo. He sent one of them flying. Then an *aguzzino* struck him behind the ear with the loaded butt of a whip. The circle of raw, furious faces around him suddenly shrank, as if he were falling down a well, and then he plunged into darkness.

A bucket of salt water slapped him awake. His head was throbbing desperately, and his body was sore in all the places where he must have been punched or kicked. He was dangling by his manacled wrists from the stub of the broken mast. Someone had nailed him there by the simple expedient of driving a spike through a center link of the chain into the oak. His toes barely brushed the deck, but he had been further immobilized by a rope passed around his waist.

The captain himself was standing there, his aristocratic face purple with anger. Beside him was a sailor with an empty bucket.

"I have no time to spare for you now, Venetian," the captain said tightly. "But you're going to regret the fact that you weren't killed outright. Because when we get out of this pickle, I'm going to have you flogged to death for all to see."

Sandro stared blankly at him, as impassive as the Turk. He was surprised that he felt no fear. There was just the dull hate.

The captain bit his lip. "I'd have expected rebellion from a Moor when the ship's in danger. But not a Christian, galley slave or not. You had nothing to gain. You started something, Venetian. You had few of the more foolish ones standing on their benches, convinced their moment had come. We snuffed it out quickly. Your infidel accomplices won't thank you. We have to keep them rowing now, but afterward we'll have the rotten apples crucified."

Sandro kept himself from looking for the Turk among the benches of rowers, not wanting to give the captain ideas. Nothing had been said about a sawed link, and the captain had not thought to question him about how he got loose. But if they survived the engagement with the corsair, they would be bound to inspect all the chains, most especially those of Sandro's benchmates.

He had spoiled it for the Turk—and botched it for himself as well. At this moment the Turk would be aching to kill him.

He looked out across the water and saw the yellow sail—no, sails, he could tell now, with one behind the other and some sort of a jib in front—considerably closer. A device of crossed scimitars was painted on them in red. The banks of oars were clearly visible on either side, churning the water to froth. A glint of brass meant a cannon. He had been unconscious for at least a half hour for the corsair to have closed the gap that much.

The captain lost interest in Sandro. With a last sour look, he rushed off to give orders. The pumps were still spewing foul water from the bilge, but the galley seemed as low in the water as ever. Now it lost even its sluggish headway as the sailing master tried to work the ship around by oars alone, both to present the bow cannon to the corsair and to avoid being rammed in the flank.

Crossbowmen were ranged along the top of the castle where they could rain down bolts on the deck of the corsair—Genoese and Venetian galleys tended to be taller than the Moslem copies of them. A lone crossbowman had been hoisted in a basket to the top of the mizzenmast, and another was bravely perched on the yard itself, like a bird.

Sandro twisted his head to see what was going on forward. The remaining crossbowmen had distributed themselves along the fighting platform—one of them on the narrow, planked top of the ram itself. Sandro couldn't tell if any of them was Maffeo. Crewmen with long pikes waited among them, ready to repel a boarding. The big bow cannon and the two smaller ones were in the process of being stuffed with scrap metal by the cannoneers; there would be time for one deck-raking blast if they were lucky.

The towering sails of the corsair blotted out the sun. Sandro could see half-naked men with scimitars clinging to the rigging. He braced himself for the coming crash. Lashed to the mast, exposed and vulnerable, unable to move, he swallowed hard as he waited for the Moor's cannon to spray the deck with shot.

All the cannon seemed to explode at once, both the pirate's and those of the Genoese galley. Sandro winced, deafened by the tremendous roar. He opened his eyes, still alive. The corsair had waited too long, fired at too-close range. From his lower hull the load of shot had flown too high and merely torn through the rigging. Sandro saw the two crossbowmen who had been stationed there fall like lead weights into the sea.

The Genoese blast had been more successful. It had strewn the deck with writhing bodies. Sandro could hear the screams of the wounded. Some of them were the Christian slaves at the rowers' benches, poor devils. Sandro could not take his eyes off the carnage on the deck. He saw the lower half of a body, a tangle of bloody guts spilling from what had been a waist. A pirate whose leg had been blown off rose from the deck on his remaining leg and, balancing himself upright, shook his scimitar at the Genoese galley. For the first time Sandro felt a stab of fear. These were not men; they were fiends out of hell.

The air hummed with arrows and crossbow bolts, like contending swarms of wasps. The crossbow's greater range was of no advantage at these close quarters; the pirates, with their curved Moorish bows of wood and bone, could get off twice as many arrows in the same time. Sandro saw a shaft thud into the body of a sailor who had been standing nearby with a pike. Another arrow embedded itself in the mast just above his head and vibrated there with a musical thrum.

There were only four men left alive on the fighting platform. One of them, incredibly, was the one who had stationed himself on the narrow spine of the ram. He flung his useless crossbow at the men crowding the prow of the enemy ship, now only yards away, and drew his sword.

The ships came together with a grinding sound. But the rams did not embed themselves. Instead, with a jolt that flung a couple of unwary brigands off the spars they straddled, the two hulls slid past each other with a scraping and splintering of planks. The Barbary captain had thrown rudder at the last moment. He didn't want to have to board the Genoan at a single, easily defended point.

Not all of the rowers had shipped their oars in time. There was a dreadful carnage as oars snapped and heavy boles drove backward to crush the chests of the men who were caught. Sandro could not find the bald head of the Turk in the confusion, but he was sure he would have had the presence of mind to drop his oar and to knock the Genoan down to the safety of the foot bench.

Pirates stationed fore, aft, and amidships swung iron chains around their heads. Grappling hooks bit deep, reining the ships up short with a jolt that Sandro could feel in his bones. Pirates in steel skullcaps and chain-mail vests swarmed over the side, scimitars in their hands and daggers in their teeth. More raiders swung down from the rigging of the corsair, which now overhung the galley's deck. A cry of battle went up.

The Genoese captain tried to rally his defenders. Sandro saw him at the head of a dozen men, pushing a wave of shouting Moors back. A pirate and a Genoese soldier staggered past Sandro, trading swipes with their swords, so close that the pirate brushed Sandro with his mesh sleeve.

Sandro struggled vainly to free himself. If he stayed where he was, he was going to get killed by an accidental slash or, worse yet, someone was going to run him through for the fun of it.

It was no safer down among the rowers' benches. Some of the Moslem slaves had gotten hold of an *aguzzino* by the legs and dragged him down among them. They were hacking at him with his own sword. A grinning pirate, his sword arm covered with blood from wrist to elbow, paused in his work to encourage them. "*Ehl, mumtaz*, brothers! Keep it up! When this is over, you'll be freed!"

The fighting swept past Sandro. The corsairs were forcing the Genoans, foot by bloody foot, back toward the sterncastle. The crossbowmen still stationed on the upper parapet were trying to give cover to the retreat, but they could no longer pick out targets below. With dozens of individual tussles going on, and with the two battle lines continually merging, all was confusion on the deck.

Out of the tail of his eye Sandro saw a hunched figure break from cover between some of the silk bales that still remained lashed to the deck and come running at a crouch toward him. At this stage of the fighting, there were few Genoans left beyond the waist of the ship. In hopes that it might be a corsair, Sandro took a chance and shouted in Arabic: "This way, brother! For the love of God, set me free!"

Too late he saw the straight sword and the cocked beret. But it wasn't a Genoan, either. It was Maffeo.

Maffeo lifted his sword, his face pale.

"Maffeo, you wouldn't!" Sandro said, the moment unreal to him. "You denied me before, but at the last you called me by name."

"You should have killed me when you had the chance," Maffeo said, sweating. "You're an embarrassment. I don't know if I'll be able to explain you away to my partners. If they talk when we get back to Venice . . ."

The point of the sword paused at Sandro's throat, giving him momentary hope that Maffeo was finding it as difficult to kill him as it had been for him to tighten his own fingers around Maffeo's neck when their roles had been reversed.

In that moment, facing death, he was ready to forgive.

"Maffeo, remember our mother," he said quietly.

"Shut up!" Maffeo blurted and swung the sword back, two-handed, for the killing blow.

A hurtling bulk came out of nowhere and knocked Maffeo sprawling. The sword went clattering to the deck. Maffeo took one look at his formidable opponent and started backing away on hands and knees.

It was the Turk, his leg chain dragging behind him. He reached for the sword, his eyes on Maffeo.

Before he could pick it up with his manacled hands, an eddy in the fighting brought a duo of hard-pressed Genoese men-at-arms stumbling toward him, backing up under the onslaught of advancing pirates. One of the Genoans, bumping against the Turk, paused to take a slash at him.

The Turk parried, spreading his wrists to catch the blade on the chain between them. Before the man could recover, he flipped the chain to trap the sword in a loop. A knee in the Genoan's crotch turned him to jelly, and the Turk, letting the dangling sword drop, spun the Genoan around, snapped the chain over his head, and broke his neck with a quick yank.

He dropped quickly to one knee to retrieve the fallen sword, but the other Genoan was already dead, run through by a corsair's sword.

"Good work, friend."

The Barbary pirates crowded round the Turk, pounding him on the back and feeling his muscles approvingly. They were a colorful lot, dressed in odds and ends of stolen finery under their light armor. Scraps of silk and satin protruded from sleeves and skirts of chain mail, a pair of Venetian slippers was sewn with pearls, a turban was made of cloth of gold. One of them wore a woman's gown, gathered up between the legs by a silk scarf to make pantaloons for fighting.

The Turk looked round for Maffeo, but he had fled.

"Let him go, brother," one of the corsairs said. "We'll get him for you. The fight's over."

They swept on, to join the horde that was assaulting the castle. It wasn't over yet. The pirates were stalled at the heavy grill that was the castle's last line of defense. They were venting their annoyance by chopping to pieces a couple of unfortunate cooks who had tried to take refuge behind the sheep pen. A battering ram improvised from a piece of the shattered mast burst through the grating, and the pirates poured through.

The Turk turned to Sandro. Without a word, he reached up and grasped Sandro's chains at either wrist. He braced a bare foot against the mast and pulled. The eight-inch spike that had nailed Sandro's manacles to the mast came out with a groan and tinkled on the deck.

"I'm sorry, *ya Turkeeya*," Sandro said.

For a moment he thought the Turk was going to strike him. Then the Turk shrugged. "*Iskit*," he said. "It doesn't matter anymore."

When the mopping up was finished, only about thirty members of the crew and the defending force remained alive. The corsairs paraded them around the deck in great good humor, amusing themselves by hitting them, tripping them, and kicking them when they were down, tearing off clothes or jewels that caught their fancy. Sandro saw Maffeo among the survivors, his hands bound behind his back, offering no resistance as they shoved him around. The other two Venetian passengers had come through it with their lives, too.

The corsairs had gotten into the wine supply. Moslems or not, they had knocked in the heads of scores of barrels, and what they were not wasting they were scooping up in the jeweled goblets they had found in the captain's quarters. A drunken pirate lurched by, festooned with gold chains and trade beads, brandishing his sword dangerously. The Turk turned his back on him in contempt.

"Don't make them mad," the terrified Genoese oarsman quavered. "For God's sake, don't attract their attention."

The rowers were still chained to their benches—the Moslems as well as the Christians. A Moorish oarsman who had complained too loudly had had his head lopped off with one casual swing of a passing corsair's sword. That had been hours ago. The Moslem slaves had become somber, thoughtful, quiet since then.

Sandro and the Turk had been sent back to their bench. No one had tried to chain them up again. But an authoritative-looking pirate in peacock pantaloons and a brocade turban wound around his steel helmet had said to them, "*Istanna*—wait."

The dead rowers—those who had gotten in the way of arrows or crossbow bolts, or those stove in by their own oars at the moment of impact—still lolled in their chains. The corsairs had done nothing to remove them. A few weapons still circulated among the rowers—the corsairs had not bothered to confiscate them—and a muttered debate was going on about the necessity of chopping them off at the ankle and heaving them over the side before they started to stink.

There were bodies and parts of bodies lying everywhere. They didn't seem to bother the pirates. There were no seriously wounded. After the battle the brigands had gone around and dispatched any they could find—their own men as well as the fallen Genoans. But they had left the corpses lying there.

A severed hand floated in the three inches of water at Sandro's feet. The Turk picked it up and flung it overboard.

"No one pumping," he said, looking at the rising water. "Soon we go down. Maybe by dark. Maybe sooner."

He looked down at the rows of chained men. He didn't have to say anything further.

The Genoan gave a whimper.

"They'll need rowers," Sandro told him. "Half their benches are empty."

He looked across at the enemy galley, still grappled to their side. There, at least, the pirates were clearing away the dead and wounded. A working party was moving methodically down the length of the ship, striking their chains and tossing them into the sea.

"Shut up, infidel dog," came a voice behind him. "They'll enslave you, maybe. But not us."

"Would you rather go down with the ship?" Sandro retorted.

The Moor got up and stood over Sandro at the length

of his chain, his fists clenched. Sandro stood up and faced him.

The Turk put up a large hand between them. "No," he said. Glaring at each other, Sandro and the Moor sat down.

"They could pump out the ship, have us row it in as a prize," the Genoan jailbird said. "There are enough of us left for that."

"Does it look that way to you?" Sandro said.

He looked over at the activity at the rail. A few narrow planks had been laid across the gunwales of the two ships, making precarious gangways. A party of bare-chested pirates, all of them dead sober, was transferring light cargo to the other ship under the steely-eyed supervision of the captain's second-in-command—traders' treasure chests, small crates of glassware or pewterware, barrels of spices. They weren't bothering with the bulky stuff—the bales of silk and furs or metal. The silk would be a waterlogged mess by now, anyway.

"They collect everything back from the men, go shares," the Turk said.

After the first orgy of looting, when the pirate captain could not have stopped his men, a guard had been put over the choicer items like the treasure chests. One of the drunks, who had started splitting open spice barrels with an ax, had been beheaded on the spot. The pirate crew was still ransacking the cabins and robbing the corpses, but if what the Turk had said was true, their trinkets would eventually be taken away from them and put in a common pool.

"What's happening now?" the Genoan asked, his teeth chattering.

Over in front of the sterncastle the corsair captain was putting a stop to the fun with the prisoners. Reluctantly, the pirates drew back from those they had been tormenting. One of the brigands, who kept on pricking a young bowman in the buttocks with his sword, desisted only after the captain grabbed his arm and remonstrated with him.

The captain was an enormous potbellied man with a

chest-length black beard. Sandro had heard his men refer to him as "al-Dubb"—the Bear.

He seemed to be choosing a couple of personal slaves for himself, common pool or not. He snapped his fingers, and an escort of armed ruffians led off a pair of the bowmen cadets, young Genoese noblemen with fuzz still on their cheeks. As an afterthought, he tossed a couple of coins at the recording officer, a hairy one-eyed scoundrel, who duly and laboriously made a mark in a ledger.

The captain ran his eyes down the line of prisoners. He crooked a finger and called one over to him. It was the Genoese master-at-arms, a broad, square-jawed man whose name, Sandro knew, was Tomaso Grazzini. During the boarding, Sandro had seen him fighting bravely with pike and sword. The captain spoke to him, working himself up all the while into a rage. Grazzini stood his ground. Then, at a word from the captain, a towering man in Berber robes stepped forward with a three-foot-long cutlass that an ordinary man might have found difficult to handle. Two pirates moved in to pin Grazzini's arms, but he waved them aside disdainfully and knelt. The Berber swung his sword, and Grazzini's head rolled on the deck.

The Genoese captain broke out of the line of prisoners to protest. Sandro had never felt anything but hate for him, but at this moment he had to admire his bravery. The captain had been wounded in the battle; a cut across his forehead had blinded one eye with dried and crusted blood, and one arm hung useless with the broken-off shaft of an arrow still protruding from it.

Sandro expected the captain to be killed out of hand. But al-Dubb merely had him seized and tied by the wrists to a pair of standing posts on either side of a doorframe of the castle. He was saving him for last.

Then, to Sandro's horror, the slaughter became general.

One by one, the archers and man-at-arms were hustled forward, forced to kneel, and beheaded by the Berber. Blood ran across the deck. The heads piled up in a heap. The tangle of headless corpses began to get in the way, and the pirates had to drag them aside by the heels.

The Berber, his arms weary, stopped to rest. His robes were drenched, and he passed a bloodstained hand across his forehead.

Al-Dubb stood scowling with his hands on his hips, his barrel chest heaving with emotion. But his fury for those who had dared to resist him was not yet spent. Next he started on the sailors, most of whom had borne arms in the fray.

The Turk leaned toward Sandro. "This Bear is a bad man," he said. "And stupid. He doesn't need to kill so many. He should give them a chance to join him first. But he lost too many men."

"He's stupid indeed," said the Moor on the bench behind them. "He should sell them as slaves. He's cheating his men."

Perhaps something of the same thought was going through al-Dubb's head. Another Genoan had been dragged forward—a ship's carpenter by the look of the leather apron—and was pleading volubly for his life. A carpenter would be worth something at Tunis or Alexandria. Al-Dubb gave a nod, and a burly pirate led the man off.

All of a sudden the remaining prisoners, who had been stunned and apathetic after seeing the systematic slaughter, began begging for mercy. The captain looked them over like a shopkeeper inspecting vegetables and selected one who had said something to attract his attention.

It was Maffeo, still wearing the flaming red cloak, though it was in sorry condition, and the remains of such finery as the pirates had not yet stripped from him.

The Venetian clothes may have made an impression on al-Dubb. He stood stroking his beard, listening and interrupting from time to time to ask questions.

"He's ransoming himself," the Turk growled. "How could he do that?"

"There's a factor of the company in Tunis," Sandro said. "He could pay over the money."

The pirate in the peacock pantaloons who had ordered Sandro and the Turk back to their bench stepped up to al-Dubb and whispered in his ear. The corsair captain listened and asked a question. The peacock turned him around and pointed down the rows of oarsmen's benches.

The captain was questioning Maffeo now. Maffeo was being vehement, waving an arm and shaking his head.

Al-Dubb came to a decision. He spoke to the officer in the pantaloons, who came down the gangway with a pair of armed men at his heels.

"*Yallah,*" he said to Sandro. "Come."

Sandro stood up slowly.

"Go on," said the Turk.

He followed the pirates to the sterncastle. The deck was slippery with the blood of the slain. It was still warm and wet on the bare soles of Sandro's feet.

"Some of the rowers say that you are the brother of this man," al-Dubb said to Sandro in Italian. "Is that so?"

"No," Maffeo cried. "I don't know him."

"*Iskit,*" the captain's lieutenant ordered. "Shut up."

Al-Dubb turned back to Sandro. "Well?" he said.

Sandro looked at Maffeo. The memory of how the point of the sword felt at his throat came back to him.

"Yes," he said.

Maffeo's face was taut with desperation. "It isn't true," he protested. "Don't believe him. These galley slaves will try anything. It's a trick."

His trapped eyes rolled around to the other two Venetians. They were sallow men, made sallower by shock. They'd been ill-used. Their sober gray robes were ripped and filthy, and one of them had an angry purple welt on his forehead. They stood numbly, trying to follow this new development that seemed to have halted the killing.

The pirate chieftain scowled his puzzlement. "Why wouldn't you want to ransom your own brother?"

"One ransom," Maffeo said. "Five thousand ducats. In gold. My factor can raise that. You won't have to wait."

Sandro was staggered. It was a princely sum. Maffeo's Tunisian enterprise must have been doing well.

But Captain al-Dubb frowned unhappily. He'd been planning on squeezing Maffeo for the extra ransom. The rowers' rumors that had been brought to him had been pure manna. He conferred with his lieutenant. Finally he turned again to Maffeo.

"All right," he said. "One ransom. But double. You pay ten thousand ducats."

Maffeo agreed at once. "Get me a pen and paper. I'll write out the instrument of exchange."

"Get him what he wants," the captain ordered a flunky. His lip curled in contempt. "Now you see what sort of people the unbelievers are," he said to his lieutenant. "They set no store by blood ties."

The lieutenant looked pityingly at Sandro. "You're unlucky, it seems, Christian." He used the derisive form for Christian, *Kafir*.

The captain was not yet through with Maffeo. "What about them?" he said, jerking his thumb toward the two Venetians.

Maffeo's eyes shifted. He would not look at his two confederates.

"For God's sake, Maffeo," one of them said, "speak quickly. We can pay you back out of the Cyprus *cambiale* that's due in Venice."

Maffeo, his face turning red, said to the pirate captain, "I don't have the funds."

"No, Maffeo!" the other Venetian burst out. "Why are you doing this? The Trebizond profits alone will pay for it!"

Maffeo stared sullenly at his feet.

Al-Dubb gave a shrug to his lieutenant. "Truly these *Maseehiyeen* do not know Allah the Compassionate," he said piously. "They'll all roast in hell."

He gave a signal to his men, and the two Venetians were dragged unresisting to the blood-soaked Berber. Their pirate tormenters forced them to their knees. They remained white-lipped, silent. The Berber took a step back for better aim and swung his sword. A head flew off and rolled to a stop at Maffeo's feet. The nerve of the other condemned Venetian broke, and he tried to crawl to Maffeo for protection. But the Berber chopped down and caught him on the move, sending a bright spurt of blood from the stump of the neck over Maffeo's shoes.

"There you are, *Masseehiyeen*," al-Dubb said contemptuously to a rigid and ashen-faced Maffeo. "No one left to talk."

He culled the remaining prisoners, selecting those who would bring a worthwhile price on the auction block, rejecting those he thought were too scrawny or too old. The Berber's scimitar flashed four more times.

"No, don't take them away yet," he said when a record had been made in the ledger used to figure shares. "I want them to see this."

He swaggered over to the Genoese captain who had been saved for later. "Well, dog, are you ready to pay for your impudence in resisting me?" he said.

The Genoese captain was weak from loss of blood, and he must have been in agony from the wounded arm that had been twisted around to be tied to the post. But he lifted his head and said defiantly, "You'll be punished for this. My ship has a safe conduct from the soldan."

Al-Dubb spat. "What's the soldan to me? I serve the king of Tunis."

"Maybe the soldan looks the other way when the king sends him a share of the booty, but every once in a while somebody has to be thrown to the wolves. Trading with Genoa's being encouraged now. You'll be disowned."

Al-Dubb laughed. "I'm disowned now, Maseehiyeen."

"It isn't too late. Turn us loose. Return the plunder. We can pump out the ship. There are enough of us to row back to Sicily. I can pick up another crew there."

"Spread him out," al-Dubb said.

Rough hands cut the captain loose from the doorposts and starfished him on the deck. Four spikes were driven into the planking and his wrists and ankles bound to them. The Berber put down his sword and took out a small knife.

"Now we'll show you how we execute those who resist us," al-Dubb said.

Maffeo tried to turn away, but the corsair chieftain said, "No, you'll watch." A pirate took a handful of Maffeo's hair and turned his head toward the spectacle. The Berber grasped the captain's nose as if he were giving a shave and sliced it off. A hideous cry came from the mutilated man.

Sandro watched, sickened. The captain took about an hour to die, joint by joint, slice by slice. When it was over, the thing staked to the deck was scarcely human. There was an earless, featureless mask of blood for the face, the stubs of limbs, a welter of butchery.

"Now you can cut off his head," al-Dubb said.

With a grin, the Berber took a single gratuitous swipe at the gory object, and the oozing ball parted from the trunk. A whoop of laughter came from one of the watching pirates, and several of the his fellows joined in.

Some of the prisoners who had been forced to stay were being violently sick. Al-Dubb turned to them and said, "I was merciful. Hammou could have made it last longer. But there isn't time."

The galley was considerably lower in the water by then. The rowers set up a wailing as their situation was borne in on them. The pirates speeded up their activity, hurrying to transfer the last of the salvageable cargo to the corsair ship bobbing at its grapples. It was an uphill balancing act across the connecting planks now.

Al-Dubb indicated Maffeo. "Take him to my cabin. Treat him tenderly. He's ten thousand ducats."

His eye fell on Sandro next. "He's a big strong one. Put him to an oar as lead stroke."

A pirate overseer, followed by a squat, powerful villain with a sledgehammer and chisel, was working his way down the catwalk, choosing replacements for the empty benches on the pirate ship. He selected Saracens and Christians with equal impartiality, solely on the basis of shoulder beef and general condition.

A blow or two of the sledgehammer freed the lucky ones—lucky, though they were going to be galley slaves again. None of the Saracens seemed inclined to stand on his right as a fellow Moslem not to be enslaved by his brothers. Those who were chosen held the chisel willingly for the overseer's assistant.

The rowers who were bypassed clamored for the corsair overseer to reconsider.

"Take me, *padrone*! Look at these muscles!"

"For the love of Allah, don't leave me to drown, *ya rayyis*!"

"*Aqdar agi ma-ak, ya sidi*? My name's Ahmed, and I'm a good man!"

The Turk was one of the first to be chosen, though he didn't plead. Sandro saw him being led off, the loose end of the chain that he had broken himself slung over his shoulder. Sandro did not see their Genoese benchmate among those who were being herded to the pirate ship.

The pirates had long since abandoned the sinking galley. The last to leave was the squat man. As he turned to go, an anguished howl went up from the benches. He paused with a toothless grin and tossed the hammer and chisel to the rower at the first bench. The man instantly began striking at his chain, while the rowers at the other benches raised a racket, shouting at him to hurry and pass the tools down the line.

Sandro was not chained with the Turk. He was taken to a forward bench that had two vacancies. A spatter of fresh bloodstains and some embedded scrap iron in the chewed-up planks told what had happened to the missing rowers.

Sandro's new benchmate was an emaciated man with the ribs of a starved greyhound. He was entirely naked, and Sandro could see that he was not circumcised. He looked up at Sandro's sun-blackened skin, at the lean features that privation had chiseled away until they resembled those of a desert hawk, and said in the Maltese dialect, "Are you Saracen or Christian?"

The pirate *aguzzino* at that moment was coming down the center walk, swinging his whip and yelling at his new charges in a mixture of languages.

Sandro gave a mirthless grin and picked up the oar. "Does it matter, brother?" he said.

CHAPTER 12

Al-Dubb sailed triumphantly into Tunis to the sound of flutes and tambours, his pennants flying to announce his spoils. As he rowed, Sandro had a good view of him standing with his motley officers in front of his silk pavilion at the poop, dressed in his gaudiest tunic and an impossibly towering gold turban decorated with feathers. Of Maffeo, there had not been a sign in two days of rowing; the pirate captain was keeping him out of sight in the pavilion's *es-shigg*—the guest section.

"Usually he puts in at the corsair base in Mahdia to avoid paying the king's *zakat*," volunteered his skeletal oarmate. "But the port officers are becoming vexed with him, so he's mending his fences."

The oarmate's name was Antonio. He spoke little Italian, but the Maltese dialect was so close to Arabic that Sandro was able to understand it with no trouble. Antonio had been captured in a raid on the Maltese coast five years ago and had been rowing for al-Dubb ever since.

A cannon boomed. Sandro twisted his head to locate the source. A puff of smoke was drifting from the walls of an enormous outjutting fortress that commanded the harbor entrance. If the harbor at Mahdia—"Auffrique," as it was known to Christian Europe—was half as well guarded, Sandro thought, it was no wonder that the corsairs raided with impunity.

"That was the signal," Antonio said, grunting as he hauled on the oar. "They'll be waiting for him when he docks. The *zakat*'s double—ten percent for the king, ten percent for the soldan. But the king doesn't always pay his tribute, either."

Sandro took another quick look over his shoulder. Tunis was a rich city, with towers and the tiled domes of great mosques rising above the jumble of waterfront buildings. It was a busy harbor with many ships. One of them, tied up near the quay toward which al-Dubb was heading, looked familiar.

"Isn't that the official galley we passed heading out— the one al-Dubb was at such pains to give a wide berth to?" Sandro asked. "How did it beat us here?"

Antonio confirmed it after a glance at the device embroidered on its stern pavilion. "That's what's keeping the Bear honest about the *zakat* on his booty," he said between gasps as he rowed. "He knows they spotted him in the Strait."

Al-Dubb's musicians stepped up their volume as the pirate galley slipped handsomely into its moorings, adding the noise of clappers and cymbals to their flutes. Al-Dubb stood confidently at his balcony, preening a little for the benefit of any admiring eyes watching from the quayside.

The sails were tucked, the oars raised. Pirate seamen prinked up in rainbow finery for a spending spree ashore made fast the lines. For the first time since coming aboard, Sandro saw Maffeo. A deferential pirate brought him out of the guest tent and took him over to al-Dubb. A change of clothes had been found for Maffeo out of the pirate's chest. He had chosen well from the plundered wardrobe of nations and looked spruce in Florentine brocade and a cap with a feather.

The two chatted amiably for a while. Al-Dubb called over a ship's boy and handed him a scrolled parchment tied with a ribbon. That would be the instrument of exchange Maffeo had written out for his Tunis factor. Al-Dubb spoke to the boy at length; the instructions would be minutely detailed. The factor would have to come see for himself that Maffeo was actually aboard, and there would be warnings against contacting the Venetian consul in Tunis or any Tunisian authorities. Ransom was a serious business, and nothing must be allowed to interfere with the order of things as practiced in the Mediterranean. If a signed and sealed ransom agreement could be abrogated by diplomatic representations, then obviously it would threaten the safety of hostages in the future. When it was all over, there might be official regrets, but for the moment the king's functionaries must not be embarrassed by overt knowledge.

Maffeo added his own instructions—giving the boy directions for finding the factor's house or relaying some warning of his own. He paused and asked al-Dubb something. Al-Dubb shook his head. Maffeo shrugged and stepped back. Al-Dubb gave the boy a slap on the rump and sped him on his way.

He didn't get very far. A couple of officials in splendid silk robes stopped him at the bottom of the gangplank and took the scroll away from him. An armed bailiff took charge of the boy while the officials read the scroll.

"The port officers," whispered Antonio. "Something's wrong."

With a roar of rage al-Dubb lumbered to the rail and began shouting imprecations at the officials. He reminded them of all the bribes they had taken in the past. Then, blustering, he started forward with the clear intention of taking the boy bodily from the bailiff and retrieving the scroll.

But he didn't get even as far as the gangplank. A detachment of soldiers came running down the pier with lances at ready. More troops blocked the exits to the quay, disciplined men in leather cuirasses and helmets. They stormed aboard, grabbing every pirate they could see. The pirates, outnumbered two to one and in a port where they were under the authority of the king, had no stomach for a fight. Four or five who made the mistake of resisting were overpowered and put to the sword on the spot.

Al-Dubb, still blustering, was led away with the rest, his hands bound behind him.

Maffeo had stood to one side, cool and detached, through it all. An officer, an ameer of a hundred with a plume in his turban, spoke briefly to him. Maffeo went off with him. His hands were not tied, and it was all very courteous, but Sandro saw that a squad of soldiers had fallen in behind him.

A few soldiers were left on guard, keeping the curious away. The oarsmen were left to sit in the sun for a couple of hours. No one spoke to them.

After awhile workmen came to strike off their chains. A deputy and a whole battery of clerks were right on their heels. These fanned out through the ship to take inventory, but they stayed away from the rowers' section.

The workmen didn't like the stench or having to stoop down near the slops that littered the deck between the benches. When their Moorish coreligionists tried to question them about what their fate was to be, they mumbled unintelligibly and moved on as quickly as they could or fobbed the starved wretches off with the meaningless cheer of an "Allah will see to it, brother, don't worry," or "Everything will be fine, inch'allah."

The man who crouched at Sandro's chains had a bluff, open face. Sandro detained him with a hand to his shoulder and said, "For the love of Allah, brother, tell me what happened!"

The workman looked over his shoulder before answering. "A naval patrol found the infidel ship foundering, with the slaves trying to keep her afloat. They found the remains of the infidel captain staked out on deck, and the slaves told them the rest of it. The Frank wasn't a Venetian—who the king is very strict about leaving alone—but he had a safe conduct from the soldan, and there was a very big trouble because the Franks have lately shown good faith by hanging some of *their* corsairs who violated a safe conduct. So everything's been confiscated, and they say the pirates are to be punished."

He finished chiseling through the link of the chain and stood up to go.

"What's going to happen to us?" Sandro asked.

The man's face closed. "I can't tell you that, brother."
He moved to get away.

"Wait. What's going to be done with the Venetian prisoner they took off the ship?"

"I wouldn't know anything about that, brother," the
man said, and left in a hurry.

A man with the characteristic gravel voice of a slave
overseer appeared, with an armed detail to back him up.
He signed a paper for the deputy. He assembled the liberated galley slaves forward of the poop, counted them,
and inspected their limbs and muscles in an all-too-
familiar fashion.

"*Yallah,*" he said when he was finished. He gave those
like the Maltese a rag to cover their nakedness and
marched them through the crowded streets to a slave
barracks in the port quarter. "*Temam,*" he said in a harsh
voice. "You'll spend the night here."

The slave quarters had once been a warehouse. It still
smelled of pepper and other spices. Guards were posted
at the doors, big green-cloaked men with orders not to
talk. But the authorities fed them that night—flatbread
and mutton and steaming semolina, enough for a hundred and fifty men. The starveling creatures fell on the
food and bolted it down with frantic haste. Most of them
had not known a full stomach for years, if ever. The Maltese, Antonio, gobbled his food so fast that he promptly
lost it. He stared tragically at the result, his chance for a
stuffed belly gone. Silently, Sandro handed over his last
scrap of bread, wrapped around a mouthful of mutton
and semolina. Antonio ate it slowly, carefully, and this
time managed to keep it down.

Sandro sought out the Turk. The big man was sitting
with his back against the wall, staring morosely at the
high, dim interior of the warehouse.

"Well, Turk," Sandro said, "how do you like your freedom?"

The Turk spat. His enormous torso was oiled with perspiration; the room had not been meant to hold so many,
and the cool of evening had not yet descended.

"Maybe they'll release the Moslems tomorrow,"

Sandro went on. "They haven't had time to sort it all out yet."

"*Imsh,*" the Turk growled. "Go away and don't bother me with your foolish talk. This little pisspot king of Tunis is more of a money counter than you Venetians."

"At least we're out of the galleys," Sandro persisted.

"The whole world needs oarsmen, Tunis included," the Turk glowered. "Or didn't you notice the galleys tied up at the dock next to us?"

Antonio came over to where they were sitting. He looked with awe at the Turk's slablike chest, but being unaware of his reputation showed no fear.

"We're to be sold tomorrow," he said.

"How did you find out?"

"One of the vendors from the *suq* who brought the food told a rower I used to sit with, and he told me."

The Turk gave Sandro a sardonic stare but did not comment.

"They're going to make a big circus of the pirates tomorrow, too," Antonio continued in a low voice. "They're inviting all the Christian ambassadors and trade agents to see. The pirates are getting the traditional treatment, so that the warning will be visible from sea for some time to come."

Sandro thought with a shudder of Venice, where in the case of particularly heinous crimes the bodies of the hanged were sometimes allowed to dangle on display from the windows of the Doge's palace, or from between the two pillars in Saint Mark's Plaza, for a few days.

"What do they do?" he said.

"They hang their skins from the walls of the city."

"They take the rouble to skin the bodies afterward?"

Antonio gave him a curious look. "No, they skin them first."

Sandro thought of ninety or more human skins flapping in the Mediterranean breezes and swallowed hard. "In England, I've heard, the heads of criminals are kept skewered on pikes on London Bridge until they rot and fall off."

"Oh, that's done, too," Antonio said. "The Jews salt the heads, so they're preserved longer."

Sandro drew a breath. "Did your friend say what happened to the Venetian?"

"Oh, the ransom will be honored. But it will go into the king's purse."

Sandro was bewildered. "I thought the object was to demonstrate to the Frankish nations that the king won't tolerate piracy by his subjects against those with whom he's at peace."

"So it will. The Venetian will be sent home safely. But the ransom was already contracted for. It would be a shame to waste it."

Antonio's manner was forthright; there was no questioning tone, no casting about of the eyes. He had not, evidently, had an opportunity to talk at length to any of the transplanted Genoese rowers and consequently remained unaware of any connection between Sandro and Maffeo. Sandro could not help but be aware that Maffeo had won. He glanced around the moldering interior of the warehouse at his fellow slaves, emaciated and half naked, already resigned to what was to come tomorrow. As these dregs of humanity were scattered to the four corners of the Saracen world after the slave auction, the story would dissipate with them.

"And the Venetian's goods?" Sandro queried.

"Who's to say? Al-Dubb had booty from many ships in his hold. It will all be auctioned off—like us."

The Turk's eyes flicked toward Sandro. His voice gave away nothing when he spoke.

"At least he keeps his skin, eh, infidel?" he said.

That night, among the sleeping bodies, the Turk edged closer to Sandro in the darkness and said in a harsh whisper, "So now, Venetian, you have nothing to keep you going. He's out of reach. Do you give up?"

Sandro had been unable to fall asleep. The images kept turning over in his mind—Maffeo walking at ease on the broad Piazza with the domes and gilded spires of Saint Mark rising behind him; Maffeo lolling in the cushions of a gondola while Lorenzo poled him toward an assignation; Maffeo in the Cavalli countinghouse giving instructions to Ippolito; Maffeo receiving guests at the head of the wide marble staircase of the Cavalli palace;

Maffeo sitting across the dining table from little Agnese, drumming his fingers impatiently at one of her bright, chirping questions . . .

His face contorted. "The soldan of Egypt is out of reach, too," he grated. "Do *you* give up?"

From the dimly seen bulk of the Turk there was no sound but breathing.

Sandro smiled grimly to himself. He grew icy calm. Somewhere in Venice was his heart's core of hate.

The sun-drenched square was filling up with people in a holiday mood—thousands of them in every sort of costume from rainbow-striped robes to plain desert cloaks and shawls, from billowing Turkish pantaloons and swollen turbans to European doublets and hose. They poured in from the narrow, twisting side streets to overflow the sprawling expanse of the old Roman forum, which had been cleared of market stalls and stands for the occasion.

From his place on the slave platform Sandro could see past the baked tiers of buildings that surrounded the square to scrub desert on one side and bright-blue sea on the other. He noticed discreet screens on some of the balconies of the more imposing buildings. From behind them the European notables would watch with Christian distaste, later to report to their governments.

Directly across from the auction block, a stage had been set up in front of the candy-striped keyhole arches of the plaza's showiest structure, a palatial jumble of vaults and towers that served the royal officialdom. The pirates waited there in a packed group under armed guard, each with his hands bound behind his back and a rope around his neck. Sandro recognized al-Dubb, still wearing his gold turban and gaudy tunic, bantering with one of his guards.

A peculiar series of structures sprouted from the stage, like preparations for an ornamental garden—rows and rows of waist-high posts in pairs, each pair supporting a light trellislike frame at a slant. At least two dozen executioners were on hand, large businesslike men wearing leather aprons over their bare chests.

"They'll be worn out before they're through," said the Turk, nudging Sandro. "Too much for them to do in a short time. They'll have to work fast and well to get through them all."

Sandro nodded with sick fascination, noting the kegs of salt waiting in readiness, the stacks of stretching boards. It was amazing the degree of organization that could be brought to bear on human affairs when an important enterprise was in the offing.

"No talking there," said one of the slave drivers without much concern. The heat and the flies had sapped his zeal, and his thoughts must have been straying to the entertainment yet to come.

A silken pavilion had been erected for the king of Tunis and his court. Sandro could see a throne on a dais. The king was taking his place, attended by courtiers. From what Sandro could make out of him, he was a ruddy man with a red beard, dressed in flowing robes of mauve and gold, with a complicated arrangement of crown and turban that resembled a mushroom encircled by a gold ring. Two little black pages in pantaloons, silver lamé vests, and turbans fanned the cool air from a block of ice toward him, while a pair of high officials in gorgeous costume had the honor of waving the flies away from the king's face with peacock feather dusters.

A trumpet fanfare blared, much in the Venetian manner, and the king leaned forward, his chin resting on his fist.

At the signal, al-Dubb was seized by four of the executioners. He tried to walk, but his legs kept buckling, and they had to lift his feet off the ground and manhandle him over to where the chief executioner stood waiting. One of his slippers fell off in transit, and the bare foot when they set him down lent a small touch of indignity to his plight.

"They're doing it wrong," the Turk said. "They should save him for last. Al-Dubb did it better."

"The king will want to leave early," whispered Antonio. "He won't want to spend the whole morning here."

"Quiet there," the slave driver said listlessly.

The chief executioner was clearly a man of importance. He bowed to the king's pavilion and strutted a little for his audience, holding up a knife in each hand. He left it to his assistants to strip the corsair captain and tie his wrists to the posts. In short order, al-Dubb was stretched out on the slanting trellis and his ankles fastened.

Sandro tried to feel sorry for him but could not help remembering the cruel death of the Genoese captain and the wholesale slaughter of the prisoners. Still, Sandro had to admit, the pirate captain was trying to be brave, attempting banter with the executioner.

The banter stopped when the executioner produced a lead crayon and drew a mark on al-Dubb's shoulder. Al-Dubb grew rigid with terror and could be seen to have soiled himself. The crowed jeered.

"What's he doing?" Sandro whispered.

"He's marking the best place to start in order to get the skin off in one piece. Anybody can skin a man, but it takes an artist to do it that way. It's called the blue-star spot. Sometimes pirates have themselves tattooed with a blue star there, for bravado."

The executioner worked slowly and carefully, to a continuous sound of screaming. An iridescent cloud of green flies soon surrounded him and his victim as if summoned by Beelzebub to add to the torment, but the executioner was not deterred from his work. Sandro thought that al-Dubb died about the time the skin was peeled down to his waist. At least that was when the screaming stopped. But the executioner, with thorough-going professionalism, continued working unhurriedly until the entire skin, lacking only hands, feet and head above the midpoint on the neck had been peeled free. He handed the dreadful trophy over to a silent man in a dark caftan for salting and stretching. It had taken about a half hour. At that, Sandro thought, al-Dubb had not suffered as long as the Genoese captain had.

The executioner, speckled with blood, turned back to the raw shape of a man on the rack and lopped off its head with an easy stroke of his scimitar. He held it up for the crowd to see, dangling it by the long black beard, then gave it over for salting. The crowd was noisy and excited. A man tried to climb the platform to steal an article of al-Dubb's clothing for a souvenir and got his fingers chopped off for his trouble.

It took the executioners until well past noon to work their way through the ninety-odd pirates. Al-Dubb was the only one to be executed alone. After him the chief executioner was joined by three colleagues, and they skinned al-Dubb's four top lieutenants together, including the Berber butcher, Hammou. The remaining pirates were flayed in three large batches by all the executioners working at once—a scene, Sandro thought numbly, out of hell's butcher shop. The first of the skins were through with their crude tanning by then and were held up on poles like banners for all to see. The king had been long departed by then. He must have slipped out soon after the mass flaying began. But his officials, there to represent the might of the state, stayed to the end.

"How do you like it, Venetian?" the Turk said. "Do you want to go back to your Christians?"

Sandro remembered what the Turk had been witness to in Damascus. By the curious arithmetic of fate, he must have been about the same age that Sandro was now. Perhaps, like a bar of steel that has not been fully tempered until it has been brought to a glowing heat and then plunged into its bath, one was not hardened for the vicissitudes of life until one had witnessed one of these pageants of horror from which God had surely absented Himself.

"I'll take what comes," he said without rancor.

The slave auction could not match the pirate executions as a spectacle, and people began to drift away. The booths of the adjoining *suq* reopened, drawing off a share of customers, and the sherbert sellers began to do a brisk business. The king's silk pavilion emptied out, and servants began to fold it up and to cart off the throne and other furnishings.

Sandro gathered that the auction was a regular weekly occurrence in the square. The pitiful remnants of al-Dubb's rowing benches were added to other, more valuable lots of slaves brought from a variety of sources—Greeks and Circassians acquired from the booming Alexandrian wholesale market, black people arriving in Tunis with the slave caravans that penetrated the unknown interior of Africa, Christian prisoners delivered here by individual sea raiders.

Though galley slaves were low-grade merchandise, Sandro had learned by eavesdropping on a couple of the slave agents that his group was going to be sold first. As al-Dubb's oarsmen, their connection with the bloody preamble of that morning had boosted their market value somewhat—the auctioneer wanted to sell them while interest was still high. Some of them might even hope to escape the benches and be bought for their novelty value as household servants or laborers.

"A gardener, that's what I'd like to be," Antonio said wistfully. "I'd like to dig in the earth for a change instead of the water."

The Turk snorted. "A scarecrow, that's what you'll be sold for."

Antonio appealed with a glance to Sandro for support.

"Don't get your hopes up too high, son," Sandro said.

Sandro's batch had been filled out further by the rowers who had been left behind on the sinking Genoese galley and rescued by the Tunisian patrol. He saw his old benchmate, the jailbird Giuseppe, roped to a couple of Moors and trying to make himself look small.

The lot had originally contained the ship's carpenter and the few other Genoese crew members who had been spared by al-Dubb, to be sold for their skills. But the two young nobles whom al-Dubb had enslaved were to be freed and returned to Genoa as part of the king's demonstration of good faith, and they had interceded on behalf of their free countrymen.

Galley slaves were quite another matter, however. They were only property. Genoa was not going to be too offended by their retention, any more than it would consider it a serious diplomatic breach for the stolen merchandise to be retained. Property could always be replaced.

"See that one over there?" said one of Sandro's

chainmates, sidling closer. "He's a wholesale dealer from
farther east. He'll pick out only the choice items. That
means a higher price on resale. The chances of getting a
soft spot in some rich household will be better."

Sandro followed his gaze and saw a portly man chat-
ting with one of the auctioneer's assistants. He was richly
dressed in the Persian mode with a splendid silk turban
and slippers with curled toes.

"No wholesalers for me," Antonio put in. "I'm going to
get picked out by a family buyer."

"Then you'd better not attract the attention of that
crowd over there," said the slave who had spoken to
Sandro. He let his eyes shift toward a small knot of hard-
eyed men with a nautical air about them. "They're all
galley owners."

He saw the portly buyer looking over in their direction
and immediately puffed out his chest and began to display his muscles.

"Aren't you going to try to catch his eye?" he whispered out of the side of his mouth to the Turk. "With a
physique like yours he'll snap you up, scars and all."

He did not know the Turk—he was one of the rowers
from al-Dubb's ship—and did not know that was the
wrong thing to say.

"Go on, preen for your master, you molded piece of
dung," rumbled the Turk. "Show him how much you like
your chains."

Offended, the man turned away. "Is it wrong for a man
to want to better his lot?" he said in an injured tone to
Sandro. "At least with a buyer like that you could get out
of this hellhole and get taken to a civilized place like Damascus."

"Where did you say?" Sandro asked.

"Damascus," said the rower.

A whip cracked in the air above their heads. "No talking!" yelled a slave driver.

The other chained men, flinching from the whip, did
not see the Turk change color, but Sandro did. Then everybody's attention was diverted as the auction got underway. Gradually, the Turk's color returned. He had
remained as still as a statue, and now his massive head

turned toward the portly man and turned away again when he saw the Damascene looking at him.

"*Fee eyh?*" Sandro said without moving his lips. "What is it?"

The Turk only shook his head, like a bull being baited by dogs in a pit.

"Damascus was leveled and rebuilt," Sandro said, meaning it kindly. "There's nothing there you'd recognize."

"You want to be a house pet in Damascus like that one, Venetian?" the Turk said venomously, his voice under control again. "Why don't you show off for the Damascene, too?"

Sandro was alarmed to see the tremendous fingers closing and reclosing at the Turk's sides. "You're not going to try anything, are you?" he said.

"No," the Turk said. "That's for stupid turds like you."

Sandro allowed himself to growl back. "Get yourself bought by a galley captain if you wish. You're too used to the oar. That's all you're good for now."

Antonio, not understanding what was going on, attempted a wan smile and said in his mongrel Arabic, "Take it easy, *ashabi*. It's not for us to say. It's up to the bidders."

"Up to God, brother," the offended one reprimanded.

"Up to the Satan, you mean," snarled the Turk.

As the auctioneer had intended, the bidding was brisk. He sold off the poorest of the lot first, to get them out of the way—the scrawny ones, the emaciated ones, the broken ones. Antonio went with a brace of Dalmatians who were as spindly and rawboned as he was. The galley captains were the only ones to bid—no private householder wanted to inflict the sight of such shamefully abused men on those he wanted to impress, not even as conversation pieces—and even the galley masters would not budge until the auctioneer offered an inducement.

"Three for the price of two, *effendis*. Plenty of good in them yet." And, stripping them even of the poor scraps they wore, he made them jump around to show how lively they were.

Sandro watched with pity as Antonio, head hanging

down and with a stricken expression on his face, was led away on a rope by a swarthy man whose feathered turban and rolling gait marked him as another corsair.

"Poor Antonio," Sandro said. "He wanted a garden."

"He'll have his garden," the Turk said roughly. "Five fathoms down and growing barnacles and seaweed."

When it was their turn, they were bought by the portly Damascene. The other bidders dropped out when they saw how serious he was.

"They look like the two strongest of the lot," he said with satisfaction as the auctioneer made out the bill of sale. Sandro looked on with apprehension when he felt the Turk's muscles, but the Turk showed a massive indifference to the proceedings. "The old one's not pretty, but that won't matter where he's going. Jaybir al-Sumit notices nothing but the stars."

"Lift!" ordered Hassan the Knout.

Sandro and the Turk heaved with all their might, and the enormous block of stone came free from the rubble. While the Turk strained to keep his shoulders braced against it, Sandro managed to slip his pry bar into the gap and throw himself against it. There was a bone-cracking moment when he had to hold it all by himself, and then the Turk got his own iron bar underneath and the two of them toppled the stone.

"What's that underneath?" cried the elderly gentleman standing behind Hassan. He was Jaybir al-Sumit himself, and this was the first time in the six weeks of being his property that Sandro had laid eyes on him. Sandro and the Turk had been consigned to the stables for the roughest, most backbreaking work that Hassan could find for them, but on this cool, clear morning, when a golden sun made even Damascus's scars tolerable, Hassan had told them that he required a couple of strong men to help Jaybir poke in the ruins.

Jaybir wore his rich robes and opulent turban like an afterthought—he was careless of material things, and it took all the art and patience of his valets to keep him looking like the great man of high station that he was. He

was thin and ascetic looking, with parchment skin and a
nose as thin as a knife blade. But there was nothing feeble about his voice; it was richly resonant—the voice of
a man who, if uncertain of the shape of the universe, was
at least sure of his place in it.

"Careful, noble sir," said Hassan. "Don't go near that.
One of the slaves will get it."

In the hollow that the block had covered was a glint of
brass. If it was the treasure that Jaybir al-Sumit was seek-
ing, then it had been overlooked by the Mongol hordes
who had sacked Damascus twenty years ago, by the wild
Black Sheep tribesmen who had poured in afterward to
pick over the leavings, and by a generation of more
seemly Syrian treasure seekers.

Sandro sprang into the hole, trusting to the Turk to
keep the block from sliding back down the slope and
crushing him, and dug with his hands. He came up with
a circular brass instrument consisting of a complicated
filigree of arcs and pointers revolving around a bottom
plate. Rubbing the dirt off with his hand, he uncovered
engraved Arabic numerals.

"It's an astrolabe, Your Grace," Sandro said. "It's engraved with the name Ibn al-Shatir."

The old patrician gave a start of surprise. "Can the
slave read?"

"I don't know, *ya sidi*," Hassan said. He scowled at
Sandro. "Hand it up."

Sandro passed the astrolabe to Hassan, who immediately had it snatched from his hands by Jaybir.

"Careful, *ya sidi*, you'll get yourself dirty," Hassan said.

Sandro was surprised to see tears rolling down the old
man's face. "And what else is there?" Jaybir said.

Sandro poked around some more. "There's a box with
its top smashed in. No gold, though, only some pieces of
parchment in bad condition. And a leather-bound book,
all moldy."

"They must have been hidden by al-Shatir's disciples
before the Mongols came," Jaybir said, mostly to himself.
"What's your name?"

"Sandro, *ya sidi*," he said, lifting his eyebrows. He

could not understand why the noble Jaybir al-Sumit would want to know the name of a stable hand.

"He's an infidel dog, *ya sidi*," Hassan said, scowling. "And I don't believe he can read. He must have heard al-Shatir's name when we got up this digging expedition."

"Can you read, *ya* Sandro?" the old gentleman said. He gave the name an Arabic pronunciation, so that it sounded like the word *sandoo*, for a box or chest.

"I can read Italian and Latin, *ya sidi*, and recognize a little written Arabic. And I can number."

"Don't tell His Nobility any more of your lies, dog," Hassan snarled. "Here, hand up that box."

Sandro rocked the chest gently in its bed of rubble. "I don't think I'd better. It's falling apart. If these parchment manuscripts are valuable, then it had better be done carefully and each fragment laid on a cloth to keep them in order."

"Hand it up, I say!" Hassan cried in a fury. "Or you'll get a touch of this across your back!" He waved his scourge threateningly.

"Stay, stay, *ya* Hassan," the old scholar said gently. He put a hand on Hassan's arm. To Sandro, he said, "What you have in that box is the real treasure, *ya* Sandroo, not gold. I'm pleased that you recognized it. How would you like to excavate it for me, taking care that nothing is damaged and putting things in order?"

"Whatever you say, *ya sidi*," Sandro stammered. He saw the Turk glaring at him.

Jaybir turned to the overseer. "Give him whatever he requires," he said. "And send him to the house when he's finished."

Sandro worked for four days at the job, making sure that he recovered even the smallest fragments and had them assembled in place and pressed between boards. He enlisted the Turk to help him, over the Turk's grumbles and Hassan the Knout's hostility, getting him out of the man-killing work in the stables. When he was ready, he presented himself to Hassan.

"Don't think you're out of my grasp, infidel dog!" Hassan told him. "Sooner or later you'll be back here. Take off your shirt."

Silently, Sandro removed his upper garment. Hassan took a judicious step back, raised himself on the balls of his feet, and swung with all his strength.

The impact sent Sandro reeling. He clawed at the wall to stay on his feet. Slowly, his back on fire, he turned to face Hassan.

"That will show you where you stand," Hassan said. "Now put on your shirt and take your pieces of ungodly writing to your master."

Jaybir al-Sumit was delighted with Sandro's work. He received him in a spacious, sunlit workroom of marble and Moorish tile, whose every working surface was cluttered with maps, star charts, and manuscripts with geometic diagrams on them.

"So, you're an educated man, as I thought," Jaybir said after questioning Sandro. "You're not used to keeping *my* sort of records, but you have an orderly mind and can do bookkeeping, and you can learn. And you Venetians know something of seafaring. How would you like to work as my secretary?"

Sandro could hardly believe the stroke of luck. To get out of the stables and out from under the supervision of Hassan the Knout! He thought of the Turk. The Turk would be stiff-necked, but he'd get around that.

"*Ya sidi,*" he said, "I have a friend in the stables . . ."

"Can he read?" the old gentleman said.

"I . . . I don't think so, but . . ."

"I have no use for a servant like that right now," Jaybir said, dismissing the subject. Sandro had to leave it at that. He understood that he had been extraordinarily favored for Jaybir even to give him a reply. He told himself that he would keep trying.

An overbearing intendant of servants took him in hand, saw that he bathed, took away his stable clothing to be burned, after making a to-do about holding his nose, and found him a new outfit of trousers, robe, slippers, and turban. Then he was told that he could go to the kitchens to eat.

Sandro ate his fill for the first time in two years. There

were fowl and lamb with eggplant, wheat and almonds, and little sweetmeats. The leavings of Jaybir's table were a feast for his servants. The intendant looked at him disdainfully while he stuffed himself.

Afterward, as he was being taken through the tiled and vaulted corridors to his new quarters, feeling lazy and satisfied, Sandro peered through every arch and doorway he passed, marveling at the beauty and luxury that bloomed so miraculously amidst Damascus's avenues of rubble.

Then, turning a corner, he got the shock of his life.

A slave girl, unveiled, was hurrying in his direction, carrying a tray. Her uncovered face was as white as alabaster, her eyes dark and enormous, her straight nose and curved lips taken from a classical statue. Though she wore harem dress—a blue deep-necked gown and trousers, he recognized her immediately. It was the Greek girl he'd seen sold to Falco on the auction block in Venice, the one he'd gotten into a fight over.

She hurried past with her tray, frightened at the attention she was getting.

"Who was that?" Sandro asked.

"She's not for you, Christian," the intendant laughed. "Just because you've been plucked out of the stables and given a meal and a bath don't let it go to your head. If you get above yourself, you're liable to have your *zib* trimmed for you."

CHAPTER 13

The Venetian was a braggart, but he was probably good for a free drink and maybe a meal, if Tom played his cards right. Tom shouldered his way through the crowd, keeping an eye out for the Greek landlord, who had thrown him out the night before for cadging. He approached the Venetian's table and stood unobtrusively to one side, listening through the tavern's multilingual din.

" . . . rubies as big as hen's eggs, palaces of ivory and gold, wealth beyond measure," the Venetian was saying in an eager tumble of words. "There is, in this country, a kind of ant the size of a small terrier that digs up gold and stores it in its nest, and when the Zamorin wishes to replenish his coffers, he simply sends men to smoke out the nest and raid it for the gold."

The Venetian's drinking companions nodded sagely and reached for more wine. There were four or five of them, not counting the sot who was asleep with his cheek resting on the table. One of them, the most reputable looking, was another Venetian from Constantinople's huge self-governing trading colony—a comfortable, well-dressed man with skeptical eyebrows—but at least a couple of them were spongers. Tom could recognize one from a mile away. The type was the same in every country he'd passed through.

They looked as if they'd heard it all before.

"Vijayanagar!" the Venetian said expansively, setting down his glass. "Isn't *that* a name to conjure with? A city larger than Rome and a hundred times as grand, with a luxury that can hardly be conceived! The king has three thousand wives, and they're all expected to burn themselves alive when he dies! The wives of the lowest peasants and fishermen wear gold bangles and gold hoops in their noses, and in the markets diamonds and emeralds are sold as we sell onions! It's from this kingdom that the Saracen traders get the pepper and cloves and other spices that they sell to *us*—and from this small fraction of the riches of Vijayanagar comes all *our* wealth! You can imagine how much is left!"

Tom had never seen Rome, but he found it hard to picture a city grander than Constantinople. He had been in the Byzantine capital for more than a week now, and he still hadn't gotten used to its eastern splendors. It must, he thought, be the most beautiful city in the world, with its miles and miles of enormous turreted walls, its gleaming rooftops and golden domes, its ancient palaces of a fairy-tale past, the marvel of the Hippodrome and the grand church of Saint Sophia into which all the cathedrals of Bristol could fit with room to spare. It made the great cities of Europe that he'd walked his way through these two years—Bruges, Cologne, Prague, Vienna, Venice itself—seem like mudheaps.

But if Constantinople was enchanted, the tavern was much like taverns anywhere—smoky, grimy, noisy, and smelling of spilled wine and unwashed feet. And the story the Venetian was telling was like many a tall tale heard in taverns like this—taverns patronized by sailors and ne'er-do-wells—after a few flagons of wine.

"Tell me, Messer Niccolo," said the other Venetian. "Have you seen these marvels with your own eyes?"

The tale-teller flushed. "No," he admitted. "I managed to journey no farther than the northern kingdoms of India, of which we have already heard, before my wife died of the plague and I was forced, temporarily, to return. But I had the account of a Saracen traveler, a reliable merchant named Abdur, whom I met in the sultanate of Delhi."

One of the spongers, an oily individual who spoke a variety of Italian that Tom was not familiar with, said with flattering ingenuousness, "But you have actually penetrated as far as Delhi, Signore dé Conti?"

Conti expanded again. *"Ma certamente,"* he smiled. "It was not easy, I can assure you. I was discovered and had to renounce my Christian faith."

Expressions of horror erupted from the others. One of them crossed himself in the peculiar way that Tom had come to recognize as characteristic of the Eastern rite practiced by the Greeks and Byzantines.

The Venetian merchant raised his eyebrows. "You renounced your faith, Messer Niccolo?" he said.

Conti smiled again, all charm. "Don't go running to tell the *bailo*, Messer Leonardo," he said. "I've had to renounce my faith more than once, traveling through infidel lands. But my confessor has absolved me. I can assure you that I remain a devout Christian."

"This sultan's kingdom of Delhi, *kyrios*," the Greek said diffidently. "They are Saracens, then, like the Turks or the Egyptians?"

"Yes," Conti answered. "And just as bloodthirsty when it comes to dealing with faiths other than their own. Except that they have no Christians to persecute. Instead, they persecute the Hindus to the south of them."

"This kingdom of Vijayanagar?" said Messer Leonardo.

"Indeed," said Conti. "These Indian Saracens are driving farther and farther south. Some day the marvels of Vijayanagar will be no more. I'm determined to see them for myself before they disappear forever."

"Admirable, Messer Niccolo," said Leonardo down his nose. "You're another Marco Polo." He gave a condescending smile. "Marco *Milione*! But if Marco had his millions, you have your billions."

"Marco Polo told the truth," Conti replied with some heat. "And he didn't tell the half of what he saw."

While Conti glared at his countryman, Tom took the opportunity to slide into an empty space at the end of the bench. Nobody paid any attention to him.

"Do you really think," said the Greek earnestly, "that this . . . Hindu . . . kingdom is in danger of disappearing before a European can lay eyes on it?"

Conti was all seriousness now. "Tamerlane gave the Hindus a respite when he sacked Delhi, carried off all the wealth that the sultans had stolen from the Hindus for centuries, and left the countryside in ruins. Just as Tamerlane gave Constantinople a respite when he sacked Damascus and Baghdad and so diverted the Saracens' resources. But the sultans of Delhi have reoccupied their throne, and they've had twenty years to rebuild. Sooner or later they'll sweep all the way south and finish their bloody work."

"Are they so rapacious, then?"

Conti gave a thin smile. "Before Tamerlane taught them a lesson on the use of power, they squeezed the Hindus they conquered like lemons. One of the sultans, Aladdin, drew up a list of rules and regulations for grinding the Hindus down: There could be no gold or silver in a Hindu house, not even a coin or a wedding bangle, and no possessions of any kind beyond the barest necessities. Half the crop was taken from them each year so that they should have just enough to keep alive on and not a scrap of food more. Another sultan, Ahmad Shah, feasted for three days whenever it was reported to him that twenty thousand Hindus in his domain had been slaughtered in a single day."

Forgetting the free meal he was hoping to wangle, Tom burst out, "Aren't these Hindus men, then? Why don't they fight back?"

Conti raised his eyes, saw a new listener in his audience, and gave a little nod of approval for the question.

"Bless you, lad, their religion tells them it's no use to strive because all is foreordained. They believe that if they're not sufficiently holy in one life, they'll be reborn as an animal or insect, but that the highest reward is oblivion—*nirvana*, they call it. They're too tenderhearted to eat beef or wear leather—the cow is sacred to them. Their highest rank, the Brahmins, even sweep the path before them to avoid stepping on insects."

"God's truth, they sound like a lily-livered lot!" said

one of the spongers. "Perhaps they deserve to have their wealth taken from them."

The merchant, Leonardo, picked up his goblet and peered through its ruby contents at the light of an oil lamp beyond. "If what you say is true, Messer Niccolo, it's a pity that those riches must go to the Saracens. If there were only some way for a Venetian galley to sail there, we could have it for ourselves."

It was Conti's turn to be condescending. "We'd have to find a way to sail around Africa to do that, Messer Leonardo," he said. "And it's well known that Africa has no bottom."

The other shook his head. "All that wealth—the spices, the gems, the goods that come from farther east—to have to come to us through the hands of Arab merchants by caravan and ship! If only a sea route *were* possible, we could cut out the Saracens entirely."

"You have it there, Messer Leonardo," Conti agreed. "I confess to being entranced by wonders, but the real wealth is in the cloves and cinnamon, the pepper and ginger! But that's what makes travels like my own worthwhile. Through such journeys—posing as an Arab if needful, as I have done—we may hope to find out some day which commodities come from India and which come from the eastern islands and from Cathay itself."

"You're only trying to find an excuse for your curiosity, Messer Niccolo."

"I confess," Conti said with a laugh.

Tom thought it time to remind Conti of his presence again. "How will you get to this marvelous kingdom, *signore*?" he said.

"Eh?" Conti jerked his head around. "Don't you have a drink, boy?" He raised two fingers in the smoky air and shouted in approximate Greek, *"Ypirétis, glígora!"*

A fat attendant appeared with a goblet of wine for Tom and refills for the others. Tom took a cautious sip. It seemed to him that it tasted of turpentine. He would have preferred English ale, or at least the bitter brew called *biere* that he had found in the Lowlands and the German lands, but it had become harder and harder to find anything decent to drink since he had crossed the Alps. Beggars, however, could not be choosers.

"I sail for the Holy Land tomorrow," Conti said. "From there I hope to cross Arabia by caravan and reach a gulf that opens into the Arabian Sea, if I can believe the accounts of the Arab travelers I have spoken to. This gulf is a great lane of commerce by which the Arab seafarers sail to the southern coast of India and to the spice islands beyond. I shall wear Arab dress and hope to take passage."

The bold assertion drew gasps of astonishment from Conti's hangers-on, with the exception of the Venetian merchant, who merely raised his bushy eyebrows again.

Tom said, puzzled, "Why would you travel west to go east? You could take ship for Trebizond, and then travel south and east."

Conti laughed hugely. "You have a rare sense of direction, boy. And I see you believe in the direct approach. Tell me, have you ever seen a map in your young life?"

"No, *signore*." Tom had handled enough of Master Philpot's correspondence, but it was all place names, like points of equal value and equal distance on a flat board, connected by the straight lines of commerce. "But it makes sense," he added.

"And so it does," Conti assured him. "Marco Polo thought so. But the world has changed since his day. The old silk route is no longer open. And then south of Trebizond one would have to pass through the land of the Black Sheep Turks, a savage people who would as soon slice you into tiny pieces as look at you. These were the lands ravaged by Tamerlane on his way to India, and they don't take kindly to strangers. And then, too, even the excellent map of the great Ptolemy tells us nothing of the obstacles one might have to overcome in order to reach this gulf of which I spoke from the north."

Tom drew in a breath. "Can I go with you?"

There was general laughter from the older men around the table. Conti said kindly, "How old are you, boy?"

Tom had to think. "About seventeen."

"*Inglese*, aren't you? Where did you learn that bastard dialect of Genoese and Venetian?"

"I . . . I just picked it up."

"What's your name?"

"Tom . . . uh, like Tomaso."

"You're a long way from home, Tom. How did you get to Constantinople?"

"Walked."

Conti stared at him in frank disbelief. "Walked?"

"Well . . . I sailed from Bristol to Bruges. Then I walked to Venice. In Venice I found a Greek ship that was short a hand and worked the rest of the way here."

"But you walked all the way across Europe—crossed the Alps on foot—to get to Venice?"

"It wasn't too bad crossing the Alps. I joined a merchant's party. They needed help with the mules. The Alpine monks keep the paths marked, and string ropes along the ridges. When the going got rough, the monks pulled us on a sort of sledge made of boughs. It was early spring, and they were starting to clear away the bodies of the travelers who hadn't made it during the winter."

"*Sorprendènte!*" Conti exclaimed. "You're a bit of a traveler yourself!"

The merchant shook his head in amusement. "What, one teller of tall tales being taken in by another?"

Conti ignored him. "And good at picking up tongues in a rough and ready fashion," he said. "Tell me, Tom, can you read, write, do sums?"

"Yes, *signore*. I was . . . apprentice to a mercer in Bristol."

"Oh, a budding merchant, are you?"

Tom lowered his eyes modestly.

The other men, who had been ready to make sport of Tom, desisted when they saw that Conti was treating him courteously. "That's why he wants to get to this kingdom of riches you spoke of, Signore dé Conti," said one of them. "I know these merchants of Bristol. They're a closed shop. The lad needs a stake in order to get started."

Conti made a decision. "All right, Tom, perhaps I can make use of you. No pay, but I'll give you your keep. Is that understood?"

"Yes, *signore*." Tom grinned with elation. Not only was

the immediate problem of his employment solved, but he was going to get to see the Holy Land, the Arabian interior which no Englishman had visited, and—if Conti's wild tale was true—a wondrous kingdom where even peasant women wore gold and where diamonds and emeralds were as common as eggs.

"Do you know where the pillar of Constantine the Great is?"

It was a well-known landmark, and one of Tom's favorite places in Constantinople. He had climbed its spiral stairs several times to drink in the view of the entire city that it afforded. From its crumbling top one could look past the sprawling rooftops and out across the Golden Horn to the walls and towers of the Genoese colony of Pera. But the really magical view came when one made a quarter turn to the right. Then one could look out across the narrow ribbon of the Bosphorus and see another world entirely—the sinister Saracen shore, where the sultan had already begun to build forts and watchtowers in preparation for the final conflict between Islam and Christianity.

"Yes, I know it, *signore*," Tom said.

"Meet me there at tierce. You can help carry my luggage. We sail at nine from the Venetian quay directly opposite."

"I'll be there, Messer Niccolo," Tom promised.

"Ho, listen to him! He's a Venetian already." Conti signaled for more wine.

The conversation became general again. The wine flowed. Tom listened, fascinated, as Conti recounted some of his adventures.

"A Saracen pilgrim from Granada whom I met in Sinai told me that the Red Sea opens out into a still greater sea by which the Arab merchants reach India directly. This must be true, since it corresponds to the map of Ptolemy. If it indeed be true, one might save oneself the trouble of crossing Arabia. But the way thither is perilous because the Saracens patrol the sea approaches to their holy city most vigorously, stopping the pilgrim ships to search for infidels. I've sailed in such a ship—a *boom*, as they call it—but not far enough south to test the route.

"The Saracens use no nails in building their ships—they sew them together with cord instead. They believe there are magnets at the bottom of the sea that draw out the nails and sink Frankish ships. The Arab mariners don't set as much store by the compass as we do, either. Instead, they rely mainly on the stars. They have a kind of instrument called the *kamal*, which is really not much more than a piece of board and a knotted string . . . but somehow they're able to measure their latitude with it . . . I'm deuced if I understand how!"

"Wonder upon wonder!" Leonardo said sarcastically. "Boards and strings that whisper a captain's latitude to him. The Moors must like to tell tall tales, too. With such an instrument one might guide oneself down the coast of Africa and discover the kingdom of Prester John."

Conti refused to be baited. "It's not impossible," he said.

Food came then, and Tom got his meal—bite-size morsels of lamb and various unidentifiable vegetable tidbits roasted on a spit, and a kind of sausage the Greeks called *pastirma*. He gobbled down the little treats as quickly as he could without being conspicuous about it, making sure he got his share. Coming from a large family helped. He felt vindicated to note that the two spongers were making their meal of the day out of Conti's snacks, too.

Messer Leonardo excused himself after a while and then some of the others. Tom hung around, getting sleepy, listening to Conti's stories until the Venetian started to repeat himself, contradicting himself on some of the details. Tom looked at him closely. Conti was making a late night of it and drinking rather more wine than was good for someone who expected to set out on a sea voyage the next day.

Tom got up. Conti's circle of listeners was down to one of the spongers and the Greek. He was talking as confidently and fluently as ever, but his eyes had gone unfocussed.

"Can I see you to your lodgings, Messer Niccolo?" Tom asked. Constantinople was a well-policed city, but a drunk could be prey in the dark streets at night. It would be a pity if anything happened to Conti, now that he had found him.

Conti waved him off. "No, no, run along. Get some rest. I'll need you to be bright and fresh on the morrow. I'll hire a linkboy to see me home."

Tom shifted his feet. "You won't forget that we're to meet tomorrow?"

Conti was all warmth. "At the foot of the pillar in Constantine's forum. At tierce." He smiled glassily, but Tom could detect no slurring of his words. "Be there in good time. The ship won't wait for laggards."

The bells of tierce had long since died away, and still Conti had not come. For the third time that hour Tom left his post at the foot of the great ruined column and made a circuit of the forum.

Flies and beggars there were in plenty, but there was no sign of Conti. Tom had taken seriously the Venetian's admonition to be there in good time and had arrived at least two hours early. So he did not think he could have missed Conti.

He returned to his post, clutching the knotted square of cloth that contained his few possessions, and sat down on a broken piece of marble. In former times the top of the column had held a giant statue of Emperor Constantine, so one of the forum beggars had told him, but when the Crusaders from Europe had stopped off to plunder Constantinople on their way to the Holy Land, they had toppled the statue and stripped it of its gold. The crater of cracked and powdered marble still remained, two hundred years later.

"Alms, young master," a crippled beggar croaked, shaking his clack dish at him. He straightened up when he recognized Tom and lifted the clever patch that had been made to resemble a blind man's scab. "Oh, it's you, the English lad. I can't see through this thing. *Chaire*, Tom."

"*Chaire*, Dimitrios."

The beggar sat down beside Tom, using his crutch as a lever and reaching under his tunic to rearrange the foot that was strapped tightly to his thigh. The beggars in the forum had at first been suspicious of Tom and his ragged clothes, but when they saw that the did not intend to compete with them, they had become friendly.

"You're doing better, Tom," Dimitrios said. "Isn't that a new shirt you're wearing?"

Tom blushed. "A lady gave it to me."

"*Kairon gnothi,*" Dimitrios chuckled. "Know your opportunities. If I had your innocent face and that mop of yellow hair, I'd soon retire from this business. What are you doing, loitering here? Don't you have anything better to do on a fine day like this?"

"Have you seen a Venetian here this morning?"

"A Venetian? Let me see. Which of them will you have? There was the servant of the *bailo* who comes through here every morning on his way to do the marketing. And there's the fat old fool of a merchant who prowls the district looking for young boys in the profession, and a small party of tourists just off a galley. . . ."

"A man of about thirty with a dark complexion. Lean and a little below middle height. A little careless in his dress but an air of consequence about him . . ."

"Ah, so you have business with a particular Venetian?"

"His name's Conti. Niccolo dé Conti. He's a merchant. Or used to be one."

"Oh, that one. The talker."

"You know him?"

"Everyone hereabouts knows him. He'll talk your ear off if you let him. I bump into him in the taverns sometimes. He never recognizes me out of my working clothes. I swear he tells better tales than any of the confidence men who work the forum, but to no purpose because he throws money away instead of taking it in. He has lodgings at the Sign of the Dolphin in the Lane of Saint John the New, which is a good sign that his purse is emptier than his talk. . . . Where are you going?"

"Thanks, Dimitrios." Tom jumped up. "If you happen to see him in the next few minutes, tell him I was here, and ask him to wait for me."

He raced off across the marble flagstones, darted around a market cart, and plunged into the dark, narrow lane. Upper-story extensions turned it into almost a tunnel, despite the Constantinople law that said you had to allow your neighbor at least ten feet of sunlight. The Sign of the Dolphin was a scurvy place where one could definitely save money at the expense of comfort, cleanliness, and a choice of bedmates. The landlord was a large, unshaven man with an eye patch and a chewed ear.

"Excuse me, *kyrios*," Tom said breathlessly, "but have you seen Signor dé Conti this morning?"

"The Venetian. *Vai*, I've seen him, and good riddance. Tried to pay me with a glass ruby. I made him empty out his purse, and I still came out short by the difference in the clipped ducat that he passed off on me."

"He's gone? What time did he leave?"

"He left before prime. His ship sailed at first light, he said."

"Thank you, *kyrios*."

A meaty hand descended on Tom's shoulder. "Where do you think you're going, *neos*? If you have some connection with that fraud, you can pay me the ten aspers I calculate he still owes me."

Tom wriggled free and streaked down the lane in the direction of the waterfront. The Venetian quay was at present unoccupied except for a round ship that was still unloading cargo and some Greek lighters of the type that plied the Sea of Marmara and the Bosphorus, ferrying offloaded goods. Tom accosted an alongshoreman.

"Did a ship sail for the Holy Land this morning?"

The man turned a broad, stupid face toward him. "What?" he said.

"*Sugkhoréte.*" Tom reassembled the question from his small store of Greek words, speaking slowly and carefully. "A ship, it left from here, go Jaffa, Jerusalem?"

The man wrinkled his brow and nodded.

"When?"

"*Hénas.* It sailed at first light. A pilgrim galley."

"Is there another ship, one that's supposed to sail at none?"

For an answer, the man turned his face in the direction of the quay, where the only vessel of any size was the cog that was still unloading, and shrugged at the idiocy of the question.

Tom's shoulders slumped. "Was there a man aboard, a Venetian of about thirty with ..." He stopped at the alongshoreman's uncomprehending expression. "Never mind. *Eukharisto.*"

He walked out to the end of the quay and stared down the length of the Golden Horn, out across the busy Bosphorus, to the blank and unresponsive Turkish shore beyond.

Along that shore, to the east, lay Trebizond and beyond that the fabled lands of which Conti had spoken. Could those lands, as strange and exotic as their people and works must be, be materially different from the solid earth he had already trodden? There would still be mountains and rivers to cross, roads to follow, people who strove and cultivated the land for the food they ate. The Turks, he had been told, were monsters, but in any land there were always people to avoid and people to strike up friendships with, and where there were people, a way could always be found to get along.

He peered at the indistinct shore with its suggestion of green growth and scattered habitation. It was not very far away. One might row across in an hour.

All of a sudden it was intolerable to be standing at the end of a quay in Constantinople when Conti was already gliding over the waters, taking his roundabout way to his kingdom of gold.

He grinned in anticipation. His two feet had gotten him this far. They would take him farther. And he would beat Conti there.

He remained outside the seawalls that night, hiding from the watchmen in a nook under the battlements. When it was dark enough, he followed the narrow strip under the foundations until he found someone's unattended boat pulled up on the ledge. It was old, leaky, and smelled of fish, but he located a board to paddle with and shoved off into the inky waters. The current of the Bosphorus bore him along, but he made steady progress.

He grounded on a gravel beach that was no different from shores anywhere. Left was east, where Trebizond lay some hundreds of miles away. He put his small bundle on his shoulder and began following the shore.

• • •

Tom stood on the heights, admiring Trebizond for a last time. The city spilled down from the tilted oblong of tableland that had given it its name to a wide blue harbor that was walled in the manner of Constantinople against attack from the sea. More walls protected its classical villas and gardens and palaces on either side, and beyond the walls were the natural defenses of two deep gorges that ran all the way to the sea. On the land side was a string of formidable forts, connected by ramparts and backed up by mountains too high and too deep for an army to cross. Seeing it spread out like that, Tom could understand how it was possible for this alien enclave, this offshoot of Byzantium with its own Greek emperor, to continue to exist on the shore of a hostile continent.

He fingered his turban, tucking a stray tuft of straw-colored hair out of sight. There were plenty of blond Saracens, he had learned, and anyone who cared to give him more than a cursory glance could not fail to see his blue eyes and the light golden down on his sunburned skin. But it was better not to stick out like a sore thumb in the Turkish lands, especially at a distance, and attract the unwelcome attention of horsemen.

The turban, manufactured from the remnants of the shirt that Mathilde had made for him, and the pantaloons and vest he had won at dice from a camel boy in Izmit, had gotten him through the Turkish domain. He had packed them away when he had reached the borders of Trebizond's narrow coastal empire, where dress was a cosmopolitan mixture of east and west, and bare heads were not uncommon, but he had donned them again when he had gone to visit the caravan campgrounds outside the city walls.

The bawling of camels and the jangle of camp life carried thinly through the air to where Tom stood. He could smell the burning dung of a hundred small fires. The caravan had not been allowed across the stone bridges that spanned the gorges, of course; a thousand camels would have made a muddle of Trebizond's already jammed commercial streets. Instead, it had settled into its regular stamping ground, where there was centuries' worth of dried camel dung for fuel and more being produced every hour. The merchants would come with pack mules after they made their deals.

The caravans came twice a year, bringing goods by the old overland routes. The Mongol hordes who had turned themselves into Persians had no love for Trebizond, but they loved the Mamluks of Egypt and Syria even less, so they had kept the caravan trails open as competition to the Red Sea route.

Tom had gradually come to understand the web of traffic that Conti had alluded to. The taverns of Trebizond were an education, where one might find oneself talking to a Janney sailor or a Trapezuntian commission agent one minute and a Turkish caravan guide the next, each with his own story to tell over a goblet of wine or the bitter black brew they called *ghahffee*. It was not hard to put the stories together.

Another Venetian named Marco Polo had taken the caravan route more than a hundred years ago, though he had veered east to Cathay instead of south to Vijayanagar, only touching India, so Conti believed, on his return journey by sea. Venice was still trying to make up its mind whether or not Marco Polo had been a liar. In any case, Christian merchants were no longer welcome on the silk road; they had to take what was deposited for them by the Saracens at depots like Trebizond.

Tom's gaze followed the long curve of the harbor again. There was a Venetian fortified castle at one end and a Genoese castle at the other, separated by the entire width of the bay and manned mostly by Greek troops supplied by Trebizond. The emperor wanted no private wars in his domain.

"Tohm, Tohm," said a voice behind him. "*Âghâ* Hasan Ali is looking for you. It's time to load the camels. Hurry, or you'll be beaten."

He turned around and saw Mostafa, the second boy, a scrawny starveling who reminded him of himself four or five years ago.

"There's plenty of time," he said. "And if Hasan Ali

tried to beat me, I'd kick his arse for him. I'm not one of his *bandè*-boys."

Mostafa laughed delightedly. "It's truly said, *ya* Tohm, that garlic is the spice that overcomes."

Tom laughed with him. He had learned early on that his name, in the queer eastern jargon that substituted for lingua franca here, was irresistibly transformed into *tohm*, the word for garlic. It was always good for an icebreaker.

"Hasan Ali's never met an Englishman before," he said. "He'll get used to it."

"Don't the English have slaves, then?" Mostafa asked.

The word for slave, *bandè*, meant something like "bound," but it could also stand for a servant. In fact, it was considered good manners, when addressing a superior, to use the word *bandè* in referring to oneself, even if one were free. Tom hesitated, thinking of English peasants bound to the land, thinking of apprentices bound to their masters. But a peasant could break his bonds by living in a town for a year; an apprentice became his own master after completing his term of service. England did not have markets where people were sold like cattle.

"Not like here," he said.

The little camel boy cocked his head, savoring the idea of a place where Hasan Ali had no power to give orders. His smudged face split in an infectious grin until he remembered his errand.

"*Yallah*," he said. "If you don't come right away, Hasan Ali will beat *me*!"

Tom gave in and followed Mostafa over the crest and down the opposite slope. Mostafa skipped ahead like a grasshopper, looking back frequently. The caravan came into view, a milling sea of men, animals, and black tents. Here and there billowing shapes collapsed as tents were struck; camels were being formed into lines while men shouted and moved among them with sticks.

"Where have you been, *pesar*?" Hasan Ali demanded. He waved a camel stick but made no attempt to hit Tom with it. Tom had once dropped the story of Mijnheer van den Vondel among the camel boys, and word had gone round that he had killed a man.

Tom, without a word, began gathering gear. It was not easy to load a reluctant camel, but he had learned to do it as well as anyone.

"You can begin by loading Ghadisè, Zenat, and the Asp," Hasan Ali said venomously. "And make sure the thongs are tight."

Tom shrugged. He always got the irascible beasts— the old *nágas*, the spitters, the biters. He would not give Hasan Ali the satisfaction of showing resentment.

Hasan Ali looked at him narrowly. "You can stop smiling, Frankish *pedar sag*! If we're raided, the caravan master won't lift a finger to stop them from taking you. You'll be lucky if you get halfway to Kharput without being skinned alive."

Tom ignored him. They were headed in the right direction, that was all he cared about. They were going to a place called Baghdad.

Baghdad was a dead city, a skeleton city, where the flat desert winds whistled through the ruins, blowing grit, where the rats peeped out of the rubble with little glinting eyes, and people went about their business furtively, muffled in cloaks.

Tom shivered, wrapping his own cloak about him and trying to get comfortable again in the little nest he had made for himself between the fallen pillars of what had been, from its extent and the tumbled fragments of carved stone, a mighty palace.

It was a good wool cloak, though grown shabby and smelling of camels. Once it had belonged to Hasan Ali, but Tom had won it from him fairly and squarely, wagering five stripes on his bare back against it if Hasan Ali had won the toss of the dice.

Hasan Ali had come to reclaim it in the night, but Tom had awakened in time, and Hasan Ali had left quietly when Tom had shown him a knife. Still, Tom had thought it prudent to depart and spend the rest of the night elsewhere.

He had gathered up a few small things to which he thought he was entitled and stolen through the sleeping

campground, avoiding the snoring camels and giving a
wide berth to the sealed tents, where a sleepless occu-
pant might mistake too close a footstep for a thief in the
night. Tom had seen what they did to thieves in a caravan; one had been caught near the beginning of the journey and left staked out with his hands and feet missing.
Hasan Ali's excursion, of course, did not count as thiev-
ery, since Tom was *kafir*, an unbeliever.

He had made his way across the blasted landscape in
the dark, crossing several of the silted canals that once
had irrigated the plain, until he had put a good distance
between himself and the caravansary. He had kept away,
too, from the miserable hovels that poked through the
rubble here and there and from the dim lights of the waterfront district that was growing itself back again on the
banks of the Tigris.

Baghdad, he had learned from the caravan storytellers
and from the raffish local traders who had come out to
look the caravan over, had once been the most splendid
city in the world. It was hard to believe, looking at the
fields of desolation. Here had dwelt the caliph, a sort of
Saracen pope. Though Baghdad was hundreds of miles
inland, two mighty rivers had brought the ships of the
ocean to its gates, and through these crossroads of land
and water all the riches of Islam had flowed.

But about a century and a half ago, by the reckoning
of Tom's informants, the grandson of a human devil
named Genghis Khan, a fiend called Hülegü, had destroyed Baghdad. According to Mongol custom, all its
people were assembled on the plain outside its walls, the
women raped, then both sexes slaughtered down to the
smallest child. The city was then reduced to rubble to
prevent its being used again. But Baghdad was not so
easily obliterated. Its location was too tempting. So people began drifting back, the caravans came again, the
traders from the sea once more brought their goods up
the great rivers, and within a century it had resumed its
place as a center of civilization.

But twenty years ago, the Mongols had struck again.
The conquerer's name this time was Timur the Lame,
known by some as Tamerlane. Tamerlane, like the latter-

day Mongols of these parts, had become a Moslem himself, but that didn't stop him from imitating his ancestors. Once more Baghdad was sacked, its people systematically butchered, the palaces and libraries and mosques, which had been so painfully rebuilt, destroyed. Tamerlane had left his own architectural legacy: a tower made of a hundred thousand severed heads.

This time civilization did not return. With Tamerlane's passing the region had fallen under the sway of Qara Yusuf, leader of the Black Sheep Turks. Nominally he held Baghdad and Tabriz, but the wild tribesmen he ruled rode in and out of the city at their pleasure, picking at its corpse. What Hülegü and Tamerlane had left, they took.

Still, the caravans and the sea traders came, visiting the place as if touching on a savage shore, to exchange the riches of the East for the riches of the West. The merchants had skulked back under the dubious protection of a Qara Yusuf, who now saw their utility. At the bend in the Tigris, near the remains of the once-immense walls of the ancient Round City, a commercial quarter was again springing up with taverns and whorehouses for the sailors and camel drivers and limited amenities for the merchant class. The natural accretion of wealth was beginning cautiously to make itself felt.

Tom struggled for sleep in his nest of stone. A tumbled masonry head as big as his whole body stared at him out of its chipped eyes from a short distance away. Overhead, the desert stars were huge and brilliant. He heard the distant shriek of some predatory bird, like the hawks of England. After a while he rolled over and fell asleep.

In the morning things looked better. A dazzling sun came up over the harsh flat land and baked the nighttime chill out of his bones. The ruins looked dusty and harmless, their blood washed away by the years. He found some water at the bottom of one of the filled-in canals and washed, then made a breakfast out of a piece of bread he had taken with him from the camp.

He followed his nose to the waterfront. The smell of water was like a pungent wine in this parched land. He admired the brick quays and the curious woven reed docks with a professional eye. As outlandish as it was, it reminded him of Bristol. A freshwater seaport, far inland, was nothing new to him.

The Tigris was broad and slow-moving, its waters a muddy brown. It was full of small traffic, with a few big ships anchored out in the center of the current. Tom studied them avidly. They were nothing like European vessels or even the Saracen ships of the Mediterranean that he had seen after leaving Venice. There were no galleys among them and nothing like a round ship. He saw a long rakish craft made in one continuous curve, like an archer's bow; a three-masted vessel shaped like a spoon with a handle at one end; a double-ended one-master with a stern as sharp as its overhanging prow; a large, dignified ship with a high poop, like a halved pear with a step cut in it. He wondered if they were sewn together, as Conti had claimed, instead of being nailed. He found it hard to believe such a thing possible, but he had learned how marvelous Saracen craftsmanship could be.

The smaller river craft were just as exotic. His eye roved to one of the craft used by the lightermen. It was nothing but a big round basket woven of reeds, large enough to carry a dozen men or even two or three horses. They had a tendency to spin round and round when caught in an eddy in the current, but that didn't seem to bother the boatmen.

He spent the morning exploring the riverfront, picking up what information he could about the schedules of the ships currently at anchor. As Conti had maintained, the gulf into which the Tigris and its sister river flowed connected with the greater sea, and these Arab seamen fearlessly sailed to India, to the mysterious spice islands—had reached even the eastern shores of Cathay itself, if the sailors' vague references could be believed.

Most of the ships he inquired about, however, sailed the Arabian coast with humble goods—rice, dates, dried fish, gum, salt. Tom pressed the search for a vessel that plied India's spice coast.

"Yes, that one there, tied up at the end of the dock," grinned an evil-looking Omani with a scimitar tucked under his belt, whom Tom found idling under the awning of one of the market stalls that sold sweetened lemon juice and other refreshments. "But you don't want to sail aboard her."

Tom squatted down beside him. "Why not?"

The Omani drew a finger across his throat. "The cook's crazy. He chops up little boys and serves them in a curry to the captain. The captain's very partial to them, especially little Frankish boys."

"What's the captain's name?"

The Omani's grin grew wider. "Sindbad." He looked around and got a laugh from his companions.

Tom stood up. "Thank you," he said.

He walked down the long stone pier, hearing the sly remarks and laughter behind him. The ship looked solid enough, though old. If it was sewn together, the stitches didn't show. It carried two leaning masts bearing tilted lateen yards made of lashed-together tree trunks. The stern was high and broad, but the deck bore no shelter of any kind except a cook's shed. A small pen amidships contained three or four scrawny goats.

Tom stood at the foot of the gangplank, looking for someone to talk to. A black sailor with a rag around his loins was perched aloft like a stork, tucking up one of the linen sails. Another sailor was emptying bilge water from a leather bucket that someone below decks was handing to him. Flies buzzed around the carcass of a decapitated goat that a bare-chested man in a long skirt was butchering with a bloody scimitar.

The cook paused in his work to gather a heap of carved-up chunks in a square of cloth and went to the cookhut. A moment later there was a terrified scream, and a boy of about fourteen, with his long white gown girded between his legs for speed, came streaking out of the cook's shed with the cook hard on his heels, brandishing the scimitar. The cook took a violent swing at the boy's neck, a swing that surely would have swept the boy's head off his shoulders, but the boy ducked and the blade just missed the top of his turban. While the cook was off-balance, the boy scurried ahead, widening his lead. He sprinted down the gangplank, tripped at the bottom with a tinkle of brass, picked himself up, and ran flapping down the pier.

The cook followed, bellowing curses. After a dozen long strides he saw that he could not catch up with his quarry and turned back. He paused to pick up the spoons the boy had dropped, ignoring Tom's presence.

Tom looked him over at close range. The cook didn't look particularly crazy—only about as splenetic as most sea cooks. He was fiftyish, with dark pouches under his eyes and a paunch that overhung the knotted waist of his skirt.

A number of sailors had appeared at the rail of the ship to see what was going on. A lean swarthy man with a neatly clipped beard and mustache, whom Tom took to be the captain, pushed past them and called down to the cook, *"Eh da, ya Ahmed?"*

"Harami!" the cook spat. "That dog of a boy is a thief. I took after him, but he got away."

"That boy was a thief, the one before him was lazy, and the one before him was too clumsy," the captain said. "We sail after dawn prayers tomorrow, and we're already short two hands. How are we to fill out the crew if you keep scaring them off?"

The cook flew into a rage. "Do you expect me to put up with every son of a camel who creeps out of the desert? And then, just when I get one of them trained, you take him away from me and put him to hauling rope!"

"Excuse me, Captain," Tom said.

The captain noticed him for the first time. "Eh? What's this? Do you want something, brother?"

"Do you sail for Vijayanagar, *ya nakhoda?*"

The captain frowned. "Yes, we sail for Calicut tomorrow, for a cargo of pepper. It's no secret. Are you an unbeliever? Where did you learn the caravan talk? And who told you how to address a captain properly?"

"Take me with you, Captain."

"An unbeliever aboard?" the cook exploded in horror. He brandished his scimitar, his eyes rolling, and a drop of goat's blood flicked to Tom's cloak. "He would defile the ship!"

"Yes, I'm *nisrani*," Tom said to the captain, using a

more neutral word. "But I've worked ships before, and I know how to follow orders."

"You've worked Frankish ships," the captain said.

"What does it matter? A rope's a rope, and a strong back's a strong back."

The cook was beside himself. "A ship made unclean by an unbeliever on it! Allah would punish us for such a sin! We'd sink to the bottom!"

"Come on up here and we'll have a talk," the captain said.

The captain spent an hour with Tom, questioning him closely over tiny cups of the bitter black brew Tom had learned to drink these past months. He skillfully drew from Tom the extent of his experience on the ship from Bristol and, with a more approving mien, the lateen-rigged vessel he had sailed from Venice. He extracted from Tom the fact that he had worked as a camel boy in the caravan that was now camped north of the city but had his own reasons for staying clear of it now. Tom, for his part, learned that the ship was called a *boom*, and that its port of call, Calicut, though it had its own king called the Zamorin, was indeed part of a loose arrangement known as the kingdom of Vijayanagar. He learned further that the captain's name was not Sindbad, but Salem, and that many of his crew, fine, deep-chested fellows, were pearl divers when they weren't working as sailors. Pearls, however, were no part of the cargo bound for Calicut. "The Zamorin has his own pearl fishers," was all the captain would say, "and he gets them cheap—as cheap as lives."

The captain returned to the subject of the caravan.

"Are you a thief?" he asked.

"No," Tom said.

"You had better not be. Here, we cut off the right hands of thieves."

Tom slept on board that night. The other sailors had their favorite spots—a soft place in a coil of anchor rope, a nook in the curve of the rail, a hatch that provided a headrest. Even the captain slept on deck, balancing himself, still as a corpse, on the officers' bench. Tom found an uncontested strip of planking and stretched out. In the morning, at first light, the sailors prostrated themselves and said their prayers. Tom saw no harm in kneeling and saying a *Pater Noster* with them. This seemed to mollify the cook somewhat. Tom overheard the captain saying to him, "It's not *kufr*, unbelief, but *jahilaya*, the innocence of one who is yet to be converted." He joined the others for a breakfast of roast goat and beans, cooked in a clay-lined barrel and served up on a sheet of flatbread. His sojourn with the caravan had taught him to eat with his right hand only and to compliment the cook with a belch, and several of the sailors nodded and smiled at him approvingly.

It was backbreaking work after that—hoisting a ton of yard, straining at heavy bales in the stifling cargo hold to trim ship—and then he was turned over to the cook for menial chores.

But there was a moment, as the desert breezes pushed the ship south, and the brown river widened, and the sands on either side turned into forests of giant reeds, for him to stand at the mast and look out over the bowsprit at the waters beyond, and whisper to himself with dizzy disbelief: "Vijayanagar!"

CHAPTER 14

"What, not finished yet?" Dona Florbella said with a sniff. "Why, you began that bedcover ages ago!"

Inês flushed. "I've been working on it every spare minute, but . . ." She looked to her mother for corroboration, but Dona Beatriz would not raise her eyes from her own embroidery. ". . . but the pattern's very intricate, with the coat of arms and the other designs, and there are all those little seed pearls that take time to sew in. . . ."

"In your *spare* minutes?" Dona Florbella said acidly. "What on earth can you have to do that's more important than Helena's trousseau?" She turned to Dona Beatriz with her large jaw set and said, "Really, Beatriz, you should teach your daughter to show more gratitude for the favors she's received."

Dona Beatriz gave her sister a swift ingratiating smile. "Don't distress yourself, Dona Florbella. It will be ready by next *terca-feira*, I promise you."

"No sooner? There's still the matching bed linens to complete before I can show it as a full set . . . and what am I to do without my new *cotte* for the procession of Our Lady of Escoda?"

"There's plenty of time for the *cotte*—have I ever dis-

appointed you?" She fluttered her hands nervously.
"You'll be the envy of all the other women there."

Dona Florbella pursed her lips. "Very well, but keep
this lazy girl working. I've already mentioned the coverlet to the *condessa*, and she's asked to see it. I can't put
her off much longer."

"*Sim, sim*, Dona Florbella, don't worry," Dona Beatriz
said placatingly.

Dona Florbella swiveled back to Inês. "As for you, my
girl, you waste too much time playing Helena's clavichordium. I forbid it. You should know your place."

She left the little room with a definitive swish of fabric. A door slammed in the distance.

Inês turned to her mother with tears in her eyes.
"*Mamãe*, how could you promise? We'll both have to stay
up all night . . . work by candlelight. . . ."

"Hush . . . you don't realize how lucky we are to have
a place in Dom Rodrigo's household. Don't anger Dona
Florbella."

"It isn't fair! Helena's lazy! She doesn't do any sewing
on her own trousseau, and now she wants me to make
her a velvet cape for church as well so she can pretend
she made it herself! She orders me about and uses me as
a maid!"

Her mother put down her sewing and reached for the
bedcover. "Let me see the *sobrecama*. . . . You've done
beautifully. This is of a quality for royalty. After the
condessa sees it, every tongue in Lisbon will be wagging
about it."

"I'll never get it finished in time!"

"I'll help. We'll work on it from either end. I can leave
the *cotte* till later."

"*Mamãe, Mamãe*, you're going blind sewing for Dona
Florbella and Dom Rodrigo! They use you like a servant,
too. Dona Florbella dismissed her seamstress, and Dom
Rodrigo's saving money by having you make his doublets
instead of a tailor!"

Her mother looked about nervously. "You mustn't say
such things. Dom Rodrigo was kind to take us in. We've
got to earn our keep."

"There's Father's pension from the Prince, that Zarco

petitioned for after Father's shares reverted. That should be enough."

"Dom Rodrigo explained about that. It was very small. He applied to have it paid directly to him as the head of the household so that I wouldn't have to bother."

"It should go to you. And there should have been money left from the estate, too."

"That's enough, young lady," her mother said almost sharply, as her uneasiness transmuted itself into a shadow of her old parental authority. "It's not for you to question Dom Rodrigo."

She had startled herself. She gave Inês a tentative smile and went on, "We're only women, *moca*, and we're not expected to understand these things."

"I'm sorry, *Mamãe*."

Dona Beatriz softened. "I know it's hard, *preciosa*. You see your cousin accumulating a lavish *enxoval de noiva* for her marriage—you're even asked to contribute your needlework to it—and we're poor as sparrows. But consider this: Helena's already eighteen, a year older than you, and for all her preparations still not actually betrothed. She's a year closer to spinsterhood, and there's nothing sadder than an old maid's trousseau."

"I know, *Mamãe*," Inês said apologetically. "Dona Florbella hopes for a proposal from the *condessa*'s second son, and that's why she's trying to impress the *condessa* with what a good seamstress Helena is."

"You see? That's why Dona Florbella spoke to you—sharply. Promise you'll show a more willing attitude."

"I promise." After a pause, Inês spoke again: *"Mamãe?"*

"Yes, *filha?*"

"Do you think Dona Florbella meant what she said about my not playing the clavichordium anymore? Helena never plays it—it just gathers dust in her rooms. I don't play very often, really! Just sometimes when I'm feeling a little lonely, I go in there when she's not around and play some of the songs from the *cancionero* that Father gave to me."

Dona Beatriz bit her lip. "I'll speak to her. But in the meantime, perhaps you'd better not play it."

"All right, *Mamãe*."

They worked together on the pearl-embroidered counterpane. After a while Dona Beatriz, without looking up, said in a strained voice, "It's beautiful, *cara*. You're wonderful at needlework. Don't think I'm not sympathetic. We should be sewing a trousseau for you at this moment."

Inês looked across the field of stitches and saw a tear fall from her mother's eye. She was trying to think what to reply when the door opened and Miranda came in.

"Helena's having a fit because you won't make her the velvet cape for church," she announced smugly. "She's gone to my mother about it."

At thirteen, Miranda was still thin as a slat and hipless, but her retreating childhood had given her the beginnings of breasts and problems with her complexion. She kept her hands clean now and was starting to take an interest in clothes.

"I told her I'd do it when I had more time," Inês said.

"She says she's got to have the cape for Sunday," Miranda said, grinning.

"She knows that's impossible," Inês said. "I haven't even started, and I have too much else to do."

Miranda lolled in the doorway. "The *condessa*'s son, Dom Sebastião, is back from his hunting trip. He'll be in church Sunday."

"Well, she'll have to wear one of her other capes," Inês said. "I can't get it done in time."

"You'd *better*," Miranda said. "Or she's going to tell Mother."

"Tell your mother what?"

"That you've been making eyes at Dom Sebastião."

"That's ridiculous," Inês said, coloring.

"She's complaining that Dom Sebastião paid more attention to you than he did to her when he came to pay that call with his mother."

"I can't help that."

"You're to be kept out of sight the next time Dom Sebastião calls. I heard Mother say so."

"Dom Sebastião was no more than courteous," Inês said, her face still hot. "He hardly spoke more than a few words to me."

"And you're not to go to church with us on Sunday," Miranda said with a sniff like her mother's.

Inês felt a pit open at her feet. She had never missed mass since her father had died, in spite of the difficulties of living in the Da Cunha household, and she made it a point to receive communion every month instead of the three or four times a year that were deemed sufficient by most people in Lisbon society.

"But ... but how can that be?" she stammered. "Not to go to church ..."

"You're to go to Madre de Deos instead of to the cathedral this Sunday," Miranda said with open satisfaction. "The majordomo's to take you with the others."

"You must have heard wrong," Inês said. "There's some mistake. Dona Florbella and Dom Rodrigo could not intend to send me to church with the servants."

She looked to her mother for support, but Dona Beatriz only began sewing faster.

"*Mamae* ..." Inês said.

"Perhaps it won't hurt this once, if it will set Dona Florbella's mind at ease," Dona Beatriz said quickly. "If the young man is ... if his attention's straying, this will give him a chance to cool off."

"*Mamae*, I swear to you, I gave him no encouragement. I'm sure he doesn't know I'm alive."

Miranda made a face and left. Inês turned to her mother.

"I didn't, *Mamae*," she said.

"I know, *filha*," Dona Beatriz said, averting her gaze. "But sometimes a young man may misinterpret ... liveliness ... especially when the girl's attractive."

"Why would a *fidalgo* like Dom Sebastião be interested in a pauper like me, without a dowry, without a trousseau to bring to her marriage?" Inês asked bitterly. "Such a marriage wouldn't be allowed anyway. The *condessa* would repudiate it."

Dona Beatriz chose another seed pearl and stitched it expertly in place. "The *condessa* and Dom Sebastião are none of our business," she said nervously. "Think about your cousin's happiness!"

"I know, *Mamae*." Inês sighed. "If only Father hadn't

died. We'd be living on a grand *fazenda* on the island of
Madeira. The news is that Senhor Zarco's now settled
there, with the title of count, with his family, and that
Senhor Teixeira's been granted the captaincy of the
northern part of the island. Even Senhor Perestrello, of
the rabbits—the one who made *Pai* so angry—is growing
rich with the *infante*'s patronage, because he's so anxious
to attract settlers! Poor Father, that was his dream for us!"

"Hush now," Dona Beatriz said, her needle flying.
"That's water under the bridge. It's no use to talk about
such things."

"And from here," Prince Henry said with an expansive
sweep of his hand, "we will point our direction into the
unknown."

He was standing at the center of an enormous compass
rose, almost an acre in extent, made of paving stones. He
was bareheaded in the hot Algarve sun, having scandalized his servants by discarding the cumbersome cartwheel hat with a liripipe that hung almost to his feet,
after it kept getting in his way. He looked animated and
vigorous, his long lantern face burnt ruddy and the sea
breeze from below the cliffs riffling through his inverted
bowl of hair.

"Who's that standing next to him?" whispered Pedro.

"That's the Jew, Jaime of Majorca," Morales whispered
back. "The *infante* persuaded him to come here to Sagres
at great expense. It's said that he's the greatest
mapmaker in the world. His father was the famous Abra-
ham Cresques, who made the Catalan Atlas for the king
of France—but all agree that Mestre Jaime surpasses
even his father."

Pedro was impressed. He didn't know much about
maps, but he knew you had to be very learned to make
one. He gave more of his attention to the geographer.
Mestre Jaime was a small, colorless man wearing a scholar's robe and a flat velvet cap. He didn't look like anybody important, but the Prince had been treating him
with deference.

"I don't see his badge," Pedro said. Jews, he knew, were supposed to wear a yellow patch on their clothes.

"Oh, he's converted, so they say," Morales replied.

"You make maps, too," Pedro said. Morales, though he sprang from no higher stock than Pedro himself, was a respected character around Sagres. Good pilots were to be treasured beyond pearls, of course—that was part of it—but Morales had been borrowed from Zarco between voyages on a number of occasions by Prince Henry himself, to share his drawings and his observations with the cartographers at the Prince's school for navigators.

Morales laughed. "Not like Mestre Jaime. I draw charts of what I see—*portolani*, with directions and distances. Masters like Jaime put such pieces of knowledge together and draw a picture of the entire world. His father's atlas was a work of art, like Ptolemy's, but instead of guessing at the unknown, it included much practical information brought back by Marco Polo and also the Arab travelers that we Christians never hear about. Mestre Jaime hopes to go even further—to give a shape to Africa itself, if Africa has a shape."

"How can he give a shape to Africa when no one's ever sailed the coastline past Cape Non?"

"Not yet," Morales said thoughtfully. "But that's not for a lack of the *infante*'s coaxing. The crew that does it will be richly rewarded."

He broke off. Pedro knew it was a sore point with him that Zarco had given up on further exploration after being awarded his Madeira domain. Zarco was concentrating on developing the rich estate he had carved out for himself as the Count dos Lobos, and Morales was reduced to ferrying workmen and supplies back and forth for Zarco and the handful of boon companions to whom he had given land grants. Prince Henry was known to be annoyed at the slow pace of colonization, but he had pushed Madeira to the back of his mind for the time being while he built up his school of navigation.

Pedro returned his gaze to Mestre Jaime. Prince Henry was moving on now, crossing the great stone circle with its radiating lines, and his entourage was moving with him, but he had his head inclined toward the Jewish

geographer in continuance of some sort of private exchange. Pedro could guess that there were some who
were jealous of Jaime's intimacy with his new patron.
Henry could not move out of doors without at least fifty
people following him around, but today, when he was
showing off some of the new buildings that had been
completed on the cliff's flat top, the crowd was three or
four times larger than usual. They were ranged around
the *infante* at various distances, reflecting their degree of
importance. Richly dressed *fidalgos* with their own attendants, members of Henry's household, visitors from
Lisbon, mariners, and large numbers of the scholars and
craftsmen he had assembled here to populate the new
town he was building. Pedro located Zarco in the crowd,
splendidly dressed in a fine new doublet and long
pointed shoes that would have been of no use on the
deck of a ship. The former squire, now followed about by
a pair of squires of his own, was trying to edge closer to
the Prince's immediate circle, where he would be noticed.

Pedro's eye lit on an imposing trio in magisterial robes
and towering conical hats.

"Who are they?" he asked.

Morales crossed himself. "Astrologers. The *infante* has
five of them here. They're skilled in the use of the astrolabe, which they use to fix the position of the stars.
Mestre Jaime himself sets much store by them. He
brought an astrologer of his own with him from Majorca,
along with a number of skilled instrument makers he was
used to working with. The Prince hired all of them, just
like that!"

"Astrologers, geographers, instrument makers—to say
nothing of shipwrights and master craftsmen!" Pedro exclaimed. "Have there ever been so many kinds of learned
men collected in one place before?"

Morales clapped him on the back and laughed. "That's
Prince Henry's object—put them all together, systema-
tize their knowledge, fire them up, and out of all these
separate talents will come one big enterprise. It's a new
idea in the world, *hijo!*"

"Is there any place here for a simple sailor, then?" Pedro asked, only half in jest.

Morales squeezed his arm. "Listen, *hijo*, they'll always need sailors. The learned men stay at home and argue. But a place isn't discovered until a human foot's been set in the sand."

Prince Henry, drawing the loose crowd with him like a magnet, had reached the edge of the huge stone circle. He stopped to point out something to those closest to him, and everyone strained to hear.

"And that long low building there, between the chapel and the observatory, will contain the workrooms for Mestre Jaime's cartographers," he was saying. "Everything they need will be at their disposal. A library will be attached, where we'll collect every scrap of knowledge, old and new: the classical geographers like Ptolemy and Strabo, the works of Herodotus, the logs of our own brave mariners showing winds and currents—everything! For example, I have secret agents in Tunis who have informed me that the Saracen caravans that bring back black slaves and gold, which they've gotten from other caravans, cross the desert in five or six weeks. So it seems clear that Africa doesn't simply end in a fiery barrier or a boiling swamp. Far past the desert, below the latitude of Cape Non, there must be green lands."

"The Terra Incognita of Ptolemy?" someone asked.

"Perhaps," said the Prince.

"Pardon me, *infante*," said a young Lisbon fop in a slashed tunic and green leather shoes that were so elongated that their pointed toes had to be hoisted aloft by lengths of cord tied to the knees. "But how can such rumors about Africa's interior help a cartographer to deduce Africa's outward form, which is all a mariner needs to know?"

Pedro waited for thunderclouds to gather, but the Prince retained his high good humor.

"All knowledge is valuable. Every crumb of information may some day fit into the puzzle. In the meantime, a mariner who sets forth from our launching point here at Sagres will be armed with all the facts we can give him."

"Can you *order* discovery then, like an omelet?"

"Ask Morales—he set out in advance to discover Madeira, and he did." The Prince searched the fringes of the crowd and spotted Morales. "Isn't that so, Senhor Morales?"

Morales removed his woolen seaman's cap and stepped forward. "Come along, Pedrozinho," he hissed, dragging Pedro with him.

"Yes, Your Honor," Morales affirmed, "but it took us two tries. And we only landed on Madeira's doorstep because we were blown off course. It was an accident."

"God grant us more such accidents," Prince Henry said. He turned to his previous interlocutors. "It only goes to demonstrate the truth of what I've been saying. Can discovery be ordered up like an omelet, you ask? No, but we can create a climate of discovery"—he seemed pleased with the phrase—"a climate in which discovery is more likely to occur."

He paused to gesture toward the rising buildings of his school for navigators and the new clifftop town that was springing up to support it.

"And second," he went on, "we can keep trying. Always go a little farther, even if it's only fifty miles." He turned back to Morales and said, with a hint of severity in his voice, "You never passed Cape Non, Senhor Morales. I can't fault you for discovering Madeira instead. But when do you return to your original quest?"

Zarco took the opportunity to move in. "I've been keeping him busy sailing to Madeira, Your Excellency. We're making much progress. Already we're laying out a port of Machico, and we hope to begin a city of Funchal—"

Henry cut him off. "A port of Machico, a city of Funchal—so far they're only names, Dom João. Where are the people? As yet, the population of Madeira consists only of the proprietors of a few *fazendas* and their servants."

For once, Zarco was at a loss. He bit his lip. "I'm trying to persuade a number of additional *fidalgos* to settle there. But it's still very primitive. There are no comforts, no society yet. They prefer to run their Madeira properties from afar."

"You only repeat what I've been saying. We need people—hundreds, no, thousands of people."

Zarco spread his hands and smiled with the old charm that had worked for him before. "Where am I to find them? I'd have to empty the prisons."

"Do it, then," the Prince said sharply. "I give my permission."

Zarco was taken aback. He opened his mouth to reply, but at that moment a dignified gentleman in clerical garb stepped out of the throng and said, without first bothering to ask leave, "I'll pass Cape Non for you, Dom Henrique."

The Prince turned from Zarco to regard the newcomer. "Well said, Fray Goncalo. I've had nothing but excuses from my mariners for the last five years."

"No excuses. I'll sail as soon as I return from the Canaries."

"I would not wish you to miss a sure chance for glory against a gamble on a will-o'-the-wisp," Henry agreed. "You're joining the de Castro expedition?"

"Dom Fernando is putting me in command of a ship and a troop of horse. I'm supplying several *cavaleiros* from my own household as well. It's not right that the Canaries should remain unoccupied by a Catholic prince and their heathen inhabitants denied salvation. By my faith, sir, the king of Castile forfeited any claim to ownership when he failed to conquer those savage people and bring them the benefits of Christianity. Those unhappy islands have been nothing but a haven for those French pirates to whom that weakling on the Castilian throne sold the captaincy. And now the Frenchmen are gone, having sold their rights to the count of Niebla, who in turn sold them to another Castilian, Guillen de las Casas, who still has done nothing to convert the natives and assert the rights of Castile. No, sir, if Castile had any claim to the Canary Islands, it's long since evaporated. Your father, the king, injures no one by taking possession. The pope will agree readily enough to Portuguese ownership when he sees the conquest has been accomplished!"

Morales nudged Pedro. "That's Fray Goncalo Velho Cabral, the commander of Almoural in the Order of Christ, of which our prince is the Grand Master. He's a firebrand, and the *infante* is inclined to trust him all the more for his fervor. I don't doubt that he'll either kill the natives or convert them, and then go on to break the barrier of Cape Non for Prince Henry. You ought to hitch up with him, Pedro my son. There'll be more glory sailing with Goncalo Velho than in serving as a ferryman for Senhor Zarco. I'd sign on with him myself if Zarco didn't have me by the balls."

"*Como?*" said Pedro, startled by the idea.

Zarco was trying to scramble back from his fall from grace. "Fray Goncalo makes my point for me," he said with a winning smile. "It's just as important to develop what's already been discovered as to make new discoveries. If we don't establish a strong presence on Madeira and Porto Santo, then we run the risk of having the Castilians or someone else move in on us, as we are trying to do with the Canaries. John of Castile may be a weakling, but he still claims that Madeira is rightfully part of the Canaries group and so part of the papal grant of eighty years ago."

"Yes, yes, Dom João," Henry said abstractedly. "See about the prisoners. I'll give you all support." He turned back to Fray Goncalo. "You're not planning to invade the islands of Lanzarote and Fuerteventura? The Castilians maintain small garrisons there."

"No," Fray Goncalo assured him. "We'll confine the attack to Grand Canary and one or two of the other islands in the group. We don't want to kill Castilians and stir up a hornet's nest. Your father forbids it. Leave politics to the politicians, Dom Fernando says. We're only plain soldiers. Later, perhaps, with the help of the Vatican, you can gain possession of Lanzarote and Fuerteventura by diplomacy."

"Good, good," Prince Henry said. "We shall all pray for your success, Fray Goncalo. When you return from the Canaries, come to see me, and I'll see about outfitting a ship for you. By that time our learned mathematicians here at the school should have completed their new tables for the position of the sun at noon at different latitudes for every day of the year. They promise to eliminate some of the errors in the old calculations. It ought to be an immense help to those navigators who are versed in the use of the backstaff or the astrolabe."

Fray Goncalo laughed. "Bless me, I'm no scientist. I'll just keep sailing south, and when I pass Cape Non, I'll know it."

Morales drew Pedro off to the side. "You see how the Prince gave Zarco short rope. Faith and discovery, that's what's important to him. What I wouldn't give to be sailing south with a set of the Prince's new calculations in my pocket! I know how to use a backstaff, I promise you! Well, Pedro son, are you going to speak to Goncalo Velho?"

"I can't desert Zarco," Pedro protested. "I owe too much to him."

"You owe him nothing," Morales said. "Do you have a *fazenda* on Madeira?"

"But would Fray Goncalo take me?"

"He'll take you. I'll guarantee it. You're a good luck charm, Pedrozinho. You're one of the sailors who discovered Madeira." He screwed up his ugly face in a wink. "And if that isn't enough, tell him you know my secrets."

CHAPTER 15

At first light Tom opened his eyes, though he had been lying awake for a quarter hour. The dream of a golden city still gripped him. The muscular legs still entwined him; that had been no dream. He lay still, watching the dark square of window brighten to pearl.

"Vijayanagar?" he said aloud.

The *devadasi* rose from the mat like a cobra, sleek and sinuous, and pointed through the open window vaguely toward the north. She showed no surprise at the sudden question, but then, she never showed surprise at anything Tom, or any man, said or did.

"But how far?" Tom said. He groped for the Tamil words. Time and distance seemed to have no meaning in Calicut. He never got a clear-cut answer.

She said something that might have meant a mile or might have meant infinity, and then inquired, with an intimate touch substituting for speech, whether he wanted to please the god Shiva with her again.

"God's blood!" he said. "You've already drawn me more times than a man should be drawn in a single night, with your temple tricks. I have no doubt you could do it again, but it's morning. Time to start a day."

She smiled and shrugged, understanding his meaning if not his English words. She stood up with a jangle of ankle bracelets and put on the two garments that were a temple girl's going-out costume—a silver-bordered skirt that was gathered between the thighs and a brief, open jacket that framed the breasts without concealing them. Her waist was impossibly narrow, like those in the temple carvings, but she swelled into opulence above and below. Her hair was shiny black in two swooping wings, and the knowledgeable brown oval of her face was decorated with a small painted spot, like an eye, on her forehead, and a jewel in one nostril. Her name was Lakshmi, and she was the nightly gift of the Zamorin.

After she had gone, he got dressed himself, a simple matter of wrapping the length of cloth called a *dhoti* around his hips and tucking it up between his legs. He remembered to leave the outer door of the jakes ajar and shout, *"Mehtar!"* into the courtyard so that the sweeper who squatted there day and night would come and empty the slop jar. That was a hard thing to get used to. He had made a mistake, when first he had been installed in this luxury, by treating the man as if he were human. That had shocked his servant, Lal, who had excitedly explained that the sweeper was an untouchable, not to be noticed. Tom wondered what Lal would think if he knew that his new master was an untouchable himself—after all, hadn't he once emptied chamber pots for Master Philpot? If the Zamorin had known that, he never would have turned him into a palace pet, yellow hair or not.

He went to look out the window. He had a fine view of the elephant stable from here—a long stone building of arches and domes, fronted by man-sized hitching posts that were carved all over with gods and animals. The location of his apartment, in the wing that overlooked the stables and the zoo, pretty much told the story. Though he had been given his own cook and attendants and the services of one of Calicut's most expensive *devadasis* to keep him happy, he was no less a pet than the Zamorin's apes and monkeys and white elephants and the tiger cub he kept chained near his throne.

He sighed and looked past the domes of the stable to the green jungle that rose behind the city to the north and east. The capital city that gave its name to the empire of

Vijayanagar lay somewhere there—that much he had been able to find out. But, like Lakshmi, no one he had talked to seemed able to tell him how far away it was, or how one got there. It was doubtful whether even the Zamorin had ever bothered to go there. Though he was theoretically under the suzerainty of the emperor of Vijayanagar—*raja*, he was called—the Zamorin ruled, as far as Tom could tell, as an absolute despot, even to the point of having small wars with the rulers of neighboring city-states of the Malabar Coast, who were also Vijayanagar's vassals.

Calicut, for all its splendors, had been a disappointment to Tom. It was true, as Conti had said, that the merchants bought and sold pearls and precious stones in the streets. And that the wives of fishermen wore gold bangles. And the temples and palaces, dripping with carved stone fantasies, were astonishing. But beyond the facade of wealth, the mass of people were poor—poorer even than the poor of England. Starving poor, naked poor. The gold bangles were all the family dowry, worn where it could be seen, accumulated through the privation of lifetimes, hoarded through the hunger unto death. Even the pearl fishers got no benefit from their finds. The Zamorin appropriated the largest and finest pearls for himself, at no compensation. The remainder were bought by fat merchants, sitting on their porches, at their own prices. It never occurred to the pearl fishers to bargain with the merchants directly. Instead they sold their catch—the part of it that was not taken by the Zamorin's agents—to a horde of naked and homeless urchins who descended on the beach whenever the log rafts of the pearl fleet came in. The boys, out of whatever small investment capital they had been able to accumulate through begging or previous pearl transactions, paid a pittance. They then went to the merchants on their porches and told how much they had spent. The merchants paid them something above and beyond that—enough for a meal or two. Tom's Arab shipmates, pearl fishers themselves in their home waters, looked on their Indian counterparts with pity and contempt. Still, they themselves bought pearls from the merchants for resale at the caravan terminini at Baghdad and elsewhere; there was enough profit for all.

Captain Salem had asked Tom to return with the ship on the Baghdad run. There were always a few beached Arab sailors at Calicut, and he would have no trouble replacing Tom, but Tom had fit in well with the crew and had proved to be a good sailor. Even the choleric cook, Ahmed, had urged him to stay aboard. "For a *kafir*, you're not bad," he had grunted. "If you'd convert to Islam, so that you wouldn't contaminate the food for Believers, you could turn into a pretty fair cook."

But Tom, having attained Calicut, was not going to turn back yet. Regretfully, the captain had paid him his wages. "You've earned every *dirhen*," he had said. "It ought to last you until we return on the spring voyage. If you're still here, you can ship on with us again."

Tom had let him think what he wished. In his mind, he had decided to go on to the fabled Vijayanagar as soon as he had tasted what Calicut had to offer.

Already he knew that Conti's colorful tales had to be taken with a grain of salt. There were no gold-digging ants, for example. The Zamorin had no such miraculous source of supply. By all accounts he was a grasping miser who squeezed gold out of others however he could. The Arab traders who maintained stations in Calicut had regularly to pay him tribute in gold; nothing else would do.

But Conti had been right about one thing: Calicut was where pepper came from. Tom had seen the vast paved warehouse yards where acres and acres of peppercorns were spread out to dry in the sun by barefoot men who raked them with their toes. More spices came to Calicut from unknown lands farther east.

At least, Tom thought, he had beaten Conti here. No one had ever seen a European before. No one had ever heard of England.

He would beat Conti to Vijayanagar, too, he promised himself. The Zamorin sent tribute there. There would be roads through the jungle and people who traveled them.

When his ship left without him, Tom set about exploring Calicut and its environs. The people were like people anywhere, despite their strange ways—willing to pause and be friendly with a stranger who tried earnestly to communicate with them through a battery of gestures and a grabbag of mispronounced words. His yellow hair and blue eyes were always a cause for wonderment, but once people got over them, they decided that he was just as human as themselves. Tom at first thought that Hindus were a kind of Christian—they had buildings he took to be churches, they had a sort of cross with bent arms that they called a *svastika*, and the first statue he saw was what might have been a bare-breasted Virgin Mary with a child. But then he saw that the stone was alive with statues, a whole pantheon of gods and goddesses and demons—deities with four arms and three heads, a god with an elephant's head, a terrifying goddess with long fangs and a necklace of skulls doing a dance on the backs of the slain. As his eye grew more sophisticated, he saw that some of the carvings were stylized representations of male and female sexual organs, called *lingam* and *yoni*, that he learned later were supposed to echo the divine principle. But one did not have to be very sophisticated to understand the carved pillars depicting whole cascades of men and women, in couples and groups, performing the sex act in every possible combination and position, and to realize that their acrobatics were intended as a form of worship. The temple girls he had thought at first were nuns or priestesses were *devidasis*, wives of Shiva, who made love to worshipers for what they would pay and gave the coin to the god.

Tom, unsure of custom and hoarding his meager pay, did not go in to the *devadasis*. (Afterward he had an inkling from Lakshmi of how lightly regarded the temple courtesans were.)

For a while he subsisted on bazaar food from the open-air vendors—*chupattis* wrapped around curried vegetables, a kneaded concoction of pulse and chiles called *chattu* that was eaten by the lowest laborers but that was marvelously filling, puffed rice snacks by the handful, fried sweets, and sticky unidentifiable confections in violent colors. But cheap as it was, it ate into his funds day by day. He could not steal here in Calicut, where people

warded off hunger by chewing betel nut wrapped in
leaves; to steal food was to steal someone's life.

With what was left of his money he thought to improve his lot with a little pearl trading, as the urchins
did. He walked some miles down the beach to where
the miserable huts of the pearlers' village sat back from
the bay. A swarm of boys was already there, waiting
for the rafts to come in. No one dared to challenge Tom;
he was bigger than any of them. The pearlers returned in
the mid afternoon—dark, wiry men and women who
were stark naked except for the net bags that hung at
their waists. They had lost a man to the sharks that day,
and there was a delay in the trading while they beat the
shark charmer. Tom found a fisher who was willing to
trade with him, a small, dark, rackabones fellow who
sized up the Arab clothes Tom was still wearing, wrinkled
his brow at Tom's yellow hair and then decided to ignore
it, and drew Tom furtively to one side. He fumbled in his
string bag and showed Tom a large, round pearl that he
offered to sell him if he promised not to tell where he got
it. "*Nahin dum*, lord," he said, putting a finger to his lips
in the universal gesture. Tom paid him a gold dinar for
the pearl, about a fourth of what he had left. The pearler
knew what Arab money was; the dinar disappeared into
the net bag, wrapped in a leaf, and the pearler was gone
before Tom knew it. He bought six more pearls that day,
small ones, for only a few silver *dirhen*, and then he
started to worry about it. He started a conversation about
pearls in general with one of the urchins, using gestures,
a little Tamil, and pictures drawn in the sand, and
learned what a dangerous thing he had done. The large
pearls belonged to the Zamorin. The punishment for pos-
sessing one would be dreadful.

As soon as Tom was alone, he knotted up the pearl in
a scrap of cloth torn from what had been his shirt, and
hid it in his drawers. It represented a major part of his
funds now—funds that could not be spent as long as he
was in Calicut. But someday he would cash it in; he had
seen what pearls were worth in Venice.

The small pearls he took to the merchants—*banias*,
they were called here. No one dared to make them angry,

and it was unthinkable to argue with them. One of them inspected Tom's merchandise, shook his head in disbelief when Tom told him how much he had paid but said he would allow him a profit, did a quick calculation on the value of Arab currency, and paid him in the coin of Calicut. The difference did not quite pay for his bazaar meal that day—he had to dip into his reserve again. He was little better off than if he had not bought the pearls at all.

He had thought, working for Master Philpot, that he had learned what it meant to be sharp, but there were no merchants in all the world like the *banias*. No matter how he struggled in their net, his situation became worse. In nine days he was out of funds, and the *banias* were offering him credit.

Tom backed away. He had seen where that could lead. There were peasant families that were mortgaged for generations to come. The *banias* owned them, their children, their plots, the fruits of all their labor—only allowing them back enough to keep them alive, at interest rates that compounded the debt. It was a villeinage worse than any that had ever existed in England before the revolt of Wat Tyler.

He went hungry for a day and thought wistfully of stealing. But stealing food in the bazaar was not practical, when the vendors hovered over their pots in narrow spaces hemmed in by other vendors, preparing meals that were meant to be borne away on a palm leaf. At best he might snatch a handful of rice from a pot or make off with a half-cooked *chupatti*. And then, with his yellow hair blazing like a beacon, he could never return to the bazaar again—would not, in fact, be safe anywhere in Calicut.

Regretfully, he sold his little Venetian knife and dined for two days on the proceeds. Hungry again, he wandered through the city, growing progressively lightheaded, looking for an opportunity to beg. Beggars there were in Calicut, but they were holy men, *sadhus*, they were called: filthy, naked creatures with self-inflicted mutilations or skewers through various parts of their anatomy. Still, their begging bowls were kept filled—by people who had nothing themselves. It was different for those who had no claim to holiness. They might starve, for all anyone cared. There was food tantalizingly in sight for Tom, food going to waste, but it was unreachable. Once he encountered a Brahmin, wearing the sacred cord that was their vestment, scattering cooked rice on the ground for the insects in order to gain merit in the next life. Tom followed, but when he tried to pick up some of the rice, the Brahmin's attendants drove him away and would have beaten him if they could have caught him. And then there was the food in the temples, offered by the *devadasis* to the god Shiva—whole banquets laid in front of a stone idol, while the girls danced and sang and offered their bodies, maintaining the fiction that the god was dining. But it would have been worth Tom's life to try to get a bite. When the dancing was over, the food was borne away—to be eaten, he was sure, by the girls and the priests.

He tried going around to the Arab merchants who maintained trading posts in Calicut. Hindus he could not fathom, but Moslems he felt able to deal with.

He almost lost his life. The Saracens here had heard of Europeans, all right. When Tom had outdistanced the two large Moors with scimitars who had been set on him by a Granadan spice merchant, it occurred to him that he must have driven the Saracens frantic. They were terrified that Christians would learn to bypass the caravan trade that was fed by Arab ships through the Persian Gulf and the Red Sea and deal with the spice purveyors of India directly. That would have put all Islam out of business. Tom, ragged and hungry, was an unlikely advance agent for the western commercial interests, but when much is at stake, reason flees. Now that the Saracens knew a Christian was in Calicut, they would not rest until he was disposed of.

He was too hungry to care. He wandered back toward the market square. He fingered the large pearl that was knotted beneath the waistband of his drawers. He had a king's ransom there, and he couldn't spend it on a few *annas* worth of food. Light-headed as he was, he began to play with a dangerous thought: He would go to one of the *banias* and confess. The greed of the *banias* would overcome the peril of dealing in the property reserved for the Zamorin; they must have ways of dealing in clandestine merchandise through the Arab traders. And grasping as the *banias* were, they always stuck to the letter of their word—he might get a few *pice* for the pearl, maybe even a whole rupee.

He had trudged halfway across the market square when he heard a shout from one side.

"There he goes! The yellow hair!"

Running feet slapped the pavement. Half a dozen large men in expensive satin loincloths, with gold ear hoops and bristling waxed mustaches, were after him. Tom recognized the livery—they were the Zamorin's palace guards.

He turned and fled. His legs had never failed him before, but hunger had weakened him, and his flight from the scimitar-wielding Moors had used up his reserves. His legs started to give out, the soldiers gained on him, and just when he was about to reach the edge of the square, another half-dozen men in satin livery appeared in front of him, reaching.

Many hands held him. He heard a confusion of voices, and more or less made out what they were saying.

"It's not paint, then? It's really his hair?"

"His eyes—look at their color! Is he blind?"

Exploring fingers hauled down the waistband of his drawers a couple of inches. For a horrible moment, Tom thought they knew the pearl was hidden there, but they missed it.

"Look at the true color of his skin! Like the belly of a fish!"

Nobody spoke to Tom. They hustled him along as if pulling a dog's leash and brought him to a waiting palanquin borne by four men in calico diapers. There was a round of encouraging smiles and gestures, and Tom understood that he was supposed to get in. They bore him to the palace in triumph, chattering like monkeys all the way.

The Zamorin turned out to be a small, brown, chubby man in a white skirt and conical hat and nothing else, sitting on an elevated cushion. He clapped his hands in delight when he saw Tom.

"So the reports of a yellow-haired alien in the marketplace were true." he said. "The king of Cochin may have a white tiger and an ape with blue cheeks and a red bottom, but he doesn't have one of these!"

Now Tom was getting fat—fatter than he'd ever been in his life. He looked down at his middle and saw that little roll of flesh beginning to overhang the waistline of his *dhoti*. He could always make it disappear by standing up straight, but he was not yet twenty years of age, and he wondered if some day he would look like some of the Zamorin's stuffed capons. He was drinking too much, too—the potent palm liquor called toddy that made your head split wide the next day.

"*Koi hai!*" he called, clapping his hands.

Lal, his servant, appeared at once, miraculously bearing a tray. He must have been waiting just around the corner.

"Your breakfast, lord," he said, his face widening like a split coconut around his grin.

He set down the tray. It was a curry of vegetables, with rice and curds. Tom sat cross-legged to eat. He could have done with a little meat, but they did not kill cows in Calicut, and Lal had tried to make him understand that only the lower castes ate other sorts of flesh. The bout with Lakshmi had left him ravenous, though, and he ate the lukewarm mess with appetite. From its temperature, his breakfast must have been ready and waiting for him for some time, with Lal itching to serve it.

"You must hurry, lord," Lal said. "The king waits."

So it was to be one of those days, when he would have to hang around, bored senseless, at the foot of the *gaddi*—the word meant both cushion and throne here—to be an object of curiosity for the Zamorin to show off. It would be different if the Zamorin talked sensibly with him sometimes, but he never showed the slightest interest in the customs of far-off Europe—didn't even seem to have any clear awareness that such a place existed past the boundaries of the Arab and Mongol lands that he *had* heard about. Tom might have come from somewhere in India's vast interior, for all the Zamorin cared, like the brace of white elephants he was so proud of.

Tom rebelled. "Let him wait, then," he said.

Deliberately, he took another helping of rice.

Lal danced around in anguish. "A summons has been sent, lord. You must make yourself ready."

"I forbid you to speak of it," Tom said. "You may go. Wait! You may bring me some toddy."

"Yes, lord." Lal touched the insides of Tom's calves in submission and crept out backward, looking unhappy.

As soon as he was gone, Tom sprang to his feet. He brushed his teeth with the tooth stick, dashed water on his face, and wound a turban around his head to minimize his conspicuousness.

Lal chose that moment to return with the toddy. Tom had forgotten about it. He took it from Lal and drank it down, while Lal, prevented from speaking, stood there with tears running down his face. He followed Tom out to the verandah, wringing his hands. Tom left him there, staring dolefully after him.

He pushed his way through the crowded streets outside the palace, not knowing where he wanted to go. He was in hot water, he knew, but he didn't care. The Zamorin would shriek at him, but it would blow over. He wouldn't be harmed. He still had too much novelty value.

He paused for a while to watch a snake charmer. Sooth, Calicut was better than an English fair! A large bony cow paused to lick the rice out of the bowl of a beggar. A troupe of naked children ran by. A very holy rich man, with a length of his skirt thrown over his shoulder like a toga and a gauze mask across his face to filter the air of insects, walked slowly on, with an attendant to sweep the path before him and another to carry a parasol for him; the crowd parted respectfully in front of him and closed again in his wake.

Tom raised his eyes above the jumbled roofs of the city to the green, dense slopes of the eastern hills.

Did he really want to return to the Zamorin's palace? Somewhere beyond the *ghats* and through the jungles to the north lay Vijayanagar, a city to make Calicut look like a backwater. He could start walking there now if he wanted to, following footpaths and asking directions on the way.

He reached to finger the pearl hidden in his *dhoti* for reassurance, and with a shock realized it wasn't there. He had been so distracted by his little contest with Lal that he had walked off without it.

Tom cursed his absentmindedness. He kept the pearl in a little locked chest beside his cot for his nightly bouts with Lakshmi, but he was always careful to have it on his person when he left his apartment. None of the servants would be brave enough to steal from him while he was high in the Zamorin's regard, but he had no illusion about Lal's light fingers, which he was sure wandered through his possessions at every opportunity to inventory them against some future contingency.

He would have to go back. Lal would be relieved that he had seemingly changed his mind, and he would have to make his appearance in the Zamorin's throne room. But he could endure it for one more day. Tonight he would send Lakshmi away, and tomorrow, before dawn, he would empty the chest of its accumulated trinkets, take what he could of his furnishings, and leave before anyone was the wiser.

He turned to retrace his steps back to the palace. But before he had gone more than a few paces, he was shoved aside by someone who was bulling his way through the street crowd, shouting, "Make way, make way! A message for the Zamorin!"

Tom looked after him. He was some sort of petty official, to judge by his bangles and brocade. He was coming from the direction of the waterfront.

A moment later four or five more officials came puffing up the hill, trying to beat one another to the palace.

Tom tried to stop one. "*Roko*, brother! What's happened?"

The man shook him off. "Big ships! Hundreds of them!"

He ran on. More people came boiling up from the harbor after the officials, spreading the news as they went, hoping to share however minutely in any reward that might be given.

In their wake the milling crowds began a contrary movement to get to the shore. A sweetmeat vendor packed up his portable shop and hurried to be among the first to hawk his wares to whatever customers were about to land. A blind *fakir* regained his vision and joined the flow. People began to spill out of houses and temples to see what was happening.

Tom followed the crowd. What could be bigger than an Arab dhow to have excited the official to such a degree? It could only be a fleet of ships from Europe!

But how had they gotten here? He knew from his travels that there was no way through the Mediterranean to Indian waters. To get to the Red Sea or the Persian Gulf, you had to pass across Saracen lands.

He was too excited to try to think it through further. He would find out soon enough.

When he reached the waterfront and pushed his way through to the sands, he saw hundreds of small boats paddling out to sea to meet the approaching fleet. Closer at hand, sweating harbor officials in calico loincloths were dragging a big *kattumaran* of lashed logs into the surf; it was their job to warn incoming ships of the treacherous sandbars around the immediate approach to Calicut and advise them to anchor a couple of miles up the coast.

Tom peered at the horizon, trying to make out the oncoming fleet. He saw distant sails of an unfamiliar shape—not the triangular sails of the Mediterranean or the square sails of northern Europe, but tall, narrow, stiff sails standing in rows like so many fans, five or more masts to a ship.

No, this was not what he had thought. It was something even stranger.

He drew in his breath. The mysterious fleet blackened the horizon like an advancing hedge. He had never seen so many ships. He counted up to a hundred, then lost track.

All the nations of Christendom could not have assembled such a fleet. Even the Venetians, with their Galley of Flanders and Galley of Barbary and Galley of Romania, accounted four or five ships to be an impressive fleet.

A war fleet—now that was something else. As a boy in Redcliffe, Tom had heard the older men say that King Henry had assembled a thousand ships to ferry his army to Agincourt. But King Henry's fleet must have consisted mostly of one-masted cogs and anything even smaller that would float—not mighty vessels like these!

For even at a distance, with those queer Venetian-blind sails no larger yet than the nails of his little fingers, Tom could tell how massive and beamy these mighty ships were. One of them, escorted by a squadron of five-masted vessels, had—Tom could scarce believe his eyes!—nine masts.

If it *was* a war fleet, then Calicut would shortly be under its dominion. A fleet like that could lay all Calicut waste with its guns without ever coming ashore. The flighty officials of the Zamorin had never seen such a force here on the Malabar Coast under the protective shield of Vijayanagar, where a war meant a day's skirmish against a neighbor with a few elephants and a barefoot battalion of men with spears.

But the possibility seemed not to have occurred to the Zamorin's ministers. A gaggle of flustered bureaucrats in their ceremonial best—silk loincloths in gorgeous colors—had arrived belatedly at the shore. Tom saw them try to hail the diminishing *kattumaran* containing the port officials—attempting to call it back so that they could be the first to make contact—but if the harbormaster could hear them, he wasn't responding. Hastily, the ministers commandeered a boat of their own, a graceless lighter propelled by eight low-caste oarsmen.

The *banias*, too, were getting a boat into the water. There were three of them, fanning themselves with palm leaves while their servants launched a small, stately craft with a thatched shelter. They saw only the possibilities of profit in everything.

For a moment he thought of asking if they needed an-

other rower. Then he remembered that he was no longer
a casteless toiler; he was a pampered creature of the
Zamorin's.

God's blood! That reminded him that he had intended
to return to his quarters to remove the contraband pearl
from the possibility of prying eyes.

He could not worry about that. Not when wonder was
being borne to him from across an unknown sea on the
wings of those unlikely ribbed sails.

He knew where the ships would land. Let the ogling
folk around him stare out to sea until the strangers responded to the harbormaster's signals and changed
course. He hitched up his *dhoti* and set off at a trot along
the bayshore.

The ground around the encampment had been trampled into packed earth by the hundreds of horses that
were going to and fro from the beach to escort the porters, and by the tough-looking cavalrymen who were
riding picket around the perimeter in squads of four.
The riders were stocky men with yellow skin and flat
cheeks, somewhat like Mongols, dressed all alike in
leather armor and conical caps topped by spikes.

Tom stood in the underbrush, as close to the compound as the soldiers would allow anyone to get, watching the activities of the strangers with admiration and a
touch of awe. He had never seen anything like it. Thousands of men, each to a task, had swarmed ashore from
the gigantic ships and erected a small city in a matter of
hours. There was a stout outer palisade of carved and lacquered wood that had been brought in whole finished
sections from the ships and fastened together, and the
clustered buildings inside had been assembled in the
same manner out of wall panels complete with windows,
door, and dovetailed expanses of red-lacquered roof. The
watchtowers at the four corners had been floated ashore
and carried entire from the beach by immense gangs of
baggy-drawered, shaven-headed men, like rectangular
thousand-legged dragons, then hoisted upright by a thousand arms hauling on pulley ropes. They were manned

now by sentries with crossbows, who beat a drum every quarter hour.

But the strangers were not at all menacing. It was just that they were as single-minded as ants. They had been firm but courteous to the swarms of sightseers who had descended on the encampment, keeping them at bay but letting it be known with pointing fingers and simple gestures that they were here to call on the Zamorin with gifts. Now the first pack train, loaded down with saddlebags, was trickling through the lacquered gate, heading in the direction of the Zamorin's palace with a cavalry escort.

"*Kya hogya*, brother, what did you see?" Tom asked the shivering pearl fisher standing next to him.

The fisher's name was Ram, and he had actually seen the strangers at close hand, as he had told one and all. He had been paddling his raft in the gulf when the great ships loomed over him, and, overcoming his fright, he had allowed himself to be taken aboard to answer their questions about reefs and anchorage. But they had spoken no known language, he told Tom, and though their interpreters had tried out a variety of tongues, they had been forced to resort to pantomime. They had shown him a statue of the Buddha, though, and seemed gratified that he had recognized it. Before putting him and his raft back in the water, they had rewarded him with gold, and he was still trying to grasp the fact that he was rich.

"*Achya!*" Ram exclaimed. "Their great ones, though they are large men, have voices like women." He thought it over. "And they do not speak, but sing all their words."

"Voices like women?"

"Yes. Or young boys. But withall, their men listen to them with great respect and obey them instantly."

"The sailors, do they have normal voices?"

"Yes. But they sing, too."

"Strange . . . where do they come from?"

"I don't know, lord."

The pearl fisher was exasperating. He had no powers of description. Tom had heard the singsong voices of the sentries as they called to one another, and the gabble of the passing horsemen, but he wouldn't have called it singing. Doubtless Ram was trying to express some other thought when he talked of women's voices, but Tom could not guess what it might be.

He tried again. "What else did you see when you were on deck?"

"Tubs, lord."

"Tubs?"

"With growing things. And pigs."

Pigs? They weren't Moslems then, at any rate. And whether the idol they had shown Ram was the Buddha or not, they could not be Christians. A third interloper had come to Calicut.

He looked out across the azure bay at the tremendous fleet anchored there like a scattering of stubby wooden boxes. So many of them! He had worked it out, from observing the number of men it took to handle those slatlike sails and the number of men who had poured out of one of the nearer ships that was unloading, that the crews and soldiers must number at least twenty or thirty thousand men.

He shifted his gaze to the nine-masted behemoth anchored just offshore that was in the process of disgorging its treasures into a swarm of bobbing scows. It dwarfed any of the round ships or visiting galleys he had grown up with in Bristol. It was wider than a Venetian great galley was long, and it was longer than any four English ships put together. It was hard to see how a ship that size could be built—but judging by the way large numbers of these yellow-skinned men worked in concert, as if they were one man with one brain, they must have shipyards at home that were adequate to the task. He could see tiny figures moving about on the broad deck and triple-tiered poop on unimaginable occupations; the reefed sails must have weighed tons, and the anchor he had seen dropped was the size of an elephant. Most of those swarming figures wore faded blue pantaloons like the porters and shirts or short belted robes tied at the waist, but among them was a scattering of others in brightly colored robes—Ram's "great ones," he supposed.

"What do they want?" he asked the fisher. "Have they come to trade for pepper, like the Arabs?"

"I don't know, lord."

"They must want *something*!"

Ram wrinkled his brow, then nodded toward the departing pack train. "Perhaps it's as it seems. Perhaps they only come to bring gifts."

Tom, frustrated, separated himself from the knot of bystanders and started down the path to the beach for a closer look at the treasure ship. Two porters staggering under the weight of a coffer that looked heavy enough to contain gold called to him in a singsong that unmistakably meant to get out of their way, and then a mounted soldier came along and wave the blade of a sword at him, shouting, *"Pu chun, pu chun!"*

Tom stumbled off the path and backed off far enough to satisfy the soldier. He looked over at the anchored ship again. Something was going on there, on the poop's topmost deck.

The swarms of sailors were moving aside to make space. A personage in a brilliant yellow robe and vermillion cape was coming out of a cabin, attended by a red-robed entourage bearing aloft what Tom supposed were the standards of these queer people—they were not banners and pennants such as Christians and Saracens used, but round emblems as large as cartwheels, raised on ceremonial lances that were three times the height of a man.

Now the lesser nobles were joining him, men in variously colored robes who seemed to be doing a complicated pavane whose steps led them to their proper places and distances.

Tom's eyes swung to the side of the ship, where davits of heavy timbers were lowering a barge that contained a number of enclosed palanquins along with a mob of men in short-robed livery who must be the bearers.

Tom gawked properly, then came to himself again. The diplomatic niceties must have been accomplished. This would be the official delegation to the Zamorin.

With the first gifts on the way, the strangers were about to come calling.

He had seen enough. He turned back from the beach and started down the crowded road to the palace.

• • •

When he made his way across the verandah, Lal was not there to wail at him and ask where he had been. That should have warned him.

The first thing he saw when he entered his quarters was the open lid of the box by the side of his cot. He had left it locked.

Then he saw Lal cowering in a corner, hemmed in by four of the Zamorin's most towering soldiers, spears in hand. He was babbling abjectly at them, and when he saw Tom he gave him the look of a drowning man.

"The Zamorin is most angry, lord. You must go with them now."

They gave Tom no time to demur. The two tallest stepped to his sides and seized him by the elbows. The others fell in behind, and they hustled him through the door.

Behind him, Lal cried, "You'll be taken to the execution yard now, lord, to be trampled by elephants. And what am I to do when that happens?"

The throne room was jammed with people when they got there, and at first no one seemed to be interested in Tom. His guards stopped inside the door and covered their mouths with their hands, as everyone had to do in the presence of the Zamorin to indicate submission. One of the guards kicked Tom's leg with a bare foot, and he did the same.

The Zamorin was lounging negligently on his cushion, as he usually did, chewing betel nuts and spitting into a gold spittoon. He had dressed up for his visitors. In addition to his wraparound skirt and conical hat, he wore bangles, pearls, and a collar of sapphires, emeralds, and rubies set in gold. All around him, like goods in a warehouse, were the gifts brought by the strangers—tall bales of silk, coffers of jewels and coins, exquisite porcelain jars that might have contained precious oils, gilded vases, exotic statuettes of bronze or gold.

The large, moon-faced man in the yellow robe and vermillion cape who sat with the Zamorin on the dais was not covering his mouth. He was there as an equal or something better. From his dress, Tom recognized the commanding figure he had seen distantly on the deck of the treasure ship.

Tom took a fascinated closer look. He saw a man who should have been about forty-five years of age, except that his skin was as smooth as a baby's. It was not that he had shaved closely—he had no trace of whiskers at all. He was large-boned, running to fat, but by no means gross. The round, saffron face was intelligent; the wide mouth firm, full of authority. His yellow-silk robe was embroidered with a marvelously wrought design of a snake and gathered at the waist by a wide, loose belt studded with panels of jade and gold.

His courtiers and ceremonial guards were ranged along one side of the throne room, an impressive display of splendid garments and perfect dignity that contrasted sharply with the Zamorin's fidgeting attendants. Among them were several sizable men in gorgeous identical silks who might have been kings themselves except for an indefinable posture of deference they showed to the moon-faced admiral.

The stranger and the Zamorin had found a way to talk to each other. The Zamorin had fetched one of the Arab merchants from the trading quarter as an interpreter, and he was talking in Arabic to a bent scholarly old man in a blue gown who had come with the men from the ships. *"Bi-la sakh, lazim ti-ftikh bi-karam balad khum,"* the blue-gowned elder was saying, and Tom found that he could understand every word. If only he had gone to the throne room that morning as he was supposed to! If he had, he might be interpreting in the Arab's place right now.

The merchant was relaying the essence of the sentiment in Tamil to the Zamorin. "He says you have no reason to apologize for your hospitality, Your Highness."

Tom bristled. By God, he thought, it was the same Saracen villain who'd had him chased by the men with scimitars that time!

The Zamorin replied, "He must not think we lack for riches or rare objects in Calicut. Tell him I fully intend to reciprocate his emperor's generosity." He fluttered his hands helplessly. "If only I could think of the right gift."

"The white elephants, Majesty," a courtier suggested.

"Are you mad?" the Zamorin frowned. His eyes roamed the audience chamber and fell on Tom. "Aha, I have it!"

He initiated a long flowery exchange in Tamil. When it was the Arab merchant's turn to translate, Tom could see that the man was torn. He gave Tom a glance of oily triumph, and Tom could tell that he was thinking about how he was about to rid Calicut of a Christian threat to Saracen monopoly. Then his face fell as he suddenly realized that Tom was going to have the inside track with the representative of an incomparably richer kingdom than that of Calicut.

The guards thrust Tom forward. The Saracen merchant temporized, his eyes shifting back and forth.

"Well?" the Zamorin said peevishly. "Why doesn't he get on with it?"

Tom spoke out boldly. "I can speak for myself, Your Majesty." He turned to the old man in blue and said, in his bastard Arabic, "The Zamorin wishes your master to know that of all the rarities he possesses, none is so rare as a sign of Vishnu's favor in the form of a man with hair of gold and eyes of sky. He wishes to present me to your emperor in token of his friendship." He added quickly, "A yellow-haired man has never been seen here, but I come from a land beyond the lands the Zamorin knows, across seas beyond the seas sailed by these Saracens, where there are many like myself."

The old man looked at him in mild surprise. "You speak the language of the Prophet, young scholar?"

"Yes, but it is not my own."

"Nor mine," chuckled the old man. He turned to the moon-faced man and spoke to him in the odd singsong tongue.

The moon-faced man responded, and Tom was astonished to find that the pearl fisher had told the truth. This stranger in yellow silks indeed had a voice like that of a woman, high and clear.

The old man translated into Arabic. "The illustrious

one wishes to know if *you* wish to be presented to the Celestial Emperor."

"Who is he?"

The old man straightened his stooped shoulders. "He is Cheng Ho, the Three-Jewel Eunuch and Grand Admiral of the Raft of Stars, who serves the Yung Lo Emperor, the ruler of the Celestial Kingdom."

Tom did not hesitate. There was nothing to choose; either he stayed in Calicut to face the consequences of stealing one of the Zamorin's pearls or he sailed with these extraordinary strangers to a celestial kingdom.

"Tell him yes," he said.

The Zamorin was growing petulant. "What are they saying?" he demanded.

The Arab merchant started to reply, but Cheng Ho cut him off with a flow of words in his woman's voice. He addressed the Zamorin eye to eye, over the heads of his two intermediaries, but he finished with a smile for Tom.

The old man translated. "The Grand Eunuch Cheng Ho, he of the Triple Treasure, thanks the Zamorin on behalf of the Celestial Emperor for this auspicious gift. It is clear that this apparition with hair that shines like the sun is an omen of good fortune, like the long-necked chilin, which some call a unicorn and some call a giraffe, or the vegetarian tiger that appears in the world when harmonious vapors proclaim heaven's favor. The Emperor will be pleased at this additional sign that a benevolent cosmos has blessed his reign."

While the Arab merchant translated into Tamil in his turn, Tom whispered to the old man, "What did that mean?"

"It means, young scholar," the old man said, "that Cheng Ho has made you his good luck charm."

CHAPTER 16

Sandro's brush hovered over the parchment, hesitated, then dipped to add the extra dot that transformed the *taa'* into a *thaa'*.

"You're doing very well, *ya* Sandroo," Jaybir al-Sumit said behind him. "Most Franks don't make the distinction."

"Thank you, *sidi*," Sandro said. "But I'm afraid my calligraphy leaves a lot to be desired. My style will never delight the eye. I can only try to make the characters recognizable."

He went on with his draftsmanship. The astronomical table was nearly complete. He needed only to fill in the last column of figures.

"That doesn't matter," Jaybir said. "The scribes can copy it out later. The important thing is to get all the numbers down properly, without transcription errors."

Sandro laid down his brush and turned with an easy smile. "That much I can certainly do, *ya* Jaybir," he said. "I had enough practice with Arabic numerals while I was growing up and learning the banker's trade. My father himself taught me—my abacus master would have nothing to do with such newfangled ideas. My father was probably the first merchant in Venice to keep his ledgers in the Arabic numbers. He saw at once how much more convenient for figuring they were than the old Roman numerals." His face clouded as he remembered. "When he was denounced anonymously through a letter placed in the lion's mouth, one of the accusations against him was that he liked Moorish things too much. We never actually had a law in Venice against using Arabic numerals, as they did in Florence after the abacus masters brought a civil action, but they're still frowned upon by conservatives."

Jaybir did not notice the troubled expression that had passed momentarily across Sandro's face; as usual, his head was serenely in the stars. "It's you Franks who always call them Arabic numerals," he corrected Sandro with absentminded pedantry. "*We* got them from the Hindus. And yes, they *are* marvelously convenient. The Roman figures—and those of the Jews and Persians as well—have no *sifr* to signify the naught. And without the *sifr* to keep the rows of tens in place, it would be impossible to do the calculations of *al-jabr* and so arrive at a true picture of the celestial motions."

"I know, *sidi*."

Jaybir gave a deep sigh. "I don't know what I'd do without you, *ya* Sandroo," he said. "These old hands are getting too palsied to make a steady line or to draw an epicycle. I think that I'd better start packing my winding sheet and make the pilgrimage to Mecca before it's too late."

"Don't say that, *ya* Jaybir. There's plenty of time to think about making the *hajj*."

He felt a genuine affection for the old man, despite their master-slave relationship. It was impossible to harbor resentment for someone whose only consuming passion was for abstract knowledge and who wore the trappings of wealth and rank with such indifference.

But beyond that it was Jaybir who had rescued him from the stables and the lash of the overseer—rescued him from the galleys, when it came to that—and given him as decent a life as a slave could hope for, with interesting work to do. Jaybir was a stern master, but kind enough in his absentminded fashion. And he was tolerant—or perhaps only too preoccupied with more important thoughts to be intolerant, which came to the same thing. He had not pressed Sandro to convert to Islam. He did not, in fact, interfere with any of his Christian slaves, despite grumbles from his relatives about the large number of unconverted infidels in his household.

It was this that gave Sandro hope that the request that he had been steeling himself to make might be granted.

Jaybir was still studying Sandro's work. He cocked his head as something new occurred to him. "Have you checked the new table against the *Zij* of Ibn-Yunus?"

"Yes, *sidi*. There were no serious inconsistencies."

"You understand the principle?"

"I think so, *ya* Jaybir. As one travels farther south, new stars appear above the horizon. The angles of known stars, including the north star, change. By measuring the changes in the altitudes, one can fix latitude. Conversely, one can use the astrolabe at a known latitude to tell time with great precision. In your *Zij*, *ya* Jaybir, you hope to refine the results of previous astronomers, like Ibn-Yunus, and the great Ibn al-Shatir whose records we excavated, to arrive at a truer value for the terrestrial degree and thus the circumference of the earth."

"One must rely on such imperfect instruments," Jaybir complained.

"Your new astrolabe in the garden . . ." Sandro began.

It would be an amazing instrument when the artificers got through fashioning it. It was going to be thirty-six feet in diameter, containing the coordinates for more than a hundred stars in its *umm*—"womb"—and *ankabut*, or "spider," as Saracens called the rete, or net. Jaybir's relatives, particularly his nephew, Murrwan, who stood to inherit from him, were objecting vociferously to its great cost.

"No, not instruments like these!" Jaybir tapped the fine Moorish example of the art that hung above Sandro's workbench. "It's the human instruments I speak of—the ship's captains who promise to make sightings and forget, the agents in foreign lands who make up any data that comes into their heads, the fraudulent travelers whom one commissions and who turn out not to be able to read a simple scale of degrees. . . ."

"You'd think that a ship's captain, of all people, would see the value of your work," Sandro commiserated.

"They're the worst of all. They're incapable of using an astrolabe. The *kamal* is good enough for them. It gets them into port, and that's all they care about."

"The *kamal*?"

Jaybir, still fuming, did not enlighten him. "A knot in a piece of string! How can that compare with the precision of a graduated adilade with a vane and a sighting hole?"

"Perhaps what's needed is a simpler sort of astrolabe for mariners," Sandro suggested. "One that's used mainly to find the altitude of the sun or stars, without all the refinements, and that can be used on a pitching deck at sea."

"Astronomy is a noble art," the old man said severely. "It wasn't meant to have any practical value, or to serve as a handmaiden for sailors!"

"Still," Sandro said, "mariners would find such an instrument of great use."

Jaybir snorted to show his disdain for any such pedestrian concerns. "I have a great lout of a sea captain coming in later this morning. It was a bit of luck—he's one of those who sail the Red Sea, ferrying pilgrims to Mecca and making the run to Calicut for spices in the off season. He left his ship at Suez and came overland across Sinai to drum up business in Beirut and Damascus. He's returning now with a load of passengers, but he'll be back in time for next year's *hajj*."

"*Bakht,*" Sandro responded. "That *is* a stroke of luck."

"I'm going to entrust him with an astrolabe. We can give him one of the old ones—the Granadan one with the dent in it. First we'll remove all the climate plates except the southernmost to avoid confusing him and then try to instruct him in its use. I fear it may be hopeless, but I'd give anything to establish the true latitude of Calicut. Hardly anything more southerly is known."

"I'll do my best to drum it into him, *ya* Jaybir. But first he'll have to be taught to take an accurate reading of local time."

A faraway look had come into Jaybir's eyes. "The map of al-Idrisi, which is excellent in most other respects,

shows the latitude of Calicut to be above that of Aden, at
the exit to the Red Sea. But I think it's farther south.
There are reports from other travelers that at Cape
Comorin, which is at no great distance from Calicut, the
north star is only a hand's width above the horizon."

Sandro made an appropriate sound of awe.

"Oh yes, *ya* Sandroo," the old scholar said, nodding.
"There are reports from sailors who fared too far south
on the way to the spice islands that the north star disappeared entirely."

"They passed below the waist of the world, then?"

"Yes, *ya* Sandroo. The equinoctial line. I'm pleased to
see that you have cast off the Frankish superstitions of a
flat earth and have formed a grasp of these matters." He
frowned. "I've also heard that in place of the northern
constellations familiar to mariners, Allah put a cross in
the sky. What could He have meant by that?"

Sandro maintained a discreet silence.

"Perhaps it's just a tale that someone invented."

"Yes, *sidi*, it must be that."

Jaybir shook off the troubling thought. "The main
thing is that the world is round, as was known long before Ptolemy. As to why people don't fall off—the favorite
question asked by ignorant persons—the answer is that
the center and the bottom are the same. If one could
drill a hole all the way through the earth and drop a
stone into it, the stone could only fall as far as the center.
And there it would remain."

"It makes one dizzy to think about it, *ya sidi*."

The old man stroked his beard. "The evidence of the
senses sometimes deceives us, *ya* Sandroo. It's much better to rely on the intellect."

Sandro dipped his brush in preparation for finishing
the tabulations, but Jaybir wasn't through yet.

"The problem of latitude's been solved in principle,"
he sighed. "We latter-day astronomers need only improve
on the results of the ancients. But how do we solve longitude?"

"I don't know, *sidi*."

"You'd be a wise man if you did, *ya* Sandroo." He
sighed again. "It seems to be inherently insoluble. Allah's

given us signposts in the sky by which we may tell time exactly and so proceed to calculate latitude. But to discover our longitude in an unknown place, we would have to have some way of telling the *difference* in time between our location and some other place on earth that is used as a reference point. But noon in Damascus is not noon in Calicut, and we can never know what time, exactly, it is there."

"A clock," Sandro suggested. "You carry a clock that has been set to the time of your departure point, and then compare it with the sky time in the other place."

The idea was so outrageous that Jaybir smiled. "What, carry one of your Christian tower clocks with its five-hundred-pound weights along on a journey? Or pack up the giant water clock of the Great Mosque of Damascus, along with the eleven men it takes to keep it in working order?" He grew serious. "Perhaps better clocks will be made some day, *ya* Sandroo, but they'll never be accurate enough for *our* purposes. Even if they could be improved and made small enough, they could not keep the time while on the pitching deck of a ship or a camel's lurching back, when the weights would swing back and forth or the water slosh around. A simple sandglass, such as mariners already use, would be more practical. But someone would always forget to turn it quickly enough, and the accumulated differences at the end of the journey could add up to errors of hundreds of miles."

He smiled benignly. The little exercise in thought had made him mellow, and Sandro was encouraged to broach the request he had been saving up.

"*Sidi,*" he began hesitantly, "you have always been tolerant toward those of your servants who are unbelievers provided only that no images or other outward displays offensive to Islam intrude in your household. I wanted to ask ... that is, there is a Christian slave girl who works in the kitchens ..."

But Jaybir had become distracted again. "The moon!" he exclaimed suddenly. "That might be the answer, *ya* Sandroo." He stroked his long white beard with a preoccupied air. "The moon does not revolve in the great celestial sphere in which the fixed stars are embedded. By somehow comparing the two at the moment of the moon's meridian passage . . ."

He went off, mumbling to himself. Sandro had seen the signs before. When an idea suddenly seized Jaybir, he became totally absorbed in it until he had worked out all its implications or—as was more often the case—saw that it rested on false assumptions. The process could take a quarter hour or it could take days—days without sleep or food with time out only for the five daily prayers that were part of Jaybir's unshakeable faith.

At the door to his inner sanctum Jaybir shook himself back into the real world long enough to pause and say with a vague air, "Oh, yes, *ya* Sandroo, when the sea captain arrives, you'll entertain him for a little while, won't you, if I don't come out right away?"

Captain Kareem was a brawny, black-bearded man with a rolling gait and a booming voice. He looked around curiously at the shelves of books and manuscripts, the collection of arcane instruments from many lands, and the huge iron and brass armillary sphere that stood in the center of the room.

"Does your master cast horoscopes, then?" he inquired with a nod at the astrolabes.

"No—he studies the stars to learn other secrets," Sandro replied.

"A pity. I thought I might have my fortunes foretold by an expert. Your master's a fine gentleman."

"Yes, he is," Sandro said.

Sandro ordered refreshments brought and chatted awhile with the captain. Kareem was an outgoing sort, who seemed not at all put out by the fact that he was being entertained by a slave. When he discovered that Sandro was a Venetian, he asked a number of trenchant questions about the handling of Venetian galleys. "They're wonderful ships," he said. "I've seen them at Tyre and Beirut. Is it true that they sail clear through the Pillars of Hercules and through the Green Sea of Darkness to the northern infidel lands?"

"Yes," Sandro told him. "Of course, they keep to the margins of the coast."

The captain's big frame shuddered. "I shouldn't care to do it myself," he said. "The southern sea's dangerous enough for me. It's said by the learned *mujtahideen* who study the Koran that a man mad enough to embark for the unknown, even on a coasting voyage, should be deprived of his civil rights."

"Still," Sandro suggested, "you sail for the spice islands out of sight of land for much of the time."

"The way's known," Kareem declared. "Has been for centuries. I keep tabs on my latitude with the *kamal* and never allow my ship to pass the *khat* that divides the world—though I've heard the tales of those who did. There's a bird that dwells there large enough to carry off a ship in its claws—the *ruq*."

"This *kamal*," Sandro said, "is it something like an astrolabe?"

"Bless you, no," Kareem laughed. "It's nothing so complicated. You don't have to be a scholar to use one. I can teach a simple sailor to use it in five minutes. Here, let me show you."

He rummaged in his robes and came up with a little rectangle of sanded wood about the size of the palm of Sandro's hand. Dangling from a hole drilled in its center was a length of knotted string.

"Is that all there is to it?" Sandro said, puzzled.

The captain seemed a little embarrassed; being in a scholar's den intimidated him. "Well, it doesn't look like much," he said defensively, "but you can use it on the deck of a pitching ship, even if you don't know where the zenith is from moment to moment, and you don't even have to have good sea legs. Try that with an astrolabe!"

"How does it work?"

"Well," the captain said, mollified, "you just take the string in your teeth at the right knot and hold the board straight out. You squint with one eye, and if the north star sits exactly on the upper corner, you know you're at the same latitude as your port of call, so you steer due east or west, as the case may be. If the star's above the board, you're too far north, so you steer south. If the star's below the edge of the board, you steer north."

"The bottom of the board must rest on the horizon?"

"Yes."

Sandro had absorbed enough astronomy from Jaybir al-Sumit to understand immediately that the captain's crude device measured star altitude from a visual horizon rather than the artificial horizon of the astrolabe, which depended on establishing a perpendicular. The *kamal* would not give an astronomer such abstract information as degrees of altitude and so would be of little interest to Jaybir, but for a navigator it would be immensely more practical.

"Here's the knot for Damascus," Kareem said, demonstrating. "I tied it last night. See, it's right on top of this other knot—Damascus turned out to be the same latitude as Baghdad. Who would have thought it? This knot near the end is for Calicut. And the last knot is where the north star vanishes. Or almost vanishes. I stay away from there."

"So once you've been to a place, you can always find it again?"

"Yes. More important, you can always find your way home again. The sailors wouldn't sign on otherwise."

"All that from a piece of board and a string!" Sandro said, impressed.

"I've seen some captains use a kind of *kamal* with an unknotted string of fixed length, and a whole series of boards of different sizes. But this is simpler."

A thought struck Sandro. "Your *kamal* keeps you on course on that part of your east-west run when you're out of sight of land. But for a Venetian captain on the north-south run of the Galley of Flanders, it could allow him to stand well out to sea until he arrived at his destination latitude."

"Why would he want to do that?" The captain's bluff face showed bewilderment.

"Well . . . I don't know. To avoid unfavorable currents or reefs. To evade pirates."

The captain laughed. "After all these centuries your Venetian captains must know every reef and unfavorable current along the west coast of the world. And from what I've seen of Venetian galleys, no pirate would dare to attack one, let alone a fleet of them. They'd best leave well enough alone and stick to coasting. I envy them."

"I suppose you're right. Only the Portuguese are crazy enough to travel south along the coast of Africa. And even they haven't dared to approach the equator."

They sipped their sherbets for a while. When it became evident that Jaybir was not going to join them any time soon, Kareem passed the time by explaining each of the knots in his *kamal* to Sandro. "Now you'll always be able to find your way back to Damascus, at any rate," he said. "That's as far north as this one shows. If you want to show the latitude for Venice or any of your infidel capitals, you'll have to get a longer string or a bigger board."

There was an embarrassed silence as he realized he'd said the wrong thing to a slave. Sandro tried to put him at his ease by admiring the *kamal* again.

"Here, you can have it," the captain said, thrusting it at him. "It's a spare. I whittled a new one on the way from Beirut. Measured out all the knots on a fresh piece of string except for Damascus, and I can do that one again tonight."

Sandro thanked him and put the *kamal* on a shelf.

"You can show it to the old man later. Maybe he can make something out of the knot representing Calicut."

"Maybe he can," Sandro said.

He had no intention of showing the *kamal* to Jaybir. It would only irritate him. There was no point in antagonizing him before making the request about Marina.

He glanced at the inner sanctum. There was still no sign of Jaybir.

Kareem followed his glance and shrugged. "Do you know what the old gentleman had in mind?"

"Yes," Sandro said.

He knew where the little bag of gold had been put aside for the captain, and he knew that Jaybir would make no objection to his paying it out, though slaves weren't supposed to be trusted with gold even for the daily marketing, unless a household official went along with them.

"Let's get to it, then," the captain said, putting down his goblet.

Sandro spent the next hour drilling Kareem in the use of the small Granadan astrolabe and explaining what Jaybir wanted of him. "You'll have to make your observation when you go ashore at Calicut," he emphasized. "But first you'll have to discover the local time with great accuracy, and to that end you'll have to read the altitudes of the three stars on the list I gave you and check the readings against one another."

The captain was bright and quick and knew the stars better than Sandro did, but he had begun to sweat out the explanation with increasing impatience.

"W'allah-i l'azim!" he finally exploded. "I can tell time well enough at night by watching Kochab revolve around the north star!"

"Kochab?"

"It's one of the guards of the north star. The bright star in the constellation you Venetians call the Horn or the Trumpet. Other Franks sometimes call it the Small Bear."

"Oh, yes?" During Sandro's years as a galley slave he had often watched the slow wheel of heaven around its hub at night, but it had never occurred to him that time could be told by watching a particular star.

The captain nodded, confidence flowing back into him after the catechism that Sandro had put him through. "You've got to memorize the position of Kochab at midnight for every two weeks of the year, but after that you can always tell time to within an hour or two by imagining a little man in the sky with the north star for his navel and seeing if Kochab is at his head, his shoulder, his feet, and so forth."

Sandro was fascinated. He had not been at sea enough years to have sorted out the sidereal positions of the great revolving dome of stars on a biweekly basis, but evidently experienced Arab sea captains took the feat for granted.

"Now it's your turn to teach me something, *ya sidi*," Sandro said, the respect showing plainly in his voice. "What's this about a little man in the sky?"

Flattered, Kareem puffed out his chest and, using his

own bearlike figure as a model, helped Sandro memorize the eight basic positions of Kochab used by Arab mariners. Sandro would have to go to Jaybir's star maps to get the rest of it, but he had an advantage over the apprentice Kareem once had been in that he could take himself through the whole sidereal revolution as many times as he chose without having to wait for a whole year to go by.

"Thank you, *ya* Kareem," Sandro said. "I won't forget. But now I'm afraid we'll have to go back to my master's astrolabe. Your method of using Kochab and the polestar for time-telling is fine for a ship at sea, but it isn't exact enough for Jaybir al-Sumit's purpose."

He smiled apologetically.

"What purpose? Oh, you explained it before—he wants to measure the world. I'm hanged if I understand how he thinks he can do that by looking at stars and writing down numbers from an astrolabe, but I promise to do my best for him."

Jaybir finally emerged as the captain was about to leave. He hadn't quite shaken off his creative trance, and he was mumbling to himself. "What a fool," he said.

"I beg your pardon, *sidi*?" the captain said.

"I should have seen it immediately."

"What's that, *sidi*?" the captain said cautiously.

"That you can't use the meridian passage of the moon to determine longitude. Even though it doesn't revolve with the fixed stars, it still boils down to the same old problem of the observer's sky."

"No one can determine longitude, *sidi*," the captain said. "You can only try to guess at how far your ship has traveled each day."

"Yes, yes," Jaybir said impatiently, waving off this intrusion of the practical. He turned to Sandro. "You explained the astrolabe?"

"Yes, *sidi*."

Jaybir questioned the captain in desultory fashion and seemed satisfied with the answers. Sandro watched him anxiously to see if his creative disappointment had left him in a bad temper, but the old man seemed to be getting lively again. Just when Sandro was about to breathe a sigh of relief, Jaybir's eyes glazed over again.

"Eclipses!" he exclaimed.

The captain looked at him with some trepidation. "What's that, *sidi*?"

"It's not the meridian passage of the moon that's the key! It's lunar eclipses!"

The captain exchanged a helpless glance with Sandro.

Sandro said soothingly, "How's that, *ya* Jaybir?"

"We've been able to predict lunar eclipses since the days of ancient Babylon. To find longitude in a distant place, all that's required is to observe a lunar eclipse and time it precisely, then look it up in an ephemeris for a place of known latitude, like Damascus. The difference in time will give us our longitude." He frowned. "Assuming we have the right value for a terrestrial degree."

"That's . . . very ingenious, *sidi*," Sandro offered.

Jaybir turned to the captain in triumph. "How's that, *ya nakhoda* Kareem? I've given you mariners a way to determine your longitude at sea—just as soon as all the tables are worked out!"

Kareem cleared his throat. "Very good, *ya sidi*. It will be a help, I'm sure. That is, to be able to tell longitude every time there's an eclipse of the moon." He looked unhappily at the battered antique astrolabe Sandro had given him. "Provided one can get the exact time from a rolling deck with one of your instruments, that is."

"You see, *ya* Sandroo," Jaybir said with a mischievous smile. "Don't ever say there's no practical use for astronomy." The glazed look returned. "I've got to work it out. See that I'm not disturbed, *ya* Sandroo."

He disappeared into his sanctum and drew the curtain behind him.

"He's a rare old gentleman," the captain said, mopping his brow.

"Yes, he is," Sandro agreed.

The morning passed, and then part of the afternoon, and Jaybir stayed hidden. A servant from the kitchen appeared with lunch for him, and Sandro told him to set the tray down on a stand outside the door.

He completed the astronomical table he had been

working on, then gave himself to the never-ending task of cataloguing Jaybir's manuscripts. On a hunch he went through the treasure trove of materials by Ibn al-Shatir that he had helped Jaybir unearth from the ruins and found a parchment diagram of positions of the moon, plotted according to a double epicycle system by which the great astronomer had hoped to eliminate Ptolemy's classic equants. He guessed that this would be of some value to Jaybir in his pursuit of his current will-o'-the-wisp and put it aside for him.

He became progressively more restive as the afternoon wore on with no evidence of Jaybir. He would have an opportunity later that day to see Marina, and he had hoped to be able to tell her that he had put his request to Jaybir.

A moment later he was blinking back tears as a full sense of his helplessness came back to him. He shook it off. The Arabs had a useful word: *qismah*. Fate. One's lot in life. He was a slave in Damascus. It was his *qismah* to be here. Venice was a shadow, Maffeo a ghost. The marble palace on the Grand Canal, his little sister Agnese, his romance with Giuditta—they were gone, as a dream is gone when one opens one's eyes.

Why did he not accept his *qismah* and convert? It would make his life easier here. Though Jaybir ruled with a gentle hand, others were not so liberal. Jaybir's nephew, Murrwan, loathed Christians. Even some of the servants made so bold as to show their dislike of Sandro and his favored position. What did he owe God—his own God—after all?

But no. Marina deserved better of him than that. His own faith had worn through, like an old shirt, but hers was not a garment that she could put on or take off at will. It was a part of her—her very skin. He owed her this last shred of his faith. If he were to renounce it, she would be left with nothing. She would be not his wife but the chattel of another Believer.

He stole a glance at the curtain to the sanctum. Perhaps it was a good thing that Jaybir had remained closeted there so long. It probably meant that things were going well, and that Jaybir would be in a good mood later on. When Jaybir began with a mistaken assumption, he tended to discover it fairly quickly.

And he would surely be pleased by Sandro's initiative in uncovering the al-Shatir manuscript. Sandro glanced at the manuscript, which showed circles upon circles upon circles in red and black ink, with squiggly notes in al-Shatir's own hand. A line at the bottom thanked Allah for giving him the inspiration to invent a model for lunar motion that removed some of the doubts surrounding Ptolemy's solution.

He could hear Jaybir moving around behind the curtain. Jaybir was probably consulting the small armillary sphere he kept in there, as a last check against the work he had done, and would be coming out soon. Sandro gathered up the manuscript.

"So this is how you loaf when my uncle's not around! He's far too lenient to you Christian parasites."

Sandro turned quickly to the doorway and saw Jaybir's unpleasant nephew, Murrwan, standing there with a sardonic expression on his face.

Murrwan was a fleshy man, with drooping eyelids that always looked bruised and a pendant nose that overhung sensuous lips. He was oiled and perfumed and wore a jeweled turban and a cloak that was richly threaded with gold.

"*Salaam aleikum, ya sidi,*" Sandro said guardedly, letting the manuscript drop.

"Where's my uncle?" Murrwan demanded. He strode into the workroom and looked around at its manuscript-lined walls with distaste.

"He's in his study, *ya sidi*. But perhaps you'd better not go in just yet. He asked not to be disturbed."

Murrwan whirled on him in an instant fury. "What? A slave dares to tell his betters what they may and may not do?"

"I'm sorry, *ya sidi.*"

"You're the one he thinks so highly of, aren't you? No doubt filling his head with your infidel filth. What's that you've got there?"

Silently, Sandro handed over the al-Shatir manuscript.

Murrwan scanned it, grunted when he saw that it contained Arabic script, and tossed it aside.

"More of that learned nonsense that occupies his poor old addled mind and prevents him from meeting his responsibilities to his family! You encourage him in it, don't you? That's the way you assure yourself of a sinecure here instead of being put to useful work in the stables or the smithy."

"No, *ya sidi*," Sandro protested. "I only do my best to serve the noble Jaybir al-Sumit as he requires. He's an illustrious scholar."

"He's a senile old . . ." Murrwan checked himself. "If you belonged to me, fellow, I'd sell you for the mines. Or give you the choice of being converted or gelded and sold for a eunuch. At least you infidel scum are good for that—it can be done without offending against the Koran. As for my uncle's female Christian slaves"—he licked his full lips—"they belong in the harem, where they can be used without constraints."

Sandro stood stiffly, waiting it out. The only way to deal with Murrwan, he had found, was to try as far as possible to be invisible to him. Murrwan had conceived a dislike for another Christian slave some time ago, according to stable gossip the Turk had passed on—a stiff-necked German monk who had been captured while on a pilgrimage to the Holy Land—and had somehow wheedled title to the man out of Jaybir. The German, determined to be a martyr, had resisted a forced conversion with which Murrwan had hoped to entertain some dinner guests. Murrwan had obliged him. The German had not survived the attempts at persuasion, and the details of his death were not pretty. Jaybir had been horrified. After that, he had refused to give or sell any of his slaves to his nephew, though Murrwan was always after him to let him have some woman or young boy who had caught his eye.

Murrwan shot Sandro another challenging glare, then turned and stormed into Jaybir's study.

The argument began immediately. It was about money and property—Murrwan seemed to be protesting Jaybir's trusteeship of some parcel of inheritance that had devolved through a concubine of Murrwan's father, who was Jaybir's younger brother. Jaybir had distributed shares to two daughters according to the precpets of the Koran, which decreed a portion even to female orphans. But Murrwan was hotly disputing the inheritance, claiming that the Koran didn't apply in this case.

Murrwan's sudden assault had caught Jaybir by surprise. Still immersed in his vision, he responded mildly. As Murrwan's voice rose, Jaybir's became more constrained. After a few minutes he excused himself with a conciliatory murmur and came out to see Sandro.

Sandro saw the distress in his face. The old aristocrat did not want a slave to hear a family quarrel.

"You can leave, *ya* Sandroo," Jaybir said. "I won't need you any more today."

"Very good, *ya sidi*." He hesitated a moment. "You might want to look at this manuscript of al-Shatir later on, *ya sidi*. You may find it of interest."

"Yes, yes," Jaybir said absently. He looked over his shoulder at the entry to his sanctum. Sandro took the hint and left.

It was too early to seek out Marina. She would be working in the kitchen under the supervision of *'amm* Arif, who kept the slave girls entrusted to his protection under tight control. He would be able to snatch a few moments with her after the sunset prayer, when she was on her way back to the slave quarters and unsupervised.

He stopped off first at the stables with a napkin full of mutton and cracked wheat that he had abstracted from the tray Jaybir had left untouched. Stealing food was theoretically a punishable offense, but the old man never noticed.

He found the Turk mucking out horse stalls, swinging the heavy shovel with an angry rhythm, the sweat rolling down his naked torso and pooling in the horrendous scars. He shoved the blade into a pile of manure and dusted off his hands when he saw Sandro.

"Is the Knout around?" Sandro asked.

"He's picking on the grooms right now. He won't be back for a while."

Sandro handed him the tied napkin. The Turk took it around behind the stalls, out of sight, and unwrapped it.

"It's all I could get," Sandro said. "There would have been more if he'd eaten and I could take the leftovers—he picks at his food like a bird—but I didn't want to disturb the tray too much in case he wanted it later."

The Turk did not bother to reply. He ate rapidly, picking up the pieces of mutton and wadding the gravy-laden wheat into balls with his fingertips. When he finished, he handed the napkin back to Sandro.

"Good," he said. "That Hassan shorts us on the rations. Nothing yesterday except bread and some stewed beans. It's almost like being in the galleys."

"Tomorrow there may be a fowl."

The Turk picked up his shovel and went back to his work. Without looking up, he said, "Did you ask him?"

"No," Sandro said. "I had no chance. I was about to bring up the subject, but his nephew, Murrwan, came in at that moment. Jaybir sent me away."

"Murrwan!" The Turk spat. "He's a bad one. Borrowed a horse the other day. The fine white *el khamsa* stallion from Arabia. Ran it into the ground. Lamed it. Then complained to the Knout that he had been sent out on a horse with a dry foot and got a groom whipped for it. Good groom—little Abdul, who was sold with that horse and lived his life for it."

"I'll try to speak to him tomorrow," Sandro said.

"Don't wait too long." The Turk seemed about to say more, but changed his mind.

"I'm sure Jaybir will give his permission. He's very strict in his morals. He prefers a slave to be married, as a preventative to indecent behavior, and if they're *kafir*, not converted, then he thinks a Christian marriage is better than nothing."

"Then I don't see the problem. One of the garden slaves is a Christian priest—that *'abb* Agostino. He could say a few words over you, and you'd be married one-two-three."

"He's a Latin priest. He couldn't marry us according to

the rites of the Greek church. Marina wouldn't consider herself married."

"Is the difference in your Christian creeds so great, then?"

Sandro pondered the efforts to unite the Eastern and Western churches that had been going on when he had left Venice. It had all boiled down to a few words of ritual.

"No," he said.

"I don't see what all the fuss is about," the Turk said. "You Christians make more of your differences than the Sunnis and Shi'ites do, and there's blood between *them*."

"With us, too," Sandro said. He thought of the barbarous sack of Constantinople by the Crusaders, with the connivance of Venice, that had taken place only two centuries before. The very horses of Saint Mark's, prancing forever in bronze, had been part of the loot.

"Why don't you just take the woman?" the Turk said. "She'll get used to the idea."

"No," Sandro said.

He would not do that to Marina. Jaybir would grant the dispensation. The Byzantine consul here in Damascus had a chaplain. They had no power to protect Greek nationals or to pluck them out of slavery, but a quiet ceremony could be arranged with Jaybir's permission. The viceroy of Damascus did not forbid discreet Christian observance behind closed doors.

The Turk scratched his head. Sandro had discussed the plan with him several times before, but he still had trouble comprehending why Sandro was willing to go to such lengths to humor a slave girl.

"Well," he said at last, "it will probably work out all right. The old man's lenient. He always gives gifts when a slave gets married and allows a small feast."

He looked past Sandro, gave a warning nod, then turned his back to him and began shoveling industriously. A moment later the overseer, Hassan the Knout, came stomping over.

"It's you again, is it?" he growled. "Why are you always loitering here? You have no business here, infidel dog."

"I'm going, *sidi*," Sandro said.

The overseer turned his attention to the Turk. "Those stalls should have been finished by now, dog! This is no *diwaniyah*, where gentlemen gather to socialize! I have a good mind to give you a few stripes to remind you of your place!"

The Turk turned around slowly and leaned on the shovel handle with his chin resting on his big scarred fists. He gave Hassan a long, steady stare. The overseer flushed and turned back to Sandro.

"Don't think I've forgotten you, you camel's son!" he said. "You may be the great man's pet for the moment. But someday I'll get my hands on you again."

He walked away, swinging his whip.

The garden blurred in the dusk to a filigree of dark shapes against a still-luminous sky. The thick banks of roses sent their heavy perfume into the air. Hidden in the trees, songbirds twittered at the last of the light. Sandro took Marina by the hand and led her down a graveled path to where they could find the relative privacy afforded by a stand of flowering hibiscus.

Few people were about at this hour. In the distance a gardener, working late, grubbed on his hands and knees in a flower bed. An elderly eunuch emerged from a side door, escorting a flock of small piping children—offspring of some of Jaybir's dependents—and herded them through a gate with hardly a glance in Sandro's and Marina's direction.

"It's only old Theodoros," Marina said. "He's a friend."

They embraced. Marina clung to him for a fraction of a moment longer than was prudent, then they stepped quickly apart.

"It's going to be all right," he promised her. "It won't be much longer."

She knew him as well as he knew himself. "You haven't spoken to him yet, then?"

"No," he admitted. "We were interrupted. I don't think he'll be in a very good mood just now. I'll speak to him in a day or two. It might be better to wait anyhow. By to-

morrow I ought to have word from a vendor I entrusted
with a message. He's a tailor who goes to the consul's
residence. He promised to make our situation known to
the chaplain, after I convinced him that this was not
some attempt to escape. The chaplain's said to be a good-
hearted man—a Father Chrysostom. He's performed this
service before. For"—Sandro's mouth twisted—"free
Greeks in the city."

He drank in her appearance while there was still
enough light to see by. The years of captivity had turned
her from the classical statue he had seen on a waterfront
auction block in Venice into a particular woman with
stored-up tragedy in her eyes. But there was still that astonishing wide brow and the straight nose that descended uninterrupted from it to the strong, full lips,
dividing the perfect ellipse of her face in two. It was
doubtful that Marina herself understood how striking she
was, and fortunately for her, neither did she conform to
the Saracen ideal of beauty. She would not speak of what
had been done to her before she had reached Jaybir's
household, but here, at least, she had been left unmolested.

Mercifully, she did not recognize Sandro as the primped
and dewy youth with whom she had locked eyes that day;
two years in the galleys had seen to that. Sandro had
never told her of that first encounter—he wanted to spare
her that shame—but he thought that perhaps someday,
when they had shared enough of a life together, he would.

"Will . . . will we be allowed to go there, do you
think?" she asked.

"Yes. Jaybir won't want the ceremony to be performed
here where it would pollute his household. But we'll
have to come back right afterward."

"It doesn't matter." She smiled. "It will be good to
speak Greek for a little while, to be among Greek people,
even if they're a grander sort than I was used to on my
little island." Her fingers flew to her lips. "But you,
Sandro, it can't mean the same to you. I'm sorry. . . ."

It was ironic, the thought flashed through his head,
that they spoke to each other in a lingo that was mostly
Arabic. Sandro had small Greek, and she had no Italian

at all, save for those words that were part of the dialect of Koine that had been spoken in the part of the Aegean where she had grown up.

"It will be good for me, too," he said, taking the risk here in the open of raising a hand to brush the hair that peeped in two black wings from under the coarse head-covering she wore. "I've almost forgotten that there's a Christian world past these shores. But the most important thing is to be with you in a place where, for a little while, we'll be free."

She touched his sleeve. "Oh, Sandro, our children will be slaves."

"Don't think about that now. It's in God's hands. We can't know what may happen someday. For all we know, Jaybir could set me free. He's freed other slaves after long service. Then any children would be free, too."

"I couldn't bear to have a child and lose it."

"Jaybir doesn't separate families."

Sandro knew she was thinking of her little brother, Lukas, the boy he had seen in her arms at the slave auction. They had been separated in Alexandria when the wholesale lot had been resold. He had been bought by a rich Egyptian, that was all she knew. She had never seen him again.

Sandro groped for her hand. "You must try to believe that Lukas is well and happy," he said. "Perhaps he was enlisted in the *Yeni Cheri*—the New Troops. They especially look for young Christian boys—take them as children and train them for a life in the corps. It's a good life."

The lie tasted sour on his tongue. The Mamluk sultans of Egypt did not employ Janissaries, and Ottoman slave agents did not travel to Alexandria to obtain the child recruits; the boys were acquired through an annual forced levy on the Christian communities conquered by the Turks.

"Do you think so, my Sandro?"

"I'm sure of it."

"He was so small. And frightened. There was no one to look after him except me after our mother died."

Sandro thought of Agnese, isolated now with only the

cold guardianship of Maffeo to remind her of what had once been a family.

"I know, *cara*," he said.

Marina shook off her gloom. *"Lypoúmai,"* she said with a determined smile. "Let's not talk of sad things." They walked on a little farther, past the hibiscus and through a geometric arrangement of flower beds to a small ornamental pool, while she dredged up gossip from the kitchens to entertain him.

". . . and the little serving girl from Famagusta got into the sugar cakes, but *'amm* Arif didn't punish her. He pretends to be gruff, but that's just his way. Instead he put her to scullion's work and sent me with the tray to Jaybir's harem apartments. I thought I never was going to be able to leave—those poor women are so starved for a new face and a little conversation. There's only eight of them now, all old and fat. Jaybir hardly ever goes to visit them, though he gives them everything they want. They're all old concubines—he never married any of them. He had only one wife, you know, and he was devoted to her. He's almost a Christian in that respect. It was a terrible blow to him when she died all those years ago, and I suppose he thought he'd be disloyal to her memory. The concubines' children are all grown up now, and the poor things are quite alone. But they're good to one another. You don't see the backbiting that goes on in some of the other apartments."

Sandro enjoyed listening to her and watching her growing animation. For a little while, immersed in the petty details of daily life, she was able to forget her plight, push back the suffocating insistence of memory—and more, to carry him along with her. Despite everything, she was a naturally healthy, lively person with a mind as sturdy as the young body that was hidden by the drab slave's garments. As long as she had her faith to hang on to—and now the haven of Sandro's own person—she would hold her despair at bay. Never, he told himself fiercely, would he betray her trust in him.

"Don't tell me you didn't sample one or two sugar cakes yourself?" he teased her. "On the way up with the tray?"

"Never!" She slapped at his hand with her fingertips. "Only the ones that were offered to me, with tea, by the concubines, but that was all right."

"I know."

"Sugar is expensive, you know, even among the Saracens, though they sell it to Christians for ten times what it costs them."

"Don't worry about it, *cara*," he laughed. "We Venetians will soon put them out of business with the sugar plantations on Crete and Cyprus."

"Don't talk to me of Venetians!" she flashed.

"Yes, *cara* . . . of course . . . I forget . . ." Sandro's face was hot.

She softened immediately. "I'm sorry, *agape mou*. I didn't mean you. There are evil men everywhere; that doesn't mean everyone's bad. And anyway, you've been wronged by your own people, too."

He nodded. He had never told her that it was Falco, the same Falco, who had sold him—he would have had to reveal too great a familiarity with what had happened on the slave quay that day—but she knew his history in general terms.

Forcing her merriment a little, she returned to her subject. "What was I saying? Oh, yes, *'amm* Arif thinks honey's good enough for most sweets; he guards his accounts jealously, and Jaybir doesn't care for sweets anyway. But it drives the chief confectioner crazy—he always wants to show what he's capable of. And now he's been borrowed with hardly a by-your-leave from the *sayyid* Jaybir by the nephew, Murrwan, to make sugar roses for a great feast."

"Sugar roses?"

"Yes, out of the rose-colored sugar from Alexandria, and you know how expensive *that* is. He's having the roses arranged in sugar gardens, with leaves and thorns and everything, for his guests. *'Amm* Arif is scandalized and not just because of the expense. You know how their holy book forbids them to make a representation of an actual living thing, not that it's always observed, and how they're horrified by our images of the Virgin and by crucifixes and call us idolaters?"

"Yes."

"Well, *'amm* Arif wants him to make the confections in the shape of imaginary flowers, ones that won't compete with God, he says, and the confectioner's almost in tears, and there was a great fight about it."

"You see," Sandro said, "there are righteous Saracens, too, at least when it comes to their own beliefs."

She gave a small perfunctory nod, though Sandro could see that the concept had no real meaning for her. "But Murrwan insisted on the roses, and so that's what they're going to be. He said that his uncle gave his approval to the cost coming out of *'amm* Arif's household allowance, but I don't think so. You know how absent-minded the *sayyid* Jaybir is—he probably just gave some vague answer without really listening."

"It's not our business, *cara*. I hope you haven't said anything like that to anyone but me. Remember that all the ears around you aren't friendly, even among the slaves."

"Yes," she said soberly, the artificial merriment gone.

"Good."

"Sandro, I'm afraid of that Murrwan."

He was instantly alert. "What do you mean?"

"He always has his eyes on me. And he comes to the kitchens more often than necessary to confer with *'amm* Arif. I try to stay out of his sight, but he always seems to turn up just when I have to be there. He asked *'amm* Arif if he'd send me with some fruit to his women's quarters—said that they'd expressed a desire for pomegranates—but *'amm* Arif sent someone else in my place, that new Adharbaijanian girl I told you about who's so anxious to get herself into trouble with the male slaves."

A chill went down Sandro's spine, but he smiled reassuringly and said, "Don't worry, *cara*, you're safe from Murrwan or anybody else as long as Jaybir's alive. Murrwan wouldn't dare to go against Jaybir—he controls the purse strings. And after we're married, that will settle the matter."

He drew her to him and they stole a kiss. It was dark enough now in the garden to conceal their closeness. Her arms tightened around him, and he felt her breath-

ing quicken. He could sense the depth of this warm
promise of passion and knew that it would all belong to
him. He broke loose with an effort.

"We'd better start back," he said.

They picked their way through the geometric paths in
darkness toward the courts of the residence. An enormous spidery shape loomed ahead of them, occulting the
stars.

"Jaybir's astrolabe," Sandro said. "Jaybir's folly, his relatives call it. By its great size, and the fact that a man can
place himself within, he hopes to attain an accuracy that
has never before been known."

The instrument had nothing in common with the
hand-held astrolabes that Sandro was familiar with, and
he was not sure how it would work when it was finally
finished. In shape it was a huge skeletal globe, and the
alidade, six times as long as a man is tall, was mounted
on a swiveling post at the center.

"He wants to know more than it's given to know," Marina said with a shudder.

"It can't be wrong to know God's works," Sandro said.

He left her at the gate to the women's quarters. The
old eunuch, Theodoros, pretended not to see. Jaybir was
nowhere around when he got back. He went to the small
room off the library that he had been given. He would
have to ask Jaybir for larger quarters after Marina joined
him. Jaybir knew all about the stars, but he did not trouble himself much to think about the down-to-earth needs
of people.

In the morning, Jaybir did not put in an appearance in
the workroom at his customary hour. Sandro pottered
around for a while, then settled down to cataloguing
manuscripts. When Jaybir still had not shown up by the
time of the noon prayer, Sandro sauntered over to
Jaybir's apartments and loitered outside. The servants
seemed to be in a turmoil, but Sandro couldn't find out
what was going on. Inside he could hear the majordomo
bawling orders, countermanding himself, then shouting
corrections, and servants scurrying around. Sandro finally

collared a footman who was hurrying from one court to another with a shoe tree in either hand.

"*Lah-za*, brother, do you know where the lord Jaybir is?"

"I can't stop, Christian. Look out of the way."

"Just tell me if he's in there."

"He went to the mosque early this morning with his nephew, the esteemed Murrwan, to speak to the *khatib*."

"What's going on?"

"The butler sent me on an errand to the shoemaker, that's all I know. Let me go. We're very busy."

Sandro went back to the workroom. Jaybir returned about mid afternoon, looking even more absentminded than usual.

"Did you have a chance to look at the al-Shatir manuscript I left out for you, ya sidi?" Sandro asked.

"No, no, all that can wait," Jaybir said. "I want you to pack up some instruments for me—the Persian astrolabe and the linear astrolabe I acquired in Baghdad. And the *Zij* of Ibn-Yunus in a waterproof pouch together with the new *Zij*."

"You . . . you won't be working on your lunar eclipse method today?"

"What? Oh, that. I won't have time. There's too much to do in the next few days. I must see about having the garments of restriction made for me—they must be unsewn, you know—and some simple sandals. They're allowed. It's all been explained to me. And supplies for three to supplement the fare provided along the way—preserved fruits, pepper and garlic, hard cheeses, twice-baked bread, that sort of thing. I'm taking only two servants with me. And bedding as well."

Sandro stared stupidly. "I don't understand."

The old man's agitation ceased. He turned a serene face to Sandro and said, "God shows the way. I'm undertaking the *hajj*."

Sandro was dumbfounded. He'd known in a general way that the pilgrimage season was approaching—the tenth lunar month, Shawwal, was almost past—but he had taken it for granted, especially after what Jaybir had said the previous day, that the old man intended to let it slip by once more this year.

"I wish I could take you with me, *ya* Sandroo," Jaybir said. "We'd get some work done along the way. But no Christians are allowed. You'd be stoned to death if you were discovered."

"B-but . . ."

"It's all arranged. Murrwan's been most helpful. Captain Kareem will take me with him as far as Jidda with the party of pilgrims he's escorting. He'll go on the Calicut from there, and we'll go by beast the rest of the way to Mecca. There'll be no problem in finding a *mutawwif* to guide us—every facility is provided for the pilgrims."

"This was the *sayyid* Murrwan's idea, then?" Sandro said slowly.

"No, no, it came to me in a flash. Allah's granted me signs that I should not put it off, and Murrwan agreed with me." He smiled benignly. "He also pointed out to me that when one is in a state of restriction for the *hajj*, one of the things that is not allowed is to argue, and the thought was so timely that we embraced and made peace with each other, may Allah be praised for granting us wisdom."

Sandro saw the old man's attention slipping away from him, and said desperately, "God is to be praised indeed, *ya sidi*, but there is something I must ask you. . . ."

"The overland trip across the Sinai will be difficult, of course, especially for someone of my age," Jaybir said, his eyes far away. "It was all explained to me by the *khatib*. I must take a burial shroud with me, as indeed most pilgrims do. If I should begin to fail, the caravan cannot wait until death actually comes to bury me. In such cases it is permitted that a shallow resting place be scooped out of the sand and for the dying person to place himself in it on his side, facing Mecca. The final rites may be performed, and one of the Faithful may say the last prayer just as if the person were already dead, and it is just as efficacious so that the caravan may go on without guilt."

"God grant that won't happen, *ya sidi!*"

"Thank you, *ya* Sandroo." Jaybir gave him a frail and saintly smile.

Sandro renewed his effort, and this time Jaybir heard him through.

Jaybir nodded. "It's good for a man to be married, *ya* Sandroo. I give my permission. Now come—we have much to do before I leave, and we'll need every moment."

CHAPTER 17

"At the top of the stairs you must do the kowtow," Ma Huan said.

"I don't like it," Tom said stubbornly. "I didn't have to do that for the Zamorin. Most of the time I didn't even cover my mouth in front of him the way everybody was supposed to."

"Nevertheless you must do it," the elderly translator said with a gentle patience that would have outwaited eternity. "It is a remarkable honor that you will be allowed to approach the Emperor so closely, but the geomancers have advised him that as the *Hsing-yeh-man Chin-mao*, the omen of good fortune from the West, you must ascend to the same step that was reached by the auspicious beast, the chi-lin."

Tom's title meant something like "Auspicious Barbarian with Sun-hair." During the four-month voyage to Chunggwe, as the inhabitants of Cathay called their vast country, he had become almost glib, in a rough-and-ready fashion, in the strange singsong language. Actually it was simpler than any of the European languages he was acquainted with and far easier to learn than Arabic. The words were simply strung together to make sense, with no case endings and no grammar to speak of. There was no past, present, or future, either. The hardest part was to learn to sing each syllable on its proper note. The wrong tone could change the meaning of a word to something entirely different—or even make it mean its opposite.

"You mean the giraffe?" Tom said.

Cheng Ho had shown him the marvelous, long-necked beast, which everybody here seemed to set great store by, in a palace enclosure. But he had not been allowed to stand and gawk. He had been hustled into seclusion, in a place just outside the walls of what was called the Forbidden City, and placed under the tutelage of Ma Huan.

"Yes, young Chin Mao," his mentor said, using the abbreviated sobriquet that seemed to have become his name. "You see, the chi-lin, which the inhabitants of the dark lands call a *zurafa*, was supposed to have been an entirely mythical beast, something like the unicorn of your own legends. When Cheng Ho was able to present a live one to the Emperor, it caused a stir. The appearance of such prodigies is considered to be proof that an emperor is favored by heaven, and Cheng Ho has been diligent in providing such proofs. Before the chi-lin, there was the Celestial Horse—a horse with the stripes of a tiger. Now there is you." His watery old eyes held a glint of humor. "And since the chi-lin was taught to perform the kowtow before the Emperor, Cheng Ho expects no less of you."

"Am I to be a pet again, as I was in Calicut?"

"No, young gentleman, you are to be greatly honored. If all goes well and you can be civilized, you will be given a house, a rank, and a salary."

There it was again—the Chinese conceit that everyone else was a barbarian. The very name they had given their country, Chung-gwe, meant the Middle Kingdom, and reflected their conviction that Cathay was the center of the earth—that no one else mattered and that they had nothing to learn from the rest of the world. Cheng Ho, with his zeal for collecting plant and animal samples and his curiosity about foreign customs, was an exception, and Tom gathered that he was much criticized for it.

"All right, I'll do my best. About the kowtow, I mean, and everything."

Ma Huan beamed at him. "Very good, Chin Mao."

Tom looked around at his surroundings. He knew that the pavilion to which he had been temporarily consigned was considered to be only an ordinary residence for a low-grade government official, but it was luxury enough to Tom. It was made in the Cathay style, with rows of tall, lacquered pillars supporting a tile roof with up-turned edges, walls that were an afterthought, and windows that were latticeworks of oiled paper. There was a staff of obliging servants, a series of spacious, sparsely but elegantly furnished rooms arranged around a courtyard, and a beautifully kept garden with a fishpond. No English earl could have lived in greater comfort.

"What kind of salary?" Tom said.

Ma Huan pursed his lips. "To begin, I would guess a stipend equivalent to that of the second grade of the ninth rank of civil servants, that is to say sixty *shih*. You cannot advance through the ranks of the civil service itself, of course, because you are not a Confucian scholar and in any case are an ignorant barbarian who could not hope to master the knowledge needed to take the examinations. But with Cheng Ho as your patron, you need have no concern. You could advance faster if you could regularize your position and be brought under the Yellow Gate—the Department of Eunuchs. Would you like to become a eunuch? It can be arranged."

"Zounds, no!" Tom shuddered. It had been an unnerving experience, on shipboard, to see a eunuch piss. They did it through a short length of hollow reed that plugged them between the legs.

"You are probably wise, Chin Mao. At your age the operation is not without risk."

Tom's curiosity got the better of him. "Did—did Cheng Ho have that done to himself in order to become Admiral?"

"No, Chin Mao. His father arranged to have it done when he was a boy."

"Jesus!" Tom exclaimed.

Ma Huan raised his eyebrows. "How else is a father to assure the future of an untutored son who cannot hope to take the *chin-shih* examinations? It's a common practice in poor families—too common in famine years, when an emperor sometimes has to punish to prevent ignorant peasants who cannot afford the *i sheng* fee from attempting the operation themselves and botching it. Cheng Ho's family was not poor, but he was a Moslem from Yunnan, and needed a head start in life."

"Cheng Ho a Moslem? But he doesn't look like a Saracen! And I never saw him doing the five daily prayers the way the crew of the ship I sailed from Baghdad did! I've even seen him burning incense to . . . to the Buddha!"

"There are many Moslems in the Middle Kingdom. I'm one myself. The word of the Prophet has penetrated even this far. But the Middle Kingdom has a way of absorbing all else and turning it into its own. I doubt that Cheng Ho remembers much of the precepts of his early years, though his father, the *hajji* Ma, once made the pilgrimage. I myself retained a fluency in the language of the Prophet, and Cheng Ho remembered my poor self when he needed a translator to take with him to the Moslem lands."

"He's a very important . . . man, isn't he? I mean, not just as an admiral."

"The Yung Lo Emperor has greatly elevated the eunuchs, to the fury of the civil service. In his father's day they were forbidden to interfere with government functions, but when the Emperor seized the Dragon Throne from his nephew, he found the eunuchs to be of great help. Cheng Ho's voyages began, many years ago, because the Emperor feared that his nephew had fled beyond the seas, and to this end Cheng Ho was given extraordinary powers to build ships, command thousands of men, and collect vast amounts of gold and other treasures to be given as gifts to foreign rulers in order to make the magnificence of the Yung Lo reign known in distant lands. He is the grandest of the Grand Eunuchs—the *Fu-shih T'ai-chien*. He is the Emperor's *San-pao T'ai-chien*, his Three-Jewel Eunuch."

Tom's head was reeling from all the titles. "How do I address him tomorrow?"

"Who?"

"Emperor Yung Lo."

Ma Huan threw back his head and cackled. "If you are fortunate you will not address him at all. Your Chinese is barbarous, and I will not be allowed close enough to the throne to correct you."

"But how do I address him if I have to?" Tom persisted.

Ma Huan became serious. "In the first place, he is not Emperor Yung Lo. That is not his name. It is the name he has given to his reign. Do you understand the meaning?"

"*Yung* means something like forever. . . ." Tom hesitated.

"Very good, young scholar. It means perpetual happiness. Thus he is the Yung Lo Emperor—the Emperor of everlasting bliss—as his father, who drove out the Mongols, was the Hung Wu Emperor, the Emperor of vast military power and the founder of a new dynasty called Ming—"

"Which means bright!" Tom cried delightedly.

The old tutor nodded, pleased. "The Emperor's *dynastic* name is Ch'eng-tsu. But he was born, simply, Hung Hsi. I will drill you in a few simple forms of address you may use without offense. No one will expect much from a barbarian. The Emperor will be as pleased as he was when the long-necked animal kowtowed."

"What's he like?"

Tom expected a careful reply, but Ma Huan was matter-of-fact. "He is a plain man, a harsh man. His father was of low origin—he began as nothing but a wandering monk—and the Emperor is sensitive about that. He is very aware that the Confucian scholars of the civil service look down on his learning and his lack of literary polish. Do not prick his pride under any circumstances."

The description did not at all square with Tom's conception of an aloof and mighty king who ruled a land that could have swallowed all of Europe several times over, and he said so.

Ma Huan acted surprised. "But that is exactly what makes him so great. He strives to make the accomplishments of his reign the greatest that the world has ever seen.

"He does things in a big way," Tom agreed, thinking of the astonishing fleet that had taken him from Calicut across vast seas that dwarfed the oceans known to Europe.

"He rebuilt Peking on a scale and with a magnificence never before imagined and made it his capital. Lumber was brought a thousand miles, while armies of workers labored for sixteen years. One hundred and twenty thousand displaced households were brought from the Yangtze delta alone and resettled in the north to provide a population. But the north could not feed so many. So he dredged and enlarged the Grand Canal so that grain ships from the south could sail by an inland route, where they would be safe from the pirates who prey on coastal shipping."

Tom had sailed a length of the Grand Canal on Cheng Ho's yacht during the final leg of his journey. It had teemed with government grain freighters, identical two-masted, squarish, shoe-shaped vessels the size of the oceangoing cogs of Europe. Work was still going on. Along one stretch where a connecting link was being widened, Tom had seen laborers covering the banks like swarms of ants, carrying off their crumbs of soil under the watchful eyes of soldiers. There was no shortage of people in the Middle Kingdom to carry out the Yung Lo Emperor's grandiose projects.

"But his greatest achievement, the one he's proudest of, is his encyclopedia."

"What's that?" Tom asked.

"A book that contains all knowledge."

Tom gasped. "Is that possible?"

"It is composed of more than eleven thousand volumes," Ma Huan said seriously. "Two thousand scholars worked for many years to complete it."

Tom tried to imagine eleven thousand books, the size of the room they would fill, and gave up. "With such a *ta-tien*," he said, relishing the new term, "a whole nation might become as learned as Oxford clerks. But surely it would take an army of scriveners to copy it out."

"Only three copies have been made," Ma Huan informed him.

"But, then ... how many people can benefit from all this knowledge?"

"That doesn't matter," Ma Huan said complacently. "The important thing is that the knowledge is there."

Tom gave it up. He would never understand these queer, opinionated people. "Let's get back to the kowtow," he said. "Exactly how is it done?"

Ma Huan rubbed his hands together with satisfaction. "There are three genuflections and nine prostrations. If you make a mistake, you will be beaten by the guards. Watch me. First you kneel and strike your head on the ground three times. . . ."

The Hall of Supreme Harmony, for all its vast size and the throngs of people in it, was as hushed as a church. Tom could not hear even a whisper as he pressed his forehead to the marble step, but he sensed a mass exhalation of breath when he completed the ritual without incident.

Cautiously he lifted his head and stole a look. The lofty spaces around him were alive with fantastic decorations—carved dragons, birds, animals, intricate painted designs—that receded into the distance to become an undifferentiated blur. The silent people standing around on the stairs and terraces or in little stalls of marble were dressed in brilliant robes whose colors seemed to denote rank, to judge by the way those of the same hue flocked together—the blues in the pens, the reds on the higher terraces. Even the tough-looking soldiers, with their swords and crossbows, wore sumptuous robes of black, dappled with spots of yellow.

The Emperor was in a red-lacquered cabinet in front of him, but the doors were ajar, and before dropping face down to the ground Tom had managed to catch a glimpse of a rather stout, cruel-looking man in a robe the color of egg yolk, with a skimpy black beard and mustache teased into long spiky tendrils.

"Does it talk?" the Emperor said.

Cheng Ho, rising to his feet beside Tom, cleared his throat for a reply, but Tom quickly answered for himself.

"Forgive this imperfect person, Sublime Majesty," he said in a pretty fair imitation of Ma Huan's dusty intonation, "but I have a few small words of the noble Chung language."

The Emperor guffawed. "Cheng Ho, you've outdone yourself. First a chi-lin that kowtows, now a barbarian who parrots human speech."

"In Your Majesty's blinding presence, even a barbarian may be illuminated," Cheng Ho said smoothly. He shot a warning glance at Tom.

"Tell him he can get up," the Emperor said.

Tom scrambled to his feet without waiting for a translation. The Emperor looked him over.

"So this is your Auspicious Barbarian with Sun-hair?" the Emperor said. "What am I to do with him?"

"He is additional proof of your virtue and perfection, and a sign that the cosmic forces favor your reign, as was the chi-lin," Cheng Ho said roundly. "No one would dare to deny that." He gave a long, meaningful look to the half-dozen ministers who stood highest on the stairs, red-robed men with white crane plaques on their chests. "First of all, the Board of Rites must compose a memorial to certify that."

The Emperor singled out a resplendent individual whose robe was worked with brocade designs of snakes. "Well, what do you say about it, Lu Chen?"

Tom had trouble following the angry outpouring. The language was too high-flown, and the words came too fast. But he caught enough to understand that the official was objecting vigorously to Cheng Ho's proposal.

The Emperor turned to Cheng Ho with a small, malicious smile. "You see, my fine seagoing Eunuch of the Triple Treasures, what am I to do? The Minister of Rites says that your Auspicious Barbarian is not a prodigy. That he is merely another species of Moslem such as those that are found trading at Calicut, foisted on you because the Zamorin barbarian did not wish to part with his white tiger."

Tom found himself getting nervous. Cheng Ho's opponents seemed to have scored a point with the Emperor. There must have been spies aboard the Treasure Fleet to carry back tales of the white tiger, and the Emperor was miffed.

But Cheng Ho remained outwardly unruffled. "He is not a Moslem, Perfect One. He eats pork. And it has been verified that he is not circumcised."

"Well, Lu Chen," the Emperor said, "do you still maintain that the Auspicious Barbarian is not worth memorializing?"

The official began to backtrack. Tom could see a sheen of perspiration forming on his forehead.

"Your servants in the Forest of Letters welcome each new opportunity to show how your harmonious virtue illumines the world and causes nature to pour forth new wonders, but—"

"Ask the worthy Minister of Rites," said Cheng Ho, "if he remembers that the former Finance Minister, Hsia Yuan-chi, now in prison, originally opposed the memorialization of the giraffe. Of course, as head of the Anti-Maritime Party, he found it hard to believe that anything as"—he paused to savor the word—"*wasteful* as Your Majesty's expeditions could bring back anything of value."

The Emperor chuckled at the sally. It seemed to Tom that he didn't care who was in the hot spot as long as he could get some entertainment out of it. Then he reflected that it was his own fate that was in the balance, in some way he didn't understand, and he hoped that Cheng Ho's wits remained sharp.

"Why don't I ask the *new* Finance Minister?" the Yung Lo monarch said.

The Finance Minister, another withered old Confucian, shot Cheng Ho a look of pure hatred and said, "We are obedient to Your Majesty in all things."

"Did you hear that, turtle-face?" the Emperor said to the sweating Lu Chen. "Memorialize this barbarian with the gold hair, and be quick about it. You might say that the sun, pleased at my reign, sent down a piece of himself as a walking reminder of Ming brilliance."

"Your Majesty's literary insights are an inspiration to us all," the old minister said faintly.

Once more, Tom was astonished at the incuriosity of these people. Not one of them seemed to have the slightest interest in his actual existence as a living person from afar. He had not been asked where his country was or its distance or what it was like. He was there solely as a mirror to their own inward-looking vision—as some mystical proof of the Emperor's virtue, if that was what *mei te* meant. If a Ming traveler had appeared in King Henry's court, with his yellow skin and exotic eyes, he would have been plied with questions about his mysterious homeland.

Another minister was talking volubly and self-confidently—this time one who had asked voluntarily for permission to speak. His name, Tom discovered by keeping his ears open during interpolations, was Chien Yi, and he was the Minister of Personnel. He was a spare old man with sliding eyes.

". . . *pu shih Chung-gwe-jen*," he was saying, stating the obvious fact that Tom was not Chinese. "Nevertheless, as he is not a giraffe, but a sort of man, it would be unseemly and inharmonious for him to have an assigned place, however small, in the great and well-regulated hierarchy by which the Yung Lo reign achieves order. The barbarian is not qualified to take the imperial examination or write an eight-legged essay, but there is provision for an unclassed grade, *wei ju liu*, with a stipend of thirty-six *shih*. . . ."

Tom pricked up his ears. The Ming bureaucracy was offering to adopt him. He was even going to be given a salary. Cheng Ho must have won.

But inexplicably, now it was Cheng Ho who was objecting.

"The honorable Chien Yi is too generous. But it would be wrong to elevate this uneducated foreigner even to the lowest rung of the ladder. Think how it would discourage the scholars. The Department of Eunuchs will be glad to accept responsibility for him."

The Emperor cast a sardonic eye over Tom. "With twenty-four offices within the Yellow Gate, each with its own ball-less Grand Director, I don't doubt that you'll find some place to tuck him away. But you'll have to pay for it yourself."

"That is a small matter, Your Perfection, when it comes to adding to the luster of your reign."

"Will you send him to the eunuch school, then?" Chien Yi said maliciously.

Cheng Ho replied with perfect composure, addressing the Emperor directly. "In the days of your father, the Hung Wu Emperor, it was ordered that no eunuch was to be given any education whatsoever. But in your enlightened reign, Heaven's Equal, the *Nei shu-fang* college for eunuchs has been opened, and as a result many eunuchs have become qualified to serve Your Majesty as something more than attendants of your household. Your Gracious Majesty himself has rewarded many of us by appointing us to high posts, myself included. Perhaps, if the Auspicious Barbarian applies himself, he, too, may someday be competent to serve Your Majesty in some responsible capacity. In the meantime, I myself will take him under my wing."

The Emperor was getting tired and a little bored. "All right, he's remanded to your custody. See that he's produced in court when I require him."

"It will be done, Your Majesty."

To the horror of all present, Tom spoke. "Thank you, Heaven's Equal."

Afterward, Cheng Ho said to him, "You should not have addressed him without being asked. High officials have been beaten to death on the spot for less. Today there were only six officials present who were authorized to speak to the Emperor directly. You are lucky that he was amused by you."

They were standing at the East Flowery Gate, at the end of one of the small marble bridges that spanned the River of Golden Water. Behind them were the golden roofs of the Hall of Literary Profundity, and to one side, at the end of the meandering artificial waterway, were the secretarial offices. Cheng Ho had chosen to leave the

Forbidden City by a side gate, without his usual eunuch entourage, but his bulky figure in its vermillion robe and flowing cape was hardly inconspicuous.

"Why didn't you want Chien Yi to give me a rank?" Tom asked.

"Once he got his hands on you, he would see that you were gradually forgotten. You would disappear into that maze of his and never be seen again, except to be trotted out, less and less frequently, at the Emperor's command. And after a while, when Chien Yi judged it safe, you would waste away and die, and a memorial would be prepared that said you pined for your homeland."

"But what about my salary?"

"You'll have no need of a salary. But if you wish, I'll put you on the books of the Yellow Gate for some trifling amount."

"I don't understand why Chien Yi would have anything against me," Tom said.

Cheng Ho stopped and put his hands on Tom's shoulders. "Listen to me, Chin Mao. You have much to learn if you want to survive. I will see that there are one or two eunuchs around you at all times, and Ma Huan can explain the pitfalls that surround you. But until you are wiser in the ways of the court, you must follow our advice without hesitation."

"All right," Tom said.

"Good," Cheng Ho said.

They resumed walking. Tom was still not used to the long robe that Cheng Ho's valet had supplied for him, but he had gotten the hang of walking without tripping himself. The sleeves were another inconvenience. They were so wide that they almost trailed on the ground, and when his arms were at his sides, as they were now, they hung past his fingertips. It made it hard to use one's hands, but he supposed that was how you proved you were a gentleman in the Middle Kingdom.

He drew out the black silk cap that he had tucked there and put it back on. His yellow hair had been drawing stares.

"Chien Yi is a spy for the Crown Prince," Cheng Ho said after due reflection. "And the Crown Prince is completely under the influence of the Anti-Maritime Party. So he tries to do everything in his power to undermine the voyages of the Star Raft."

"You mean," Tom said, fascinated, "that the Minister of Personnel spies for the Crown Prince against his own father?"

Cheng Ho laughed. "Have you not heard of such things in your own country?"

Tom thought of the old, bloody story of the murder of the second Edward in Berkeley Castle by the queen and her paramour and the connivings to gain control of the young prince. Perhaps there were such dark deeds behind every throne.

"Yes," he admitted.

Cheng Ho nodded. "When the Emperor leaves the capital on one of his campaigns, he leaves the government under the control of the Crown Prince and four advisers. Chien Yi is one of the advisors the Emperor designated. They have acquired an unhealthy taste for power."

"But their power comes from the Emperor, not the Crown Prince."

'They know the Emperor is estranged from the Crown Prince and that their hold on power is precarious. The Emperor always preferred his third son, Kao-hsu, the Prince of Han, and he has never forgiven those who persuaded him to make his eldest son Crown Prince instead. So Chien Yi and the Anti-Maritime Party wait, and feed the Crown Prince's ambitions as far as they dare."

Tom's head was beginning to swim. "Why doesn't the Emperor just elevate his third son?"

"Unfortunately, the Emperor was forced to exile his honorable third son."

"Why?"

"For plotting against the Crown Prince. He falsely denounced the Crown Prince's advisers. The Emperor threw them all in prison, with the exception of Chien Yi. He's slippery as a snake. Then it was learned that the third son had conspired with Chi Kang, the head of the palace guard, the *Chin-i-wei*."

"The Black Robes?"

"Yes."

"What happened?"

Cheng Ho fell silent and drew his cloak about him. They were passing a group of red-hatted Confucian scholars, hobbling along with their hands in their sleeves. The scholars kept their eyes on the ground to show their disdain for foreign things, but Tom noticed one or two of them sneaking a glance at him. When they were gone, Cheng Ho resumed talking.

"The Emperor had no choice but to kill Chi Kang and send his third son back to his fief in Shantung."

"And then he released the ministers—the ones who were falsely accused?"

"No. He is furious with them for not being guilty."

"For *not* being guilty?"

Cheng Ho looked at him as though he were an idiot. "Yes. And thus forcing him to exile his son."

It was too much for Tom. "Then the Anti-Maritime Party is weakened?"

"No, it is strengthened."

"I give up, Cheng Ho. Just tell me what to do and I'll do it."

They had arrived at a small cemetery outside the walls. There were no crosses, but the purpose of the place was unmistakable. Cheng Ho put out a hand and stopped Tom.

"This is the eunuch's cemetery. Yung Lo himself dedicated the temple in honor of Kang T'ieh."

"Who was Kang T'ieh?"

"He was a great general who had served Yung Lo's father well. Yung Lo left him in charge of the Forbidden City while he was away on a hunting trip. It was a dangerous honor, because General Kang knew that his enemies would spread the story that he had made *hsing chiao* with the Emperor's concubines. And he was correct. The Emperor was furious when he returned because the stories had already reached him. General Kang met him outside the gates, and before the Emperor could order him seized, the General told him to look in the bottom of his saddlebags. The Emperor did, and he found a silk package containing the General's manly parts. General Kang had wisely hidden them there before the Emperor's departure."

"Jesus!" Tom said.

"The Emperor paid tribute to his loyalty by making him *San-pao T'ai-chien*, the Chief Eunuch. I served under him when I was a boy."

Tom knew why Cheng Ho had told him the story. It was to impress a lesson on him. Cheng Ho's next words confirmed this.

"So you see, Chin Mao, you must be on your guard at all times. My enemies are now your enemies, and they will use you to try to get at me. The Emperor's temper is uncertain. I'd feel safer if I could take you with me, but your presence may be called for in court. Ma Huan will instruct you in all things while I am gone."

Tom didn't like the idea of being cut adrift in this dangerous place. "Where are you going?"

"To the old capital, Nanking. My shipyards are there, on the Dragon River. I must begin immediately to build a new fleet. I dare not delay. I've been given the authority, and thirteen provinces are being taxed to pay for it. I must get the seventh expedition of the Starry Raft underway before my enemies can undermine it."

"Another expedition—so soon?" Tom found the idea staggering. "Will it be as big as the last one?"

"Bigger. More than a hundred ships this time. Perhaps thirty thousand men. I aim to go farther than I've ever gone before."

Tom gulped. "How far?"

With the utmost seriousness, Cheng Ho said in his high voice, "Perhaps all the way to this Europe of yours, Chin Mao."

"But . . . but you can't. There's no way to get around Africa. Everyone says so—my people and the Arabs. And even the sailors on your own ships that I talked to."

"I think there's a way, Chin Mao. I've thought about it for many years. There's an old Chinese map that shows the Dark Land as a triangle, ending in a southern sea. After all, we Chinese have always known that Africa doesn't join our continent, as the Arabs think. And that means

that your western seas and our eastern seas must be connected, somewhere very far to the south."

"But the seas boil away down there," Tom protested,
remembering what he had always been told growing up
in Bristol. "That stands to reason—it keeps getting hotter
and hotter the farther south you go." He thought of the
fears of his Arab shipmates on the way to Calicut. "And
. . . and there's a giant bird called the *ruq* that carries
ships away and magnets under the sea that draw out a
ship's nails."

"These are tales for children," Cheng Ho said severely.
"We have sailed below the girdle of the world, and it begins to get cooler again. We know how to sail by the
southern stars, and we are not afraid." He relented
enough for a smile. "We, too, have legends of a *peng* bird
that carries off ships and whose great wings darken the
sky."

Tom blushed. Then, as the full import of Cheng Ho's
words sank in, a vivid picture began to paint itself in his
mind. He saw the immense fleet of gigantic Treasure
Ships, each inconceivably huge to an English eye and
hardly resembling ships at all with their stiff, slatted sails
and boxy bows, sailing up Bristol Channel while people
lined the shores, gawking. What would the good people
of Avon and Gloucestershire make of Cheng Ho's fantastic armada, with its strange yellow faces at the rail and its
thousands of infantry and cavalry? Would they believe
that these incomprehensible strangers had come not to
plunder, but to bring gifts?

"Would you like to come with us?" Cheng Ho said.

Tom's heart banged at his chest. "Would I!"

"You'd be an invaluable help when we got to European
waters. From your descriptions of the climate, many of
your western nations must lie above even the latitude of
Peking. Our yin-yang expert and our chief navigator will
certainly want to query about the nature of the coastlines
we'll encounter. But most of all, we'll need your services
as an interpreter. You're the only one we've got. Do you
know any western languages besides your own?"

Tom thought ruefully of his rough waterfront Spanish,
the odds and ends of French he had picked up at Master

Philpot's, his smattering of Flemish. It didn't matter. An Englishman could make himself understood anywhere in Europe by talking loud.

"I can manage," he said.

Cheng Ho thumped him on the back in a surprisingly western gesture; Saracens never did anything like that. "What good fortune!" he beamed. "I knew you would be useful the first time I saw you in Calicut."

They walked on in companionable silence. Tom's thoughts soared. He had reached the East—gone farther than any Englishman had gone before. He had outdistanced even Conti. And now he was not only going home, he was going home in style! He fingered the rich silk of his robe, eyed the precious jade of the girdle he had been lent. How they would stare in England! He had left as a weaver's son from Bristol. He would return as an officer of the Admiral of the Triple Treasure, an ambassador of the mighty Emperor of the Middle Kingdom!

After awhile he noticed that they were taking an unfamiliar direction. "Aren't we going back to Ma Huan's house?" he asked.

Cheng Ho steered him by the elbow into a courtyard. An elderly gatekeeper sprang to his feet and bowed them in. Tom stared at the opulence around him. Ahead was a dragon screen, a porcelain barrier against demons, and beyond it the round portal that the Chinese called a moon gate. He stepped through it with Cheng Ho into an inner courtyard. The house concealed within was a thing of beauty. Carved red pillars supported a triple-layered roof with curling eaves, delicate latticework, and carved designs of herons and lotus blossoms. The faces of servants peeped past the edges of screens.

"No, Chin Mao," Cheng Ho replied. "Now that you've been commissioned as an official translator of the Treasure Fleet, and a member of my staff, you must have a house of your own."

"This . . . this house belongs to me?"

"Of course, Chin Mao." He nodded in the direction of a lanky, blue-smocked individual who had begun to trail after them and who fell all over himself to bow as soon as he saw that Tom had noticed him. "This is your number one servant, Wo. He will manage the household for you and see to all your needs."

Tom walked through the rooms in a daze. Every detail seemed to have been arranged with thought and grace. Bowls of fresh flowers, artfully arranged, were placed on all the low surfaces. The aroma of cooking food drifted from a kitchen somewhere in back. Cheng Ho must have had it all planned before the audience with the Emperor.

They had reached the inner rooms of the house. "Everything has been chosen with great care by the Department of Eunuchs," Cheng Ho said. "They tried to provide everything you will need. I hope you will find all to your liking."

A beautiful young woman in flowing robes emerged from a doorway. Tom's jaw dropped at her perfection. She had a small, symmetrical face of smoothest porcelain, poignantly delicate features, and eyes like ebony brushstrokes. Tom ached for her on sight. He had been without a woman since India, and he was afraid his longing showed. Whoever she was, she was too wellborn for the likes of him, with her elaborate hair and jade combs and fine silks.

To his amazement, she sank to her knees in front of him and bowed until her forehead touched the floor.

Tom stood dumbfounded until Cheng Ho said, "Tell her she may get up, Chin Mao."

"Who . . . who is she?"

"You may speak," Cheng Ho said.

She raised her porcelain face toward Tom. "I am Lanying, master, your number one concubine," she said.

Ma Huan dipped another piece of duck in brown sauce and popped it into his mouth. "Truly, Chin Mao," he said, chewing industriously, "you set a table that could not be bettered by the imperial kitchens themselves."

Behind him, a hovering Wo looked pleased. In actual fact, Tom had learned, Wo had begun his career as one of the six thousand cooks employed by the Forbidden City's Court of Imperial Entertainments, his talents submerged there until the Yellow Gate had rescued him. The gangling majordomo clapped his hands, and a servant brought another tray of porcelain bowls, each filled with some small, exquisite culinary masterpiece.

Tom poked around on his plate until he found a small cube of plain mutton buried among the savories, and picked it up with the ivory sticks that he had had to learn how to use in order not to scandalize the servants. It wasn't enough to make a mouthful. There wasn't a piece of meat you could sink your teeth into here. Everything was cut up small before you got it. Tom had spoken about it to Wo, to no avail. Wo had let him know obliquely that only peasants and Mongols tore at meat with their teeth.

Ma Huan reached for a helping of transparent noodles. "And sixty-nine courses!" he said. "My own cook has gotten too old and tired to bother, even for guests. He feeds me on dishes he sends for from the Longevity and Compassion Restaurant on Old Grandfather Heaven Street when he can get away with it. He thinks I don't know. But you can't mistake their lotus seed soup."

Waste, Tom thought. That was another thing. Sixty-nine courses for the two of them, when not one dish in ten would be sampled. It wasn't much better when he dined alone—though Wo usually held it down to about twenty courses. He had spoken to Wo about that, too, but servants were the masters here.

He was being unfair, he knew. The leavings would go to the servants. They would have their feast, too. And some of it, made unidentifiable, would go to him in the next day or two as well. Every scrap would be made use of. But still, he couldn't help thinking of his lean days at Master Philpot's or the hungry weavers at Redcliffe. In the Middle Kingdom eating was the national pastime. Even the poor had their street-corner noodle stands, open day and night, and their hole-in-the-wall restaurants where they stuffed themselves on fried tripe, salt fish, and blood-and-offal soup.

"Eat, Chin Mao, or you'll never get fat," Ma Huan said genially.

Tom conveyed a ball of minced pork and spices to his mouth with the ivory sticks. One bite and it was gone. Here in Cathay, where spices were so plentiful, it was hard to remember what a king's ransom they fetched in Europe.

"Have you heard from Cheng Ho?" he asked.

"A dispatch was received by imperial post a few days ago," Ma Huan said. "The work on the Dragon River is going well. They have already laid the keels for the first two Treasure Ships and about twenty of the Tower Ships and Sea Hawk ships. The diviners have selected fortunate days, *hao jih tzu*, for laying down the next batch of vessels. Cheng Ho believes that in another fortnight or so he can leave the work in the hands of his chief designer, Chin Pi-feng, and return to Peking for several months. He's been gone too long, and the Anti-Maritime crowd have been stirring things up lately."

Tom had been worried about the same thing himself. His presence had been required at the court several times during Cheng Ho's absence, and he had been taken there, with all due pomp, by the eunuch vice admiral, Hou Hsien, and made to stand in boredom with the giraffe at the right of the throne. But during the last few visits, Chien Yi and some of the other officials associated with the Anti-Maritime Party had been bolder about showing their hostility. They had taken to referring to Tom, in his presence, as a "bones-outside"—a Chinese term of opprobrium for foreigners.

The Emperor, it was true, had kept it from getting out of hand. He was still on Cheng Ho's side. He had reprimanded the Anti-Maritimers when they had gone too far in breaching decorum. But it seemed to Tom that he had done so in an increasingly tired and perfunctory manner. He didn't look well lately.

And now the Emperor was gone—he would be away from the capital for several weeks on one of his punitive expeditions against the northern Mongols. The Crown Prince was in charge during his absence.

"I'll be glad when Cheng Ho returns," Tom said. "Some Anti-Maritime thugs tried to force their way in here a couple of days ago. The servants beat them and threw them out."

Ma Huan was instantly alert. "You should have told me. I'll have some eunuch guards posted in the garden."

"Do you think that's necessary?"

"Something's been giving the Anti-Maritimers too much confidence lately. It's best not to take chances."

Wo was fussing around the low table again. The servants arrived with several more courses—a gelatinous soup, rice noodles with sweet soya, dessert meats. Wo poured more wine.

Ma Huan took up a porcelain spoon and helped himself to some soup. "Don't worry, Chin Mao," he said. "Construction's gone too far at the shipyards to be stopped. By this time next year we'll be safely on the high seas."

Tom toyed with his wine. He was tired of food and tired of talk. He wished that Ma Huan would be gone, so that he could be alone with Lan-ying.

"Here's one that I like," Tom said. "I'll have it made into a ring for you."

He took a large emerald out of the coffer and held it up to the light. It sparkled like green fire. Lan-ying gasped with pleasure, then shook her head firmly. "No," she said, "you must not."

Tom played with her fingers idly. He was propped up on one elbow on the low platform of plaited rush and floss silk that served as his bed. Lan-ying lay beside him, one hip pressed against him. Though she was naked, the elaborate hairdo, held in place by pins and combs, was intact. He was able sometimes to cajole her into taking it down, but she didn't like him to see her without it. The bed curtains were drawn, and the house was silent, though he was sure that somewhere there was a watchman awake.

"Why not?" he said lazily.

He could afford it. The emerald didn't represent a hundredth part of his wealth. Cheng Ho had been right. He didn't need a stipend. The coffer of jewels had been sent by the Emperor as a gift to the Auspicious Barbarian the day after his first interview. Other gifts—from those eager to curry favor with the Emperor or those who wished to show that they allied themselves with Cheng

Ho's faction—had arrived with gratifying regularity since.

He would be a rich man when he returned to England. The emerald alone was worth more than his father had earned in a lifetime.

"Because," Lan-ying said, snuggling against him, "it will make your other concubines jealous. You neglect them. You should spend time with each of them in turn. It's your duty."

"I don't want to spend time with each of them in turn. I want to spend time with you."

"It's not right. You make them feel useless."

"I give them presents, too."

"It's not enough. You should make *fa-sheng gwan-shi* with them more often. It would give them more face in your household. They are ashamed in front of the servants."

Tom laughed. "You're a funny burd, Lan-ying. In England a woman would scratch my eyes out for doing what you suggest."

"It's for my good, too, my *ai jen*. It would make my life in your house happier. The other women would be friendlier to me."

"Who's been unfriendly with you?" he demanded. "I'll put a stop to *that!*"

"No, no, lord, you mustn't!" she said with alarm showing on her faultless face.

"I'll make you my wife," he grumbled. "Then nobody will be able to say anything."

"But if you made me your wife," she said reasonably, "you would have to appoint a new number one concubine. And spend more time with her."

"The devil take it! I'm damned if I understand it!"

A slender arm snaked around him. He could feel her teacup breasts flatten against his chest. "And you'll be happier with me, lord," she breathed in his ear. "You won't get tired of me so soon."

"I'll never get tired of you," he said gamely. His breath had begun to quicken.

She reached down and joined them. "Go to Small Enclosed Pearl before the others," she whispered. "You've only taken her once."

"All right," he agreed. "But first . . ."

When he woke in the morning, his bed was empty. Lan-ying's perfume remained in the room, but she had departed some time during the night, taking with her all her pins and combs, her robe, and her sandals.

He sat up, feeling vibrant and alive despite the small amount of sleep he'd had. A golden morning sun was doing its best to burst through the oiled paper panes of his windows. He could hear the birds making a commotion in the garden. The servants must have been up and about for an hour. Everything in the Middle Kingdom was in full swing at the crack of dawn.

He missed Lan-ying. He had hoped that she would stay with him here and have breakfast with him, but that was a rare concession by her. It would only add to the disharmony in the household, she said, to flaunt the special favor he showed her.

He could hear voices raised in the outer courtyard. He frowned. Whatever it was, the servants would take care of it. He wondered what was keeping Wo. He had a sixth sense for telling the precise moment when his master awakened. He would be here any moment with a breakfast tray—tea, fruit, jasmine cakes, a plate of plain noodles in broth, bean curd gruel. Tom never ate anything but the tea and a piece of fruit, but that made no difference to Wo, who kept bringing the same tray morning after morning.

There was a whisper of felt slippers on the floor, and he turned to see Wo standing there, but without the tray.

"Master must come right away," he said. "Ma Huan is here with eunuchs." He looked frightened.

"What's this about?" Tom said. He had sent Ma Huan home in a palanquin last night, drunk as a lord. The old reprobate should not have been up to any activity until noon at least.

But Wo vanished without answering. Tom took a moment to use the pot, threw on a robe, and hurried across an interval of courtyard to the reception room. Ma Huan was standing there, looking agitated, and with him were a pair of armed eunuchs in leather corselets and helmets.

"The Yung Lo Emperor is dead," Ma Huan said, wringing his hands.

"*What?*" Tom said.

"The army has returned to Peking with his body," Ma Huan said. "The Crown Prince has moved quickly—so quickly that he must have known in advance. He has already named his reign Hung-hsi and taken the dynastic title of Jen-tsung."

The eunuchs moved their feet and muttered. Tom recognized one of them as a bodyguard of Cheng Ho who had been detached to the service of the vice admiral when Cheng Ho had departed for Nanking.

"What does this mean?" Tom said.

Ma Huan inclined his head to listen to the sounds in the street. Tom could hear a horse troop passing by with a clatter of hooves, a jangle of armor, and shouted military commands.

"The Anti-Maritime Party has wasted no time," Ma Huan said. "Chien Yi must have reached the Crown Prince's ear immediately. All the ministers who were thrown in prison by Yung Lo after third son slandered them have been released and their families have been pardoned."

The eunuch guard whom Tom had recognized twittered breathlessly, "It's terrible, terrible, Chin Mao. Hsia Yuan-chi has been released, too."

"Yes," Ma Huan said. "Cheng Ho's old enemy, who was Finance Minister when the expeditions began. There's no doubt that he'll take command of the Anti-Maritime Party again!"

"What can we do?" Tom cried.

"A relay of messengers has been sent to Nanking by the fastest horses. Cheng Ho will be on his way as soon as the news reaches him. But I fear it will be too late."

Tom said gruffly, "You said yourself that construction of the seventh fleet's gone too far to be stopped. At least the voyage will give us a breathing space." He thought of what Cheng Ho had told him. When the Ming Empire reached Europe, it was going to change the world. Nothing would be the same, ever again. "And when the Star Raft returns," he went on, "it's going to bring back more glory than ever was imagined. That ought to change some minds around here!"

"What I said would have been true if Yung Lo were still alive," Ma Huan replied.

Tom noticed that despite the lessons in names and titles the old tutor had given him, he was using the name of the dead Emperor's reign for the Emperor himself.

"Jen-tsung can only seize glory for himself by killing his father's dreams."

The imperial order came the next day. Hsia Yuan-chi's call for economy and retrenchment had prevailed:

"All building of seagoing ships for intercourse with barbarian countries is to cease forthwith. Henceforth it will be an offense punishible by death to build such ships. The Middle Kingdom has no need to communicate with foreigners."

CHAPTER 18

Marina reached out with a white arm to part the *saha*, the dividing curtain that turned the back end of Sandro's room into harem. Though made of old scraps that she'd sewn together, it was nevertheless respected by the rest of the household.

"Don't go," Sandro begged.

She smiled sadly. "I must, my love," she said. "You know that."

He sat up and nodded his head in rueful acknowledgement. "Yes," he said. "But it doesn't make it any easier."

"I'll be back in the evening," she said. "I'll save my portion, and we can eat together."

"I wish we could be together all the time, *cara*."

"We're lucky to have what we have," she said. "Don't tempt fate."

Sandro checked any bitter reply. He could not share her serene and radiant acceptance of whatever came her way, but he had no wish to cast shadows on her happiness. Marina had bloomed since their marriage—a hurried but valid ceremony in the house of the Greek consul's chaplain, Father Chrysostom, with a Moslem guard waiting impatiently outside. She had left the female slave quarters immediately and moved into Sandro's quarters off Jaybir's library. She had turned the bare little room into a home for the two of them, brightening it with flowers culled from among the wilted daily cast-off floral arrangements from the residence hall and begging odds and ends of rugs and furniture from the intendant's staff. There was even a shrine—a small wooden icon that had been slipped surreptitiously to her by Father Chrysostom. Sandro prudently hid it every morning after she left for the kitchens and resurrected it for her return.

He forced a smile. "You're right, *cara*. I only wish I had more to offer you. If Jaybir were here, there'd be a feast of leftovers, with maybe even a meat pastry or two."

She bit her lip. "It's the same in the kitchen. 'Amm Arif used to look the other way sometimes if a slave were hungry and sampled something, but now he doesn't dare. That bailiff of Murrwan's watches everything like a hawk. He even threatened 'amm Arif with the loss of a hand if anything's missing."

The gruff head cook had sent tidbits to the newlyweds at first, but not anymore. Murrwan's stinginess had made itself felt within a week of Jaybir's departure for Mecca. It was emblematic of the new state of affairs that 'amm Arif was no longer master in his own kitchen. All the slaves were hungrier these days. It tormented Sandro that Marina, despite his own relatively privileged position, was acquiring a pinched look. He himself was feeling the new parsimony in the upper servants' mess where he had been accustomed to take his meals, and he was no longer able to smuggle food to the Turk.

"Things will get better again when Jaybir returns," he told her. "He won't like what's been going on."

She touched his face with her fingertips. Her wide clear brow was serene again. "God will protect us, *agape mou*. Don't trouble yourself. Hasn't He been good to us so far?"

"Yes, *cara*," he said, almost meaning it this time. He kissed her, drawing her close. The warmth of her sturdy body was the only reality in this hellhole of bondage.

As if she sensed what he was thinking, she said softly, "It doesn't matter. As long as we're together. They can't take our thoughts from us. They can't take God from us."

"*Cara*, is something wrong?"

"No," she said quickly. "It's just that Murrwan is providing a feast for some of his friends tonight. Those rowdy ones who go about the city making mischief for the innkeepers. He'll be in and out of the kitchen all day, poking into everything and causing difficulties for *'amm* Arif and the sub-chefs."

"Try to stay out of his sight as much as possible," Sandro said with a frown. He struggled for his few words of Koine. "*Lathe biosas*—isn't that how the saying goes? It's best to escape notice in life."

"Don't worry—Murrwan hardly looks at the women in the kitchen anymore. Jaybir must have had a talk with him before he left. He knows *'amm* Arif will report any improprieties when Jaybir gets back. He's boiling about that threat from the bailiff—he'll report that, too. Anyway, Murrwan's just bought a new pair of slave girls for his own harem with some of the money he's been skimming off, and it's said that he's much occupied with them."

"Be careful all the same," he said. But he felt mollified by her words. Thank God the old man was a bit of a prude and that his head wasn't entirely in the clouds.

"I'll ask the Virgin to look after me today," she said with a smile. "How will that do?"

"I'll say a prayer with you too, *cara*," he said.

"You don't have to," she said. But he could see that she was pleased.

"Nonsense, it's the same Virgin. She doesn't care what language a good Christian addresses her in."

He knelt beside her in front of the little icon. Marina had propped it up in a small niche that once had held a bronze lamp, and had lain a few flowers in front of it. It was a painting on wood in the eastern manner by some village artisan. It showed a Virgin with huge eyes and stiff, elongated limbs holding the Child in the crook of one arm and with the other pointing the Way in the attitude known as the *Hodegetria*. The heads were framed by halos with a cross within, like cartwheels. The work, though crude, had strength in it, and the halos were done in real gold paint.

He stumbled through the Greek words with her. There would be some in Venice who would call him a heretic, he thought, but he didn't care. Surely Marina's burning certainty was worth more than his own worn-out faith.

"Is that wise?" he said when he saw that she was wearing the small Greek cross that Father Chrysostom had given her with the icon.

"I'll keep it hidden," she said, dropping it into her bodice. "*Chaire*, my love."

"*Chaire*," he said.

He worked hard through the morning, continuing the vast job of putting Jaybir's library in order. Some of Jaybir's staff, the copyists in particular, were taking advantage of the old scholar's absence to loaf, but Sandro, who had come to see the importance of the work, was determined to push it forward. The copyists complained bitterly when he heaped assignments on them, saying that Sandro, a slave, had no right to give them orders, but by a combination of cajolery and threats of Jaybir's displeasure, he managed to keep the work from coming to a standstill. The great library would be Jaybir's monument and his bequest to the scholars of the ages. Sandro was sure there were few like it in the world, both in Saracen and Christian lands.

He paused for the morning meal, eating sparingly so as to have something more to contribute to his evening meal with Marina. The higher-ranking slaves he ate with, in a small hall at the rear of Jaybir's apartments, had become accustomed to seeing Sandro take his second meal of the day back to his quarters on a tray, but the scanty first meal, which had become scantier under Murrwan's regime, usually offered little in the way of portable morsels that could be saved for later. Today it was a thin gruel of cracked wheat with a small sheet of flatbread. He tore the bread in half, reserving a share.

"It gets worse and worse," complained one of his messmates, a creaky relic named Taiyar, who had been Jaybir's valet but who now was a supernumerary footman. "Have you heard the story of the miser who trained his ox to eat less and less each day, but just when he had the animal accustomed to a single piece of straw, it died."

A mutter of agreement went round the table. "There's bound to be a feast when the master gets back," another slave said, "to celebrate his becoming a *hajji*."

"*Kharuf mahshi*," said another. "That's what I want. If I can taste *kharuf mahshi* just once more in this life, I'll die happy!"

"Aim your wishes higher, Aboud," someone else said. "We were given *kharuf mahshi* at the last *Id al-Fitr*."

"He's been gone two months now," said a man named Harith, who served as one of the butler's assistants. "Shouldn't he have returned by now?"

"That shows how much *you* know, Harith," said Aboud. "It's a long and perilous journey, even with the best of escorts, and he must remain for the final *tawaf*. He might not return for another month."

"Then, too, he might have decided to visit Medina as well," put in the old footman.

"A *hajji* came to the gate this morning," offered an assistant to Jaybir's kennel master. "He asked to be taken to the residence."

"I'll wager he didn't get very far," Taiyar scoffed. "The nephew regards these itinerant *hajjis* as little more than beggars trading on their status. He's given orders that none of them are to be admitted."

"That's where you're wrong," the kennel assistant said. "The chamberlain came out to see him, and he was taken to Murrwan."

"I wonder what that was about. Perhaps he had news of Jaybir."

"He didn't say. He's still closeted over there with Murrwan."

An artisan who had been doing tile work in Murrwan's quarters that morning lapped round the last of his bowl like a dog and raised his head for the first time. "He's sent for a *qadi*."

"What?"

"Murrwan's sent for a *qadi*. And a notary as well."

Old Taiyar snorted. "When a scoundrel searches out

the fine points of the law, watch out. What's Murrwan want a *qadi* for?"

"He's always in debt," Harith suggested. "Maybe his creditors finally caught up with him."

"The two of you should learn to curb your tongues," the tile worker said uneasily.

"Why?" Taiyar challenged him. "We're all friends here. There's none of Murrwan's servants around to carry tales."

"Not at the moment, no. But that kind of talk's a bad habit to get into."

"Ask the Christian. Remember how none of us trusted him at first. What do you say, *ya* Sandroo?"

"He's right," Sandro said. "It's best to keep your mouth shut."

He finished his gruel and stood up. One or two pairs of eyes looked longingly at his leftover flatbread as he gathered it up, then flashed discreetly away.

"*Ma'a salaama, ya* Sandroo," they murmured politely in turn.

"*Allah isalmak,*" he replied.

At noon, allowing enough time after the muezzin's midday call to prayer for the workmen to finish their devotions, Sandro went to the garden to check on the progress being made on the enormous standing astrolabe that Jaybir had left him in charge of. Today was the day they were supposed to install the *ankabut*—the "spider"—and that was going to be a tricky job. The thirty-foot cage of welded bronze strips had been propped up under temporary shelter while the artisans attached pointers for no fewer than one hundred and eight of the fixed stars in the revised catalog that the Persian astronomer al-Sufi had adapted from Ptolemy's *Almagest*. The calibrations for a spherical astrolabe, of whatever size, would be infinitely more exacting than for the more usual flat version.

He found none of the bustling activity he had expected. The crane that had been erected atop the wooden scaffolding that enclosed the astrolabe's openwork womb remained idle. A single workman with hammer and chisel knelt chipping away at the circular stone pavement that had been incised with decorative Kufic script to show terrestrial coordinates.

"*Eh da?*" Sandro cried. "What are you doing?"

The man lifted his head. Sandro recognized him vaguely as one of the outdoor handymen who had been appropriated for Murrwan's household staff some weeks ago over the protests of Jaybir's head gardener.

"*Ahlahn!* I've been told to take up the paving stones. A flower bed's going in here."

"There must be some mistake. Where are the men who were supposed to install the bronze sphere?"

"The bailiff sent them away. The sphere's going to be melted down and sold to a dealer in bronze."

"That can't be! This is a mathematical instrument designed by the lord Jaybir to crown his life's work."

The man shrugged. "The *sayyid* Murrwan gave the orders himself."

"He'd never dare to go against Jaybir!"

"Haven't you been told at the big house yet?"

"Told what?"

The man got to his feet and looked across at the main residence, shading his eyes against the sun. "There they go now. I guess they're going to break the news at the harem first."

Sandro saw Jaybir's Negro chamberlain hurrying along the farther walk in the company of Murrwan and his hulking bailiff. They stopped in front of the gate of the harem where Jaybir's old concubines were pensioned off. It was as much of a home as the old man had had for a good many years.

"A pity for them," the handyman said.

A eunuch guard appeared at the gate. Murrwan and his bailiff pushed past him and went inside. The chamberlain, after taking a moment to say something to the eunuch, followed. The eunuch had made no attempt to draw his weapon or to resist. He stood indecisively, his hand on the hilt of his scimitar, his shoulders slumped. Sandro recognized him as old Theodoros, Marina's friend.

"What's going on?" Sandro asked.

The handyman didn't answer. He waited with his head cocked, listening.

A few moments later, a scream came from the harem. It was followed by the sound of wailing voices, a primitive keening that raised the hackles on the back of Sandro's neck.

"May Allah have mercy on him," the handyman said. "It was not his fault that he could not complete the *hajj*."

"What are you saying?" Sandro said in a whisper.

"Jaybir. He died in the Sinai. They left him buried in the sands."

Sandro pottered around in the library until late afternoon, awaiting Marina's return. By then word of Jaybir's death had filtered through the entire household. The servants and slaves went about their tasks in a subdued manner, without the easy sociability that even Murrwan's stewardship had not been able to erase these last two months. Sandro was unable to find out anything further until a cleaning man came in, dusting in a desultory way and obviously bursting to talk.

"Have you heard anything, brother?" Sandro inquired.

The man looked out toward the corridor and back again. "The brothers are here," he said. "They're squabbling. Murrwan's taken possession in the name of his father, who's the oldest, because the old man's in his dotage. But the other brothers say that since Jaybir left neither children nor parents, they're entitled to share one-third, by the law of the Koran. Murrwan's promised to settle with them by money alone."

"Will he move into Jaybir's house?"

"Not yet. Not till things are settled. He's going around with his bailiff and the chamberlain, looking for things to sell off."

When Sandro was alone again, he mentally reviewed the contents of Jaybir's library. It had been ignorant of Murrwan to decide to melt down the garden astrolabe for its bronze, but surely even Murrwan could see the value of the old astronomer's matchless collection of books and ancient manuscripts. The whole was worth much more than the sum of its parts. Its value to other scholars would be unprecedented, particularly if the work of cataloguing it, which he had begun, were finished.

He examined his own stewardship of the precious hoard and could honestly find no fault with it. And then it came to him that he himself was a valuable part of the library. He was the only person familiar enough with the entire collection to be able to evaluate it properly. If it were sold to some wealthy savant, Sandro himself would have to go with it.

But what about Marina? He thought it through. Islam was humane. The buyer surely would not separate a man from his wife. Marina would be sold with him. And anyway, the buyer would see that it was to his own advantage to keep his librarian content, even if Murrwan put a high price on Marina. Educated slaves were not donkeys, to be beaten to improve their efforts. They had to give of their wits voluntarily.

He permitted himself a modicum of optimism in his imaginings. He could not hope to find an exceptional master like Jaybir again, but the man who acquired this treasure of books and instruments would have to love knowledge for its own sake. It would not be a bad thing to work for another scholar.

Careless of who might see him, he crossed himself and said a prayer for Jaybir. Perhaps God would be merciful. Jaybir might have been an infidel, but he had been a good man.

It was almost time for the second meal, the *r'ada*. Sandro listened for the gong that would announce it. Marina would be here soon, with her portion wrapped in a napkin. He got ready to go to the servants' mess to collect his own dinner.

Murrwan arrived just then, with his bailiff and the chamberlain in tow. With them was a sallow, musty man whose eyes darted up and down the walls at the books and manuscripts piled on the shelves.

None of them took any notice of Sandro. He was a slave, a piece of furniture. He stood quietly against the wall, arms at his sides.

"Well, *ya* Sehim, what kind of price are you prepared to offer me for the lot?" Murrwan said.

The musty man walked over to the nearest shelves and began pulling out books and scrolls at random. Sandro winced. He was going to have to file them all again.

"It's a large collection, *ya* Murrwan," the dealer said.

"Yes, yes," Murrwan said impatiently.

The dealer shook his head. "It's too large for me to handle alone. You'll have to bring in other dealers. I'll go through it and see if there's anything worthwhile. Some of the old manuscripts might be worth something as antiquities. The newer things that were copied out here won't have much value. The calligraphy's undistinguished. It's just workaday lettering for study or reading, like students' study copies, of no interest to anyone else."

Sandro found himself close to tears. What the seedy dealer was holding was Jaybir's own *Zij*, the astronomical table he had updated from the *Zij* of the great Ibn-Yunus. It didn't look like much, but it would be of incalculable value to any astronomer who knew how to use it.

"What about the instruments?" Murrwan asked.

"I don't deal in instruments. You'll have to get someone else." His eyes roved over the astrolabes and armillary spheres. "There're a few genuine antiques here, I think. But there's a lot of junk, too." He picked up the *kamal* that Captain Kareem had given to Sandro. "What's this? It's only a piece of wood like the ones used by sailors. Your uncle must have been a bit of a pack rat."

He tossed the *kamal* aside.

"I know what you're doing, *ya* Sehim," Murrwan said unpleasantly. "You only want to skim off the cream of what's here and leave me with nothing to interest other dealers."

Sehim spread his hands. "I'm a businessman, *ya* Murrwan. I can only take what I can make a profit on. You can unload the rest a little at a time on the shopkeepers in the Street of the Books. What they don't take, you can sell to the used parchment dealers."

Sandro could contain himself no longer. He stepped forward, to Murrwan's annoyance and the astonishment of the others. It was, he told himself, to Murrwan's advantage for him to point out the value of the collection.

In such a case he could be forgiven for speaking out without permission.

"Excuse me, my lord Murrwan," he said, getting the words out quickly before he could be stopped, "but it would be a great mistake to break up Jaybir al-Sumit's library. In fact, it would be a tragedy. It's a unique accumulation of knowledge. It would be worth much more if it were all kept together."

Sehim stared at him coldly. "Do you allow your slaves to scold you, *ya* Murrwan?" he said.

Murrwan was growing purple. Before he could say anything, the chamberlain stepped between him and Sandro. The chamberlain was a decent sort, a dignified, unimaginative man who had served Jaybir for many years.

"The Christian's only trying to be helpful," he said. "He worked here every day and ought to know what's here, at least. He might be of some help in inventorying the material."

He turned his head and gave Sandro a warning look. Sandro took the hint and stepped back, out of the way.

"You!" barked the bailiff. "Clear out of here! We'll deal with you later!"

Sandro returned to the room he used as living quarters. He could hear the voices in the library but could not make out the words. Murrwan and the dealer seemed to be coming to some sort of agreement. The voices moved closer, and he heard Murrwan say, "What's in here?"

"Oh, it used to be a storeroom or something," the chamberlain replied evasively. The three of them entered. Sandro removed all expression from his face.

The bailiff kicked aside a low table that Marina had salvaged from a junk heap and stared curiously at the meager furnishings. Sandro was glad he had remembered to hide Marina's little icon that morning. He hoped they wouldn't poke around too thoroughly.

"You live here?" Murrwan said.

"Yes," Sandro answered.

The chamberlain cleared his throat. "The lord Jaybir wanted to have him close by for convenience."

"It's been turned into a rat's nest," Murrwan said.

"You'll have to clear it out." His eyes fell on the dividing curtain. "What's back there?"

"That's a *saha* strung across there," the chamberlain said. "The back of the room is harem. The Christian lives here with his wife."

"Christian dogs don't have wives," Murrwan said. "They have Christian whores."

He motioned with his hand and the bailiff ripped the curtain down. Sandro forced himself to remain still.

"Slaves take on airs, it seems, when you allow them out of their barracks." His lip curled as he looked over the straw matting and coverlet that served as Sandro's and Marina's bed, the wicker hamper that contained their few possessions, and the vase of flowers and the mended wall hanging that Marina had put up in an attempt to brighten the place.

"I'll see to having it tidied up here," the chamberlain said stiffly. Sandro could feel his pity.

"See that all that trash is thrown out," Murrwan said. "The woman can go back to the female slave quarters."

"But my lord, married slaves . . ." the chamberlain began.

"There's no marriage unless they're married in Islam," Murrwan snapped. "Haven't I made myself clear?"

Sandro felt his innards knot in despair. There was no way he could warn Marina. She would come and find everything gone.

"What about him?" The bailiff jerked a thumb at Sandro.

Sandro waited while Murrwan thought it over.

"Put the useless dog to work in the stables," Murrwan said. "Hassan will know how to knock the insolence out of him."

He swept out of the room, taking the dealer Sehim with him. The chamberlain, with an apologetic glance at Sandro, followed.

"You heard him," the bailiff said.

"Can I take my bedding?" Sandro said.

"All right, but be quick about it."

Sandro breathed a sigh of relief. The icon was hidden there. He managed to hide it under his tunic without the bailiff seeing. The bailiff was too busy plundering the hamper of Marina's few trinkets.

A short time later, the bedding rolled up over his shoulder, Sandro reported to the stables. Hassan the Knout was waiting for him with a crooked smile on his face.

"Welcome, infidel dog," Hassan said. "I told you that sooner or later you'd be back."

Sandro pitched hay, ignoring the smarting sensation in his back. The violent activity had opened up the fresh laceration again, making it bleed. Hassan liked to add a stripe every week or two so that his back never healed completely.

"The bastard!" he growled. "Some day I'm going to put this pitchfork through his fat gut."

Beside him, the Turk, his massive torso oiled with sweat, heaved another forkload into the loft. "You don't know how to wait, Venetian," he grunted. "You never did. Be glad you're not poor Marouf. He was caught eating a carrot meant for the horses and got five."

"Marouf's an idiot," Sandro said. "It wasn't worth it for a carrot."

"You're the idiot. Keeping that Christian idol of yours. If I know where you hide it, somebody else is going to stumble on it too."

"It's not an idol. It's a picture of Our Lady."

"An idol's an idol, and an idolater's an idolater. You Christians are no different from the black fellows who carry their mother stones around with them. And you know how they're punished when they're caught."

"I'm keeping it for Marina," Sandro said. "I want to be able to tell her that I still have it."

The Turk spat into the straw. "You haven't been able to get word to her yet?"

"She knows where I am. One of the eunuchs told me when I saddled the horses for the hawking party yesterday. I'm going to try to see her today."

"Don't be a fool. You can't trust a eunuch. They're terrible gossips. You'll be caught."

"She'll pass along the garden path that goes past the

paddock at the far corner of the stables. There's only a low wall there. She's serving at one of the drunken dinner parties that Murrwan's been throwing to show off the palace he's made for himself out of Jaybir's wing. I'll be waiting when she goes by on her way back to the kitchens. We'll have a few minutes to talk."

"Don't go, Venetian. Forget the woman."

"She's my life!" Sandro cried.

The Turk looked at him narrowly. "You've lost a life before. You can let another one go."

"No. Not this time."

The Turk paused in his labors. "Listen to me, Venetian. The Greek woman is gone as far as you're concerned. Forget her. Murrwan is set on adding her to his harem. If he hasn't done it yet, it's because of his conceit. He's made up his mind to convert her to Islam first. He's already boasted to his friends."

"I'd kill him before I'd let him touch her."

"You could be skinned alive for even saying that."

"I don't care."

"It won't be so bad for the woman if she's sensible. If he converts her in front of witnesses, it means he won't use her and throw her away. It would make him look bad. He won't make her a concubine, but the slave girls in his harem aren't treated too badly, even after he gets tired of them. They eat with the other women—better than the household slaves eat."

"He can't make her renounce her faith."

"Don't be so sure. There are ways to make a Christian deny his beliefs in the sight of God, and Murrwan knows them."

"What do you mean?" Sandro demanded.

But the Turk would say no more.

Sandro waited at the angle of the wall, shivering in the chill of the night air. He had satisfied himself that he was well hidden. The tumbled stones of an earlier paddock wall had never been removed, and scrub vegetation had been allowed to spring up in the rubble beyond the manicured boundary of the garden proper. He had a good, moonlit view of the garden path at this point, where it meandered close to the paddock.

He had spied on the processions of food and drink wending their way past and the singing girls with their instruments and the unveiled dancers who had been hired for the night. Murrwan had provided well for his guests. Marina had gone by a quarter hour ago, but Sandro had not intercepted her. He did not want to interfere with the delivery of the tray, but if she were a little late returning to the kitchen, 'amm Arif would not care.

It had given Sandro a pang to see her. She had taken the precaution of wrapping herself in a drab cloak, draped over her head to give her the same shapeless look as the older serving women. She would hardly attract a second look from Murrwan's male guests, whose attention would be reserved for the scantily clad entertainers. But on the path, hampered by the heavy brass tray, she had allowed the edge of the cloak to fall away from her face. Sandro had been shocked to see that she had grown even thinner and paler, the cool serenity of her expression replaced by lines of weariness. Her movements seemed spiritless, unlike her usual self. They had been working her hard. It must have been shattering for her to have found him gone and not to know where he was; to have her small, safe world snatched from her without warning. His mouth tightened. He would fix *that*, at least. He could see no way out for them, but he knew that seeing him, whispering together for a few pitiful moments, would give her a renewal of hope.

As if she had sensed his presence, she lifted her chin valiantly and resumed the proud carriage that he knew. An effort of will had erased the tired lines. He could only guess at what she was thinking at that moment, but he knew he loved her.

But that had been a quarter hour ago. Sandro began to worry. She should have returned by now.

He listened for sounds from the house. It was a hundred yards' distant, but the noise of the party carried well in the still night air. They were getting rowdy in there. He heard the caterwauling of a singing girl over the jangle of thumb cymbals and tambourines, followed by raucous male laughter. Then another girl began a lewd song to the accompaniment of an oud. Sandro raised his head hopefully at the crunch of footsteps on gravel, but it was only two serving women being shooed along by a eunuch. Neither of them was Marina.

He waited another half hour, growing restive. The last of the kitchen staff straggled back—the four men who had borne the oversize brass warming platter carrying the whole roast lamb—but there still was no sign of Marina. Why were they keeping her there?

A burst of laughter and another rattle of tambourines made him nervous. He poked a cautious head out of his hiding place and started to edge closer to the house.

A sound behind him made him turn his head, and he saw a bulky shape raise itself powerfully to the top of the paddock wall and drop heavily to the ground. A large clump of fingers wrapped itself around his arm. "Where do you think you're going?" the Turk said.

"Let go of me," Sandro said. "What are you doing here?"

"I knew you'd lose your head when the woman didn't come."

It was like struggling with an iron statue. Sandro got the Turk a little off balance, then found himself propped up in the powerful grip again. "I only want to get a closer look," Sandro said.

"Leave it alone, Venetian," the Turk rumbled. "We'd better get back to the stable before we're missed."

"You know something, don't you?" Sandro wrested himself free. "Tell me, for God's sake!"

"I hear gossip, too. I rattled your eunuch around till he talked. Tonight's the night Murrwan's going to try to force a conversion. He's even got a ne'er-do-well *khatib* there to make it all proper."

"I've got to go to her!"

Sandro turned. The Turk reached for him. Sandro picked up a large rock from the rubble at his feet and swung it with all his might. It caught the Turk on the side of the head. He dropped with a thud of solid meat against the earth and did not get up. Sandro could not see any movement, but he backed away in case one of

those mighty arms came to life and grabbed him by the
ankle.

He kept off the path, keeping to the shelter of hedges
and trees as much as possible. The party had gone quiet,
which he did not like. He paused to look up at the tall
lighted archways, throwing geometric patterns of shadow
through their grilles. As he drew closer he heard a snatch
of instrumental music, which stopped abruptly as if
someone had told the player to halt.

He flattened himself against a tree as someone went
by the scalloped arcade that fronted the building. Something made him remain where he was a moment longer,
and a eunuch came out of the harem gate, looked
around, and went back inside.

And then he was inside the tiled corridors that he had
known so well when they had belonged to Jaybir. No one
was about. He crept up a flight of marble stairs toward
the hall that Jaybir had used for hospitality. At the top he
shrank back against the balustrade. A single footman was
standing in the pointed archway that gave onto the guest
hall, but he was watching what was going on inside, and
his back was to Sandro.

All at once, Sandro was aware of how he must look
and, still worse, how he must smell. He wore an old
shirt, a clout between his legs, a dirty rag wrapped
around his head for a turban, and an odor of horse manure clung to him. No one seeing him would take him
for a house servant, even for a moment. The instant anyone came along, he was done for.

A trickle of ice ran down his spine. He could hear a
woman sobbing inside, sobbing against a silence that was
somehow the sum of fifty held breaths.

"Take it!" shouted a furious voice that he recognized as
Murrwan's. "Take it in your hand and throw it down!"

"Please . . ." Marina's small voice replied brokenly.
"This is a great evil. Why are you doing this . . . ?"

"Take it, you bitch!" Murrwan cried in a fit of rage.
There was the sharp crack of a blow, and Marina
screamed. The fifty held breaths were expelled.

Sandro, forgetting everything, charged across the landing. The footman heard the slap of bare feet and turned

around. Sandro rammed a shoulder into him, bowling him over. He burst into the chamber and stared wildly about.

For a moment of arrested time, the scene engraved itself on his mind. The banqueters were sprawled around on cushions amidst the remains of their feast, flushed with food and drink. A middle-aged man had left off pawing a dancing girl whose wrist he had imprisoned, his attention diverted by his host; a young debauchee was licking his lips avidly. But here and there some of Murrwan's guests had the grace to look ashamed of what they were witnessing. Murrwan was waving a large brass crucifix, his face livid. Marina stood with her head bowed before him, her hands at her sides. The mark of the blow was still red on her cheek. Her cloak had been taken from her, and she wore a simple linen gown that had been ripped down at one shoulder by rough handling. The little ivory cross that Father Chrysostom had given her hung exposed to view.

No one had noticed Sandro yet. All eyes were riveted on the tense tableau.

A murmur of helpful advice came from the onlookers. "Leave it off for now, *ya* Murrwan. You need to let the *khatib* reason with her."

The advice infuriated Murrwan further. He ripped the cross from Marina's neck and ground it under his heel.

"There!" he exploded. "The thing's done! You've renounced your god!"

"No, *ya* Murrwan," objected a puffy-faced man who looked as if he might be the *khatib*. "She's got to trample it underfoot herself."

"No," Marina said in a shaking voice. "I won't." She stared defiantly at Murrwan. "Father save me," she whispered in Greek.

Murrwan raised a hand to strike her again. With a sob, Sandro lurched from the archway and went for him. Heads turned, men shouted in confusion. He had time to see that Marina was looking at him, her face unastonished. Then there was a clatter of dishes underfoot as he knocked over bowls and platters spread out on the long cloth on the floor. Hands grabbed at him. The recovered

footman had staggered into the hall behind him, babbling, "I don't know how he got by me, master!" Sandro
clubbed away the hands that were restraining him. The
galleys had made him stronger than any of these soft
men. For a moment he thought he was going to get
through to Murrwan and get his oak-hard hands around
his neck.

Then the weight of numbers bore him to the ground.
A dozen daggers were raised. The men were very excited. Sandro thrashed around without effect, waiting for
the blades to fall.

"Hold!" Murrwan cried.

The daggers remained poised. A blade that had been
pressed against his neck withdrew an inch.

Murrwan walked over and kicked Sandro in the ribs.
"It's the infidel dog who calls himself her husband. I was
too lenient to him."

"A rebellious slave should die," the *khatib* said.

"No," Murrwan said. He was breathing hard. "He'll
have the pleasure of watching his whore lose her faith.
And she'll know he's watching."

A rain of blows to the head left Sandro stunned
enough to handle. They dragged him to a pillar and
bound him upright, bleeding from a dozen cuts made by
the broken crockery he'd fallen on. He shook his head to
clear it. Murrwan was advancing on Marina again with
the brass crucifix. He had regained control of himself,
and he spoke with a dangerous calm.

"I'll give you a last chance. Will you renounce your
false god?" He bit his lip and seemed almost to wheedle.
"All you have to do for now is to cast down the cross. You
can make the profession of faith later. I'll give you time
to get used to the idea."

Marina cast a glance toward Sandro before replying.
Their eyes locked, as they had that day long ago on the
slave quay. She turned to Murrwan, trembling and pale,
but with her head held high. "I can't deny God," she said
quietly.

Murrwan could not back down now in front of his
friends. Sandro could see that he was holding another explosion of temper back. "It's true, isn't it," Murrwan said

to the *khatib*, "that the intention is not as important as the deed?"

"That's correct, *ya* Murrwan," the *khatib* said. "It's like *salat*. If by an act you show your submission to Allah, the belief may come later."

Murrwan clapped his hands, and a servant sprang to attention. "Bring me that brazier of charcoal," he said.

Skewers that had held pigeons or chickens were still lying across it. The servant started to remove them, then dropped them with a howl. A couple of Murrwan's guests, the type who thought that sort of thing was funny, laughed. The servant found some napkins and folded them into thick pads, and carried the brazier over to Murrwan.

"I saw this done once to a Frankish priest," Murrwan remarked conversationally. "A very stubborn man. He lectured us at length about the three Christian gods. But his faith lasted about one second when he was given his cross."

He fanned the coals with a mat until they began to glow a dull red.

Sandro grew frantic. He struggled against the cords that bound him. "Marina!" he cried. "Do what they want!" He dredged up a phrase in Koine so that they would not understand. "*He glossa omomoch, he de phren anomotos!*" It was something her father had told her when the men of her island had been required to swear allegiance to the new megadux. "My tongue has sworn, but not my mind."

"Silence him," Murrwan said.

A pair of servants forced his mouth open while a vengeful footman crammed a napkin into it. Sandro tried to bite and got a crack on the side of the head for his trouble. The gag that went around his face covered his nose, and he found it hard to breathe. His chest heaved with effort.

Marina's eyes, wide with grief, came to rest on Sandro's face. "Sandro, Sandro, you don't believe after all, to ask me to do such a thing."

Murrwan picked up the brass crucifix and thrust it deep into the glowing coals. He left it there while a servant got a bellows and began pumping it. The coals brightened, turned cherry red, then orange. In a few minutes the color of the brass itself began to change, grow coppery. The servant spit on his finger and touched it gingerly to the shaft of the cross. He jerked his hand away hastily, to a hiss of steam.

At a nod from Murrwan, the *khatib* and the footman came around on either side of Marina and took her by the wrists. She made no attempt to resist. She had used up the last of her defiance in that last utterance. Now she was like a snared animal, not even shrinking from the hands of the trapper. Her eyes darted from side to side, unseeing. Her body was rigid with terror—terror not of what might be done to her, but terror that she might weaken. "*Kyrie, Kyrie,* give me strength!" she moaned through chattering teeth.

Stop, Sandro tried to cry through his gag, but only a muffled bawl came out. He heaved himself against his cords, only making them cut more deeply into his flesh.

Using a pair of tongs, Murrwan plucked the glowing crucifix out of the brazier and, with the *khatib* helping him to pry Marina's hands open, slapped the shaft against her palms. Marina screamed. They forced her hands to close around the shaft and stepped quickly away from her. There was a sizzle and the smell of burning flesh.

A gasp went up from the guests when she did not immediately drop it. She stood there swaying, the crucifix held in front of her, the tears running down her cheeks and her teeth bared in a ghastly grin, while the smell of cooked meat grew stronger.

"*Kifehya!* Drop it!" the shouts came.

Murrwan's face went ashen. Then Marina's knees buckled and the crucifix fell from her hands. A sigh came from those present. Marina crumpled to the floor, but her eyes were open and full of tears.

"No," she wailed. "No."

"So," Murrwan said hoarsely, "you could not keep faith with your god after all."

No, don't listen to him, Sandro wanted to say. He could see the terrible red bars across the palms of her hands, the curled-up fingers.

"Put ointment on her hands and bandage them," Murrwan said. "Take her to the harem, and prepare her to be brought to my bed tonight."

His face was flushed, and he seemed very satisfied with himself. He did not seem to notice how many of his guests wore expressions of distaste on their faces.

Slave girls took Marina away, helping her to walk. They were veiled, but they managed to look frightened nevertheless. Marina went with them docilely, like a sleepwalker, her eyes gone utterly dead.

Murrwan remembered Sandro. "Give him a beating and lock him up," he said. "In the morning he'll be gelded. If he survives the operation, he can be sold at a better price. I don't want to see him again."

The night seemed very short. Sandro huddled in a corner of the stone shed he'd been shut up in, nursing his bruises. The beating hadn't been so very bad. They didn't want to weaken him too badly and lower still further his chances of living through the surgery that would take away his manhood. The doctor would come shortly after first light with four strong men to hold Sandro down, they'd told him. It was a Persian doctor, very skilled. It would be over in a moment.

It was totally dark, a blackness so complete that Sandro was disoriented. He kept smashing into walls when he tried to walk about, no matter what direction he'd thought he'd pointed himself in or how carefully he counted his paces. The shed had no window; it had been meant only for storage. There was only an oak door made of planks two inches thick, with a heavy bar across the outside. For the first few hours he'd tried to break the door down, pry it open, loosen a plank. But they'd left him nothing in the shed, not even a bench to sleep on— not that he would have slept. He had only his fingernails and the meat of his shoulders, now sore and bruised from ramming them against the door. After he'd given up on the door, he'd tried digging. He had only his fingers for that, but he'd managed to dig down more than a foot before he discovered that there was a stone sill that ran all the way around.

Now he could only wait and try not to think. But he thought all the same. When he thought about himself, it kept going round in circles and coming out at the same place. The only thing he could think of that he might do was to rush the Persian doctor and attempt to kill him. He wouldn't succeed, of course, but he might make the doctor so angry—or at least unnerve him so much—that the operation would kill him. Then he realized that the doctor wouldn't come in first; he would send in the four strong men and not enter till they had him subdued. But thinking about Marina was worse. Those thoughts didn't go around in circles. They kept going out in all directions and finding new destinations. And each place they ended up was worse than the last. Sandro kept seeing her with her bandaged hands and her dead eyes, sitting unresisting while the women of the harem bathed her and brushed her hair and annointed her with rosewater. And then he could see a fat eunuch taking her, naked, to Murrwan's door and pushing her gently inside. And then . . . Sandro rammed his fist against the stone wall so that the pain would make the thoughts stop, but the thoughts wouldn't stop. And then he tried thinking about killing Murrwan, but that didn't work either because he knew that the thoughts about killing Murrwan were not real, and the other thoughts were.

But the worst thought of all was the thought that he had failed her, that he had been helpless to protect her. He could not forget the grief in her eyes when she had looked at him and seen him not as what they had been to each other, but as one of those who, with a devil's argument, was attempting to make her abjure her faith. If he did not die in the morning, then for the rest of whatever sort of life remained to him he would carry the knowledge that Marina, for the rest of whatever sort of life remained to her, would remember him in that light.

There was a suggestion of change in the darkness about him. Sandro looked about and saw a dim outline of the door in a place where he had not thought the door was. A predawn light was tracing the ghostliest hairline crack around the edges.

The next quarter hour was as long as the night. Sandro heard the bar being withdrawn and a creak of hinges as the door was pushed slowly open no more than a foot or two. They were being especially cautious of him. Sandro prepared for his last hopeless rush.

A dirty gray light spilled into the shed, and an enormous man entered the shed and closed the door behind him. "It's me, Venetian," the Turk said.

Sandro had seen the huge discoloration on the side of the Turk's head before the light went. So he hadn't killed him after all.

Sandro straightened from his crouch and said, "Are you one of the four the Persian butcher enlisted?"

"He'll be here soon. Come on. We've got to get moving."

"You'd better get back before you're missed. *Yi rooh.* I'll take my chances on giving you a few minutes' head start." The Turk expected nothing from anybody, but Sandro owed him that much.

"You forced my hand, Venetian. I've killed that lousy Hassan. I strangled him with his own knout. I've got the money he kept under a stone in the floor and clothes for us. His body won't be discovered till the sunrise prayer. We'll have to leave together."

"You go. I have something to do here."

The Turk sighed. "God left out the wits when He made you. You've decided to go to the harem, haven't you? You can't get past the eunuchs. They'll save the Persian the trouble of gelding you. And then they'll put your head on a pike outside the gate."

"Maybe I'll get far enough to see Marina. Maybe I can yell loud enough so that she'll hear. Or at least know I came. Maybe I can say something to give her back her faith."

The Turk nursed one of his ponderous silences for a while. Then he said, "You can forget about the woman."

"I told you no to that before," Sandro said. He heard his voice turning ugly. "Now, get going. Before the alarm is raised."

"The woman's dead."

"What?" Sandro said stupidly.

"She's dead. She killed herself sometime during the night. After Murrwan left her to bathe."

Sandro was finding it hard to breathe. He put out a hand to steady himself against the wall. "How . . . ?" he croaked.

The Turk spoke reluctantly. He had been through with the subject, but he made an effort to reply. "You know that by custom, when the master withdraws, the girl he's chosen for that night is allowed to keep any money she finds in his clothes. She found his little jeweled dagger. She was very determined. She couldn't manage the dagger with her hands as burned as they were, so she wedged it in the drawer of a heavy chest and threw herself on it." He paused. "Hassan came to tell me about an hour ago. He knew you and I were thick. He thought he was waking me up. He didn't know I was already awake. It was better luck than I'd hoped for. I took my chance then."

Sandro's breath came back with a huge involuntary intake that left him dizzy. The Turk might have thought it was an effort to speak.

"If it's any consolation to you, Venetian," the Turk said with what for him was a great and surprising delicacy, "the women in the harem don't think she killed herself because she was violated by Murrwan. Tribal women will do that sometimes. They think she killed herself to atone to her God for abandoning him. So at least she died in the belief that she was finding her way to God again." When Sandro didn't respond, he added, "I got that from Hassan. He enjoyed telling me. The eunuchs had fetched him to the harem to help deal with the body, and everybody was running around. They were too distracted to mind their tongues."

"Shut up," Sandro said. "I don't want to hear any more."

"All right," the Turk said. "*Yallah.* We'd better get going. We don't have much time."

"You don't know anything about her beliefs. Suicide was a sin to her. So she died in despair."

The Turk ignored the outburst. He returned to the practicalities. "We'd better head for the coast. That's our only chance. We'd better stay away from Beirut. They'll be looking for us there. The thing to do is to work our way down the coast to Gaza. We can mingle with the pilgrims returning from Mecca. They'll be filling Gaza for the next month. Then we can try to find a pilgrim ship. One on its way back to Granada, if possible. The sultanate has a long arm for runaway slaves, but Granada values its independence. Perhaps we can lose ourselves there for a time, until you can slip across the border to the Christian lands and I can find my way to Morocco."

"Go by yourself."

"Didn't you hear me? The woman's dead. There's no reason for you to stay behind any more."

"I'm going to kill Murrwan."

"You stupid turd!" the Turk exploded. "Haven't you learned anything yet?"

"I've learned to hate, *Turkeeya*. You taught me that."

"I didn't teach you enough. Hate is to keep you alive, not to kill you."

"I don't want to live."

"Yes, you do. To kill your brother."

"He can live. A present from Murrwan."

The Turk pondered this. At last he nodded. "Yes, I can understand that, Venetian. Kill Murrwan and leave your brother walking around in the world. Something to hate. At least for the few minutes before you die. But you've lost your chance to kill Murrwan. He's lost his taste for his inheritance for the time being. He had a horse saddled in the middle of the night and left for Baghdad, while the servants clean up for him here."

The Turk's matter-of-fact words struck a chord in Sandro's mind. Dying was as pointless as living. Perhaps, when Maffeo was dead, having Murrwan to hate would make life supportable.

"All right," he said. "Let's go to Gaza."

CHAPTER 19

"I'm to be made commandant of Nanking," Cheng Ho said wryly. "That's my consolation prize for the canceling of all future voyages."

He tossed back his cup of rice wine in one gulp, and Tom followed his example. Ma Huan and the vice admiral did the same. They were all way ahead of him, though he had been no laggard. Eunuchs liked to drink.

"At least you're keeping your head attached," said the vice admiral, Hou Hsien. His title meant nothing nowadays, but he had been allowed to keep his Grand Eunuch status. "You weren't turned over to the Board of Punishments as a way of signaling the change of maritime policy. Our new Son of Heaven doesn't have the taste for blood that his father had."

"True, true," Ma Huan said, nodding sagely. "Yesterday two officials from the Han-lin Academy presented him with a memorial scolding him for having sexual relations with his concubines during the mourning period for Yung Lo, and all he did was send them to prison."

"Stupid men," said the vice admiral. "Hung-hsi's lenient, but there are limits."

Cheng Ho poured himself another cup of rice wine and stared moodily into it. He showed no effects from all the drinks; his big frame absorbed alcohol easily.

"If I've managed to keep my head attached, it's no thanks to the Anti-Maritime Party," he said. "Ever since Hsia Yuan-chi was released from prison, he's been agitating to have me executed."

"He's been given leave to report in secret to the Emperor on the failings of other officials, you know," said Ma Huan. "Only Grand Secretaries and the Minister of Personnel are supposed to have that privilege. It's a situation that will bear watching."

The vice admiral held out his cup and got a refill. "Hung-hsi's only been on the Dragon Throne for ten months," he said, "and he's trying to undo all of Yung Lo's works. He tried to have the encyclopedia burned, but the scholars hid it—two officials were beaten for that. He's reinstated all the ministers Yung Lo put in prison. And now he wants to abandon the Forbidden City and transfer the capital back to Nanking. He's already ordered all the Peking agencies to be redesignated as *hsing-tsai*—auxiliary—as they were while the Forbidden City was being built."

Tom ventured an opinion. Cheng Ho allowed him liberties when they were alone or in the presence of trusted intimates like Ma Huan and the vice admiral; otherwise he played the part of an amusing mascot of the Department of Eunuchs.

"But . . . being appointed commandant of Nanking is a good thing, isn't it?" he blurted. "I mean, if the Emperor intends to move the capital there . . ."

"No, Chin Mao," Cheng Ho said patiently. "Chu Chan-chi, the Crown Prince, was sent to Nanking last month, and he's in charge there. It's clear that he'll go on running things no matter who becomes commandant."

"Chu Chan-chi's a poet—and a good one, at that," Ma Huan said with a hiccough. "He's not interested in governing. Pay him lip service and he'll give you a free hand."

Cheng Ho's broad face grew thoughtful. "Don't mistake the Crown Prince, my friend," he said. "He may be content to leave the details to others, but he's a man of vision. He's summoned me on many an occasion to ask about the lands beyond the sea. He's commissioned a geography book out of his own budget. I think he'd like to see the voyages continue—but he's too diffident to say so."

"Get him on our side, then," said the vice admiral. "Perhaps he'll put in a word for us with the Emperor."

"No," Cheng Ho said. He shook his head decisively. "The Anti-Maritime Party is in the saddle. They have the civil service on their side. The Emperor will never change his mind. He's only forty-eight years old. Face it, my true and loyal companion, the dream is dead for our lifetimes."

"The shipyards on the Yellow River . . ."

"Have been put to work making grain ships for the Grand Canal. In very short order our capacity for making seagoing vessels will disappear. Our most able men are drifting away. The profession of our chief naval architect, Chin Pi-feng, is now illegal. I've given him a pension, but my own revenues are drying up."

"It's crazy!" Tom burst out. "The Middle Kingdom was the most advanced seagoing power on earth! You were on your way to mastering the whole world! And you've thrown it all away!"

Cheng Ho gazed at him sadly. "Perhaps your people will be the ones to conquer the sea now, Chin Mao. But I'm afraid you'll never see that."

"We'll have to take him to Nanking with us, Cheng Ho," said Ma Huan. "We don't dare leave him in Peking, exposed to the malice of the Anti-Maritime Party."

"I'm not afraid," Tom said. "And besides, wasn't it ordered that I always be available to the court, like the giraffe?"

He was thinking of Lan-ying. He had become accustomed enough to the way of things in China to understand that she was part of the household furnishings. He did not know what might happen to her if his Peking establishment was dissolved.

"The Hung-hsi Emperor is not interested in you, Chin Mao. You've never been called to court. He wishes to forget about your existence. You'd best be out of his reach before one of his new ministers decides to help the forgetting along in a more forceful manner."

"But . . ."

"He doesn't want to leave his concubine," Ma Huan said peevishly. "That's all there is to it."

"Oh, if that's all, take her with you," Cheng Ho said with a wave of his hand.

"You eunuchs forget about these things," the old man said.

Cheng Ho laughed. "And you, too, ancient one, have you forgotten?"

"I still keep a bed-warming girl," the old scholar grumbled, "though that's all I use her for. To remind me."

Cheng Ho and the vice admiral laughed uproariously. Tom felt uncomfortable. He could never understand how a eunuch could enjoy ribald humor so much. If it had been him, he would have been resentful.

"Cheer up, my yellow-haired barbarian," Cheng Ho said. "Nanking's not so bad. You may even decide you like it better than Peking."

Ma Huan said gloomily, "The Anti-Maritime Party will migrate to Nanking like a swarm of termites after the Emperor moves the Dragon Throne back there."

"We'll cross that bridge when we come to it," Cheng Ho said. "At least I'll be in charge of the garrison. And we'll have a eunuch for Nanking Minister of War."

He broke off as a servant leaned and whispered in his ear. "It's a shadow-cloak from the Forbidden City," he said, rising. "He's brought information."

Tom kept his face as closed as the others. Shadow-cloak, *ying-wai t'ao*, was a euphemism for spy, but except for the delicacy about terminology, nobody made any bones about spying itself. The eunuch espionage network extended even into the imperial bedchambers, giving the Yellow Gate an advantage not possessed by their Confucian rivals despite their resounding official titles.

Cheng Ho returned a few minutes later. "The Emperor's been taken ill," he said. "Ill enough so that he's sent a messenger to Nanking to recall the Crown Prince."

Tom waited under virtual house arrest for the next two days. "Ma Huan says it's not a good idea for me to show my face in the city," he fretted to Lan-ying. "The Anti-

Maritime Party's got roving toughs in the streets. If the Emperor dies, there'll be riots."

She gasped at the forbidden speculation, and the pastel blush drained out of her cheeks. "There are things that must not be spoken of, lord," she said, with a nervous glance at the flimsy screen that enclosed them.

"All right, all right," he grouched, "but with the morning audiences canceled, there's a lot of unrest in the city."

"You don't need to go out, lord," she said, tracing his face with a finger. "Everything you need is here."

"And what's happening with Cheng Ho?" he complained. "Nothing's been seen or heard of him since yesterday. Shouldn't he be *doing* something?"

"Try one of these honey fritters," she said, raising the sticky confection to his lips.

He brushed the tidbit aside. "I guess it's all right to say the Heaven-sent's indisposed," he said. "Everyone knows that. But what made him take ill so suddenly? Unless that memorial criticizing his sex life made him apoplectic. Or unless he ate something that disagreed with him. Or . . . you don't suppose . . ."

"Please, lord," she said, almost in tears.

He grinned at her. "Don't worry, little flower, I'm not going to utter treason. Let's try one of those honey fritters now. You first . . ."

Ma Huan arrived about noon with two eunuch bodygards. The old scholar was agitated.

"The Emperor's dead. It's official. His valedictory edict's being distributed now. Just think of it—a reign of only ten months!"

Tom remembered Yung Lo's death, and all the crazy edicts against seafaring. Was the world going to turn topsy-turvy all over again?

"Where's Cheng Ho?"

Ma Huan looked around, and drew Tom into a corner of the garden. "He's on his way to Nanking. He left yesterday, secretly. He hopes to arrive before the messenger who was sent to the Crown Prince when the Emperor became ill."

"How can he do that?"

The old man looked around again. "It has been ar-

ranged that the messenger will arrive late. This time it is
Cheng Ho who will get to the new Emperor's ear first,
not the Anti-Maritime Party politicians. You must hurry,
Chin Mao."

"Hurry? What are you talking about?"

"You're to leave for Nanking immediately. The relays
of horses are waiting. You'll have an escort to smooth the
way."

"Me? But why?"

"You'll join Cheng Ho and the Crown Prince on the
trip north. It will be a long journey. There'll be plenty of
time to fill Chu Chan-chi's ears with tales of lands beyond the sea. Your yellow hair will be worth a thousand
scrolls."

Tom felt an exultant fire race through his veins. "Does
this mean that Cheng Ho thinks he has a chance of per-
suading the new Emperor to resume the voyages?"

"It won't be easy. Chien Yi and the other Anti-
Maritime ministers are still in power. The Crown Prince
is young and unsure of himself, and he won't know at
first how to resist them. And he'll be inheriting a lot of
other crises that he'll have to deal with immediately—
floods, famine relief in the provinces, the scholar shortage, the spreading of the Vietnam war. All of these will
compete for a budget that's being eaten away by infla-
tion. But it's known that Chu Chan-chi looks favorably
on overseas exploration. If we get to him early, in time
we may be able to persuade him not to let our maritime
capability wither away."

"I'll ... I'll do what I can!" Tom promised. He was
flushed and excited. "I'll tell him about the English ...
and ... and the Portuguese ... and the Genoese and Venetians! If he doesn't get the Middle Kingdom moving
again, they're going to sail into his backyard instead of
the other way around!"

He looked back toward the entrance screen to his
quarters. First he would have to say good-bye to Lan-
ying. That would not be easy.

Ma Huan followed his glance. "Don't worry, Chin
Mao," he said understandingly. "The Yellow Gate will
look after her while you're gone."

AFTERWORD

The story of Pedro Costa, Sandro Cavalli, and Tom of Bristol—which is also the story of Henry the Navigator and Admiral Cheng Ho and the age of discovery—will be continued in the next volume of this saga, *The Voyagers*.

My publisher, Bantam Books, commissioned this story of the men and women of the 15th century, which will take at least three volumes to tell, a few years ago. In that time I have researched scores of primary and secondary sources and written more than two thousand manuscript pages. Yet, I feel that I have only barely scratched the surface.

The world in the age of discovery was very different from ours, yet the *people* were, I believe, very much the same—very human in the same ways that we are: brave, cruel, intelligent, profane, spiritual, hopeful, downtrodden, ultimately triumphant and tragic in their humanity.

I hope that this glimpse into that world has been enjoyable for you, and I invite you to return with me in the sequel, *The Voyagers*, which will be published next year.

Paul King
July 1992

The saga of the bold men and courageous women who sailed in search of a new and fabulous world continues in . . .

THE VOYAGERS

The year is 1423. Far out in the Atlantic, Portuguese sailors find a lush, fertile island paradise and call it Madeira. Following them into the unknown is young Tom of Bristol, who travels the treacherous caravan routes toward the sandal-scented Orient. Pedro de Costa seeks to convince his prince to let him sail for the dreaded Cape where, legend has it, seas boil with death for the unwary. Inês Alves, cheated of her inheritance and robbed of her good name, faces a journey to the ends of the earth to help colonize the island of Madeira. And Sandro Cavalli, the nobleman shanghaied into slavery, will cling to both hatred for the brother who betrayed him and love for a beautiful young woman in order to survive in a distant Arab land. . . .

Turn the page for a preview of **THE VOYAGERS** by Paul King, on sale in Fall 1993, wherever Bantam Domain Books are sold.

A caravan from the south had deposited another load of returning hajjis in the streets and alleys of Gaza, placing a further strain on the already overcrowded inns and eating places. The pilgrims were everywhere, many still wearing the togalike garments of restriction, chattering to one another about the wonders they had seen in Mecca and competing in accounts of their acts of piety at the sacred Well of Zamzam and the three pillars where the devil was stoned, and their exploits on the day of the Standing.

Sandro Cavalli hung around Goliath's Well, waiting for the Turk to return from his expedition to the waterfront, moving frequently from place to place so that he wouldn't attract the notice of Gaza's aggressive street hawkers, or invite conversation from some overtalkative hajji.

He kept an especially sharp eye out for the flimflammers and confidence tricksters who preyed on the pilgrims passing through. The hajj gave them an annual flock of sheep to be sheared. While the majority of pilgrims were destitute at this stage of their journey, quite a few had managed to hang on to some portion of their travel money. The local confidence men were adept at separating them from it on one pretext or another, and the special danger from them was that they became professionally inquisitive about their quarry in order to find a wedge for swindling them. Sandro knew he could not stand close scrutiny. On the other hand, he did not think he provided attractive game for a flimflam artist. In his shabby and threadbare cloak he didn't particularly look like one of the hajjis who was likely to have any money left.

His eye wasn't sharp enough. He'd let his attention stray to the clear blue bowl of the sky and the bracing salt smell of the sea breeze with its promise of freedom beyond. A shifty one-eyed fellow sidled up to him and said, "I guess you'll be anxious to get home now, hajji."

"What. Uh, oh, yes."

Sandro knew, unhappily, that he had failed to react to the honorific the way most fresh, new hajjis did—like a cat purring over a bowl of cream.

"Salaam, hajji," the man said. "I'm Achmed—*al-Ayn*, as they call me."

"Uh, salaam, Achmed, uh, al-Ayn. I'm Ali, uh, bin Yusif," Sandro said, making a botch of the name he had been using on the flight from Damascus.

Achmed the Eye pounced. "Ah, Ali. Are you a Shi'ite, then?"

"Uh, no . . ." He added hastily, "Though of course we all revere Ali. No offense."

"That's all right. I'm not a Shi'ite either. But we're all Moslems together, aren't we?"

"Yes, yes, very true."

Achmed's single eye roved over him, stopping here and there. "I can't place your accent, brother. Where did you say you were from?"

"Oh, I've lived in a number of places. I, uh, spent some years as a child in Tunis."

Sandro took care to place himself as far away from Damascus as possible, though his life in Jaybir's household had made him familiar with Damascene ways and doubtless affected his Arabic pronunciation. But Tunis was safe, in case he had to fend off more questions. He had visited there as a small boy with his father, after all, and corresponded with the House of Cavalli's factor there.

And he had been sold into slavery there.

The House of Cavalli ranked as one of the greatest of the mighty Venetian merchant houses, its far-flung commerce carrying the Cavalli name to the various ports of Europe and throughout the Moorish lands. Alessandro Cavalli, the tall, handsome younger son of the powerful and wealthy Girolamo Cavalli, had been born into a gilded marble palace within sight of the Grand Canal. But fate had turned Sandro's life from one of remarkable privilege into one of utter privation.

Because Sandro's unscrupulous older brother, Matteo, had cared little for anything but his own base pleasures, their father had chosen to ignore tradition and train the younger Sandro—who had a keen interest in the business as well as a keen mind—as his successor as overseer of the Cavalli enterprises. But Signor Cavalli had realized neither the boiling malice spawned by his decision nor just how immoral his older son had become. When the elder Cavalli unexpectedly died, Matteo had told Sandro that the youth was suspected of having poisoned Girolamo and was to be brought before the ruling Council of Ten on charges of parricide, a judgment that would mean certain execution. Sandro had been shocked by such a terrible accusation, but before a trial could take place, the perfidious Matteo had snatched control of the family power and fortune by arranging for Sandro's abduction by an equally unprincipled Genoese trader.

Thrown first into a fetid dungeon and then into the rat-infested bowels of a merchant ship, Sandro, then barely eighteen, his hands accustomed to a pen or a lute, had been forced to labor for two years as a galley oarsman, chained to his seat day and night, slaving under unimaginably brutal conditions. When by an odd twist

Sandro had finally learned of his brother's treachery, he had vowed to escape and exact revenge—and try to regain what was rightfully his. With the help of his benchmate, a powerful and dangerous Turk whose own endurance was fueled by rage, Sandro had nearly succeeded, but the two of them were taken prisoner by Barbary pirates and sold at a slave auction.

Their new owner had been an Arab scholar, a stern master but kind enough in his absentminded fashion. Jaybir al-Sumit had rescued Sandro from the stables and the lash of the overseer—had rescued him from the galleys, when it came to that—and had given him as decent a life as a slave could hope for, teaching Sandro about astronomy and mapmaking and even permitting him to marry a fellow slave he had fallen in love with, a beautiful Greek woman named Marina. But Sandro's relative good fortune lasted only a year, and then the hand of fate had lashed out with another blow when Jaybir died and his odious nephew, Murrwan, became the new householder. Sandro had been thrown back into the stables, his marriage—one between "infidel slaves"—declared invalid and his wife, Marina, tortured into renouncing her Christian faith as a prelude to her being included in Murrwan's stable of women. But Marina had quickly put an end to her physical and spiritual agony by killing herself, and the Turk, dealing his own blow, had killed the brutal stable overseer. Sandro and the Turk had fled the compound and escaped to Gaza—where they now awaited the next turn of the wheel.

Qismah. Fate. The Arabs were great believers in fate. One's lot in life. It was Sandro's *qismah* to be there. Venice was a shadow, Matteo a ghost. The marble palace near the Grand Canal, his little sister, Agnese ... they were gone, as a dream is gone when one opens one's eyes. The past three years had erased nearly every trace of the high-born, advantaged youth; in his place stood a man hardened and strengthened by travail and pain—a man capable of anything.

•   •   •

Sandro pulled himself back from his reverie and quickly refocused his attention on his companion. This was no time to be lax, especially with a canny character like Achmed.

Ah, Tunis," Achmed said. "I've had the opportunity to perform services for many pilgrims from Tunis." His eye came to rest on Sandro's hands, still thickened and callused by his years as a galley slave, despite his subsequent soft service with Jaybir. "You look as if you've had a hard life, *ya* Ali. But all must be well now, if you've managed to attain the blessings of the hajj."

It was too late to hide his telltale hands from this unsavory little man. In Saracen lands a galley slave was likely to be a Christian, just as in Christian lands one was likely to be a Saracen, and in the far-reaching territory of the sultanate there were bounties for escaped slaves.

"I was captured by the Franks during a sea voyage a long time ago," Sandro said with assumed candor. "They made me a galley slave, may God destroy their race. But, praise Allah, I was able to escape when the Franks were attacked by one of our corsairs."

"That explains your accent," Achmed said. "Living among the cursed Franks all those years."

"Yes," Sandro said. He moved to get away, but Achmed plucked at his sleeve and held him fast.

"Do you have a place to stay in Gaza, *ya* Ali?"

"I don't have money for an inn," Sandro said to squelch his interest. "I just slept in a doorway last night."

That was true enough. The majority of pilgrims passing through Gaza wrapped themselves in blankets in the streets or pitched tents on the outskirts.

"I can arrange a bargain for you on sharing a tent with a group of hajjis from Fez," Achmed persisted. "Very fine people, very pious."

"Thank you, *ya* Achmed," Sandro said, trying politely to disengage himself, "but I won't be here long enough for it to matter."

"Ah, then you've got passage on a ship. Are you with a group?"

"No," Sandro said. "That is, I was with a group, but I got separated. I'm traveling with another pilgrim now. . . ."

"Where can I find you later, if I can come up with something to your advantage? I know all the captains. I can get you aboard a pilgrim vessel at very low rates, taking the place of one of the charter passengers who died on the hajj." He struck a virtuous pose. "I swear to you, as Allah is my witness, that I don't want a single *dirhen* for commission. It's enough for me to know that I'm doing a service for God by helping one of His holy pilgrims."

"I . . . I won't need passage," Sandro floundered. "I may . . . that is . . . I may just walk."

"Walk?" Achmed exclaimed in horror. "You've done enough walking, my dear brother, by the look of those sandals." A glint of interest came into his eye. "How far?"

"To . . . to Egypt. Only as far as Suez. There are pilgrim ships there."

"Oh, then you're going west. Not north or east, say to Baghdad or Damascus?"

"No," Sandro blurted. "Not north or east."

Achmed gazed at him speculatively. "*Ya akhi*, my dear brother. I love you as I love my own hand. You won't find a ship any cheaper in Suez than I could arrange for you right here. I'll look for you tomorrow. Will you be here again, at the Well?"

"Uh, I don't know where I'll be."

"I'll find you. In the meantime, if you're short of money, do you have any souvenirs of Mecca you'd like to sell? A vial of holy water from the Well of Zamzam? Or a pebble from the Stoning?"

"No."

"No souvenirs. That's too bad. Most hajjis have something or other. Well, it's what we take away in our hearts that's important, eh, *ya Ali*?"

"Yes," Sandro said.

He finally got rid of the man when the little sharpster spotted a prosperous-looking pilgrim who had two slaves to attend him. The pilgrim tried to brush him off, but Achmed the Eye kept circling around in front of him till he finally stopped. Sandro could not leave the vicinity of Goliath's Well when the Turk would be looking for him there, but he made a wide detour and came around the other side, where he could lose himself in a dense fringe of vendors' stalls with hundreds of people milling around them, and still keep an eye on the tumbled masonry basin that was Gaza's chief tourist attraction.

The Turk returned shortly before noon and spotted Sandro after a quick scan of the crowd. He motioned Sandro to meet him in a side street, and after a few moments joined him there.

"I've got us passage to Granada," he said. "We're part of a big, prepaid pilgrims' tour group with three ships. Some of the passengers have switched accommodations to be with friends they made in Mecca, so the hajjis on any particular ship aren't necessarily familiar with all their shipmates. The captain wasn't averse to making a little extra money on the side. Here's your boarding pass. It belonged to an old man named Kazimi from Málaga who died on the voyage out. Don't show it to anyone but the boatswain—he's in on the bribe. But there'll be passengers who'll remember Kazimi."

He handed Sandro a small wooden tally with a name and a number painted on it in Arabic script.

"We sail tomorrow morning," the Turk said. "Till then, keep your head down and don't talk to anybody if you can help it." He looked Sandro over critically "You may get by, Venetian. The sun's burnt you dark enough these last weeks. You were getting fishbelly white, playing the scribe for the old scholar. Just don't let anyone see your *zib*—though that may be hard to manage on shipboard."

"Don't worry about me," Sandro said. "I won't give us away."

The Turk scowled. "You'd better get rid of that Christian idol of yours. Now—right away. You won't be able to keep that hidden during a sea voyage. I was a fool to let you go back for it."

The Turk had had little choice. Sandro remembered how crazed he had been on the morning of their escape. He had refused to leave without his late wife's icon, and had risked capture for both of them by taking the time to dig it up from the corner of the stable where he had buried it.

"No," he said. "I'll be careful."

"You've rowed a load of Christian pilgrims. You know how a habit of thieving attacks even honest men at sea, for some strange reason. And it's always trifles—handkerchiefs, pens, a spoon. You turn your back for a moment, and it's gone—under the robes of someone you've just been talking to."

"I'll keep it on me all the time. I'm not crazy enough to leave it lying around."

"What about when you're sleeping? There are hands feeling around for purses."

"I'm a light sleeper. Remember? It's a habit we acquired on the rowing benches."

"By Allah, you're still as stupid as ever. I ought to take it away from you."

"Try it and I'll kill you." Sandro's hand stole to the dagger under his cloak. It was a fine, sharp weapon that had belonged to Hassan the Knout.

The Turk studied him for a long, tense moment, his face growing darker with fury. Sandro's grip on the dagger handle tightened. The Turk, for all his rational talk, was capable of anything—even starting a scuffle in the midst of a crowd of pilgrims.

Then the bulging veins subsided and the Turk laughed. "I believe you would, Venetian. You're mad. They say that God looks after madmen. I hope that's so."

They walked on down the narrow, crowded lane. "We'd better buy some supplies," the Turk said. "There's still some of Hassan's money left, though I didn't let that villain of a captain see it. We're supposed to have our keep during the voyage, but it's never enough. They feed these pilgrims swill you wouldn't give to a dog."

"All right. Give me some of the money. I'll get some flour and beans and a little cauldron we can share. Some dried meat and some fruit for the first few days. We can get more whenever we make port. And a water cask. We each ought to bring aboard our own water cask."

The Turk drew them into a doorway and counted out coins. "Meet me in the alley where we slept last night," he said. "If anyone's taken that niche in the wall we used, I'll throw them out. It's a good spot—hidden from the ends of the alley, but you can see anyone coming from either direction."

"You're too suspicious, *Turkeeya*," Sandro said. "We got away, didn't we?"

The Turk bared his teeth in a jagged smile. "Maybe," he said.

A rattle of armor awoke them before dawn. The Turk grabbed his arm. "Listen," he said.

Voices were coming from the head of the alley, low purposeful voices speaking a language that was not Arabic. A horse whinnied and someone quieted it. Sandro caught the words, *"Burada bekleyiniz."*

"Mamluks," the Turk said. "My old comrades in arms."

The soldiers moved down the alley, leading their horses. The horses' hooves were muffled, by the sound of them—probably wrapped in burlap. They stopped at one of the sleeping forms that lined the alley and shook it awake. Sandro heard a voice of protest, then someone saying, "He's not one of them. Go back to sleep, fellow."

Another voice whined, "Give me my bounty now. You promised me a bounty."

Sandro's insides curled up as he recognized the voice as that of Achmed the Eye.

"You'll get your bounty when we find the men, ratface," someone answered. "After you point them out to us. If they're what you say they are."

"They're looking for runaways," the Turk said. "Look at those silks and plumes. They're a Damascene regiment."

"It's us they're after," Sandro said. "It's my fault. We'd better get out of here."

They disentangled themselves from the water casks and provisions they'd curled themselves around to protect and started to get up.

"Wait," the Turk said.

More soldiers were coming from the other end of the alley, blocking that route of escape.

"I hope you're ready to die, Venetian," the Turk said. "I'm not going back."

"What can we do?"

"Wait till they get here. Kill one if you can. That'll throw them off. Don't try to break through that lot coming from the other side. Then we'd have one lot chasing us and another lot to block us. Go the other way. That way they'll tangle with one another and get in one another's way. When we reach the head of the alley, we'll run in opposite directions. They won't know who to follow for one or two seconds, till the officer tells them how to split up. We'll meet at the ships, just before boarding—if we're still alive."

It was all delivered in a crisp military tone. The strategy was professional. The Turk seemed fresh and years younger—almost happy. Sandro caught a glimpse of the formidable soldier the Turk must have been before life had swatted him with misfortune. That part of him had been buried in the darkness within him, but it hadn't died.

They pretended sleep, wrapped in their blankets like the other pilgrims lining the alley. Sandro's hand was on his dagger. He knew that the Turk had a short-sword hidden under his rags; it had been a relic of Hassan's own military service. All during the dusty trek from Damascus, the Turk had sharpened it on stones whenever he had a chance.

The footsteps stopped. Sandro sensed someone standing over him. He opened his eyes a slit and saw boots, flaring pantaloons, a short robe. A soldier bent over the Turk and shook him. "Hey, fellow, wake up!"

The Turk suddenly grabbed the front of the man's robe and yanked him down. Before the soldier hit the ground, the Turk had him skewered. A powerful leg shot out and sent a water keg rolling under the horses' feet. The horses shied and whinnied, knocking against the soldiers who held them. The Turk leapt to his feet like a uncoiled spring, jerked his sword out of the dead man, and slashed at the soldier nearest him.

Sandro, at the Turk's first move, had whipped his blanket at the eyes of the man standing over him and, while the man clawed at it, sank his dagger into his belly. The horses were still pawing the air, their hooves flailing at the Mamluks who were fighting to hold onto the reins. The second group of soldiers at the far end of the alley had started to run toward the action. Sandro got past the flank of a bucking horse. He saw the Turk take a moment before fleeing to cut the skinny throat of Achmed the Eye. "Here's your bounty, cockroach!" he heard the Turk snarl.

Then he himself was running for the mouth of the alley. All was confusion behind him, with the sound of clashing horses and cursing men all in a tangle. As he reached the corner he flung a look backward to make sure that the Turk had broken free and saw him pounding after him, the bloody sword held straight out where it could be swung in an arc at any pursuer who got too close. Sandro veered to the left and headed for another opening in the maze of alleys. Dawn was breaking with a great rosy splash, and the sleepers in the streets were beginning to stir. Sandro saw people sitting up to stare at him and realized he was still holding the dagger. He thrust it out of sight beneath his cloak and turned his run into a fast walk. He ducked through a crevice in the row of mud walls and found himself in a narrow, shuttered defile. Goggle-eyed women stared at him from the roofs, and a man's angry voice shouted at him. He took several more turns through the maze, eventually emerging into a minor thoroughfare where sleepy shopkeepers were unshuttering and the proprietors of a few rude eating places were crawling out of their holes and setting up matting on the ground and unfurling patched canopies.

He stayed off the well-trafficked streets and kept to the side streets and back alleys, killing time. He bought some fruit and a skewer of lamb for breakfast with some of his remaining coins. On further thought he bought a grimy blanket and a worn pilgrim's scrip from a ferrety little urchin who had probably lifted them from a sleeper and filled the scrip with bread and fruit so that he wouldn't be conspicuous when he went aboard the ship. He regretted the loss of the water casks and the other provisions, but he had gone hungry and thirsty before; the captain, no matter how cheese-paring, would not let his passengers starve. Once he saw a troop of Mamluks crossing an intersection he had been about to enter; he turned his back and studied a rug seller's wares until they had gone by.

At the appointed hour he went to the beach where the ships were anchored. Sailors were rowing boatloads of pilgrims out. Two or three hundred hajjis, their possessions piled next to them, stood about on the sands, waiting their turn. Sandro looked for the Turk and didn't see him.

He made himself known to the bribed boatswain, who gave him a sidelong look and said in a low tone, "Where's your friend?"

"He'll be along soon," Sandro said. "I'll wait here till he shows up."

He surrendered his wooden tally, and the boatswain pretended to check off his name and the name of his father in the register. The tally disappeared under the man's clothing, but Sandro was given a boarding tag to hang around his neck. He lost himself in the crowd of waiting pilgrims; he was sure the Mamluks were out looking for him, but even if they rode by this beach, he didn't think they'd recognize him. They wouldn't expect to find an escaped slave in the midst of a tour group where people were supposed to know one another.

He waited through the morning while the sun climbed higher and the sands grew hotter. The crush of pilgrims dwindled. It was down to just a few more boatloads now, and the Turk still had not come.

A hajji standing next to him offered him a drink of water from his bottle. Sandro accepted with thanks.

"I don't remember you from this ship, brother," the hajji said. "Were you on one of the other vessels?"

"Yes," Sandro said.

"It was marvelous, wasn't it?" the man said. "Did you visit the sacred cave?"

"No."

"Ah well, that's not required, as long as you perform the *wuquf* and your other duties. You stoned the devil, didn't you?"

"Yes," Sandro said.

"Of course," the man apologized. He laughed. "I myself was able to squeeze into the cave—I'm skinny enough—but there was one fat merchant from Gibraltar who got stuck, and it took all the rest of us to pull him out. Not that there's anything to see in the cave, but just think—the Prophet saved from his enemies by a spider!"

"Yes, it's wonderful."

"Still, I'll be glad to get back to my little orange grove in Almería. Travel is interesting, but there's no place like home. When I think of the discomforts, the dangers we've undergone ..." He shook his head. "The rest of the world isn't as civilized as Granada."

"No."

"Gaza, especially. I'll be glad to get out of this place of violence. Just think, only this morning, not very far from where we're standing, an escaped slave killed two soldiers and an innocent businessman of the town."

Sandro stiffened. He hoped his face hadn't betrayed him. So word had spread so soon. It made things more dangerous for the Turk. It was fairly safe here on the beach among the hajjis, but everyone in the town must be looking for the escapees and scrutinizing every passing face. That must be why the Turk hadn't shown up yet. He was probably holed up somewhere, waiting for a good moment to make a dash for the ship.

But he didn't have much time. Sandro looked out at the anchored galleys. The ship's boat was coming back again. There couldn't be more one or two loads of stand-ees left on the beach.

"I can see you're as impatient to leave as I am," the hajji smiled indulgently. "I don't blame you. But there's nothing to worry about. The slave didn't get far. They caught up with him and killed him."

BANTAM DOUBLEDAY DELL
PRESENTS THE
WINNERS CLASSIC SWEEPSTAKES

Dear Bantam Doubleday Dell Reader,

We'd like to say "Thanks" for choosing our books. So we're giving you a chance to enter our Winners Classic Sweepstakes, where you can win a Grand Prize of $25,000.00, or one of over 1,000 other sensational prizes! All prizes are guaranteed to be awarded. Return the Official Entry Form at once! And when you're ready for another great reading experience, we hope you'll keep Bantam Doubleday Dell books at the top of your reading list!

OFFICIAL ENTRY FORM

Yes! Enter me in the Winners Classic Sweepstakes and guarantee my eligibility to be awarded any prize, including the $25,000.00 Grand Prize. Notify me at once if I am declared a winner.

NAME _____

ADDRESS _____ APT. # _____

CITY _____

STATE _____ ZIP _____

REGISTRATION NUMBER **01995A**

Please mail to: LL-SBA

BANTAM DOUBLEDAY DELL DIRECT, INC.
WINNERS CLASSIC SWEEPSTAKES
PO Box 985, Hicksville, NY 11802-0985

OFFICIAL PRIZE LIST

GRAND PRIZE: *$25,000.00 CASH!*

FIRST PRIZE: FISHER HOME ENTERTAINMENT CENTER
Including complete integrated audio/video system with 130-watt amplifier, AM/FM stereo tuner, dual cassette deck, CD player, Surround Sound speakers and universal remote control unit.

SECOND PRIZE: TOSHIBA VCR *5 winners!*
Featuring full-function, high-quality 4-Head performance, with 8-event/365-day timer, wireless remote control, and more.

THIRD PRIZE: CONCORD 35MM CAMERA OUTFIT *35 winners!*
Featuring focus-free precision lens, built-in automatic film loading, advance and rewind.

FOURTH PRIZE: BOOK LIGHT *1,000 winners!*
A model of convenience, with a flexible neck that bends in any direction, and a steady clip that holds sure on any surface.

OFFICIAL RULES AND REGULATIONS

No purchase necessary. To enter the sweepstakes follow instructions found elsewhere in this offer. You can also enter the sweepstakes by hand printing your name, address, city, state and zip code on a 3" x 5" piece of paper and mailing it to: Winners Classic Sweepstakes, P.O. Box 785, Gibbstown, NJ 08027. Mail each entry separately. Sweepstakes begins 12/1/91. Entries must be received by 6/1/93. Some presentations of this sweepstakes may feature a deadline for the Early Bird prize. If the offer you receive does, then to be eligible for the Early Bird prize your entry must be received according to the Early Bird date specified. Not responsible for lost, damaged, misdirected, illegible or postage due mail. Mechanically reproduced entries are not eligible. All entries become property of the sponsor and will not be returned.

Prize Selection/Validations: Winners will be selected in random drawings on or about 7/30/93, by Ventura Associates, Inc., an independent judging organization whose decisions are final. Odds of winning are determined by total number of entries received. Circulation of this sweepstakes is estimated not to exceed 200 million. Entrants need not be present to win. All prizes are guaranteed to be awarded and delivered to winners. Winners will be notified by mail and may be required to complete an affidavit of eligibility and release of liability which must be returned within 14 days of date on notification or alternate winners will be selected. Any guest of a trip winner will also be required to execute a release of liability. Any prize notification letter or any prize returned to a participating winner, Bantam Doubleday Dell Publishing Group, Inc. its participating divisions or subsidiaries or VENTURA ASSOCIATES, INC. as undeliverable will be awarded to an alternate winner. Prizes are not transferable. No multiple prize winners except for Early Bird Prize, which may be awarded in addition to another prize. No substitution for prizes except as may be necessary due to unavailability in which case a prize of equal or greater value will be awarded. Prizes will be awarded approximately 90 days after the drawing. All taxes, automobile license and registration fees, if applicable, are the sole responsibility of the winners. Entry constitutes permission (except where prohibited) to use winners names and likenesses for publicity purposes without further or other compensation.

Participation: This sweepstakes is open to residents of the United States and Canada, except for the province of Quebec. This sweepstakes is sponsored by Bantam Doubleday Dell Publishing Group, Inc. (BDD), 666 Fifth Avenue, New York, NY 10103. Versions of this sweepstakes with different graphics will be offered in conjunction with various solicitations or promotions by different subsidiaries and divisions of BDD. Employees and their families of BDD, its division, subsidiaries, advertising agencies, and VENTURA ASSOCIATES, INC. are not eligible.

Canadian residents, in order to win, must first correctly answer a time limited arithmetical skill testing question. Void in Quebec and wherever prohibited or restricted by law. Subject to all federal, state, local and provincial laws and regulations.

Prizes: The following values for prizes are determined by the manufacturers' suggested retail prices or by what these items are currently known to be selling for at the time this offer was published. Approximate retail values include handling and delivery of prizes. Estimated maximum retail value of prizes: 1 Grand Prize ($27,500 if merchandise or $25,000 Cash); 1 First Prize ($3,000); 5 Second Prizes ($400 ea); 35 Third Prizes ($100 ea); 1,000 Fourth Prizes ($9.00 ea); 1 Early Bird Prize ($5,000); Total approximate maximum retail value is $50,000. Winners will have the option of selecting any prize offered at level won. Automobile winner must have a valid driver's license at the time the car is awarded. Trips are subject to space and departure availability. Certain black-out dates may apply. Travel must be completed within one year from the time the prize is awarded. Minors must be accompanied by an adult. Prizes won by minors will be awarded in the name of parent or legal guardian.

For a list of Major Prize Winners (available after 7/30/93): send a self-addressed, stamped envelope entirely separate from your entry to Winners Classic Sweepstakes Winners, P.O. Box 825, Gibbstown, NJ 08027. Requests must be received by 6/1/93. DO NOT SEND ANY OTHER CORRESPONDENCE TO THIS P.O. BOX.